Covenant

roberta clark

the

the GOLD Covenant

roberta clark

Gold Imprint
Medallion Press, Inc.
Printed in USA

Published 2007 by Medallion Press, Inc.

The MEDALLION PRESS LOGO
is a registered tradmark of Medallion Press, Inc.

If you purchased this book without a cover, you should be aware that this book is stolen property. It was reported as "unsold and destroyed" to the publisher, and neither the author nor the publisher has received any payment from this "stripped book."

Copyright © 2007 by Roberta Clark
Cover Illustration by Adam Mock

All rights reserved. No part of this book may be reproduced or transmitted in any form or by any electronic or mechanical means, including photocopying, recording, or by any information storage and retrieval system, without written permission of the publisher, except where permitted by law.

Names, characters, places, and incidents are the products of the author's imagination or are used fictionally. Any resemblance to actual events, locales, or persons, living or dead, is entirely coincidental.

Typeset in Baskerville

Printed in the United States of America

10 9 8 7 6 5 4 3 2 1
First Edition

DEDICATION:

In memory of
Richard and Robin
who started it all.
Never forgotten.

CHAPTER 1

The Red Lion had just reopened for business when Barcineh walked in. His small body moved stiffly, back rigid, as if supported by a brace, steps slow and deliberate giving the impression of someone much older than his twenty-six years. He made his way to the bar, ordered a draft lager, then carried it to a corner table next to the window. From here he would have an unobstructed view of the customers as they came in, as well as of the activity on the sidewalk outside the pub.

It was the right place to meet, a good choice. Safe.

Meticulous attention to detail is necessary in these matters. Wasn't that why he was here? Why he'd been successful where others had failed? Pulling his shoulders back against the laddered chair, Barcineh adjusted his tie and collar, and brushed at pieces of lint on his frayed lapels. After today he would burn the clothes he was wearing, the shabby cotton shirt, the suit so threadbare its pinstriped pattern was barely distinguishable. He would start over with tailor-made trousers and jackets befitting his new position.

The sunlight played on the glass of lager in front of him, changing the color of the translucent liquid from gold to amber, and amber back to gold. It amused him—the brilliance—the appropriate brilliance of the color. He picked up the glass, took a sip, and put it down again, then lifted an index finger to brush the underside of his dark mustache. His tired, deep-set eyes drifted from the glass to the slab of timber that served as a bar and, at the moment, a game table for the publican and his early customers. Heavy studs and massive beams gave the interior a constricted look, as did the low ceiling that was, in places, low enough to present an obstacle even to Barcineh. The musty odor of dry rot mingled with the smell of fresh-baked pastries drifting from somewhere in the back recesses of the ancient building. It was pleasing, a reminder of home.

Barcineh was happy. Although he knew it was too soon to indulge in such an emotion, how could he stifle the sense of well-being, the pride of accomplishment? Why shouldn't he allow himself this small premature satisfaction? It would be over soon enough. Only one last contact to be made. One last duty to discharge so that all would seem as normal.

the **GOLD** *Covenant*

Although the pub was growing full and noisy, he still had a clear view of each new arrival. The two who had just walked in held his attention longer than any of the others, even though neither fit the description of his contacts. They'd stood in the doorway, studying the other customers with mild interest, as though deciding on the fitness of the place before entering. One of them was almost a foot taller than Barcineh, a good hundred pounds heavier. The other was small by comparison, five six or seven, an inch or two over Barcineh's height. They were workmen, laborers. He was expecting white collar.

When they moved directly to the bar, he shifted his attention back to the entrance with a degree of relief. The relief was short-lived. Minutes later, pitcher and glasses in hand, the two men cut through the crowded room, plunking themselves down at his table without speaking to him. Overriding the immediate sense of intimidation, he said, "I am most sorry, sirs, but those seats are reserved for some gentlemen who are expected momentarily."

The larger man's eyes, almost lost in the puffy expanse of his red face, fixed on Barcineh. "Are they now?" he said, making no move to vacate the chair. Instead, he took out a large handkerchief, spread it on the table, then placed the pitcher and glasses on top of it before turning to his companion. "What ya think of that, Maurice? The man wants for us t'make way for a couple a blokes what ain't even 'ere."

"Maybe his friends they lose their way," the other man said. His pleasant smile bared a row of small pearl-like teeth. "Perhaps we can help to find them?"

"No, no, not at all a necessity. I am sure they will arrive shortly. The time was of no exactitude."

While trying to convince himself there was no reason for it, Barcineh was growing apprehensive. He was acutely aware of his scalp. It was cold and the skin growing taut, painfully taut, restricting the blood vessels, making him feel light-headed. His nerves were on edge. He hadn't had time to recover from the long journey overland—and the sea voyage. It was foolish to expect so much of himself, not to allow himself a rest before making this last contact.

The vest was heavy under his clothes, the weight of it pressing down on his shoulders, pressing him to the chair. He didn't trust himself to stand and walk away from these two. He needed control. Balance. Perfect balance.

The big man polished the rim of his glass, inspected it, picked up the glass, then emptied half its contents. He turned his attention to Barcineh as he removed another folded linen from his pocket, dabbed at his lips, wiped the cloth over the rest of his face, blew his nose into it, then stuffed it back where he'd found it. "Feelin' a might edgy, are you?" the man asked. "'Nother beer help? We'll see to it you don't lose your seat."

"Thank you, no. That is very kind, but I am not yet

ready for another."

"You don't 'ave to upset yourself over the seats, you know. There won't be anyone else arrivin' this evening."

"They will be here," Barcineh insisted. "Soon. It is arranged."

"I don't believe he uses the correct phrase," the other man said, turning to his large friend. "You think perhaps he expect someone with more class?"

"Oh, I see," Barcineh laughed nervously. "My apologies. I was to—that is—the trains are running late out of Waterloo Station today."

The response should have come immediately. Instead there was silence. The two men smiled at each other, making Barcineh feel foolish as well as frightened. "Again, I apologize for the mistake," he said. "You are, of course, welcome to stay at the table. I will move when my friends arrive."

" 'E sounds like a friggin' spy, don' 'e?" The big man picked up his glass and tapped it against the pitcher of lager. "You just don't understand," he said. "They're bloody not comin'."

The smaller man shook his head and smiled sympathetically. "It is a most unfortunate business," he said. Reaching into his rear pocket he pulled out a crushed box of Gaulois, emptied the pack on the table, then picked up one of the bent cigarettes and began coaxing it into shape as he went on. "You should have make a more reliable choice of occupation, Monsieur Barcineh."

At the sound of his name, Barcineh's small remaining hope collapsed.

"You do not look well, *mon ami*. I think you will feel better when you are relieved of your burden, yes?" He lit the reshaped cigarette and shoved the rest back into the box. "Forgive me, I have not made the introductions, eh? I am called Maurice Lepine; my colleague is Kenneth Farr who, like me, is a man of great compassion. He is very anxious to—how you say?—give comfort."

Any thought of running was out of the question. He was carrying too much weight—it was a matter of balance. He had practiced with the vest for a long time but, still, balance was impossible without absolute concentration. Under these circumstances, even walking would be difficult. He could cry out but what good would that be? A disturbance would only bring the police—and then the others. If he fell into their hands, he would be sent back where he'd come from. And, after what he'd done, anything would be better than the death that waited for him there.

"You've made some nasty enemies, little man," Farr said, "the kind what can close doors in any bloody direction you decide to run. So, if you're thinkin' of it, you might give it a second go 'round."

Farr picked up the white linen, tucked it in his pocket, and the two men rose from their chairs. Barcineh

the **GOLD** *Covenant*

tried to get up but his energy was exhausted, his legs unable to bear his weight. Farr's hand circled Barcineh's back, anchored itself under his arm, and lifted him from his seat. With a nod to the customers at the next table, and rolling his eyes to indicate the smaller man had exceeded his capacity, Farr half-carried, half-pushed him toward the stairs that led down to the exit at the rear of the pub. It was a short but steep flight and Barcineh found it hard to maneuver without his knees buckling. He clung desperately to the banister, determined not to disgrace himself by falling.

What had happened to his contacts? Where were they? And who were these men? Did they want only what he was carrying? The gold? Or could they know about the other? There weren't many who would dare to steal a syndicate gold shipment. Still, it was possible. He hadn't been as clever as he should. It was the journey—the fatigue. If he hadn't worn the vest—hadn't been so anxious to make delivery—he could have run, could have tried to get away. Or, failing that, would have had something to bargain with, something to trade for so meager a thing as his life.

But, if it wasn't the gold—

If they knew about the other . . .

They crossed the alley behind the pub and entered a dark hallway through a paint-chipped door that had been propped open with a crushed can of Pilsener beer.

Maurice let the lock click into place after him, shutting the light out of the narrow passageway.

"Gentlemen," Barcineh pleaded, "surely, I can give you the vest here. I have no desire to cause trouble, only to walk away and leave you in peace. A simple thing to ask."

"The stairs, *monsieur*. Move."

They went up single file, Maurice in front, the larger man behind. Between them, drawing on a primal will, Barcineh dragged the dead weight of his legs up one stair at a time. At the third level, they walked to the rear of the unlit corridor and entered a dim, sparsely-furnished room. There was an unmade bed shoved sideways against the faded rose wallpaper, an ancient wardrobe closet leaning for support on the corner wall, and, under the single closed window, two chairs and an oak pedestal table holding a blue glass lamp and a brass ashtray overflowing with butts and ashes.

Maurice crossed the room and drew the shade down under the limp, grayed-white lace of the curtain. He switched on the lamp and turned to look at Barcineh, his face reflecting a cold pallor from the blue glass.

"Perhaps you will tell me," Barcineh said, "what has become of my friends?"

"You don't 'ave friends in this business," Farr said impatiently. "Let's get on with it."

As Barcineh began to unbutton his shirt, Farr grasped him with his immense hands, hefted him like a

the GOLD Covenant

side of beef, and slammed him against the wall. "You're carrying a pretty good load for such a little fellow," he said. "What d'you guess 'e weighs, Maurice?"

"At present, who knows. *Au naturel*, he look to be about ten stone, *c'est vrai*?"

" 'E should be about ten stone all right, but it'll take a bit a trimmin' down to get 'im there."

"Did I not say we would make you more comfortable?" Maurice smiled. In the blue light, his white teeth looked decayed.

His huge partner reached down, pulled Barcineh up by his lapels, and, with hardly a pause, wrenched the jacket and shirt from his back like pieces of offending lint. "We're through talkin'!" the man growled.

Thrown off balance by the weight he was carrying beneath the clothes, Barcineh staggered against the wall and tried desperately to keep his legs from collapsing again. When he'd steadied himself, he reached for the top button of his vest.

Farr stopped him, clamped his neck to the wall with one meaty hand, and, with the other, pulled a slim gold bar from one of the slots in the vest. "Not good for your 'ealth," he said, "luggin' this kinda weight on a body size a yours." He tossed the bar to Maurice and then systematically looked through each of the remaining seventeen, deep, narrow pockets.

When he'd finished, he unclamped his hand from

Barcineh's neck and turned to Maurice, his angry face a dark red. "It's bloody not 'ere. It's just the bloody gold."

"Are you certain?"

"A course I'm certain, you soggin' little frog. Whatta you take me for? Some a the pockets is empty. 'E's ditched the stuff, I tell you."

Unaffected by the big man's loss of temper, Maurice turned his attention to Barcineh. "Maybe, you like to bargain, little man, eh? You think it's worth your miserable life? These little trinkets you smuggle in with the gold?"

Barcineh's mind was racing. How was it possible they knew? How?

It didn't matter now. He had to think. Maybe there was hope after all. Obviously, these men weren't after the regular shipment. And, they'd believed he was still carrying the other pieces—the necklace and the dagger sheath. They didn't know he had already made the delivery. Perhaps he could make a bargain. He nodded at Maurice and said, "Locker. Victoria Station. In my jacket, the key—."

"Bugger the talk," Farr snapped at Maurice. "We been through the locker. We been through 'is filthy knickers. We been through 'is room. Show 'im the roll a bills we found. I say 'e's already made the delivery so what're we bloody waitin' for?"

"Ah, *mon ami*." Maurice sighed and shook his head. "You think there is value in your filthy underwear? Or did you think we settle for this?" He shrugged and pulled a pouch out of his pocket.

Barcineh recognized it and the roll of bills that came out of it. It was true. They had already been through his locker—his bag.

"Is this what they pay you?" Maurice went on. "You make a bad bargain, *mon ami*. You cannot carry enough gold to buy those pieces. Maybe you like to tell us who cheats you? Maybe you like to tell us about the next shipment?" His eyes changed—deadened.

It was a look Barcineh knew. His legs sagged but he pressed his back against the wall and held himself upright. It would be fruitless to argue with them. Their faces were like others he'd seen: fixed, immutable, wanting him to hope, to add to the pleasure of their game. That he would not do.

Nor would he steal from his people again. He had stolen once—two small artifacts only. Surely no more than his share. Hardly enough to be noticed—the price of his freedom—a small thing to ask.

But to tell these men more would be worse than stealing. It would be a betrayal of his people. It would destroy their heritage, their cities, their lives. He'd had his chance. He'd broken the rules and now he would not question or struggle. Life gives only one course for survival and when we make a mistake there is no going back. These men were only the instruments of his fate.

roberta clark

He thought it would come quickly from the big man, Kenneth Farr, but again he was wrong. Maurice opened a drawer in the table and took out a pair of leather gloves. He slipped them on and then took out a polished coil of stainless steel. The metal was several feet long, a quarter of an inch wide, and paper thin. With a few deft moves, he twisted the strip into a loop and then walked over to where Barcineh was standing.

"Try it," he said. "Go ahead. It should give you confidence, *non?*"

Barcineh touched the edge of the metal. It was razor-sharp. He had hardly felt anything, but as he withdrew his finger he saw a thin flow of blood oozing from the cut.

"You see?" Maurice said. "Clean. Quick."

"You want me to strip 'im first?" Farr asked.

"*Mais, non.* There would be no point to this lesson. We must let Monsieur Barcineh bear the full weight of his crime. Then, perhaps, if there is something he would like to tell us, he will have the encouragement, *non?*"

Pulling a short piece of cord from his pocket, Farr said, "I like your sentiments." He tied Barcineh's hands behind his back and, supporting his weight, forced him to stand erect as Maurice slipped the garrote over his head and attached it to a hook on the wall above him. The wire was then adjusted so the razor edge lay perpendicular to the flesh of his neck.

"You see now, *mon ami*, how much more pleasant it would be to honor a simple, reasonable request?" He turned, walked back to the table and removed the gloves.

Barcineh closed his eyes but after a few minutes nausea and dizziness forced him to open them again. Farr had made himself comfortable on the bed, having first laid a handkerchief over the pillow. Maurice sat next to the table. He dumped out the contents of his crushed pack of Gaulois next to the ashtray, chose a moderately undamaged one, and lit it.

"It is curious that you express no regrets," he said, smoothing out the remaining cigarettes as he replaced them in the box one by one.

"Those who do not try regret," Barcineh whispered, feeling the bite of metal as the muscles of his throat contracted. "I regret nothing."

"We're about t'change your mind," Farr said, "an' you bloody well will, you buggering little sod. You've put some very important people to a lot of bloody trouble."

"It's an interesting way to die," Maurice said, blowing a cloud of smoke toward Barcineh. "As long as you retain consciousness, you will retain your head. It is unfortunate that the weight of indiscretion is so heavy, *comprenez?*"

Barcineh tried not to think about the weight of the vest. Thirty-four kilos. Over seventy-six pounds of gold. It had been a happy as well as tolerable burden before. Now it dug into his shoulders, tearing at muscles and nerves, pulling the bones out of sockets. His knees were like a fragile crust of earth crumbling beneath him. He could not remain standing for long; already he could feel the compression of his vertebrae. Each time he swallowed, the wire seemed to tighten at his throat and there was a dampness dripping from his neck into the collar of his shirt and down the hollow of his spine under the torturous garment.

He stared straight ahead at the wall—at the patterned rows of pink flowers twining from ceiling to floor—finally fixing on one faded rose level with his eyes.

They were waiting for him to weaken, these men. Waiting for him to cry and plead. Waiting for him to dishonor himself. He had done that already. It would not happen again. He would not give them that satisfaction. Better to be done with it quickly. For only a moment he wondered what it would be like—the head parting from the body. And the soul. If there was a soul . . .

It would take one last effort, the concentration of all the strength he had left. Slowly, and with great determination, he balanced on one foot, gradually sliding the other up to the baseboard to steady himself. Then, closing the room and the two men from his sight and his mind, he kicked his foot against the wall, thrusting the full weight of his body against the steel blade.

CHAPTER 2

"Look, Hal, I pay you to get me the people who can get me the people I want."

"Some people can't be got, Ivar."

Ivar Whalen shoved his glasses to the top of his head and massaged the paper-thin flesh around his eyes—dark eyes sunk deep in dark sockets in a pale face. He looked worse than usual, Lawrence Halvern thought, but then he never looked really well except on camera. Next thing he'll do is rub his forehead to let me know he's fighting a headache. Public or private, his motions were ritual.

"You're giving static, Hal," Ivar said, pressing his fingers against his temples. "You suddenly need a *TV Guide* to remind you what we do here? We do presidents, premiers, kings, dictators, Popes. God almighty!"

"We haven't done him yet."

Ivar's hollow cheeks folded into a network of vertical creases. "So give me credit for patience," he laughed.

"We have room to move up, Hal boy, you and I."

"My ceiling's always been lower than yours."

"Sure it has. That's why, when there's a doubt, *I* call the shots."

Halvern had been dragging his feet on this one. He knew Ivar could read the slightest tinge of guilt on his face and was enjoying his discomfort. It wasn't malevolence; it was Ivar's way of keeping tuned up. The man was a specialist in reaction, an expert with a needle, nice bedside smile, this isn't going to hurt a bit, knowing it's going to hurt like hell. Only his performance was usually in public, in front of millions, on his once-a-month special, *Power Line*, NBC television.

Lawrence Halvern and Ivar Whalen had been together since they'd both started—still wet out of college—at a local station in Michigan. The relationship had always been the same: Ivar the flier, Hal the spotter. It was that symbiosis that kept them together and, in the years before and after *Power Line's* inception, had made Hal indispensable to Ivar—that and Hal's slow fuse and quiet efficiency.

"Look, old buddy," Ivar went on in his cotton-swab-after-the-needle voice, "your instincts are reliable, good for the long haul, but there are times when reliable isn't enough. Nobody's everything. We need each other."

"This is beginning to sound like a marriage proposal."

"It's a reminder, Hal, a reminder. We have a show

because when I want something nobody talks me out of it. We have ratings because when I know something's right, I won't let it go. That's why I can afford three ex-wives and you can send those two daughters of yours to fancy Ivy League colleges. Now all I'm asking is for you to earn that nice fat salary. Just plug me into the connection. I want Sheppard Wilde before anyone else gets him, and I know this Nikulasson woman is the right connection. Maybe the only connection. If you can't even deliver the small-fry, what-the-hell-good are you?"

"Okay, Ivar, you've made your point, but I've already talked to her. She's not interested."

Halvern felt a drop of perspiration drag a slow trail along his sternum under the starched white front of his shirt. He stood up, refreshed his glass from a pitcher of ice water on Ivar's desk, and began pacing the room. It was a simple desire to let the air circulate more freely inside of his shirt and his beige sharkskin suit but Ivar was likely to mistake the action for nervous tension. The man was always projecting. It didn't bother Halvern. That's why they'd been able to work together for the last twenty years without any major differences.

"So," Ivar said, "what you're really telling me is you can't do the job. Right?"

"Maybe I'm getting too soft for this kind of work."

"The soft is temporary. I know you, Hal. The woman's had a couple of bad breaks, so what? It happens.

roberta clark

Make it work in our favor. How's she fixed for money?"

"Husband left her nothing," Halvern said, settling down in his chair again. "A few debts, at most."

"Husband? I didn't think she was married to the guy."

"No contract, if that's what you mean, but there might as well have been. She'd almost cleared off his debts when her father was killed in the plane crash. The father's estate should be worth a fair amount when it's settled."

"They never found the body, Hal boy. That usually causes complications—delays. The kind that tie up estates for a long time. The kind that might leave our Miss Nikulasson with some heavy expenses."

"There's a trust her father set up for her when she was a child—after his wife died. It won't pay all the bills, but it's enough to take the edge off."

"Hal boy, a woman can always use something for the entertainment fund—clothes, trinkets, trips to Bermuda."

"Believe me, I've tried. She doesn't care about the money."

"Everyone cares about money."

"I'm telling you, she's turned it down."

"How much have you offered her?"

"Twenty-five-thousand," Hal said. "Half in front."

Brows lifted and there was a momentary spark of white in the dark sockets of Ivar's eyes. "Make it twenty-five in front with a twenty-five-thousand-dollar bonus. If you tell me she'd turn that down, you'd be telling me

the **GOLD** Covenant

she's stupid."

"What I'm trying to tell you is, you ought to be more realistic about Wilde."

"If I were realistic, I wouldn't be in this business."

"If I were realistic, I'd put my money on God before Wilde."

Ivar reached up and disengaged his glasses from a wiry profusion of gray hair—his trademark—and fixed them in place on the bony parapet that served as a nose—another mark of distinction that made him a frequent subject for caricature.

"What's bothering you, Hal?" he asked. "If I didn't know you better, I'd think you were afraid of Wilde."

"Maybe I am," Halvern answered, a little surprised at his confession.

"Well, I'm not," Ivar said, slapping a hand on the desk. "And I'm going to pay your way back to prep school if you don't pull this one off for me."

"Why not shoot for next season? Maybe we'll get a handle on Wilde by then."

"Are you hearing me or am I talking up my own ass? We're not waiting until next season. Somebody else will have him by then. Now! I'm saying now. This season. The handle we've already got—Katherine Nikulasson."

"Now you're going to tell me everyone has their price," Halvern said, "and you're going to be wrong."

"What I'm telling you is what you and I both know.

Everyone has a rot spot—soft—easy to get a thumb into."

"*You* know it," Halvern said. "Me, I'm not so sure."

"Find it, Hal boy. Get your thumb in deep. Give her a reason to go after him."

Halvern reached for the pitcher again, using the seconds to reorganize his thoughts. "What's going on, Ivar? You're not leveling with me. This Nikulasson pitch has nothing to do with the show. There are better methods of getting through to Wilde so what in hell's so important about doing it this way?"

"Believe me," Ivar said, "it's important."

Ivar waited until he heard Halvern leave the outer office, then flipped the switch on his intercom. "You can come in now, Gehreich," he said, "and bring the scotch with you."

The door to his private inner office opened. A man—fifty or so, medium height, with even features, the kind you can't remember after he's left the room—came in and sat in the chair Halvern had vacated only minutes before. He plunked the fifth of Scotch on the desk between them, loosened his brown tie, and smoothed his gray thinning hair with the palms of his hands. His stomach was making the kinds of noises that indicated the recent consumption of a heavy, indigestible lunch.

"We've got a problem here," Ernest Gehreich said, sitting back with the drink he'd carried in with the bottle.

"What kind of problem?" Ivar asked.

"Your Mr. Halver-en," the man said, drawing out the last syllable in a nasal twang. "He's gonna be a large boil-on-the-ass problem."

Ivar took his time, let his eyes wander with distaste from the man's olive-green suit to his sallow complexion which looked even more jaundiced next to the drab gabardine. Lousy choice of color, he thought. No excuse for lack of style—it's just unadulterated sloth. He poured himself a scotch and fished a couple of ice cubes out of the pitcher before saying, "Hal's all right. And you know damn well he gets the job done."

"Sure sounds like an ass-dragger on this one, wouldn'ya say?" Gehreich shoved a hand into his pants pocket and pulled out a package of Rolaids. He ripped off the green wrapper and popped two mints into his mouth while he waited for an answer. Failing to get one, he sighed heavily and continued. "Well, me, I'm not so sure of your Mr. Halver-en as you are."

"Your approval isn't part of the deal, Gehreich. This isn't exactly one of your regular department assignments."

"Trouble with civilians, they're full a questions. All kinds a questions. Can't keep their noses in low gear for more'n a minute at a time. I don't like workin' with 'em. Too damn risky."

"Seems to me, you're in the wrong business if you don't like risk."

"There's different kinds a risk—different odds. I like t'keep control on 'em, know what I mean? Especially when they got anything to do with the goddamned entertainment industry."

"Why don't you file your complaints with someone who's more sympathetic?" Ivar said. "Empathy isn't a virtue I like to cultivate." With that, he put down his drink and shuffled the stacks of paper on his desk, his way of signifying the end of the meeting. To his annoyance, instead of rising, Gehreich reached for the scotch and replenished his almost empty glass.

"You know—" his voice relaxed into a leisurely drawl, "—I'm not so sure you appreciate what I've been doin' for you all these years. Your organization couldn't function on the wrong side a mine. We pave the way—give the State Department the motivation they need to make things happen. Things that might otherwise take months or even years. Without us, your guest list on *Power Line* would read like the Podunk telephone directory."

"Nothing's free," Ivar snapped. "It's been pay-as-you-go all the way. And just you remember, this time there's no department to back you up. You do it my way or you do it alone."

"Then make damn sure you got your finger in the right hole, Whalen, 'cause we've got a lot ridin' on this—

the GOLD Covenant

on your amateur crew. See to it they don't foul up and get themselves killed. Amateurs are always gettin' themselves killed."

"Don't you think that's rather overstated?"

"Under! Mr. Whalen. Under! And the really shitty thing is when they fuck up it's someone like me always has t'do the cleanin' up after 'em."

"You know something, Gehreich? With a temperature of a-hundred-and-six, you could be a genuinely warm human being."

"It's a cinch you ain't got the corner on that market anymore'n I do," Gehreich said, slouching back into this chair. "Listen, I've got six more months before I hang it up once and for all and start collecting my pension. Got a one-way ticket for the Bahamas and a nice little Catalina 30 waitin' at the dock. With my experience, I'll soon have her fitted out with something young and nubile that's waitin' on her back for a free ride into the never-ending sunset. I'm gonna be real unhappy if anything happens to spoil my pretty little dream. I might even want to spoil things for you."

Ivar leaned across the desk and fastened his eyes on Gehreich. "Let's get one thing straight right now. Not only is this deal costing me, it's my ass on the line. Mine, Gehreich! You deliver as promised or that pretty little dream of yours'll sink into the ocean along with your golden sunset and your sexual aberrations."

roberta clark

It had taken Lawrence Halvern two days of digging and a bit of luck to place himself in a better bargaining position for his third try at Katherine Nikulasson. After waiting in front of the apartment for almost an hour, he finally spotted her a half-block away. He made no move to get out of the limo. If she caught one glimpse of him before she passed the stop light at the corner, she'd be off in another direction. He wasn't going to let her get away this time, now that he had the bait to land her.

Carrying an overnight grip in one hand and a brown paper package in the other, she was making brisk progress along Central Park West. Halvern wasn't the only one watching the rhythmic movement of her long legs and nicely-shaped compact body. The elderly doorman, Melton, had spotted her, too. Except for the few minutes it took to whistle down a cab for one of the Plaza regulars, he'd kept an unwavering eye on her, his chest gradually inflating to its limited capacity, his shoulders rising and broadening under the gold epaulets, years dropping from the sagging jowls as they lifted the corners of his mouth. Melton's unequivocal admiration played across his face like the Times Square news, and, as inured to show business flash as Halvern had become, he found it easy to empathize with the old man.

the **GOLD** *Covenant*

A moment later, Melton's expression changed to annoyance. Katherine had stopped in response to a shout and was waiting as a man dodged through the stalled traffic to cross over to her side of the street. He was a Wall-Street type—dark vested suit, leather briefcase—only the overly effusive greeting seemed out of character. She gave it a right-hand block and held him at a distance while they talked.

Melton sidled over from the Plaza entrance and, eyes still intent on the two of them, bent stiffly to speak into the open window of the limo.

"See that?" he said.

"Sorry," Halvern said, leaning forward on the seat. "I don't understand."

"That! Her stiff right arm. Ain't nobody gets past it. Found that out when she was just seven, first time I gave her a pat on the head."

"Likes to keep a distance, does she?"

"There's distance and there's distance," Melton said. "If you know what I mean."

"I'm not sure that I do."

"There are times when it comes in mighty useful. Take that fellow she's talkin' to there—fancies himself an old friend—family retainer—that kind a thing. Well, he ain't none a those. 'Cept maybe old. There's ambulance chasers and coffin chasers, know what I mean? Neither one of 'em's the type you'd want to snuggle up to, and that fella's a bit a both."

"You sound like a very discerning fellow."

"I've been opening doors all my life, Mr. Halvern. There's doors and there's doors—you know what I'm saying?"

If it hadn't been for Melton, Halvern would have come up empty-handed again in the meeting with Ivar scheduled for this afternoon. Katherine had been out of town for almost a week. The most Melton would reveal about where she'd gone was that it was unreachable by phone. He did, however, give Halvern the day and time she was expected home, after buying his highly embellished story about legal business regarding Gustav Nikulasson's estate and the urgent necessity for locating her about the settlement.

The old man started to move back to his station under the French blue canopy, paused, seeming to remember something else he wanted to say, and sauntered back to the limo.

"I know you lawyer fellows got a lot a dirty work to do, but I hope you're bringing her some good news this time, Mr. Halvern. She's had more'n her share a bad lately."

"Her fortune may be changing, Melton."

"Glad to hear that. She's like my own daughter. Not that I ever had one, mind you, but there's having and there's having. You know what I mean? No, guess you wouldn't. Too young! Twenty-three years. Come September it'll be twenty-three years since she and her father moved in." Cautiously straightening up from the waist, he added, "Told you she'd be on time, didn't I?"

"You were right," Halvern said, feeling unaccustomedly guilty over the contrived story he'd given the old man.

Melton scurried back to his post through the midday-rush of pedestrians as Katherine approached the entrance.

"Have a nice weekend, Miss Katherine?"

"A busy one. Nice to see you back at the post, Melton. I missed you last Friday."

"Never would've deserted, but Betty wouldn't let me out of the house. Said August was the best month for turning a dribble-sized cold into pneumonia. Looks like you picked up some sun."

"Gardening. The yard has gone wild since I moved back to the city. Have to get it in shape for the real estate people." She held out the brown paper package. "Some cuttings for Betty—Beach Plum and Bristly Rose. Not sure how well they'll do in this climate but it's worth a try. Tell her the rose is pink."

"That's her color all right," he said, handling the package like a fragile treasure. "Shame you have to sell the place."

"It's part of the past now," she said, then changing the subject, added, "You could use some sun yourself. Sick-leave doesn't take the place of a vacation."

"There's a man from the lawyer's office over there.

roberta clark

Been waiting to see you since eleven-fifteen."

"Almost an hour? Expensive time for a lawyer to squander."

"Said it was important legal business. 'Bout your father's estate," he added over his shoulder as he moved across to the curb to meet an arriving taxi.

She turned to see Halvern walking toward her, a sheepish grin on his face, right hand outstretched, left hand holding a large manila packet.

"Mr. Halvern." There was a tinge of metal in her voice and in her dark green eyes.

Halvern smiled and nodded toward Melton. "He's a nice old guy."

"And he's the only reason I'm going to talk to you. I wouldn't want him to know you'd taken advantage of him. It would spoil his day."

Halvern planted himself in front of her. "He's very fond of you," he said. The comment did nothing to change the unrelenting look in her eyes so he tried another opening. "It seemed a harmless deception for a desperate man."

"Is that part of your job? Doing impersonations for Ivar Whalen?"

"It's not what I do best."

"Good, because you're going to need a new act," she said and started to move around him toward the entrance.

"I promise I'll get one if you'll do me one simple

the **GOLD** Covenant

favor." He shifted his position to block her path again. "Won't take more than five minutes of your time."

"What is it?"

"Take this file upstairs with you and skim it over. I think you'll find it extremely enlightening."

"Manila envelopes have an affinity with blackmail, Mr. Halvern. I wouldn't find that interesting or enlightening."

Once more, she tried to slip around him but, anticipating her move, he side-stepped with her. "It's nothing like that, I promise you," he said. "Look, I'm not asking to come up with you. If you decide to talk to me after you've read it, give Melton a call down here. I'll wait in the car for twenty minutes."

"You said it would take five."

"Time to think . . . in case you need it."

"I won't," she said, feinting to the right and then moving left. "Don't waste your time."

"Wait! Please."

"You'd save yourself a lot of bother, if you'd just find someone else to run your errand."

"I've already invested too much in you, Miss Nikulasson."

"Every investment doesn't pay off."

"Give it a chance, will you? I told you there were things I do better than impersonations."

"I'm sure there are, but I'm not holding auditions."

"One of those is research," he went on, talking fast,

trying to keep a grasp on her attention. "I have a sample in this envelope. Some information that was never printed in the newspapers. Unreported highlights about the crash of a private plane in the Mediterranean—a plane that belonged to Sheppard Wilde and was carrying Gustav Nikulasson and Kevin Arman. That's worth at least five minutes out of your day, isn't it?"

He could feel the sudden anger and see the effort it took for her to control it. Wrong move, he told himself. You've blown it again.

"All right, Mr. Halvern," she said, taking the packet, "five minutes."

His shoulders sagged in relief as he watched her enter the building and fade into the shadows of the lobby.

CHAPTER 3

The elevator ride up to the tenth floor had given her a chance to skim through enough of the file to realize it was worthy of a more careful reading. It also made her wish she'd allowed herself more time. Five minutes—real smart ass, Katherine. Next time try not to box yourself in.

She crossed the hall to her apartment and unlocked the door, feeling a slight resistance when she tried to open it. *Damn, they've fallen over again—have to find a better place to stack them.* Pushing the door gently, she slid a heavy pile of books over the hardwood floor in front of it, toppling a second stack in the process.

Inside, she cleared a path to the intercom. She pressed the button for Melton, and, while waiting for him to answer, restacked the books against the wall farther from their precarious place next to the front door. The overgrown library had long ago surpassed the storage capacity of the apartment. Her father, she thought, would have given up his bed if it had ever come to a choice.

The brisk sound of the buzzer brought her to her feet again. "Melton, would you put Mr. Halvern on, please."

"Sure thing, Miss Katherine. He's right outside pacing the leather off his wing-tips."

A minute later Halvern's voice came through sounding tentative. "Have you decided, Miss Nikulasson?"

"Where did you get this information?"

"I assure you, it's accurate."

"It's also classified."

"Did that stop you from reading it?"

"There are pages missing."

"Sometimes we have to settle for what we can get."

"Put Melton back on. And give me five minutes to change."

With luck, the elevator would add on a few extra minutes getting down and then up again with Halvern. Time enough to get out of her travel clothes and into Levis and a chambray work shirt. The two items—her indispensable uniform—were still strewn on top of the bed where she'd tossed them on Friday morning. Pushing aside a stack of bills and unopened bank statements, she placed the file on top of the bureau where she could continue reading it while she changed.

Several minutes later, she picked up the pile of papers, walked into the foyer to leave the front door ajar, and then went into the kitchen for something to appease the hunger pangs. It was the neatest room in the apartment, the only room where she didn't indulge her natural tendency to let things pile up. The refrigerator yielded a lone carton of milk which was light to the touch and sour to the smell. She poured it down the drain and checked again for anything immediately edible. The most she could come up with was a saltine cracker, the last one in the cupboard, and a piece of moldy cheese which had been stuffed into the butter cooler, and, when trimmed, was less than half-a-mouthful.

On the memo slate next to the vintage porcelain counter, she wrote, *everything!*, then walked back to the study which opened directly onto the foyer. The room was dusty—everything was dusty—she hadn't even noticed it until now. There were dozens of framed photographs on the walls, most of them connected with thin trails of cobwebs—testimony to a deliberate neglect and avoidance of the memories they contained. Since John's death and then her father's, she'd felt more and more that her own life was held together by nothing stronger than those flimsy webs. She had always been isolated in one way or another but this was the first time she'd ever been conscious of it, maybe even frightened of it.

Katherine padded barefoot across the balding oriental carpet and stood beside the ancient, oak, leather-inlaid, hulk of a desk that had been Gustav Nikulasson's pride. She let her fingers slide over the smooth surface, savoring the faint smell of wood and leather that held so many memories. Gustav's powers of concentration had been phenomenal. As a child, she'd been allowed to use a corner of the desk for school lessons, even while her father was working. Banishment from it for a period of one month was the harshest punishment she'd ever received. It happened only once, when a wadded paper cannonball misfired and upset a cup of coffee, resulting in the loss of several valuable manuscript pages. She had always been an expert on how far to go, but this was more than even Gustav would tolerate.

She never jeopardized the sacred privilege of the desk again. From that time on there was always, at the least, a serious pretense of study. Though her father rarely spoke to her or noticed what she was doing during those times, she knew he wanted her there—another presence in the room. She understood, now, more than ever, it was a reaction to loneliness, to the void her mother's death had left in his life. The loss had been devastating to her, too, at the age of seven, but seven-year-olds are resilient, quick to heal. For her father, the loss had been irreconcilable.

Now, he was gone, too. The very thing she'd dreaded as a child—that he would leave on one of his trips and never come back—had really happened. It had been a long time since she'd had a nightmare like that, a long time since Gustav had packed her along with him, and a long time since he'd realized how emotionally dependent she'd become. His breaking of that dependency when she was sixteen had been necessary but it wasn't an experience she liked to remember.

There's never any sense in trying to erase memories or to hasten the numbing process. It's all a question of time and the prescribed medicine—work—and Katherine had more than enough of both. The library, as well as the rest of the apartment, was cluttered with cartons, manuscripts, photographs, and relics. They were stacked in the corners of her bedroom, in front of the over-loaded, ceiling-high book shelves in the oak-paneled living room, on top of sturdy antique trestle tables and leather sofas and chairs, and in Gustav's bedroom which had been turned into a storeroom, all waiting to be sorted and catalogued.

Every room in the apartment smelled of dust, but of a special kind: of brittle vellum and faded parchment, of worn leather, and of the crust of ancient pottery. It was a smell of childhood and security and love and she made no apology for it or the mess when Lawrence Halvern entered the study.

"I assume you wanted me to come in," he said apologetically, gaping at her bare feet and over-sized shirt as though he had intruded at an awkward moment. "The door was open and you didn't answer the knock."

"Yes, I'm sorry, I didn't hear you," she said. "Do

you mind if I take a few more minutes with these files?" She moved around the desk and sat down on the over-stretched cane seat of an ancient swivel chair.

Halvern wandered around the room looking at the photographs, as she shuffled through the stack of papers on top of the already-cluttered desk. When she'd had time to collect her thoughts, she tapped the edges of the papers, making them even, and slipped them back into the envelope.

"If it's Sheppard Wilde you want," she said, "why spend all this time on me? Why not ask him yourself?"

"We've tried. We need a key to get in," Halvern said, settling into the one empty chair in front of the desk, "and Ivar Whalen believes you're the key."

"I don't think Sheppard will consent to a filmed interview. Even for the daughter of an old friend."

"Surely you're more than—" The look in her eyes stopped him abruptly and he slid at once into another tack. "All we want you to do is try, Miss Nikulasson. Sooner or later someone is going to get him, and Ivar is determined to be first."

"It's disillusioning to think the great Ivar Whalen needs help," she said, smiling, "especially from me."

"Miss Nikulasson . . ." He slid forward on his chair and continued in a confiding tone. "Ivar would be the first person to admit he can't do it alone."

Katherine bit her pencil to stifle the involuntary grin.

the **GOLD** *Covenant*

Too involved in his thoughts to notice, Halvern went on. "When Ivar needs help he asks for it. He's not what most people think."

"And what do most people think?"

"Well, he's been accused of being everything from an imperious egotist to a megalomaniac, but, I'll tell you something very few people know, it's a front. Sure, he grates on people—no one knows that better than Ivar himself—but it's what his public wants—to watch the other guy squirm."

"He has the ratings." It was a flat noncommittal statement. "Maybe he should be content with the show business crowd. And politicians. They don't need coaxing."

"We have to fight them off. Those aren't the people who make a show different, make the audience switch over from the hot soaps and the Saturday-night movie. Hell, you can catch all the same faces on any talk show. They're on a goddamned merry-go-round. Look, Ivar wants this bad enough to up the ante to twenty-five thousand, all expenses paid, no limit—within reason, of course—and a twenty-five thousand dollar bonus if you land him. Plus—and this is something you might have some use for—access to the network's resources and entree in England. What've you got to lose?"

"A friend. And time."

"Then you had no second thoughts after reading the file? You aren't the least bit doubtful about that friendship?"

"How do I know your information about the plane crash is accurate? It's difficult to believe Shep wouldn't have filled me in on all of those details. If they were factual."

"The network has unimpeachable sources—that is a fact—and you would have free access to those same sources. Don't you think it would be worth some of that valuable time of yours to find out why Mr. Wilde didn't fill you in on the details?"

Katherine swiveled around in her chair and looked out of her tenth floor window. She could almost see the haze of August heat rising from the sidewalks below. Not a bad place to leave for the summer, and she already had her airline ticket. A ticket she had planned to cancel. Why was it so difficult to say yes to this man? She turned back and looked at him, wondering how deep his polished veneer went—where the genuine Mr. Halvern began if there still was one. He certainly had done his homework. He'd been right, too—about the questions, the doubts—and it didn't make her fond of him.

"What do you say, Miss Nikulasson?"

"It wouldn't be honest to say you've gone to all this trouble for nothing. I am impressed with your file. The information isn't a complete surprise, but it does lend weight to what might otherwise be called rumor. I also feel compelled to tell you I already have an airline ticket to London and arrangements to stay at Sheppard Wilde's estate."

the **GOLD** *Covenant*

"But that's marvelous. We'll reimburse you for the ticket, of course . . . and any other expenses incurred."

"You don't understand. I'm not agreeing to go on your behalf. I have very strong reasons myself for wanting to visit Shep, reasons that need no impetus from Ivar Whalen or anyone else. What I'm saying is under those circumstances, you'd have no guarantee of getting your money's worth."

"If I were afraid of being short-changed, Miss Nikulasson, I wouldn't have come to you in the first place. Do you mind if I call you Katherine? It'll save time."

She smiled. "Valuable time."

"You're a good risk, Katherine. Do you want to see the dossier I have on you?" He pulled a notebook from his inner coat pocket. "Makes pretty good reading."

"I prefer Raymond Chandler."

"Too bad," he said, smiling as he flipped over a few pages. "I rather enjoyed it. How many schools were you bounced out of? Very impressive."

"I wasn't good at institutions, and that seems an odd reason for considering me trustworthy."

"The point I was making was that Ivar is thorough. He's only influenced by what's relevant. Your professional reputation is impeccable, your articles in *Cross Atlantic Magazine* have depth as well as polish and—something Ivar would never give you the satisfaction of knowing but which I'm going to tell you anyway—he has most of them on file in his office."

"If I accepted your offer—" she said, reluctantly, "—and couldn't persuade Mr. Wilde?"

"Let's say half the bonus for your time."

"Just like that—even though I wouldn't give a wooden slug for my chances of getting an agreement—an all-expense-paid vacation in England, plus twenty-five thousand dollars, plus half of another twenty-five if I fail. You're not spending your money wisely, Mr. Halvern."

"You forgot to mention the resources."

She hadn't mentioned them but she hadn't forgotten them either. Shep Wilde was a powerful man with powerful connections, and if she had any hope of finding answers to the questions raised in Halvern's file and in her own mind, she was going to need some power of her own. Halvern was offering her something she couldn't refuse and yet she still hesitated, still wondered if she would be the one to regret the choice.

"Look, Katherine, I know how you must feel—as though you're betraying the hospitality of a friend for base motives and all that kind of thing—but I can't imagine anyone being less vulnerable, or more sympathetic to the profit motive than Mr. Wilde."

"I agree with you on the first count—Shep needs protecting like a Bengal tiger in a deli—but he might surprise you on the second count. Profit has never been his prime motivation."

the **GOLD** *Covenant*

"Great! Just what Ivar wants. Simply to show the public what Wilde is really like."

"Ivar wants to nail him—publicly, for whatever reason he's trumped up in his contentious little mind."

"You're reading too much into this. It's only a request, after all. We're not asking you to serve a subpoena."

He said it pleasantly enough, as he had everything else in this meeting, but Katherine didn't want to like him. She tried to focus on some weakness, some aggravating habit. So far, other than that he worked for Ivar Whalen, she hadn't been able to find one. His sandy-brown hair was untinted, slightly gray at the temples, with the kind of cut that isn't done on a template. His face was clean-shaven with a healthy outdoor glow, his eyes bright-blue and unwavering, no pot at his belt-line, suit immaculate.

"Are you married, Mr. Halvern?"

"Why, yes. Happily."

The qualifier did it. Only people who were doing a selling job needed one.

Halvern looked puzzled. "Marriage is another institution you find distasteful, I take it?"

"Not at all." She smiled, stood up, and offered her hand in an unmistakably final gesture. "I have a feeling we'll meet again," she said.

"You are weakening then?"

"Call me tomorrow."

"I don't want you to feel rushed," he said. "You can

have until Thursday if you want."

"I don't need until Thursday."

The truth is, Mr. Halvern, she thought, *I don't need until tomorrow either.*

CHAPTER 4

Katherine was out of Heathrow and into a cab before the first load of baggage hit the conveyor belt. Waiting for luggage was a hassle. She never traveled with more than she could carry on. Halvern had offered her the use of a limo but she'd refused. Those *Power Line* resources had to be used with restraint. Even if there were no unseen strings attached, the idea of becoming accustomed to their use might make it difficult to break the connection with Ivar Whalen. She didn't want a long-term association with the man—one of Halvern's last-ditch offers—just the temporary use of NBC's entree. Without it, the success of her trip would have been in doubt, or, more likely, the trip canceled until she was better prepared.

She'd been out of the fast-paced world for too long. It takes time to get up to speed, to get the gears slicked and working, but there isn't always time to wait. When an opportunity like this comes along, you've got to convince yourself you've been moving too slowly. The body waiting for everything to be nice and pat inside the head, using that for an excuse.

There were too many unanswered questions about her father's death and Shep had side-stepped all of them, as had everyone else connected with the investigation. The only information she had was from news releases. Gustav Nikulasson and the pilot, Kevin Arman, had gone down somewhere in the eastern Mediterranean Sea. It was a conclusion based on their flight plan, the time of the last radio contact, and the failure of the search parties to find any trace of wreckage. Halvern's file had confirmed the ownership of the Lear jet, Wilde Enterprises. It had also confirmed the fact that Sheppard Wilde had left England in the plane with Kevin Arman two days before the crash. There had been no explanation for why he hadn't been on the return flight with Kevin and Gustav.

It was disturbing enough not to have heard this directly from Shep, but even more disturbing was the fact that Gustav's latest research and manuscripts had gone down with him. There had been no record of his work in the personal effects forwarded to her in the States—clothes, books, typewriter, recorder, camera equipment, but no tapes or photographs and no current notebooks or papers.

the **GOLD** Covenant

Never, never would her father carry all of his work with him on a plane. There had to be copies on the ground—in a safe place. It was a religious rite with him. It was what kept the plane in the air whenever he flew. It was his only indulgence in superstition. Sacred copies on the ground. He could laugh about it but he could never ignore the necessity for it. It kept him alive. It had until four months ago.

She hadn't seen much of her father over the last two years. His work, the fourth volume in his *History of Ancient Civilizations*, had kept him buried in an eastern sector of Turkey. She guessed it was in the vicinity of the Shamiram aqueduct near Lake Van but he'd never corroborated this. His silence during that time had convinced Katherine he was onto something important. He was always silent until his work was completed. It insured privacy, time to substantiate his findings and to thoroughly document them.

When the crate containing his effects had arrived, her anticipation was at its peak. The following months brought nothing but disappointment. She read every paper, every notebook, but there wasn't a hint of his findings.

If it hadn't been for his letter, the last one she received from him, there would have been no reason for the disappointment. She knew the letter by heart. Most of it had read like a travelogue but at the end he hadn't been able to contain himself.

roberta clark

There's a missing century here, Kat, enough to keep me busy the rest of my life. I keep hoping you've done with the dead and come back to the living. John is gone. There is nothing more devastating or more final than that. I know the need—the compelling desire—to bury oneself with the dead, but it must pass. You can't grieve forever, my girl. If you've had your fill of that self-imposed exile, get yourself over here for a look. Shep is flying in next week, maybe you can thumb a ride.

She'd asked herself a thousand times if she had thumbed that ride, would Gustav still be alive. It wasn't a logical conclusion. More likely, she would have been on the plane with him when it went down. She knew that, but, either way, she was left with the feeling she'd deserted him.

After his death, she had packed her belongings, moved out of the small house on the coast of Maine, and rejoined the world. The papers he'd accumulated in the apartment had occupied all of her time for four months. Gradually the guilt had been replaced with regret. Regret for the two years she'd wasted, as her father had said, in her self-imposed exile. It had been a debilitating indulgence, keeping her in a suspended state of non-living for too long. It was time to shift into high gear again.

Since the accident, there had been several letters from Shep Wilde with invitations to spend some time at his estate in Wiltshire. She had hoped to know more about her father's discovery before accepting the offer,

the **GOLD** *Covenant*

but the last of Gustav's papers had revealed no more than the first. It had been disappointing, at the least, but the real frustration lay in trying to find out why there was a complete lack of material on his current project. And why Shep—who she knew had been on the site—had raised a stone wall on her questions. Prying information from him would not be easy, not if he was determined to keep that information from her, as she was convinced he was. She needed an advantage, and the arrangement with Ivar Whalen might give her that needed edge.

She had also needed a push. There hadn't been a hope of getting answers with an ocean between them, but still she'd delayed crossing it for months. For so many reasons.

No, she wasn't being honest with herself. The reasons had been merely rationalizations. It was Shep she'd been avoiding.

Seeing him again—

Now she was here, remembering past decisions, mistakes, all the things she hadn't let herself think about for a long time. If there was anything she should understand—should recognize with absolute certainty—it was a closed chapter . . . an ending . . .

This trip was strictly business.

The cab turned onto York Road and rolled into a line of cars emptying passengers at Waterloo station.

"We're in for it," the driver said, reaching over with her change. "It's a sure thing you'll be needin' your

roberta clark

umbrella while you're here. Take my word on that."

"I didn't bring one," she said. "Maybe I'll get lucky."

It started raining before the train to Salisbury pulled out of the station.

CHAPTER 5

The Wiltshire countryside had been drenched with the summer shower, but when Katherine stepped off the train at Salisbury the clouds were drawing back like a gray curtain behind the towering spire of the cathedral. People hurried past her along the platform and out of the station, briefcases and umbrellas dangling from their arms, rushing to shelter as though the emergence of blue sky were only a fleeting promise and not to be trusted.

She walked out of the building and stood with luggage in hand as the waiting taxis rolled up to the curb. One of the cabbies hopped out, hitched up his baggy corduroy britches, and lifted the visor of his cap, scanning the ten-forty-five efflux of commuters rushing past him. His eyes lighted on Katherine, briefly, passed over her, and then, almost as quickly, returned. He tugged the cap back into place with a deft twist of his hand and walked over to her. A broad smile revealed an uneven set of teeth and multiplied the profusion of freckled creases around his blue eyes. He touched his visor. "Miss Nikulasson?"

"Yes," she said, feeling she ought to have recognized him.

"I were figurin' there'd be a heap o' luggage, but otherwise you fit the description nicely. Are there more bags in the waitin' room perhaps?"

"No, this is it. Who gave you the description?"

" 'T'were Mr. Wilde's housekeeper did that. I'll be drivin' you to Stowesbridge if you're ready now. Let me carry them bags for you."

Taking them from her hands without waiting for a reply, he scooted ahead, held the door open for her, then shoved the bags onto the front seat and slid in beside them.

"It's a good run out to Stowesbridge," he said, shifting into first and making a flying take-off that pinned Katherine to the upholstery of the back seat until he finally settled into fifth gear. "Always like to let 'er out a bit on my last trip."

"I hope you're not being prophetic."

"Not a bit of it," he laughed. "It's the last trip o' the day I were referrin' to."

A clear blue ceiling was opening above them as they left the traffic of the city and drove out into the green sprawl of farmland. The cab sluiced along the narrow rain-soaked road, not in the least intimidated by the slippery surface or by the high hedgerow obscuring the oncoming traffic.

When they finally hit on a straight-away, she relaxed her grip on the seat and began to breath freely again. "Do you have suicidal tendencies?" she asked him.

"It's the twits, like him in front o' me there, what have those leanings, see. Imagine gettin' out on a public thoroughfare with no trace o' aptitude for it." As if to underscore the statement, he whipped around a small car, sending a spray of muddy water onto its windshield. "If you're feelin' edgy, I can slow 'er a bit."

"Don't do that. You'll throw your timing off. I'll be into the spirit of it by the time we get there."

"I've been makin' this trip regular of the last few months. Door to door I know every stitch o' the road."

"That's a comfort," she said, wondering if the reddish fringe of hair flapping wildly below the brim of his cap would manage to escape its roots. "I didn't realize Mr. Wilde did so much entertaining."

"It weren't, by my experience, the usual way o' things. As to the entertainin', I don't think I once caught sight o' Mr. Wilde hisself. You sure you'll be catchin' him at home?"

"About as sure as I am we're going to make it in one piece."

This seemed to inspire him to new heights of daring. He skidded ahead of an Austin-Healey as they rounded another curve and, leaning on the wheel, slid back into his lane, out of the path of a loaded hay wagon, brushing the overhanging crop into the open window and covering Katherine with damp slivers of hay.

"You're wasting yourself," she said, scooting up to a sitting position. "Stirling Moss couldn't touch you."

"You've a fine eye for talent. A racing career—now that's a decent way to make a livin'."

"But your wife wouldn't hear of it?"

"Was me old mum wouldn't have it. Said I owed it to her not to get twisted into a tin like a bloomin' sardine. As for a wife, Mum'd sooner o' seen me in a sardine tin as standin' at the altar with another woman."

"Is that a fact or a test of my gullibility?"

"Oh, it's a fact, look. You'll be knowin' the battleship yourself when you get to Stowesbridge. She's cook and head of household for Mr. Wilde."

"You can't mean Flo Short?"

"Ah, then you've already been fired on."

"She doesn't so much fire as take command. And I like her—as much as you do. You're Cuppy Short, aren't you? Didn't you drive for Mr. Wilde years ago?"

"Fourteen year ago to be exact. Fancy you rememberin' a thing like that."

"It would have been difficult to forget. At that age I had a better appreciation of your unforgettable driving skills."

the **GOLD** *Covenant*

"Now that shows solid good sense. Fourteen year ago—that'd be before I went on my own. You must o' been no more'n a child back then."

"Not exactly a child, but very young. It was the last time I visited Stowesbridge with my father, Gustav Nikulasson. Do you remember him?"

She caught his eye in the rear-view mirror, suddenly serious and a little curious as well.

"He were a fine gentleman, your father. I was certain sorry to hear what happened."

She nodded silently and looked away, surprised the tears were so close to the surface.

"I seen him not more'n a week afore the accident," Cuppy went on. "Lookin' fit to go another fifty year, he were."

"A week before the accident? Are you sure? He was working in Turkey—for the past two years. He didn't usually leave a work site until he was finished."

"No mistakin' it. I drove him up to the house myself."

"How long was he there?"

"I couldn't be sayin'. I didn't rightly see him leave."

"Did your mother talk about the visit?"

"My mum? She's close-mouthed as a bachelor in the company of a spinster when it comes to Mr. Wilde's affairs."

"Yes, she is. I remember."

It's odd, Katherine thought, Gustav hadn't mentioned leaving Turkey. And Katherine couldn't imagine him coming to England without letting her know. Was it possible Cuppy was confusing her father with someone else? No, that wasn't likely either.

With only a slight reduction in speed, he made an acute right-angle turn onto a gravel lane which threaded through a mat of wild flowers under an uncultivated growth of shrubs for a quarter of a mile. The end of the private road was marked by a tall iron gate—open. Beyond lay the manor house, Stowesbridge, surrounded by a trim lawn and a formal rose garden.

Slowing to a sedate five-miles-an-hour, the cab rolled around the circular drive and came to a stop directly in front of the waiting Mrs. Short. She was tall and thin-nosed, with long shapeless limbs sprouting out of a sturdy figure. Ignoring the driver, she opened the car door and smiled broadly at Katherine.

"It's a relief to see you've arrived safely, Miss Katherine." A sharp glance at Cuppy and she had made her point. "Mr. Wilde says 'es most sorry 'e couldn't be 'ere to welcome you, but you're t'feel at 'ome and ask for anything you like."

"Thank you, Mrs. Short. It's nice to see you again."

"You'll be 'avin' the same room as you had before. Most prefers the front rooms, but I remember you liked t'look out on the hayfields and the stream, and even the kitchen garden." She bent down and peered into the cab. "You carry them bags up the stairs," she said to Cuppy. "I'll be wantin' a word with you."

Katherine entered the house expecting the austere formality which had impressed her when she was younger. The dark foyer—as large as an apartment in Manhattan—the hand-carved banister, English landscapes and portraits in oil which lined the staircase and the second floor gallery; they were all the same and yet different, warmer, less like a museum.

Mrs. Short started up the stairs after Cuppy, speaking in a firm but decorously soft voice. "I weren't fooled none, my lad. I seen the cloud o' dust you raised all the way from Beckfirth road."

"A remarkable thing, Mum, seein' it's been rainin' the dust into mud for the past hour."

"Has it now? Then it makes me shudder to think how fast you were goin' to be turnin' the mud back to dust."

Cuppy put the bags down in the center of Katherine's room, gave her a wink, lifted his protesting mother off her feet, and swung her around. "Don't know what I'd do without 'ee, I'm sure." He set her down, then made a hasty exit under a hail of threats.

"What that lad needs is a wife to put 'im right." She straightened her gray blouse and skirt, and smoothed her gray hair over her ears. Placing an overnight case on the bench at the foot of the bed, she started to open it.

roberta clark

"Please don't bother with that. I'll unpack after I've had a walk."

Katherine crossed over to the window and looked out at the fields. Nothing seems to change here, she thought. The magnificent view was just as she remembered it, acres of grass sweeping down to a broad, flat valley, cows grazing on the green hillside, a dark border of trees cutting boundaries and shading a stream which ran diagonally across the cultivated land.

"Did Mr. Wilde say when he'd arrive?"

"This evening. Mr. Evan Babcock is about the grounds somewhere. I'm sure he'd be pleased to show you 'round."

"Evan Babcock?"

"Some sort of assistant to Mr. Wilde he is. Been here three weeks now. Spends most of his time buried under papers in the library."

"Mrs. Short, has my father been to Stowesbridge in the last two years?"

"Several times. With Mr. Wilde. Deep into some sort of business they were. Wouldn't let no one set foot into the library. You'd think they kep' the crown jewels in there."

"Did my father leave anything here? Boxes? Papers?"

"Not as I know. Now the library—knee-high in dust it must be by now—but you'd want to be seein' Mr. Wilde about that." She puttered about, looking for motes of dust, checking over the linens, the freshness of the flowers in the bedside vase, the supplies in the adjoining bathroom. Finding everything in order, she excused herself to go back to her other duties.

Fifteen minutes later, Katherine left her room and went downstairs. The doors leading off the foyer were all closed. She stood for a moment, trying to remember where each of them led. The formal living room was to the right of the front entrance; next to it was the library which adjoined Shep's study. Directly opposite those rooms were a salon which also served as a music room, and a large dining room. Beneath the stairway, a long hall led past the huge kitchen, storage pantries, and laundry room at the rear of the house. She chose this back exit as the quickest way to the fields. Jeans tucked into boots, blue shirt tied at her waist, she was anxious to get outside for a walk, to work the kinks out of her body after the long flight.

The kitchen garden sloped away from the house, ending at a weathered rail fence. She followed it down the gentle incline to the stream hidden in the thick growth of trees. The ground was still spongy from the rain but the clouds had retreated to a ribbon above the horizon, a black mourning band in a brilliant August sky.

She moved into the shade, continuing along the soggy banks under the branches tangled overhead. Sun filtered through the leaves, reflecting on the water, a kaleidoscope of light and shade, luring fish to the surface—luring Katherine with thoughts she wanted to keep in check until she talked to Shep. He'd been a good friend to Gustav for so many years and Gustav trusted him—more than anyone else he knew. She wanted to hold on to the belief Shep would never betray that friendship but her faith had been slowly eroding since Gustav's death.

Why hadn't he mentioned her father's visits to Stowesbridge? Why the secrecy? And why hadn't Gustav written her about his trips to England? Or asked her to join him here?

From the other side of the trees, she could hear the steady clacking rhythm of machinery. A reaper or thresher, she thought, and continued walking downstream in the direction of the sound. The vague brown shape was still indistinguishable through the dense foliage when the serenity around her was shattered by the magnified roar of the motor. It was strange machinery for a Wiltshire farm to be employing. Amazed, she saw the machine rise into the air. A gust of wind enveloped her, churning leaves and water, whipping her hair into her face.

Directly above, a blur of rotor blades and the dull-brown outline of a helicopter lifted over the trees. As it angled away across the field, two men were visible inside the open cockpit, one of them clutching the frame, lean-

the **GOLD** Covenant

ing backward, precariously, through the opening.

She stepped out of the shade, shielding her eyes from the sunlight, wondering why the fool wasn't buckled into his seat. The copter reached the lower meadow, hovered unsteadily for a moment, then slid into a steep upward arc as the man clung like an acrobat to the metal bars. Suddenly, as though struck in the midsection, he collapsed, and, with arms flailing at the air, seemed to be wrenched backward out of the cockpit.

Katherine watched, horrified, as the man somersaulted once then plummeted silently, his body a lifeless puppet silhouetted against the clear rain-washed sky.

CHAPTER 6

Katherine sprinted across the field, her boots sinking in hay stubble and wet earth, her eyes pinned to the place where the man had fallen. There was nothing there now. Nothing visible. His body had sunk into the tall uncut grain of the upper meadow as if into a pale yellow sea. For a moment she thought of turning back—to call for an ambulance from the house—but that would take too long. If he had survived, the 'copter would be the fastest way to transport him to a hospital. Expecting it to put down, she was surprised to see it pull up, instead, gaining altitude as it circled—like a hawk deprived of its prey.

The 'copter hovered, swinging from side to side, seeming to survey the land. Was he looking for help? She stopped running and waited. Why didn't he come down—make himself useful? Then she realized he wasn't looking for the body. Someone behind the glare of the windscreen was watching her. The instinctive alarm was instantaneous, the sense of vulnerability more frightening than anything she'd ever experienced. Until the 'copter began to glide toward her.

In seconds, noise and turbulence churned the air around her and she was running back to the trees, feet pounding into slippery bog, skidding, sliding out of control. Her heartbeat accelerated, audibly pumping blood into her eardrums. She fell—hard—face flat in the wet earth. In front of her, tufts of grass flew up, exploding with a sharp crack.

She slid her hands under her shoulders, waiting, her fists tightening until the nails dug white ruts into the palms. This isn't happening, she thought. It can't be! But there was no mistaking the cracking sound. It was shots—from a rifle—and she was the target.

The machine roared overhead and moved away, following its racing shadow over the field. She scrambled to her feet and was heading for the closest shelter when the 'copter lifted over the broad stand of oak trees, then circled back. Too fast—too God-damned fast—she'd never make it. The terror was beyond emotion—she could taste it, smell it, feel it pushing through veins and into flesh. It drove her on, kept her moving, kept her from losing her forward momentum or her balance. That would be fatal. Then the same sharp crackling again and divots were flying into the air yards away.

"You bastards!" she shouted, her voice lost in the battering roar that filled the air.

Where are the trees? God! So far away! Keep moving, Kat, she told herself. Just keep moving. Don't think. Don't think about the lousy creep up there. Don't think about anything. Just move. He's not going to win. Can't let him win.

She dove and rolled, and found herself in thick green shade, but the leaves and branches splintered around her as the beat of rotors pounded directly overhead. She pulled herself up, clutching at the trunk of a tree, and pressing closely to the rough bark, her legs limp, her lungs gulping air and exhaling in long, ragged breaths. Okay, Kat, you made it this far. That son of a bitch up there is not going to cancel you out.

She had no idea how clearly she could be seen from above but her chances had to be better if she kept running. It couldn't be easy—flying that heap and trying to hit a moving target. Letting go the support of the tree, she followed the bank of the stream, using the profusion of bushes to steady herself along the slippery edge. The maelstrom of branches and leaves and the deafening roar of the rotor blades moved with her. The shadow of the chopper sifted through the tops of the trees, seeming to cut back and forth with ease across her path

Her eardrums throbbed from the unrelenting pressure of the noise and from the inner pressure of tension.

the **GOLD** Covenant

The pulsing beat of her heart kept her moving. Combined with the beat of blades, boots, and snagging limbs it propelled her through the maze of uncultivated brush.

There was a dull heavy thunk and chunks of bark flew off a tree on the opposite bank—clipped by another bullet. This time not close, not nearly as close as the other shots had been. He was shooting blind, but that didn't make it less dangerous. All he needed was the glimpse of a moving form in the trees and a little luck.

The earth was loose and wet under her boots, sucking at her ankles, adding pounds to her weight. She tripped, fell, lay still for a moment, letting the cool soft mud soothe her flushed face. How far had she walked before this madness began? Could she have passed the house already? Somewhere near Stowesbridge the stream angled away and meandered down to the pasture. She would have noticed if she'd come to the turn. Or would she? And did it matter? She couldn't leave the shelter of the trees even if she was near the house.

The persistent buzzing swept over her, again and again. Hearing it overhead was almost reassuring because, if he landed . . . Don't think about it, Kat, just keep moving. She dragged to her feet and began walking, clinging to the vines and branches for support. Her legs were leaden clumps without sensation, too tired to keep going and yet answering the mechanical impulses of her brain. Why hadn't anyone seen what's going on out here? Or heard the racket? Were there no police in Wiltshire? Was this the kind of entertainment they're accustomed to? A sunny afternoon of army maneuvers? People dropping out of helicopters?

Just a glimpse through the branches—the fence was there, ahead, to her right, maybe a hundred yards away. It was a flash of hope—an instant—before light and shadow became a blur as the earth gave way under her feet and she tumbled headlong down a steep incline.

CHAPTER 7

The stop was abrupt and extremely painful. Katherine held her breath for a moment, then exhaled slowly to convince herself she was still alive. Not sure if the pain was the result of a bullet wound, she tried to move and immediately discovered the real source—thorns—sharp barbed leaves cutting through her thin cotton shirt. She buried her face in her arms, relieved and exhausted, but unable to stop the furious beat of her pulse.

Above her, the noise was fading—the steady clatter of rotors—growing more distant, not circling, not putting down. She lay still, following the sound with her eyes. Through the branches she could see the indistinct image of the helicopter, shrinking then vanishing beyond the low sweep of hills to the south. She expected it to return as it had the first time, lifting over the trees, suddenly, its turbulence thrashing the foliage beneath.

But there was only the muffled purling of the stream and, somewhere above, a bird stirring the branches. The minutes dragged by as she listened, knowing she had to move, had to start trusting her senses again.

She slid her hands under her shoulders, and pushed herself up. At once, her entire body felt as though it had been pierced by needles. She cried out and dropped to the ground again. The sprawling bed of holly surrounded her. Its needle-sharp barbs were embedded everywhere in her clothing. She tried pulling a leaf from her shirt sleeve but a half-dozen others bit into her hand in the process. It would be far easier to get the business over with all at once. This time, with jaws clenched and determined, she wrenched herself loose then rolled over onto the soft mud at the bank of the stream. The earth felt soothing and cool but, with that, it brought an acute awareness of discomfort—of the pain in each scrape, bruise, muscle and joint that, until now, had been diffused by her preoccupation with survival.

Close to her face, the shallow water churned over smooth glistening rocks. She cupped her hands and drank. Then, after gingerly splashing the water on her forehead and neck, she stood, trying to recover her bearings. Moving out of the shadows into the now strangely-silent meadow, she searched the vacant sky for the predator. When it didn't appear, her fear changed to anger.

Tears came—silent, hot, stinging, spilling over her bruised face. She reached up to blot them with the edge of her sleeve, and was shocked by the condition of her hands. It was the first good look she'd had at the damage. Her hands and arms were cross-hatched with scratches and clotting blood, her boots and jeans were caked with heavy brown earth; her chambray shirt was covered with mud and small blood-smeared perforations.

But she was alive. The man out there in the field— my God—what must he look like? It must have been a ten-story drop. He couldn't have survived it even if he hadn't been shot. And she was sure he had been, remembering the way he fell—as though he'd been ejected by tremendous force. She had to go back, had to find him. Or get help. Which? The sky was clear now but how long would it stay that way? How long before the helicopter came back? Maybe it was watching her now— waiting for her to leave the shelter of the trees. She could feel the adrenalin flow again at the thought.

"Katherine?" The voice came from a distance, from the rise of land above and behind her. "Is that you?"

Startled, she turned, shielding her eyes from the sun, seeing only the outline of a tall slim figure moving along the embankment. It was Sheppard. No mistaking that. She'd never been so relieved to see anyone. "Shep!" She waved and ran toward him along the lower path.

As he moved closer, there was a noticeable change

roberta clark

in his expression. Then he was skidding down the rain-soaked embankment in long strides. The sight of him—of help—dispelled the reserve strength that had kept her going beyond her normal capacity. Her knees buckled involuntarily. She dropped onto the damp grass.

"For God's sake, Katherine, what happened to you?"

He knelt beside her, his hand on her shoulder, a look of shock in his eyes. She was staring at him inanely—at his clean face, as handsome as she remembered it, at the starched white shirt and sharply creased pants. It was funny—the contrast—it all seemed very funny. Only for some odd reason she seemed to be crying instead of laughing.

"Easy now," he said, putting an arm around her.

His concern only made it more difficult for her to regain control. Annoyed with herself, she pressed the fingers of both hands against the bridge of her nose until the tears stopped.

"You're hurt," he said, at the same time trying to assess the damage. "How bad is it, can you tell me? Is there anything broken?"

"Oh God, Shep, I'm so glad to see you."

"Katherine—?"

"No, nothing broken. I'm all right, really." But her breathing still had a ragged edge to it. She said, "Just give me a minute."

"You look like you've been chased by a bull."

"Not exactly. It was a helicopter. No horns—just bullets."

"Helicopter! Bullets! Are you serious?"

"Never more! Some God-damned bastard chasing me like an animal. He had a rifle, Shep, and he killed someone. Out there in the field. That's why—that is, I *think* that's why he was chasing me. I saw the whole thing."

"Easy, girl," he said, gripping her shoulders. "Let's go over that again. Someone killed?"

"Yes—killed! Shot! Right out of the helicopter."

"You're sure he's dead? Did you see him?"

"I didn't get close enough for that, but yes, he's dead. I'm sure he was shot before he fell. Shouldn't we be calling the police or an ambulance or something?"

"Not until I've seen what's happened. I'll take you back to the house first."

"No, I want to go out there with you."

"I don't think you should."

"If I don't go, it'll take the rest of the day for you to find him." She stood up and started back along the path leading to the fields. He watched silently, shaking his head as the distance between them grew.

When she finally turned and waited, he caught up quickly, falling into step beside her. "I see you're still the same mule-headed Swede," he said.

"What in hell's going on around here, Shep? Why is it you didn't hear anything? The damned helicopter made enough noise to wake the next county."

"I did hear it. When I drove up to the house it was hovering above the oak trees. Looked for a moment as though it might crash. When it picked up altitude and headed south, I went inside. Mrs. Short said you were out for a walk—saw you heading down to the stream—so I came out to find you."

"You must have heard the shots then."

"No. How many men were in the chopper?"

"I only saw one."

"Look here, Kat, are you sure he was shooting at you? That he wasn't just buzzing over to scare you?"

"He did a damn good job of both. If I hadn't been close enough to get under the trees, those bullets would be in my back instead of in your hayfield."

Shep took a firm hold of her arm, forcing her to stop. "You sure of this? You couldn't be mistaken?"

"Mistaken!" She stared at him, hoping to find something in the black pit of his eyes that would convince her the question hadn't been an accusation. "You're serious, aren't you? Damn it, Shep, I'm not an idiot. Don't you think I know when I'm being shot at? Look at me. This wasn't caused by hysteria."

"That's beside the point. It's virtually impossible to fly a chopper close to the ground and fire a rifle at the same time."

"God damn it, Shep. Some poor guy gets killed in

your hayfield not more than an hour ago, I almost get my ass shot off, and that's all you can say?"

She pulled free of his grip and started walking, keeping a beat ahead of him. After a few moments of angry struggle with her temper, she readjusted her speed. When they were side-by-side again, she said, "All right, if what you say is true, it might account for the poor marksmanship. Then again, there may have been more than one man up there. Since I was preoccupied with my health, it wasn't an ideal time for noting details."

"It would be wise to settle on a clear explanation before the police arrive. They're going to ask the same questions."

"I imagine they'll have a few questions for you, as well. About the war games in your backyard."

"I'm sure they will," he said, without emotion. "I wish you'd gone back to the house. It's possible the chopper could pop up again."

She glanced at Stowesbridge in the distance but continued walking. "I'd rather be with you if it does."

They had reached an area similar to the place where she first left the stand of trees. Moving out into the open field, they searched the ground for some sign of her footprints. Finding none, she looked for something else that might help to recall the exact direction she'd run during those confusing moments after the man tumbled from the helicopter.

"Do you remember which way you were facing?" Shep asked. "A landmark of some kind?"

"It's hard to tell. Second hayrick, maybe, the large one."

The huge block of hay stood out against the bordering hills, reminding her of the momentary crazy hope the man might fall into it. They walked toward it silently, keeping pace with each other, their eyes searching as they moved over the soggy chaff-covered field. The steady output of energy seemed to be burning off the residual emotions of the past hour, leaving her with a sense of unreality.

No longer weighted with clouds, the hills laid a sharply-etched green mosaic against the afternoon sky, distant and serene. The sun was still high. The dampness of the hayfields reflected its rays like flecks of gold in a river bed of sand. After ten minutes of searching, she began to wonder if she'd imagined the whole thing—if she'd imagined that somewhere in the center of that pastoral beauty, a man lay dead, killed by a rifle shot or crushed by a fall, or that she had almost been destroyed because of it. She fought down the growing reluctance to go on. A film of perspiration covered her body, its salty dampness biting into each open scrape, making her grateful for the occasional stirring of warm air.

As they waded into a section of uncut grain, her foot became mired in a spot of ankle-deep bog. Wilde stopped and waited until she'd stamped some of the heavy clay from her boots.

"The mowers haven't been through here," he said. "It'll be harder to find him in the tall grass."

"We could cover more ground if we separate," she said, veering off in another direction.

Reaching out to stop her, he said, "Perhaps that won't be necessary. Wait here."

He moved away, quickly, but before she could question him she saw what had drawn him—a touch of brown tweed, out of place in the pale expanse of ripened hay. Again, clearly, she saw the image against the sky, the limp figure wrenched from the cockpit, from its grasp on life. What would the fall, or bullet, have done to the body? This hadn't been a pristine, clinical death—like John's—the only kind of death she'd ever seen.

At first, she watched from a distance. When curiosity overcame her deflated confidence, she moved closer, stopping a few feet away when she saw Shep kneel beside the crumpled form. For a moment he stared, quietly, then placed his hand at the side of the man's neck. Shep was preoccupied, still unaware of her proximity, as he searched through the pockets of the man's clothing. The tweed jacket yielded a billfold. He flipped through it and removed a piece of paper which he unfolded, scanned, and stuffed into his own pocket.

"Isn't that frowned on?" she said, moving up behind

him. "Tampering with evidence, or whatever?"

"Kat!" he said, looking up, his eyes more concerned than annoyed. "You should have waited back there. There's nothing we can do for him."

At first glance, the man lying face-up on the grass looked unexpectedly serene. A closer look made her realize how violent the fall had been. His legs were twisted grotesquely, as if he were a discarded doll. One arm was oddly disjointed, raising the shoulder to an unnatural angle. A shapeless smear of red on the crushed grain stalks had spread like a shadow beneath his head. The front of his white shirt was soaked with blood from the powder-burned hole in his chest. There was no doubt now about the shots. Someone had guaranteed he wouldn't survive the fall. She felt light-headed and looked around for a place to sit.

Shep stood up and put a supporting arm around her. "I'll walk you back to the house," he said. "There's no need for you to wait here."

"You know him, don't you? Who is he, Shep?"

"Evan Babcock. You didn't meet him when you arrived?"

"No. Mrs. Short said he was somewhere on the grounds. I never saw him." She glanced at the schoolboy-face, hard to believe he was dead and not just sleeping. "He's so young."

"Not as young as he looks."

"He could pass for seventeen."

"He's thirty-one."

"His face . . . he looks . . . so . . ."

"Angelic?"

"Yes."

"He wasn't. He had a temperament that ensured permanent unemployment."

"But he worked for you."

"Off and on. He hated routine."

"Obviously, nothing is routine around here," she said. "What kind of work did he do?"

"That was dependent on the business at hand." Taking a pack of cigarettes from his pocket, he offered her one. She shook her head. Lighting one for himself, he said, "If I remember right, you used to smoke. Wasn't it Grace Academy that expelled you for setting a dormitory on fire?"

"It was a waste paper basket."

"I see," he said, smiling at what she knew was the memory of unstated details.

"About Evan . . ." she said, bringing him back to a subject he seemed to be avoiding. "We were talking about his work."

"Yes, well, it's difficult to be specific about someone whose talents were, what you might call, diversified. He's been extremely useful on a variety of projects over the past years. Look here, Kat, you seem a little unsteady.

roberta clark

Let's move away from here and rest awhile. A few minutes one way or the other won't matter much now."

She followed him over to the partially-covered hayrick where he pulled down two dry bales from under the canvas tarp. They sat facing each other, each studying the other for the first time since they'd met near the house.

He hadn't changed. It was uncanny. How long had it been since she'd last seen him? Eight years? Nine? He'd always been the same: his features hard-edged, his sharp eyes rich with a brown pigment that blended into the black of the pupils, a deep Bedouin tan that obscured his origins. He was tall, trim, muscular—still, far too attractive. And she still felt the same basic magnetism. She'd expected—hoped—it would have faded along with her youthful infatuation.

"You look tired," he said. "How long since you've had any sleep?"

"Night before last, if you're talking about quantity. If it's quality you mean, make it two years."

"The last few years haven't been easy, have they?"

She shook her head, wanting to change the subject but knowing her voice would be unreliable.

"It's good to see you, Katherine," he went on. "I'm glad you finally decided to come over. I have a lot to tell you."

"I know," she said, unable to handle it just yet. "Can we talk tonight—after I've had a chance to pull myself together?"

the **GOLD** *Covenant*

"Of course. I think you'll sleep better."

"That's why I'm here," she said. "Do you have a handkerchief?"

"A towel would do you better."

He handed her a folded white linen which she used and stuffed into her jeans. "And a long hot bath."

"You look like you could do with a double shot of brandy as well as some cleaning up, however it might be better if the inspector had a first-hand look at what happened to you."

"All right. I'll settle for the brandy. And I'm ready to start back, if you are." As they headed off in the direction of the house, she nodded toward the pocket where he'd stuffed the paper from Evan Babcock's billfold. "Something to do with your latest project?" she asked.

"Evan was doing research for me—has been for the past month—and I prefer to keep it private. It's of no interest to the police."

"Wouldn't they rather decide for themselves?"

"They'll never know unless you tell them and that's for you to decide."

"Just how private is it? There might be a price on my silence."

"That sounds like blackmail."

"It *is* blackmail," she said with unabashed pleasure. "Makes us both guilty under the law, doesn't it? You for removing evidence, and I for—"

roberta clark

"Larceny!"

"Yankee finesse."

"You've been down-east too long," he said.

"Maybe. I'm here to find out."

"I was hoping you had another reason for coming here."

"I do," she said.

CHAPTER 8

Mrs. Short entered the living room wiping her hands on her apron, then used the apron to wipe a spot of dust off the brass sconce on the wall next to the door. "There's a call for the inspector," she announced, almost as an after-thought.

Andrew Caucutt sighed, placed his notebook on the table, rose from the couch spilling bits of pastry onto the floor. He excused himself with a silent shrug of his shoulders.

Katherine, minus boots, was sitting with legs comfortably tucked under her on a deep-cushioned velvet chair—the chair draped with a sheet by the meticulous housekeeper to protect it from her muddy clothes. Between the two facing divans in front of the fireplace, a Sterling tea tray sat on a burled ash table with only the crumbs attesting to the provision of tarts and biscuits placed there less than an hour before.

Rising, Wilde crossed to a black-enameled liquor cabinet. "You may as well clear away while you're here, Mrs. Short," he said. "It's time Katherine had something stronger than tea."

"Yes, sir. I'm drawing her bath now, assumin' they're through with trompin' her about the fields and askin' their questions." With the empty teacups and platters piled on the tray, she marched out of the room.

Wilde set a decanter and glasses where the tray had been, then poured a large shot of vintage brandy and gave it to Katherine.

"Keeping a clear head didn't help much, did it?" she said. "I don't think the inspector was impressed with my memory. Amazing how quickly we forget details, or is it that we never notice them in the first place?"

"You did better than most, under the circumstances. And I appreciate your silence about the paper in Evan's pocket."

"That was my end of the bargain," she said, smiling. "Yours is yet to be paid."

They both fell silent as the inspector returned to the room followed by two men in almost identical dark blue suits.

"May I offer you and your men a glass, Inspector?"

"Thank you, no, sir," Caucutt said, answering for the three of them. "These two lads just arrived from C.I.D. Sergeant Moss and Sergeant Aaron, forensic.

the GOLD Covenant

They'd like to get started on Mr. Babcock's room immediately, if you don't mind, sir."

"Of course. Top of the stairs. On the right."

When Moss and Aaron had gone, Caucutt returned to the table for his note pad. "I think we've done for the moment," he said, glancing through it. "You did say Evan Babcock was not a regular employee. Is that correct, Mr. Wilde?"

"That is correct."

"And you have no idea what other business he might have been engaged in?"

"I never asked him."

"Well then, we'll see what his baggage turns up, eh?" He pulled his cap out of his hip pocket, shoving the note pad in its place. "By the way, sir, the call was from Scotland Yard. Superintendent Hopkins will be delayed until the morning. He'll be wanting to talk to both of you then."

"We'll be here, Inspector. Is there any news about the helicopter?"

"Nothing useful. It looks as though our pigeon has flown the channel."

"That's going to make things difficult," Wilde said.

"Afraid you're right about that but we've alerted C.A.A. and Interpol. Never can tell when you'll hit on a bit of luck."

Catching Katherine's eye, Wilde held up the brandy.

She lifted her full glass and shook her head. He replaced the decanter in the cabinet then turned to Caucutt. "I think it's time we excused Miss Nikulasson, don't you, Inspector? She's been more than cooperative."

"That she has," he said, turning to Katherine. "Good of you to put off your cleaning up until we'd got our metal detector chaps on the right track. But then, I'm sure you're as anxious as we are to see those men snagged."

"It will have been a pleasure to help." She rose from her chair, gathering up the muddy sheet to take with her. "I'm sure I'll see you again, Inspector."

"Are you certain you won't have the doctor look you over?" Wilde asked when she reached the door.

"There's nothing more serious than a few scratches, and the only medicine I need is this—" she held up her brandy glass, "—and that talk you promised me. Then a good night's sleep."

Neither the bathroom nor the bedroom had changed in any major way since Katherine had occupied these same rooms years ago. It was a toss-up which she liked better, the view from the back window or the enormous footed tub. When she came upstairs the tub had been full, steaming, and almost too hot to get into. Once in, the temperature was therapeutic, completely obliterating time, resurrecting memories.

Her first visit to Stowesbridge was still lodged in her mind like an irritating sliver of fish bone—a summer's visit fourteen years ago which had affected her life permanently. She'd been a sixteen-year-old misfit who thought being out of step with the rest of the world was an advantage that gave her the ability to handle anything. Gustav had been unable to keep her in school. The education he'd given her had been thorough but basic, the best he could do while working and traveling. He'd always assumed she would fill in the gaps someday so her announcement she was not going on to college brought on the most serious battle they'd ever had. It was then Gustav had discovered her rebellion was based not on self-confidence but on fear. Her dependence on him—which had begun with the early loss of her mother and which Gustav had allowed to grow out of proportion and out of control—had to be broken. Going away to college was imperative and he knew it would take something special to convince her of the need.

His solution was a peaceful sojourn in England. He'd been collaborating with Shep on his latest project and it was quite natural he and Katherine should spend a month at Stowesbridge. The prospect couldn't have been more exciting for her: one month at the country estate of Sheppard Wilde, notorious, attractive, wealthy, a bachelor and—although he couldn't have been more than thirty at the time—older man. It was her chance to prove to her father how sophisticated she had become and how unreasonable he was in asking her to spend four years in college with impossibly immature students. If she hadn't been so impossibly immature herself, she would have recognized the conspiracy.

From the first day they arrived, Shep seemed to have an uncanny ability—enhanced, she was sure, by Gustav's expert coaching—to pinpoint the deficiencies in her knowledge on every subject. Painfully worse was the proficient way he tucked her into the proper chronological cubbyhole, then made her feel like she belonged there, a coddled child who had been hand-carried through life, one who, contrary to the impression she wanted to convey, was terrified of independence. She had been furious with him, not for just being amused, but for being right.

It was clear afterward. Always too soft himself to cut her down to a realistic size, Gustav had found the perfect person to do it for him. It had been the worst summer of her life, but, as Gustav had hoped it would, it gave her an insight she'd lacked. It opened her eyes to new possibilities, a life of her own, one she might otherwise not have known.

It had also confused her feelings for Sheppard. Four years later, there'd been a week in Gstaad with him, a week which stretched into months of travel, of being together—the best months of her life . . .

But she'd ended them. Afraid of losing her new autonomy. Of falling back on something she had only just escaped. Afraid she was returning to an adolescent worship that might, in reality, be a desire for dependence. After all, he was an older man, a father figure.

God! He was barely older than she was now.

He didn't push, didn't run after her. They had stayed in touch—could hardly have helped that with Gustav the link—but the underlying reserve remained.

She met John when she'd sold her first article to *Cross Atlantic Magazine*. He was an assistant editor, just starting. They were the same age. There'd been more to their relationship than that, of course, but now, looking back, it was hard to remember the beginning. They'd been together only one short year before his illness.

She sat up, flipped on the tap, and hit the threatening tears with a splash of cold water. Couldn't afford to get maudlin. That would only plunge her into a morass of self-pity. More important, maudlin would be a handicap if Sheppard Wilde became an adversary, and that was a definite possibility if he didn't give her some straight answers to her questions.

He may be holding the best hand, but she had one good card up her sleeve, the one provided by Halvern. The one that just might make it possible for her to dig out the truth—without Shep's help.

While she was in the process, she might just nail him for that *Power Line* interview. Bag the unbaggable Sheppard Wilde and deliver him to the intractable Ivar Whalen. The idea became more appealing with each doubt he'd raised. A great deal more appealing than it had been before she'd arrived in England.

Katherine found her pajamas on top of the folded-back quilt at the foot of the high oak-framed bed where Mrs. Short had laid them out. After slipping into them, she sank gratefully onto the soft mattress and reached for the brandy glass she'd left on the bedside table. Cognac, not her favorite, but the saturating warmth was welcome. She tossed it down in one stinging swallow and lay back to enjoy its relaxing effect. It didn't work. She felt as though she'd been wired with caffeine instead.

The silence gave energy to thoughts that ran irrepressibly through replays of the afternoon. Forced from her memory by the Inspector's endless barrage of questions, the details became a ganglia of unrelated facts which only added to her confusion. It was no use trying to nap; she needed that talk with Sheppard. She pulled the robe over her pajamas and left the room to look for him. Below, in the foyer, Mrs. Short was ushering Inspector Caucutt to the front door.

the **GOLD** *Covenant*

As Katherine approached the second floor landing, she saw him step back into the house over the older woman's impatient objections. His suit jacket was wrinkled from the summer's heat, straining over the expanse beneath it. He lifted his cap and adjusted the knot on his tie without taking his eyes off of her as she descended the staircase. "You're looking a great deal better, Miss Nikulasson."

"I feel a great deal better."

"Like to give you this," he said, handing her a small card. "My number at home. If any other detail comes to mind, you can ring me up there."

"Did you find anything helpful in Mr. Babcock's room?"

"We'll know after we've sorted it all out. By the by, Miss Nikulasson, it'd be wise to stay close to the house until we get this business cleared up."

"Thank you, I will," Katherine said, wondering why Shep wasn't here to see the inspector out.

"I'll be leaving one of my men near the house tonight. Don't like to see you ladies alone."

"Alone?"

Her question went unheard as Caucutt leaned out of the front door and signaled an officer to bring the car around. That done, he turned back to them and said, "See you tomorrow then. Good night, Miss Nikulasson, Mrs. Short."

Mrs. Short closed the door after him and bolted it. "Mr. Wilde had some business in London," she said, in answer to Katherine's unspoken question. "At the club in St. James. I expect he'll be back in the morning to see the superintendent."

He'd left without telling her! No message. No apologies. She was both disappointed and curious. His business in London had come up very suddenly at a rather unconventional hour. And rather coincidentally, considering the events of the afternoon.

"Mrs. Short, how well did you know Evan Babcock?"

"Well as I had a likin' to."

"Did my father know him?"

"They were never here at the same time, as I recall. One was always goin' out when the other was comin' in."

"Do you remember who was going when the other was coming?"

"That I do. Your father first—every time."

Katherine glanced at the library. Babcock had worked in there and so had Gustav. Now, Shep Wilde wouldn't let anyone set foot inside. Something of Gustav's work was in that room. It had to be. Why else would he have come to Stowesbridge before it was finished? Why else had he left nothing of his writing among the things that were returned to her?

"I think I'll sit up and read for awhile, Mrs. Short," she said. "I'll be fine if you want to go to bed."

"If you're sure, Miss Katherine. I wouldn't mind poppin' in early like."

Katherine went into the living room, and waited until she heard the housekeeper's footsteps fade away down the hall. When she heard the kitchen door close, she retraced her steps. At the library door, she gripped the knob and tried to turn it. It didn't respond. Always kept locked, Mrs. Short had said.

She studied the latch for a moment, then turned and started up the stairs.

CHAPTER 9

Wilde took the glass of scotch from Beck's tray and made a thorough survey of the room before he entered. Smoke curled up into the dimly-lit cavernous atmosphere below the dark-paneled ceiling. The reading lamps seemed extraneous—here and there cones of light enveloping slumped figures draped with rhythmically rising and falling newspapers. Most of the armchairs were empty. Forster hadn't arrived yet.

He found a corner where he could watch the arched entry to the club lounge, and sank into soft-worn leather. Pulling out a cigarette, he lit it and tossed the rest of the pack on the table next to his chair. Time to sit and think was not what he wanted. All the thinking about his meeting with Forster had been done in the car on the drive to London. That left Katherine Nikulasson.

She'd grown even more beautiful—if that were

possible. He'd tried to forget—to push her into some remote corner of his mind—but Katherine wouldn't be pushed, wouldn't be forgotten. Amazing she had such a long-lasting effect on him. No one ever had before. Difficult as she'd been, he wasn't certain he really wanted to forget her.

Over the years, since he'd last seen her, he had regular updates from Gustav. There had also been her occasional letters and rarer telephone calls and an indirect contact through her published articles, which he never missed. Even at a distance he continued to feel a closeness to her he knew was not reciprocated. There seemed to be a reserve on her part, a residue of distrust—of herself—that kept him at a distance. With time, he'd hoped to see that barrier dissolved. Instead, she had met someone else.

And now the circumstances were widening the gap even further and the reserve was in danger of turning to animosity. It was damned unfortunate her visit had been so poorly timed.

He drained the glass and motioned for Beck.

Forster had just entered the room. He stood in the archway peering into the gloom for a destination. His gray hair was rumpled and in need of a trim; his exquisitely-tailored suit looked slept-in; his white shirt drooped from under his vest, spilling over the top of his trousers. He moved slowly across the room, checking the occupant of each chair as he progressed, his great beak of a nose giving him the look of a large myopic bird in search of a worm. There was no use trying to flag him down; he couldn't see anything beyond five feet without his glasses and, as usual, wasn't wearing them.

Recognition finally came when he entered the limited radius of his perception. "Wilde!" he said. "By God, I'm glad to see you."

"David." A brief handshake took care of formalities. "You've heard from Hopkins?" Wilde asked, crushing out his cigarette in the crystal ashtray Beck had provided the moment he lit up.

"Pulled me out of conference. Damned inconsiderate." Forster's face was flushed, as though he needed to loosen his tie. "Devilish bad timing. The whole situation, I mean. Devilish bad."

"What did he tell you?"

"Evan Babcock murdered—Stowesbridge. How much more is there?"

"I'm not sure yet. Have you given him anything?"

"Told him I'd find out what I could," Forster said. "Thought it best to drag my feet a bit. At least until I heard from you."

"Is there anything on the record?"

"Chances are slim as a twig Babcock was ever officially recognized by the department. Not with the kind of work he did. And not bloody likely he'd turn up in the files. What in tarnation was the lad up to?"

"It looks as though he was branching out. Making an independent deal."

"Thought he was loyal. Upsetting, damned upsetting! How could he do that?"

"He couldn't. That's precisely why he's dead." There was a momentary twitch of Wilde's tight jaw, but no change of expression. "The damned fool should have known better."

"Look here, old boy, you didn't. . . ." Forster's voice trailed off in sudden embarrassment.

There was no reply, only the momentary hint of disappointment in Wilde's eyes. He remained silent when Beck approached them, emptied and polished the ashtray, then placed two full glasses on the table between them and tottered off with the empty one.

"Damn!" Forster said, when the old man was out of hearing. "That was a bloody awful thing to say. Fit of nerves, I expect. Sorry, old man."

"Could Babcock have been working with anyone in your department without your sanction?" Wilde asked. "We need to go in the right direction without stirring up too much dust."

"My department? Not possible. I'd have heard."

"Can you be that sure?"

"Let's say it's damned unlikely. I could tell you what's going on in the minister's conjugal bed."

"Or not going on."

Forster smiled. "Don't bet on that," he said, the smile broadening.

Wilde let it fade before he pulled out a packet and dropped it on the table. "You'll be needing this."

"I thought I had the complete proposal."

"You do. This has more to do with current events."

Forster picked up the manila envelope and squinted at it closely before sliding it into the inside pocket of his jacket. "If this Babcock affair gets out of hand," he said, looking discouraged, "we're going to lose what little support we have in government. They could pull out or bollix up the whole thing. Or cut us out completely. And, if the Turks get involved, you'll have their whole bloody army on your tail and I'll be out to pasture—permanently."

"Not if we move fast."

"You're talking about the Foreign Office, complications, red tape. You know what I'm up against."

"I can't wait," Wilde said, pulling out another cigarette, lighting it, and inhaling deeply as he watched a new arrival enter and settle into a chair on the opposite side of the room. "It's been six months since we had the first shipment. Four months since we had to take care of the Gustav Nikulasson cover-up," he went on. "The news should have cooled off enough by now for the department to back away. It's time to move. Delays mean trouble. You're either in or out, David."

the **GOLD** Covenant

"Yes, yes, I know. Too much invested. Can't let it slip away."

"You have my latest report. Everything's in order. Let's go with it. My butt's paralyzed. I don't like sitting on it for extended periods of time."

"Right, then. Understand your impatience completely. But remember, old chap, you've never dropped anything this big in my lap before. Give me one more week on it. Let this Babcock thing cool off a bit, too."

"Superintendent Hopkins will be out tomorrow. Unless the investigation can be side-tracked, cut the week in half." He shoved a paper across the table. "I found this on Babcock's body."

Unfolding the paper, Forster laid it under the lamp shade, then pulled out his bifocals and adjusted them on his nose. The topographical map came into focus, but he continued to strain for the correct viewing angle until he realized there were no names printed on it. The only marking was a small area shaded with a yellow pen.

"Well, I'm damned. Didn't expect it would be Babcock who'd take the phony bait." He carefully refolded the map on its original creases and handed it back to Wilde. "Have the police seen this?" he asked.

"No. I lifted it before they arrived."

"Not a clue who he was dealing with, I take it?"

"It was someone he underrated," Wilde said. "Only a man with firsthand knowledge would see the map was useless. That's why he didn't buy. Unfortunately, we don't know whether Evan sold him any real information before they parted company."

"This could get sticky. Damned sticky!"

Forster touched the highball glass to his forehead, waiting for a solution to present itself. Wilde remained silent. His eyes offered no more in the way of sympathy than the austere eyes of Gladstone glaring down at them from his heavy gilt frame.

"Perhaps the whole thing is better shelved for the present," Forster finally said.

"It's your decision, David, but make it final. I have to know within the week."

"Look here, old boy, you wouldn't think of going it alone, would you?"

Wilde's face was expressionless—that was answer enough.

"What if they find something in Babcock's effects?"

"I've taken care of that. They'll only find what we want them to find."

"I suppose there's no need to ask if you've seen the *London Times* today," Forster persisted. "I would have thought that might put a damper on the plans."

"Why would it?"

"Good God, man! The Syndicate took his head off—decapitated the poor sod for a miserly forty kilos of gold."

the **GOLD** *Covenant*

"The Syndicate doesn't operate like that," Wilde said.

"How can you say that? Did you read the article? The greasy little barbarians took the man's head with them. Kassem probably has it mounted on his mantelpiece by now."

"It wasn't Kassem. If he ran the Syndicate like that, he'd be out of business in less than a day."

Forster sat back and pushed the bifocals to the top of his head, which in turn pushed his hair into an upright fringe behind them. His eyes blinked rapidly in adjustment. "I don't understand. If it was a simple case of robbery, why would they make such a disgusting mess of the man's body?"

"I don't know what happened in that room or whether it had any connection with Evan Babcock's murder—" Wilde said, tucking the folded map into his jacket, "—but two things are certain: it wasn't simple and it wasn't the Syndicate."

"Dash it all, Wilde, I don't see how you can be so sure of anything. I don't mind telling you I'm scared. Damned scared. If you make one wrong calculation, our heads will both end up like that carrier's—as ornaments on someone's mantel."

"You knew the risk when we started. Nothing's changed."

"The risk was always on paper. That's changed. The problem with a desk job, old boy, is you grow accustomed to security."

"Your ass couldn't be more secure in a nappy, David. I've arranged for the boys from C.I.D. to turn up a small bone before Hopkins arrives at Stowesbridge. All you have to do is corroborate the evidence. You'll find everything you need in that packet I gave you."

"Well, I'll do my best, but you'd better have thrown him a convincing bone if you expect to keep him from chewing off our collective asses."

Diverted for the moment, Forster unfolded his gangly body from his chair. His joints complained audibly, but, out of the harsh yellow light, his face regained a modicum of life. He polished off his scotch and waved Beck away, indicating they were leaving. "Coming to the Lewellyn's reception on Saturday?" he asked. "I'll have your answer then."

"I'll be there. With a guest. One you'll be interested in seeing again."

"The Duval girl? Lovely creature that."

"Katherine Nikulasson."

"What? Katherine? Good God, man, here in England?"

"Arrived this morning."

"It's been years—" He stopped abruptly with a new thought. "Is she going to be a problem?"

Wilde picked up the pack of cigarettes and shoved it into his pocket. Smiling, he said, "I've never known a time when she wasn't."

CHAPTER 10

It was long past office hours. Katherine had started to hang up the phone after the sixth ring, when a click at the other end stopped her.

"Hello?" she said. "Is anyone there? I'm trying to reach Mr. Kimball. Hugh Kimball."

"Too late. He's slipped the coils of bondage. All the serfs are gone at this hour, except for me, that is."

"And you are?"

"Oh, sorry. Farris. I'm from central personnel pool. Doing a spot of filing for Mr. Kimball."

"Will the office be open tomorrow?"

"Saturday? Couldn't possibly say for certain, seein' there's nothin' certain in this world."

"Would you be able to make an educated guess?"

"Could do, I suppose. It's likely some poor bloke will have to put in a few hours of honest labor. Not likely it will be His Lordship. The ride is always smoother at the top of the waterfall."

Katherine laughed. "Do philosophers always work the night shift?"

"Fertility of thought flourishes in the loneliness of night," he announced happily, sounding as though he'd waited years for the opportunity to say it. Returning to business, he asked, "Would you like me to put a message on Kimball's desk?"

"Thank you, no. No message."

After hanging up, Katherine dialed the private number listed beneath the other. She hadn't wanted to bother the man at home, but with the weekend coming up, the delay would be too long.

"Good evening." This time the voice was stiff and formal. "Kimball residence."

"This is Katherine Nikulasson. I'd like to speak to Mr. Kimball, please."

"I'm sorry, Mr. Kimball is not at home."

"Where can I reach him?"

"He's away for the weekend. However, he does sometimes ring up for his messages. Would you like to leave one?"

"Just tell him I called."

"Would you spell the last name, please?"

Katherine spelled out her name. "You might also tell him it's business on behalf of Ivar Whalen concerning *Power Line* and it's important I get in touch with him as soon as possible. He has my number here."

So much for resources, she thought, tucking the small brown book back into her purse. It was ten-thirty and the sky had finally darkened into a semblance of night. But nights were all the same. Maine. New York. England. It didn't matter where she was. Nights were filled with remembering and the desperation to forget. Now came the anger at herself for two years lost. The time she could have spent working with Gustav. How could she have been so stupid? Hadn't the last few years taught her never to depend on the future? Today is all—nothing else is certain.

There had been reasons why she'd avoided being near her father during the last two years. He would have expected her to accept what happened, to put it behind her, and to go on with her life. That would have taken a strength she didn't have anymore. Maybe never had. And she was tired of pretending when, in reality, she'd been afraid. Afraid for the entire five years of John's illness. Frustrated by her helplessness, her inability to relieve or to end his pain. When death was imminent, she dreaded and yet prayed for it. When it happened, she despised the feeling of relief and the guilt that came with it, and so couldn't allow herself the freedom she now had. Acceptance and freedom would have repudiated John's existence.

That, she realized, was her rationalization for unqualified retreat. In fact, the retreat had been a penance she'd imposed on herself. But even the most painful memories fade as the simple process of living goes on and, with time, acceptance is inevitable. Oddly, the realization of that had helped her through the more recent loss of her father.

Until Halvern handed her those papers.

In spite of her bravado, she wasn't sure she was up to that level of intrigue. She was sure, however, she had to try. There was a great deal that needed explaining. She wasn't going to be side-tracked or patronized. The most dangerous thing about Sheppard was his way of inspiring confidence. Her father had trusted him more than any other person, but she wasn't as trusting as Gustav had been, nor was she impressionable anymore.

After tossing about in bed for almost an hour, she gave up trying to sleep. Her inner clock was still on New York time. The afternoon's draining experience might have been enough to make up the difference if it weren't for the wakefulness that comes with an over-worked imagination along with over-reaching the point of exhaustion. Unless she did something more than passively wait, it was going to be a sleepless night. The symptoms were all too familiar.

Sheppard was gone until morning. It was an invitation to nose around. There might not be another. She didn't bother with the robe. It was too warm. Her pajamas—a nicely broken-in striped broadcloth salvaged from John's effects—were modest enough for an empty house. Shep liked privacy. Except for Mrs. Short and the occasional sojourns of the late Mr. Evan Babcock, none of his other employees lived in the house.

She headed across the hall to Evan's room. It was unlocked. The police were finished with it, having been over it with a sifter, according to the irritated complaints of the housekeeper. It was unlikely they'd missed anything but worth a look.

The windows had been closed, leaving the room hot and stuffy with the smell of stale tobacco. She flicked on the light—a vintage ceiling fixture—and glanced around. Between the two large front windows stood the enormous postered bed covered with a quilt in dark tones of green. A bank of pillows rested against the headboard; a stack of paperback books sat at one side. The room was a warm white, a quiet background for the oil paintings which hung on two of the walls. Standing at the center of another wall was a large wardrobe, a collection of drawings by Daumier on one side of it. On the other side was a large print of Picasso's *Three Musicians*, a painting she'd first seen at the Museum of Modern Art when she was a child. It had seemed frightening to her then and she'd renamed it *Spook with Empty Clothes*.

It still fits, she thought, giving it an offhand glance as she approached the mahogany wardrobe to open the double doors. Hanging on the rod were four suits of varying color and weight, several shirts, two windbreakers, and a khaki raincoat. She went through all the pockets and found nothing more interesting than a linen handkerchief and a stainless steel fingernail clipper. Two pair of leather shoes—brown and black—riding boots, several pair of tennis shoes and two tennis rackets rested on the green paper-lined shelf beneath the clothes. Equally unrevealing, beyond Mr. Babcock's preference for sports. On the right, four drawers, lined with the same deep-green paper, held extra shirts, undergarments, socks, and pajamas. She closed the doors and walked over to the bed, where she flipped through the stack of books. Nothing—not even a bookmark.

The drawers of the bedside tables were filled with tissue boxes, magazines, aspirin tablets, writing pads, pens and pencils, all neatly lined in the same way—all but the bottom drawer in the table on the left. She wouldn't have noticed it if it hadn't been the only place that looked touched by human hands. The green paper had been carelessly fitted, or maybe incorrectly replaced after being lifted or removed for some purpose.

She carefully emptied the contents of the drawer onto the top of the table, then lifted out the lining. Nothing. If there had been anything there, either the police had found it or Mr. Evan Babcock had removed it himself. Disappointed, she sat on the edge of the bed, scanning

the **GOLD** Covenant

the room, her eyes drawn repeatedly back to the Picasso print. Strange, the memories it triggered—her mother, an emerald green dress, a single strand of pearls, dark hair pulled back into a French knot, a pale hand holding hers, the soft thoughtful voice: *They do seem a spooky lot, don't they! It's quite an appropriate title.* Then her laughter, always a conspiratorial bond between them. *Offended? My goodness, no. Mr. Picasso would be delighted, I'm sure.* Turning away the onrush of memories, she replaced the items in the drawer in the same order she'd found them, then stood and smoothed out the quilt.

A quick check through the bathroom revealed nothing but the usual supplies; the large walk-in closet was completely empty. Where was his luggage? He must have used luggage of some sort. At home, hers was shoved under the bed where it rested in an accumulation of dust balls. She bent over to peer under the box spring. The floor was bare; not even a wisp of dust lay on the hardwood. *Face it, Kat, you have struck out.*

As she started toward the door, her eyes were drawn back again to the Picasso print. There was something different about it. She walked over and stood in front of it. Something was wrong—something out of place. She stared at it, trying to remember. The music. *The spook has the music.* That's it! The figure on the right, the one that looked like a spook to her childish eye, was the one with the music—the *only* one. In this print, the flutist also had a sheet of music propped on the stand in front of him.

She moved to one side to see if the rectangle was in relief. Immediately her pulse began pounding. She reached up, carefully lifted the frame from the wall, and laid it face down on the bed. After loosening the backing, she pulled out the print and ran a hand over it, testing the surface. The extraneous piece of paper had been attached with rubber cement. Almost shaking with excitement, she peeled it away from the print. The single white sheet, letter sized, had been folded in half and enclosed in a small piece of ink-blotched Mylar.

She switched on the bed lamp and held the paper under the light. It was a Xeroxed copy of two photographs. The photos were of a man—in one, holding a gold jewel-encrusted dagger sheath, in the other, holding a wrought-gold necklace also studded with gems. The pictures were poorly lighted and the copy was even worse, but there was no doubt in her mind the photographs were of her father. And they were recent. He'd aged since the last time she'd seen him.

She folded the paper back into its Mylar wrapping and tucked it into her pajama pocket. Then, after rubbing off the residue of rubber cement, she replaced the print in the frame and hung it back on the wall. When she was satisfied it looked untouched, she switched off the lights and went out to the hall.

the **GOLD** *Covenant*

The house was quiet. Mrs. Short had finally retired to her room after providing the policeman at the gate with an unrequested pot of coffee and a plate of biscuits.

There wouldn't be a better time to invade the library and the prospect had suddenly become very enticing. There was now the real possibility of finding not only the original photographs from which Babcock had made the copies, but, with them, perhaps even a manuscript. If her father *had* been at Stowesbridge—as Mrs. Short said—then, considering his unwavering dedication to work, he would have brought with him some part of that work.

Her mind turned over another possibility—one much more disturbing. If Evan Babcock's visits followed Gustav's it would mean that Evan had access to Gustav's papers. He might even have been carrying copies when he was killed. If that were the case, it would put an entirely different light on Shep's actions this afternoon. His reasons for removing the papers from Evan's pocket could have been to prevent her seeing them, or worse, to prevent his being implicated in the murder.

She had to get into the library. Violating a host's privacy was not common courtesy, but then the circumstances were not at all common. They *were*, however, compelling. She'd been a witness to murder, had been a target herself, and given no hope of answers to any of her questions. After four months of waiting! This was a case of priorities—of absolute necessity—not subject to the harassment of conscience, she told herself. The justification was there. If it was wrong, apologies could come later. All that mattered now was getting into the library before the opportunity slipped away.

CHAPTER 11

Moonlight sifted through the two vertical windows on either side of the front entrance, washing the oriental carpet and hardwood floor of the foyer with pale gold. At the bottom of the stairway, a dim night lamp had been left burning. It was adequate for the job, but Katherine had failed in her attempt to force her way into the library.

She stuffed the plastic Visa card and other makeshift tools, scavenged from her cosmetics kit, into her pocket and leaned against the door wondering what to do next. Break-and-entry was not for amateurs, and there was no time for lessons. The only other alternative was access from an outside window, but for that she would need an accessory—preferably someone with professional know-how.

Moving quickly through the front rooms, she quietly closed and locked any of the windows left open for ventilation. That done, she hurried through the dimly lit hall to the back of the house. Outside, with only a slight hesitation over her inappropriate attire, she decided the back door should be left unlatched behind her as a precaution against failure.

Mrs. Short's rooms were in the right wing, adjacent to the kitchen. No light issued from her windows. A nearly full moon gave the sky a lingering glow of twilight. The air was still, warm and heavy with the fragrance of japonica and of the bordering privet hedge in full bloom. Katherine walked around the house, following the path between the low stone wall that surrounded the swimming pool and the high chain-link fence of the tennis court.

Reaching the front of the house, she made a quiet but visible pretense of trying each window, apparently oblivious of the police car parked at the end of the circular drive. She worked her way around to the well-lit front entrance. Failing an entry there, she renewed her efforts on the other side. At the sound of crunching gravel under heavy shoes, she whirled around, feigning fear and surprise at seeing a young man approaching.

"No need to be frightened. It's Constable Chapman, 'ere."

"You gave me a start. I've been jumpy all afternoon."

"Yes, ma'am, I'm surprised to see you out of doors at all. You don't appear to be dressed for it." He seemed embarrassed at the sight of her pajamas and bare feet but tried to hide it. "Is there a reason you're wanderin' about so late, Miss? Don't mean to be alarming you, but after what's 'appened, it's not a good notion to be out 'ere without the benefit of company."

"I was having trouble sleeping. Thought a breath of fresh air might help, so I went out to the back garden. Unfortunately, I locked myself out. Stupid, wasn't it?"

"Not at all," he said, puffing up at the opportunity to come to the rescue. " 'Appens all the time. 'Ere, we'll just ring for Mrs. Short and 'ave you in in a jiffy."

"Please don't do that. The poor woman's been harried to death all day. It would be such a shame to wake her."

"Look now, it's all in the job."

"I know, Constable," she said, looking as dejected and helpless as she could, "but the truth is I hate to let her discover what an idiot I've been."

"Right then, can't be 'avin' the old girl thinkin' a thing like that." Having agreed with her, he seemed at a loss how to prevent the discovery.

"With your professional knowledge, couldn't you help me open one of the windows at the back of the house?" she suggested. "That way I could just slip in with no one the wiser."

"Oh, I don't know about that. The inspector would chew my . . . a . . . let's just say 'e wouldn't be delighted to 'ave one of his men guilty of 'ouse breakin'."

roberta clark

"He'll never know. I promise you."

"What say we just ring for Mrs. Short," he said, moving toward the front door bell. "I'm sure she wouldn't mind at all."

Katherine moved into his path. "I've already put her to so much trouble. Look, you really wouldn't be breaking in. I'd be the one crawling through the window. All I need is your expertise on the lock."

"Well, now, there must be better ways to 'andle the situation. Let's just 'ave a look 'round back, shall we? Maybe the door isn't locked. They get a bit sticky in their old age."

Damn, she thought, had to play it safe. I'm just not cut out for this kind of thing—can't seem to get away with anything. "You're right," she said, grasping at one last straw. "I'll go back and have a look myself."

"I'd better give you an escort 'round."

"No! Please. I don't want to be a bother."

"No bother at all," he insisted. "Come along now."

"Constable Chapman," she said, holding her ground, "if you walk me around, there'll be no one at the front gate and, to put it bluntly, that scares hell out of me. I promise, if I can't get the door open, I'll tap on Mrs. Short's window and ask her to let me in. There's very little trouble I can get into between here and there."

He hesitated, then reluctantly said, "All right then, but if you need me . . ."

the **GOLD** *Covenant*

She was already walking away. "I'll be fine. Really."

Should have managed on my own, she thought. It doesn't pay to complicate matters. When she reached the library, she stopped to inspect the windows more closely. They were double-hung—the kind she had at the old house in Maine—and not impossible to open with the right tools, but they were also high and that could be a major problem. There might be something in the garden shed sturdy enough to stand on. With luck, even a ladder.

The shed was on the far side of the house and she had just passed the back entrance when she heard the sound of someone else's footsteps. Turning, she saw a beam of light flickering near the patio wall from the direction she'd just come. Quickly, she backtracked and ducked into the recessed niche shading the back door. She took a deep breath to steady her hand, shoved the door open, and tripped the lock. Before she closed it behind her, she stepped outside and watched the thick lumbering figure approaching along the garden path. There was no doubt it was Chapman, probably having second thoughts about his duties. Quietly, she pulled the door closed and waited under the eave. As the beam from his flashlight grew brighter, she turned, pretending to struggle with the door.

"No luck then?"

She swung around. "Constable! For a moment I thought . . ."

roberta clark

"Didn't mean to startle you again. Thought it best to see you got in all right. 'Ere, let me give a 'and with that," he said, handing her the light. "It might need a bit of muscle put to it." He leaned his shoulder against the door, firmly, then pushed as he tried to turn the knob. There wasn't a creak in reply to the effort. "Seems you were right, Miss. We'll just 'ave to wake Mrs. Short then."

"I've already tried. She must be a sound sleeper."

"Best let me give it a try then. I'm a bit 'eavier on the 'and than you are, I expect."

"I do feel an awful fool. The woman's had such a trying day." Katherine's face reflected genuine disappointment. Reluctantly, she reached for the bell.

"Hold on then."

She dropped her hand at the relenting sound in his voice.

"The window?" she asked.

"Mind you, I'm not saying it's a good idea, but there can't be too much 'arm in breakin' the rules now and again. Let's just 'ave a go at it, shall we?"

A less determined man might have given up after a few failures but Chapman wasn't the type to quit, especially when he'd committed himself to the rescue. After five minutes of fumbling, he finally flipped the latch and pushed up the lower frame. Having reminded her to relock it when she was inside, he gave her a boost over the sill and stood outside watching until she'd carried out his instructions.

Katherine waited until she heard the plodding footsteps retreat along the garden walk, then turned to look around the room. Again, she had to wait until her eyes became accustomed to the dark before daring to move. In the faint moonlight seeping through the panel of windows, a flat pattern of furniture took form out of the shadows. Gradually, the nebulous shapes evolved into mass.

At the desk in the center of the room, she switched on an antique brass lamp. The desk was a dark rosewood with an ancient swivel chair—much like the one Gustav had used—behind it. In front of it were two wing-chairs with a round wood-inlaid table between them. Facing a large corner fireplace, a sofa with its brushed-velvet upholstery showed signs of heavy use. Along the back of the sofa stood a trestle table loaded with stacks of journals and books. To the left of the fireplace was a drafting table, a chair, and a taboret filled with drafting materials.

The top of the desk seemed much too neat by her standards. On one side was a small, exquisite, porcelain clock encased in the forepaws of a pair of bronze lions. On the other side she found a moroccan leather box which, on examination, contained nothing more interesting than the household accounts, memo pads, pencils, and pens. The drawers, as she expected, were locked.

Her father's desk had a release button on the underside. It was possible this one might have a similar mechanism. Reaching under the desk, she slid her hands along the smooth surface and, to her immense satisfaction, found a series of control buttons on the right-hand side. More than a little wary, she pressed one, but before she could try the drawers again the purring sound of a motor filled the room. From an opening in the ceiling, a large screen rolled down in front of the desk. The second button activated a projection system which flashed a series of topographical maps onto the screen at a touch. The maps displayed coded legends but no identifying marks of any kind. Each covered ten square miles or less. Impossible to pinpoint an area that small without a key.

The system didn't surprise her. Maps were integral to Shep's business, as was secrecy. He was considered a geological wizard—a man with incredible luck—but his reputation was built on knowledge combined with tireless energy and a tenacious will. His wealth came from small percentages of some of the richest mineral finds in the world. Semi-retired for several years, he was still in demand though he now worked on the more highly selective basis of his own interest.

It seemed unlikely any of the maps were of the area where Gustav had been working, but it was worth checking out, if possible. She took a pencil out of the leather box, tore a sheet of paper off the pad, and copied the coded legend on the first map. After finishing with that, she jotted down a sampling of the site notations and characteristics, then went on to do the same with the other maps. When she was done, she tucked the paper away. She pressed the first button again, watching apprehensively as the apparatus retracted into its overhead slot. Sliding her fingers over the panel to the next switch, she was amazed to see a section of bookshelves at the center of the facing wall swing open. "My God, *Cat and Canary* time!"

The steel door framed by the shelves resembled the time-lock mechanism of a bank vault. A closer examination confirmed it was impregnable, beyond even the talents of Constable Chapman. Back at the desk, she looked underneath for other controls. There were none. The same button brought the heavy section of shelves rumbling back into place, the sound seeming to echo beyond the room. Feeling edgy, she stood still and listened but there was only the ticking of the porcelain clock. The sound was mesmerizing. It brought sudden overwhelming awareness of fatigue. The deep, consuming weariness that usually came at night and only in the restlessness of her sleep.

She thought about going back to her room. There was nothing else she could do here. Anything of real importance would be stowed inside that steel vault.

At the paneled door leading to the foyer, she looked for the latch that would release the bolt. There was none. It was a keylock deadbolt. She felt her heart sink as she grabbed the knob, twisting it frantically, knowing it wouldn't respond. The only way to open the door was with a key. It's the window again, she thought, and this time I really am locked out of the house.

She stared at the dutifully relatched window, wondering if Mrs. Short and the constable would be likely to exchange stories in the morning. If they did, she'd be hard put to explain her actions. Plunking down in a chair, she tried to think of a plausible excuse for the implausible night-meandering.

Her eyes wandered sleepily over the large collection of books that lined the rosewood shelves. So many beautiful volumes, a wealth of information, tucked away in tidy order—at least those that were not obviously much used. Could there be something revealing there that might shed light on the map locations? An Atlas? Diary? Personal journal? Or a manuscript? In no hurry to wake Mrs. Short, she might as well check it out.

A ladder fitted to a track in the ceiling put all of the hundreds of volumes into reach. They were filed alphabetically in sections according to subject. When she'd finished the first level, she climbed the ladder and started around again. At first she rummaged only through the books that had been hurriedly shoved onto shelves, but soon found herself absorbed in others regardless of how they'd been filed away. The variety and breadth of the collection was fascinating.

the **GOLD** *Covenant*

On the second wall, three shelves from the top, she found the complete work of Gustav Nikulasson. Fourteen volumes of first editions with some later editions in duplication. She pulled one out and leafed through it. The inscription on the title page was scrawled in her father's almost illegible hand: *Sheppard—integrity in friendship.*

Here it was again, the evidence of Gustav's trust. Certainly he had greater reason for it than she had for her suspicions. His trust was the outgrowth of a long association; her suspicions were based on little more than rumor. It was no contest. Experience should always take precedence. But still, there were those feelings, perhaps stirred by unverified sources with questionable motivations but, nevertheless, difficult to ignore. Something was wrong, a great deal unexplained. Her doubts were not going to be completely resolved until she had that explanation.

She slammed the volume back into place, gripped the shelf and started to slide the ladder along the track to the next section. The mechanical noise of the casters muffled the sound of the key in the latch.

There was no warning before the library door swung open.

CHAPTER 12

Katherine grasped the edges of the ladder to keep from falling. Although she knew there could be only one person standing in the doorway, the unexpected glare of light from the foyer struck her with a shock as jolting as a current of electricity. She struggled to regain the equilibrium and composure she'd lost along with her balance. After what seemed a torturous number of minutes, she turned, smiling, to face Sheppard.

"Couldn't sleep," she said, trying to keep the defensive tone from creeping into her voice. "Thought I might find something interesting to read."

She watched like a treed cat as Shep closed the door behind him. Unhurried, he lit a cigarette, regarding her with neither anger nor amusement. He tossed his suit jacket onto one of the wing chairs and sank leisurely into the other, stretching his long legs out in front of him with ankles crossed.

the **GOLD** *Covenant*

"It seems I've made an untimely entrance," he said. "Tell me, Katherine, are those your pajamas or the latest in Ukrainian resort wear?"

"Neither." She brushed her thick auburn hair back over her shoulders, climbed down the ladder and propped herself against the bottom rung. Her deep green eyes returned Shep's blank stare with equal lack of emotion.

"I suppose," he said, "it would be fruitless to ask how you got in here."

"I suppose it would."

"Would it be equally useless to ask why?"

"I've already told you why."

"So you have—something to read. And have you found anything suitable?"

"Your library runs to the heavy side. I was hoping for something along the line of a Chandler or a Charteris."

"The sitting room upstairs—shelves are full of them. Have you forgotten?"

"It was locked. Didn't want to bother Mrs. Short. I feel rather guilty about all the trouble I've put her to today."

"Any pangs of guilt about breaking into my private study?"

"None at all! But I feel damned embarrassed at getting caught."

"It doesn't show," he said. "Was it worth the trouble?"

"I think you know the answer to that."

"If you're having difficulty sleeping, I have some

pills upstairs."

"I don't like pills. You said there were things you had to tell me. You said I'd sleep better after."

He reached into his trouser pocket, pulled out a set of keys, and tossed them to her. "There's a bottle of scotch and some glasses in the taboret," he said, picking up his jacket and laying it on the desk. "And you might find a chair more comfortable."

Leaving her perch on the ladder, she went to the cabinet, unlocked it, and took out the scotch and two glasses. She felt his eyes following every move, reminding her of the past, of the way that probing look had ruffled her composure when she was younger. She'd have to keep those memories in check. And stop running around in pajamas.

"Shall I pour here," she asked, "or is this going to be a long night?"

"You need your rest. We're going to a reception in London tomorrow night."

She poured two glasses of scotch, brought them over and handed one to Shep before settling into the chair opposite with her legs curled under her.

"What reception?" she asked.

"I don't think you know the Lewellyns. Ian and Michelle?" Katherine shook her head. "They're entertaining one of your U.S. senators and his wife. Thought you might enjoy meeting some people—and an old friend as well."

"Not sure I'm ready for that."

"Gustav was afraid you'd become a recluse. Is it true, Katherine?"

"I hadn't thought of it that way. After John died, things just went on in a kind of natural extension of what they'd been. It wasn't a conscious decision."

"I see. You cut yourself off from your father—from everyone—for two years without a conscious thought about what you were doing."

Katherine's back went rigid. She uncurled her legs and sat up straight. "Would my father still be alive if I hadn't? You're too easy on me, Shep. Why don't you talk about all the other *might have beens* and *why didn'ts*?"

"Easy, Kat. It was a thoughtless remark. I'm sorry." He waited, silently, until she relaxed again, then said, "You loved John a great deal?"

"I don't know, Shep. I sometimes wonder if we had a chance to find out before he got sick."

"But you stayed with him."

"Do you know what it's like? You stay because you care about him, because he needs you, because he'd do the same for you. You both think that'll make everything all right, bearable, and maybe it does at first. But after awhile there's a change. He begins to resent you. Resents your being there, resents his needing you, resents being a burden, resents having to die. Then he tries to destroy the thing that keeps you there, so you begin to wonder if you're staying out of caring or out of guilt because it's him instead of you. You block out the present. You try to remember the good things. Then he's gone and you can't remember anything but the pain." She turned away, "Sorry," she said. "I shouldn't have let go like that."

He watched her for a moment, silently, then said, "You've been missed, you know. I've been tempted, more than once, to come over there and bring you back forcibly."

"Maybe you should have followed through."

"Some things should never be forced." His eyes were dark and his voice almost angry.

It hasn't changed, she thought. After all the years, nothing's changed between us.

She took a sip of scotch and put the glass down.

"Would you like some ice?"

"No," she lied, keeping her manner detached under his steady gaze. "I just want information, Shep. Where do we start?"

"You've been in no hurry up to now. Supposing we drop business for the night and give ourselves a new start."

"And how would we do that?"

"Well, for openers . . ."

He stood up, walked over to her, bent down, tilted her face with his hands, and kissed her. A slow, soft, tender kiss.

It brought painful memories—emotions she wanted to deny and which she found, instead, stirring, warm, and undeniably alive. She watched him silently as he returned to his chair, crushed out the stub of his cigarette and lit another.

"It seems," he said, smiling at her, "I've stumbled on a way to render you speechless. It wasn't what I intended."

"What had you intended, Shep?"

He studied her for a moment as if trying to decide how to answer. "Have I told you how good it is to see you again?"

"Something to that effect."

"I'm sorry about the afternoon, Kat. We'll put it right, I promise you."

She sat in silence, wondering if what she was feeling was an emotional misreading, an aberration of fatigue. She was out of sync—had been for a long time—not ready to distinguish between fact and fancy. Especially where Sheppard was concerned.

"I really am glad you're here," Shep went on. "It's rather like having a second chance."

"Shep—"

"I know. It's not the time. Let's just say, for now, you're not the only one who could have made better use of the past few years."

"What have you been doing for the past few years?"

"I thought we agreed to put off talk about business."

"Then you have been working?"

"Off and on."

"With Gustav?"

"Off and on."

"You were there—on the site—when he took off on that last trip. Why did you stay behind?"

"I was working." His hand massaged the lines of his tanned forehead, then combed through his dark brown hair. "It wasn't the first time your father made use of the plane when it was available. He often made short hops with Kevin Arman for supplies, tools, whatever was needed. Kevin was a good pilot, Kat. You know that."

"Yes, I know. And my father was a fanatic about preserving his work. Why was there nothing left of it on the site? I can't believe he had every scrap of writing with him when the plane went down."

"He had a meeting in Athens with his editor," Shep explained. "Some of the work was going back to New York with him. Some of it was going into a safe deposit there—in Athens."

"There are reports—official reports—that say the plane wasn't flying the route indicated on the flight plan. How do you account for that?"

"I haven't seen those reports but there could be a number of reasons why they might have been off-course. Mechanical or electronic problems. Weather."

"There's speculation they were shot down by Syrian

aircraft. That the reasons were political."

"Gustav? Arman? Political! Come now," he said, smiling. "You can't possibly believe a story like that."

"Not about them. But it was your plane. An observer might assume you were in it."

"A wild theory, Kat. And where did you see this mysterious report? It has the familiar ring of MI6 or CIA. Perhaps that's why you finally accepted my invitation. They've pressed you into service, have they?"

"I'm not a company man. Strictly free-lance." She shifted positions in her chair to adjust for the circulation in her legs. "And I'm wondering why nothing you've said so far is in keeping with your promise to help me sleep better."

"After so many years, I would have thought you'd be more interested in Gustav's personal life than professional."

"I've been immersed in the personal aspects of his life for months. Are you the one who packed his things and shipped them to me?"

"The entire lot."

"He left nothing here? In all of those trips he made to Stowesbridge? Surely he would have made use of that marvelous safe deposit you have right here in this room behind those lovely steel doors."

"You certainly have been active in the short time I was away." He got up to refresh his glass. "Did you manage to crack that lock as well?"

"And if I did?"

"Then, I suppose, I should ask if you found anything useful. Anything of an incriminating nature."

"If you thought I'd really been inside that crypt, I doubt we'd be sitting here having this friendly little chat." She wanted to break his cool reserve but was afraid of losing her own in the process. "You were his friend, Shep. Why is it I don't believe you? What was Gustav working on? Why isn't there a trace of it left?"

"Has it occurred to you Gustav may have wanted it that way? There are good reasons why I can't talk about his work. And even better reasons why you should forget it."

"Why? Why shouldn't I see his papers? They're here, aren't they?"

"I didn't say that."

"Then show me what's inside the strong room."

He moved across to the desk and sat on the edge of it looking at her thoughtfully before he spoke. "We've been friends for a long time, Katherine. Sometimes that has to be enough."

"It was enough for Gustav," she said, "and he's dead."

Sheppard flinched. A profound sadness swept over his face giving Kat a momentary regret but, just as suddenly, the look was gone. Wondering if she'd imagined it, she stood, waiting for what might be a more revealing response. He said only, "Good night, Katherine."

the **GOLD** Covenant

She walked to the door, opened it, and left the room without looking back.

CHAPTER 13

Cradling the receiver against his shoulder, Ernie Gehreich pulled a panatella out of his shirt pocket and ripped off the cellophane wrapper. He bit off the tip and spit it over the end of the bed, then lit the slender cigar, savoring the smoke as it drifted out of his mouth and curled up to the stained ceiling.

Damned idiots always put you on hold. Keep the peons waiting. That's all these MBAs learn at their big-deal Ivy league schools. He hated working with civilians. If everything went according to plan, he'd never have to again. *Power Line* had been the perfect cover. Worth the investment, the years of cultivating connections and setting up pipelines. Worth waiting for someone like Katherine Nikulasson to come along. There was going to be a lot of flack when it was over but he wouldn't be around to see it. He'd be long gone, a speck on the South Seas with nothing but naked brown bodies for company.

As for Mr. Ivar Whalen, he could have the flack—exclusive—a going-away-present from Ernie Gehreich.

Gehreich swore into the silent telephone receiver and shifted it to his other shoulder. One thing about *Power Line*—they give you a decent hotel to park it in. This place is a goddamned sump hole. The greasy little sons a bitches could have provided something more tolerable in accommodations.

The room made him feel claustrophobic. The pattern of the wallpaper was too large for the space. Its faded dingy-gray flowers and the thick uneven layers of enamel paint that covered the woodwork and doors reminded him of the dumps he'd lived in with his grandmother. He'd hated old things since he was a kid. They were oppressive. Angie had never understood that. She collected antiques—fuckin' damn antiques—the entire time they were married. After the divorce, she sank every cent of their community property into her own antique shop—every cent of what he'd risked his hide for all these years just to keep her ass in bric-a-brac.

From where he lay, Gehreich could see into the cubbyhole that served as a bathroom, the corroded fixtures, the chipped porcelain, the rust stains in the tub that ran from the taps down to the drain. Angry at the sight, he stood and kicked the bathroom door, slamming it shut. It didn't help; it only made the room seem smaller.

He dropped the phone on the bed, moved to the half-opened window, and shoved it up as far as it would go. Before he had a chance to turn around, it slipped down to its original position. He cursed under his breath before pushing it up again, then propped it open with a wooden chair, the only piece of furniture in the room other than the bed and bureau. The air was warm and stale with the smells that rose from the narrow alley below, but it was better than the stifling atmosphere of the room. The back of the pub, directly across the alleyway, was locked and barred. He should have remembered closing time and stocked up on something cold to drink.

Disgusted, he turned away from the window. There was a faint crackling sound coming from the abandoned receiver. He rushed to pick it up.

"Kimball?" he yelled. "That you?"

"Thought you'd hung up. Almost did myself."

"Yeah, well, what do you expect when you keep someone waiting for fifteen fuckin' minutes?"

"Long as that, was it? Sorry, old boy," Kimball's high-pitched voice came over cheerfully. "Afraid you caught me at an awkward moment—fish on the line—that sort of thing. You know how it is. Can't let them get away when they're almost hooked."

"Have you heard from the girl?"

"Yes. She left a message tonight. I thought I'd wait until morning to ring her up."

"Good. The timing couldn't be better," Gehreich

said. "Remember, we don't want her to panic and run, so be careful what you tell her."

"I'm not an idiot, Mr. Gehreich. I think I can handle it properly."

"Yeah? Tell me about it. I've seen more screw-ups by amateurs than a two-bit whore sees in a lifetime. Difference is when you screw up it's not your delicate ass in the line of fire."

"I don't like you, Mr. Gehreich. And if you don't like the way I handle matters, you can tell Ivar Whalen to get someone else on this end. I don't relish working with supercilious bores anymore than you like screw-ups, as you so eloquently put it."

"Keep your goddamned britches on. You don't have to take me home to mother."

"She'll be ever so grateful," Kimball said. "Now can we get back to business? What exactly do you want me to do?"

"Arrange a meeting with the Nikulasson dame. As soon as possible. I'll take it from there."

"I don't understand how you can protect the girl when you can't even get near her without my help."

"You don't have to understand," Gehreich said. "That's my business."

"Will you be at this number tomorrow?"

"Get back to me before eleven. I'm checking out of this dump."

Gehreich dropped the phone in the cradle then picked it up again. "This is room five-eighteen. I've got ten bucks here for a couple of cold beers. See what you can do, will you?"

Assured something might be possible, he hung up and relit his cold cigar. After puffing on it for a few minutes, he put it out again, went into the bathroom and turned on the cold water tap in the tub. When the pipes were cleared of rust, he jammed the plug in and began unbuttoning his shirt. He hung the shirt on the bedpost, removed his shoes and socks, then his pants, which he carefully folded on the creases before setting them across the foot of the bed.

A loud knock shook the door, catching his shorts mid-way between hips and knees. Quickly he pulled them back up and shouted, "Take it easy. I'm coming." He made a move toward the door and then stopped. It was too soon for the cold beer, even with the ten-dollar impetus. He listened for a moment. It was quiet. Too quiet. His Browning automatic rested in the shoulder holster draped over the opposite bedpost. He started for it. Too late. The door splintered open. He froze in place as a hulk of a man hurled into the room and spun around to face him.

"Just stand where you are, mate," the man said. "No sudden moves."

He was huge, a half-foot taller than Gehreich, per-

the **GOLD** *Covenant*

haps fifty pounds heavier. Other than his bulk, he had no visible weapon. If the bastard doesn't have one, Gehreich thought, he must figure he doesn't need one. Weighing the odds, Geherich decided the Browning was his only chance. His lighter frame might give him an edge with speed.

He was wrong. The first blow hit him on the side of the head before his hand could wrap itself around the butt of the revolver. He sprawled forward on the bed, somersaulted to the other side, then came up in a crouch, his right ear splitting with pain. The bed was between them now, the weapon in reach.

"I can read you. Move careful, mate! Just ease away from the 'ardware."

"Fuck off!" Gehreich shouted as he went for the weapon again. In his peripheral vision, he saw the mass launch itself across the bed. His hand wrapped around the cold steel but the mass hit before he could use it. He was aware of pain—his brain exploding—a second before he lost consciousness.

When he came to, his face was pressed into the grit of the carpet and his hand still gripped the revolver. He fumbled for the trigger as he tried to move but the feeble attempt was paralyzed by the heavy knee at the base of his spine.

"If you was t'let loose a the piece, maybe we could 'ave a little chat. Friendly like. What do you say?"

"Go fuck yourself," Gehreich spat out as the pressure increased on his back.

"You're beginning to repeat yourself, mate. Don't say I didn't ask you politely."

A sudden chop and pain hit every nerve in Gehreich's hand, exploding up through his arm and shoulder and neck. He heard himself scream. It disgusted him—as if he were removed from his body—watching his own weakness.

"There's a good chap. Turn over gentle-like and sit up nice and easy."

Gehreich did as he was told. He needed time to think—time to clear his head. His ears were still ringing from that first blow, but, slowly, through a haze of bruised nerve-ends, the pain began to subside.

The big red-faced man towered over him, the Browning automatic shoved into his belt, legs planted a foot apart, meaty arms half-cocked, hands like sledge hammers resting on his hips. Behind this solid barrier of muscle stood another man, smaller, darker, with a smile as friendly as the snarl on a rabid Doberman. He was holding a thin strip of metal in one hand.

"What in hell do you apes want?" Gehreich asked. "Who're you working for?"

The smaller man said, "Enrique Quisette." His accent was thick, French.

"I don't believe you."

"Believe what you like, *monsieur*. The fact remains

the same."

"We had a deal," Gehreich said. "Quisette gave me his word."

The Frenchman laughed, his dark skin even darker next to the white-pebble teeth. Gehreich was furious. He'd been double-crossed by that asthmatic pansy, Enrique Quisette, after all the work he'd invested. His anger fired him off like a jet. He pressed his one good hand against the floor and catapulted himself headfirst into the rock-hard gut in front of him. Caught off-guard, the big man staggered backward giving Gehreich the split second he needed. He rolled away and sprang to his feet holding the revolver in his left hand and cradling his right against his body. The pain was terrible; the hand, broken or dislocated, was useless. He motioned the two men toward the far wall, then edged slowly toward the clothing on the bed. His body was sweating but he felt cold. He fought to stay conscious. Fuck the clothes, just get out.

"Don't try it, mate. You won't get past the door."

The two men were moving, the distance growing wider between them.

"Stay together!" Panic heightened Gehreich's voice. The Browning was heavy, awkward in his left hand. He leaned on the bedpost for support, momentarily closing his eyes. The big man picked up an ashtray and hurled it in one single motion. It struck Gehreich's right hand in a flash of glass, cigar butts, ashes, and pain. He remained conscious but he could focus on nothing but nerve ends and the radiating agony in his right side. Instinctively, he dropped the weapon and grabbed the crumpled hand. The big man moved in fast and delivered a sharp blow to Gehreich's neck. Gehreich's knees buckled.

They lifted him onto the bed, half-conscious. He struggled for words but something was stinging his neck. He swallowed and tried to speak again but it was too difficult.

"Greed!" the Frenchman said, shaking his head. He was sitting on the bed next to Gehreich. "There's no room in this world for people who do not know their place, *mon ami*."

Gehreich was almost in tears with the growing pain in his ears and the hot trickle of blood at his neck. He was sweating heavily, furious with himself for being caught off-guard. Distracted. It was the fuckin' damned ancient wreck of a hotel that did it. There had to be a way to reason with these two creeps. He lifted his left hand and motioned weakly.

"You have something you want to say?" The dark man smiled, then loosened the metal noose.

"Quisette needs me.—" Gehreich's voice was little better than a gasp, "—to get to the girl."

"You make the great mistake, *monsieur*, to over-emphasize your importance. You also make the mistake to ask for more money. Quisette does not like people who renege on their contracts."

"People who try to bloody 'old 'im up, is more like it," the big man added.

"Okay, so I didn't know the rules. Is that a hanging offense, for God's sake? Tell Quisette the original deal is fine with me."

"We'll tell 'im, mate, but first you tell us all about the plans you've made."

"It's not set yet," Gehreich said, his voice reduced to a coarse whisper.

"You tellin' us you ain't made contact yet?"

"No! I told you, it's just not set."

"Mr. Quisette's not goin' t'like that."

"Listen t'me. We can deal. I can make it worth plenty—"

"There is only one thing we desire, *monsieur*, and that is delivery of the girl, as you have promised."

"You'll have her," Gehreich said. "Kimball's arranging a meeting but I'll have to be here to finalize the details. He's going to call me in the morning with the time and location."

"Perhaps we can relieve you of the tedious waiting," the Frenchman said, putting enough pressure on the metal collar to bring Gehreich to his feet. "And, perhaps, at the same time, we find a way to make you more comfortable in this heat?"

"Hey, wait! God! I've got a stash, I'm tellin' you. Not just money . . . it's big! You won't be sorry—"

"That's right, mate. There's only one bloody sod's goin' t'be sorry 'round 'ere." The man smiled and stepped into the bathroom. He turned off the tap on the overflowing tub, released the plug to let some of the water drain out. Then he jammed the plug back into place. " 'Is Worship's bath is ready, Maurice. What say we give 'im a coolin' off?"

Maurice flipped off the noose and waited.

"Jesus! Jesus!" Gehreich pleaded. The tears spilled down his cheeks and mixed with the sweat and the coagulating blood on his chest. "Don't do this!"

The big man moved in on Gehreich, gripped the broken hand in his with a paralyzing pressure, and hoisted him over his shoulder. He carried Gehreich into the bathroom, then lowered him into the cold water. Before Gehreich could recover, the metal noose was biting into the softness of his throat again. He sat as tall as he could while Maurice wrapped the noose around the shower knobs, but, gradually, as the Frenchman pulled it tighter, the metal cut into the carotid artery.

Gehreich couldn't speak. His eyes were wild with fear as he watched the water slowly change color around his legs. Cloudy pink growing redder as his mind clouded over. He thought about Angie, ass-deep in antiques. Thought about himself—dead in an ancient, rotting, broken-down tenement in London.

CHAPTER 14

Katherine climbed out of bed feeling stiff and irritable after a restless sleep. A gentle morning breeze ruffled the curtains at her window, bringing with it the clean fragrance of the meadow and garden below. Looking out at the fields, she could see the mowers already at work. The upper field remained serenely quiet within the cordoned boundaries marked by the police. The ropes, fastened to a series of stakes, were the only reminder of yesterday's madness—those and the condition of her body.

The scratches on her arms, still red and irritated, as well as the bruises on her legs would probably be souvenirs for at least a week. The worst of it was the summer heat—covering up was not conducive to comfort.

With a groan, she lowered herself to the floor, then gently stretched her muscles, discovering in the process numerous aches and pains, some of them old ones returned.

roberta clark

The most familiar was the problem with her back.

The lifting had done it—before she'd learned the correct procedure. *Get help!* the doctor angry with her, *You don't need avoidable complications.* But John was so light—had lost so much weight in the last year—and he hated having anyone else in the house. Dying is private, he'd said. A very private occupation.

Feeling a degree more limber after showering, she rummaged through her things for something in the line of camouflage wear. She hadn't packed a large variety of clothing—a habit developed over years of traveling with her father. He'd always given her an equal share of their luggage allowance along with the freedom to fill it as she liked, but with that freedom she'd had to accept his only proviso: take responsibility for your choices without complaint, however foolish those choices might be. It didn't take many trips to realize that excess clothing and clothing that needed more than minimal up-keep were not only a pain in the backside, but also a deprivation of something more useful. Esthetics didn't travel well in a duffle bag.

Whether she'd had an alternative or not, it was too warm to be concerned with covering up the bruises on her legs or the network of scratches on her arms. After pulling on a pair of khaki shorts and a pale green shirt, she brushed and clipped her hair back at the nape of her neck, then left the room to go downstairs. The phone

the **GOLD** *Covenant*

rang as she reached the landing. She stopped to listen as Mrs. Short rushed in from the patio to answer it.

"It's for you, Miss Katherine," the housekeeper said, leaning over the newel of the staircase to look up at her. "A Mr. Hugh Kimball."

"Thank you, Mrs. Short. I'll take it in my room. Is Mr. Wilde up?"

"He's having coffee with Superintendent Hopkins, outdoors on the terrace. I'll bring your breakfast out when you've finished with your call."

Kat hurried back to her room, grabbed the receiver off the hook and sat on the edge of the bed, waiting briefly for the click of the downstairs phone. "Mr. Kimball," she said, "thank you for returning my call so quickly."

"Not at all, not at all. Spoke with Halvern in New York—Thursday—Friday—memory's a bit rusty, I'm afraid—said to give you *carte blanche*." The caller's voice was a contralto, Katherine would have guessed a woman's instead of a man's, and there was no regard for grammatical formalities in the staccato delivery. "Looking forward to meeting you, Miss Nikulasson. Fill in a bit. Show you around our little factory. Anything I can do to help—anything at all. . . ." It was an unfinished statement as well as an unstated question. "Breach the wall and all that sort of thing."

"We'll give it a try," Katherine said, smiling at the outpouring of energy from the high-pitched voice. "I haven't been briefed on your office, Mr. Kimball, so if I ask too much of you, please tell me."

"I like to think we can do most anything at all in the way of gathering information—cutting through red tape. We'll give it a go. Do our best. Not disappoint you."

"A man was murdered here yesterday. Evan Babcock."

"Saw the papers this morning. Rather thought that would have something to do with your call."

"He was a student at Oxford at one time—I'm not sure of the years—and a sometime-employee of Sheppard Wilde. I'd like you to dig up as much as you can about him: background, travel, work, friends, police record—if he has one."

"Right. Anything else?"

"Yes. I'm going to send you a Xerox copy of two photographs. I'd like the artifacts in them identified, if possible. I'm also enclosing some notations from a topographical map. I need to know if they're standard keys or if they're some sort of code. And, please, Mr. Kimball, be discreet. I don't want anyone to know where you got the photos or notes, or why you're gathering information on them."

"Needn't fear on that account, Miss Nikulasson, we are the model of discretion. Would it be possible to arrange a meeting for sometime today? The sooner I have the material, the sooner you'll have results."

Katherine thought for a moment, then said, "Perhaps

the **GOLD** *Covenant*

this evening. I'm going to be in London at a reception in Brompton Square—the home of Colonel Ian Lewellyn. I could arrange to slip away for a short period of time."

"Perfect! I'll be back in London early this afternoon. Reception's honoring Senator Marshall and his wife. Had the news release for a week. Colonel Lewellyn's a man who appreciates a dash of good press. Should be a simple matter to wrestle an invitation for myself. Do away with complications. Save having to synchronize watches—all that sort of rot."

"Before I forget, there's one more item. Can you find out if reservations were made in Athens last May for Gustav Nikulasson and his editor, Mikhail Czerny—or anyone else from Rhodes-Corinthian Publishers?"

"Good as done. That the lot, then?"

"For now. I'll look forward to seeing you tonight."

"You'll hear from me if I hit a snag."

"Mr. Kimball, if you should call when I'm out, leave a number where I can reach you. I'd rather there were no messages."

After the conversation with Kimball, Katherine went downstairs, where she found Sheppard on the patio with Superintendent Hopkins. They were seated at a table under a vine-covered trellis overlooking the pool. The table was covered with a linen cloth, set with white china, a silver coffee urn, and a fresh bouquet of roses. There was an untouched setting between them. Behind them, the inviting water of the pool glistened under the intense glare of the sun. Both men rose from their chairs as she approached the table.

Wilde's expression gave no hint of the way they had parted last night. "Good morning, Katherine. Come join us," he said. "This is Superintendent Hopkins of Scotland Yard."

"How do you do?" Hopkins said, offering a lean, liver-spotted hand. He appeared to be in his early sixties, round-shouldered, eyes sharp in spite of their deceptively soft blue color, fine hair thinning evenly over a pink scalp. His summer suit showed the ravages of the hot drive from London.

"Did you rest well?" Wilde asked. He pulled out a chair for her and the two men settled down again. "I rather expected you to sleep in this morning."

"Old habits are hard to break," she said. "Have they found the helicopter yet?"

"Afraid not," Hopkins replied. "We believe they crossed the channel near Southampton. We haven't been able to zero in on a destination. Once the trail is cold, it's a bit like searching for the proverbial needle in the haystack."

He looked up as the patio doors swung open and Mrs. Short wheeled out a cart. She placed several chafing dishes on the table, replenished the urn with a pot of fresh brewed coffee, and refilled their cups. "Will you be wantin' anything else, sir?" she asked.

"No, thank you, Mrs. Short," Wilde said. "Have you managed to reach Cuppy yet?"

"He's a hard one to pin down, but I'm still tryin'." She parked the cart beside the table, brushed away a few crumbs, and went back into the house.

When she'd left, Wilde lifted one of the lids and offered the dish to Katherine. "You must be hungry this morning after such an active night."

Katherine smiled without replying, bypassed the bangers and smoked herring and helped herself to a small serving of scrambled eggs and a home-baked roll. Turning to the superintendent, she asked, "Have you any idea why Evan Babcock was murdered?"

"We're looking into several possibilities. Mr. Wilde and I were just discussing—or should I say having a disagreement about some of them. Did you know Evan Babcock, Miss Nikulasson?"

"We never met."

"You left the house shortly after you arrived, correct?"

"Yes. I went out for a walk."

"And where was Mr. Babcock at that time?"

"Mrs. Short said he'd gone out. She wasn't sure where."

"Did you hear or see anyone at all in the fields before you saw the helicopter lift off?"

"No, there was only the sound of the engine. At the time, I thought it was a tractor or a thresher. Superintendent, what were you and Shep in disagreement about?"

"Merely conjecture, mind you, at this point. However, Evan's business was the point of contention. In my opinion, there's cause to believe he was in the smuggling trade—drugs in particular."

Drugs! That was something totally removed from what Katherine had expected. She looked at Wilde's enigmatic face then back at Hopkins. It was tempting to tell him about the Xerox she'd found in Babcock's room—the one of her father holding the two art objects—but she held back. It was her only lead. If she gave it up, she'd be on the outside again. She didn't trust the police to give her the same information she might get from Kimball. The picture could always be turned in later; they'd never know when it had been discovered unless she told them. For the moment, it was more important to her she have immediate and direct access to the information. And that Wilde not know she had it.

"Why do you think someone killed him?" she asked Wilde. "You must have known him better than anyone."

"I don't know why he was killed. I do know Evan wouldn't go near the drug market," Wilde said, reaching for a pack of cigarettes.

"How can you be so sure?"

"No reason other than what I know of Evan's character."

"It's not like you to be subjective," she said. "Didn't you tell me once, a long time ago, subjectivity was a female weakness?"

the **GOLD** Covenant

"The longer I'm around, the more often I find it necessary to apologize for past prejudices," Wilde said, smiling. "But the fact remains, I know Evan was too smart to get involved in the drug racket."

"Sometimes smart lads get impatient," Hopkins said, "take the short-cut. Then it's not easy to let go once they've grown accustomed to the fancy life-style."

"Evan doesn't fit that picture," Wilde said. "Unless he was leading a double life."

"Not as uncommon as you'd think."

"Isn't it possible he was killed because he refused to do business with someone?"

"Perhaps, but it's highly unlikely," Hopkins said. "The syndicates keep a low profile. What you're suggesting wouldn't be reason enough for a killing—not one that would attract so much attention. I think you simply find it unacceptable that Babcock was capable of dealing in drugs. It's anathema—like incest or child abuse."

"That may be true," Wilde said. "It's difficult, as well, to accept one's own mistaken judgment. I suppose that's why I prefer to wait for the final proof . . ."

He paused as Mrs. Short opened the patio door. "There's several gentlemen to see the superintendent."

"Tell them he'll be there directly."

Hopkins pushed away from the table. "As Miss Nikulasson discovered yesterday, this isn't a nice covey of people to have mucking around the country. She's lucky to have escaped with nothing worse than a few scrapes and bruises. While you're having coffee, I'm going to have a look around," he said, turning to Katherine. "I'd like to talk to you again when I've finished."

"I'll be here all morning," she said, "but I'd like to get into town after lunch, if that's all right with you."

"We'll be through with our questions long before noon."

Hopkins followed Mrs. Short into the house, leaving Katherine and Shep alone. She pushed her plate away, and picked up the coffee pot. "Another cup?"

He nodded, crushed out his cigarette and lit another. "I've been asking myself why I don't pack you off to the States again."

"I've been here less than twenty-four hours."

"And very nearly got yourself killed during that time. I'd as soon you were in a safer place until we have things sorted out here."

"Is that the reason you want to send me home? Or is it because of what happened last night?"

"Which offense in particular were you referring to?"

"Did I give you that much of a choice?"

"I stopped counting a long time ago."

"Have I been as bad as all that?"

"Someday you might stop and ask *yourself* that question," he said. "In the meantime, why don't we call a truce? It doesn't matter about the library. If you wanted a look around, you could have asked me. As for your parting barb last night, I guess I can't blame you for feeling the way you do."

"Damn it, Shep, why is it I always end up with the urge to apologize even when I don't want to? I meant what I said last night. The reason I came here was to clear away all the doubts about my father's death and you've only added to them. And now there's this Evan Babcock murder. I don't believe, anymore than you do, that he was involved in drug dealing, and I don't for one minute believe your reasons are as subjective as you would like the superintendent to think."

"And your reasons, Katherine? Would you like to explain what they are? Since you didn't know Evan, they can't be subjective either, can they?"

"Maybe they are. I know you well enough to remember how particular you are about who you hire."

"Well, it looks as though I may have slipped a bit," he said. "Look here, we've gotten off to a rotten start. Let's try to put it right, shall we? Would you like me to drive you into town this afternoon?"

"What I have to do would bore you."

"Good," he laughed. "It's time we had a change."

"All right then," she said, her mood softening with his persistent good humor. "Do you know where I can buy a dress to wear to the reception tonight? I need something with a bit more cover-up than what I brought with me."

"I know just the place. Long sleeves, lace up to the chin, that sort of thing. Is that what you want?"

"Close enough."

"Pity," he said, enjoying the undamaged perfection of line she presented as she rose to stack the plates and serving dishes onto the cart.

"What else might Evan have been smuggling?" she asked.

"Are we back to that? Look here, Katherine, whether it's drugs or not, it's still dangerous. That's why I've asked Mrs. Short to see if Cuppy's available. I don't want to alarm you unnecessarily, but if you're going to stay on, I want someone with you whenever you leave the house. Until this business is done with."

A very convenient way of keeping me on a leash, she thought. I'll be damned if I let him do it.

CHAPTER 15

Katherine found Wilde waiting for her on the landing. He was standing to one side, scanning the roomful of guests, looking elegant and relaxed in black tie and dinner jacket. Whether he was in a salon in London or a remote corner of an undeveloped country, he always seemed to belong. People treated him as though he did belong. She envied this rare quality, especially now, with the internal battle she was waging with herself.

Although the room was spacious—high ceiling, glass paneled French doors open to the terrace—she felt claustrophobic. She hated nothing more than crowds—parties, polite conversation. She'd been removed too long from all of that. Solitude had become a habit even before she was aware of it. Now she was struggling to keep the habit from becoming a compulsion.

She moved around the circle of people gathered in

the archway between the entry and salon and joined Wilde, slipping her arm through his. He turned to smile at her but his eyes were serious, the way they had been all evening.

"Great dress!" he said.

The deep blue jersey clung to the curves of her body, the high neckline bare of jewelry, the long sleeves cuffed with wide silver bracelets. The bracelets had belonged to her mother, as had the matching silver-and-onyx earrings which were almost lost in the dark auburn hair skimming her shoulders.

"You're damned lucky I was with you," he went on. "I think you would have passed it up if I hadn't been."

"You're probably right." The dress did a wonderful job of concealing the previous day's damage, but it concealed little of the figure beneath. She hadn't enjoyed attracting this kind of attention for a long time. His open admiration only added to her discomfort. "Have you decided where to begin?" she asked.

"At the bar. Always."

The reception was well under way when they had arrived. The salon was filled with comfortably ensconced embassy regulars who preferred to talk—and drink—in a sitting position, and who were secure enough in status to let the party come to them. The nucleus of activity had drifted outside through the French doors to the three beautifully landscaped patios which ran the length

the **GOLD** *Covenant*

of the narrow lot in graduated steps. The bar and buffet occupied the first level under a canopy of lights. The high masonry wall surrounding the yard was covered with a mass of vines, ivy, and wild roses. Its aura of permanence brought a twinge of melancholy which passed with the touch of Wilde's hand on her arm.

"Looks like I may have been wrong about the bar," he said. "That's Colonel Lewellyn moving up on the right flank."

Katherine watched the man cut his way across the room like a knife through a plate of spaghetti. Lean and compact, Lewellyn bore the scalded complexion of an outdoor man whose fair skin has never acclimated to the sun.

"Sheppard!" he roared, converging on them, immediately turning his beaming smile on Katherine. His self-assurance transformed a fairly homely face into one that could easily qualify as handsome. "Pleasure to see you."

"Quite clear where the pleasure lies," Wilde said. "Katherine, this is Colonel Lewellyn, our host. In spite of first impressions, he's quite harmless."

"Colonel Lewellyn" She offered her hand which he accepted and held.

"Delighted, but it's Ian. Never waste time on formalities. And while we get better acquainted, let me give you a personal tour of our notorious residence—top to bottom."

"Notorious? Does that mean you have a ghost?"

"Some houses have ghosts, this one has scandals. One for each infamous era of its lifetime, and one for each room. Where would you like to begin?"

"Katherine and I have already established the agenda," Wilde said, "and you, old chap, are about to be taken into tow."

"There you are!" The throaty female voice emanated from a statuesque brunette in a low-cut white lame dress. "You Tartar, you were supposed to come to my rescue thirty minutes ago."

"Haven't you given up yet, Michelle?" Wilde said. "Ian has a built-in resistance to diplomacy."

"A Sinclair never gives up. It's inbred, muh dear. Like insanity. As for you," she said, giving Wilde a peck on the cheek, "don't bother with any of those tired excuses for why we never see you."

"Man's a farmer," Lewellyn said. "Farmers never holiday."

"Farmer, my ass," she snapped, loud enough to cause several heads to swivel, then turned to Katherine. "You must be Miss Nikulasson. I met your father, years ago. Wonderful man. Lovely man. God, I hate airplanes. Ought to be a law against leaving the ground with both feet at the same time. I've been after Ian to give it up for as long as we've been married but it's a disease. Incurable. It must have been devastating for you."

the **GOLD** *Covenant*

"It was," Katherine said.

There was a moment of leaden silence before Wilde's arm slid around her waist with a reassuring nudge. At once her tension relaxed.

"It would seem," Lewellyn spoke with pointed emphasis, "that there are others among us who have short-comings along the lines of diplomacy."

Impervious to Lewellyn's disapproving scowl, Michelle went on with the conversation. "We must get together and make up for Shep's negligence—hopefully on a less hectic occasion. And assuming he doesn't chain you to a milk pail or plow or some such."

Katherine laughed. "I'm sure there's no danger of that."

"I wouldn't count on it," Wilde said.

"Listen, darlings, will you excuse us for running off? The senator's looking for Ian and I've promised to deliver."

"Don't go away," Lewellyn told Katherine. "We'll have that tour after I've talked to the old boy. Duty first, and all that. I've been assigned as official travel agency for our visiting senator and his wife, you see. They're taking a respite from the pressures of a grueling fact-finding trip," he added with a touch of sarcasm as Michelle nudged him in the direction of the patio.

Wilde switched from his hold on Katherine's waist to a light touch of her arm. "I doubt we'll see either of them again tonight," he said. "Come along. I caught a glimpse of Forster in the corner."

"David Forster? I haven't seen him for years."

"You'd know him anywhere. As always, he won't know you from less than a foot away."

David Forster was among the regulars in the salon, in the farthest corner, securely out of the path of his more sociable wife, Teliah. But he did see them coming. With glasses firmly in place on his beakish nose, he had risen from the comfort of his chair, patiently waiting for them. He grasped Katherine in a warm embrace, then stood back to look at her. "By God, you've got the old man in you all right, but you've turned out a damned sight prettier."

"You never change, David," she said. "You still sound like C. Aubrey Smith. I've missed you."

"Why don't you come see us more often?" At once, his undisciplined brows contracted in thought while his hands waved the comment aside. "Never mind—you're here now. Still writing those fascinating articles of yours, are you?"

"There haven't been many in the last few years, but I've been trying to pick up the pace since I moved back to New York. And you, David, are you still traveling a great deal?"

"Not like the old days." He removed his glasses, then ran them over the ruffled front of his shirt. "It isn't the same anymore. Sit down here. We're not going to let this young lad spirit you away until we've had a talk, eh?"

the GOLD Covenant

"If it wasn't for your advanced age, David, I wouldn't let you have a minute alone with Katherine. Even so, I'm putting you on limited time so make good use of it. Now, what can I bring you from the bar? I need some excuse to leave the two of you alone for awhile."

"Scotch," Katherine said, "with ice."

Wilde grinned. "And you, David?"

"I'm on rations—nursing it along. Teliah's got eyes on her elbows."

Katherine settled into the deep boxy chair at right angles to David, watching with a twinge of misgiving as Wilde moved away toward the bar, leaving them to rehash old memories. David Forster had acted as liaison between her father, the government, and the British Museum in several important acquisitions. His interest in Gustav's work had often taken him into the field as a friend and observer for extended periods of time—usually when his wife, Teliah, was on tour with the Royal Ballet Theater. His visits had been especially exciting for Katherine. Unhampered by a total absorption in work, as Gustav was, David had always included her in his exploratory side-trips into territory that would otherwise have been forbidden a young girl alone.

"You're wondering what to say about John and Gustav, aren't you?" she asked.

His fingers laced over the front of his dress-shirt while he stared at her through his thick lenses as though he were appraising a shard of unearthed pottery.

"Or wondering whether you should mention them at all?" she went on. "I'm not uncomfortable talking about either of them, David. Really."

He seemed ill at ease, reluctant to begin, giving her the sense that he must know what Gustav had been working on and where.

"What I'm thinking, my girl, is what a rotten time you've had of it these past five years. Losing both of them that way. Devilish bad turn of luck."

"The rotten times were in small proportion to the good. The trick is to remember *that* when you start to feel cheated."

"Wish I'd had a chance to meet the boy. Gustav said he was a fine lad. Approved of him one-hundred percent."

"I don't think he ever quite approved of our not getting married."

"Why didn't you? You're not one of these modern women, are you? The kind who think marriage has all the depth of a piece of paper?"

She laughed. "You're reading from the same script as my father."

"Right you are. It's not easy for crusty old codgers like us to slough off the conventions of a half-century. All the same, it's damned stupid of me to run on like that."

"I don't mind. It's just that, sometimes, convention isn't suited to circumstance."

the **GOLD** *Covenant*

She looked down at the rough red scratches on her hands without seeing them. Katherine had wanted to be married to John, but the decision had not been hers. The thought she was staying with him through some feeling of obligation had been intolerable to him. The only way he could be sure she *wanted* to stay was knowing she was free to leave.

"Here now," David said, clearing his throat noisily as he leaned to one side and then the other searching his pockets for a handkerchief. "We've got off on a dark slice and it's all my fault. Teliah would have my scalp if she knew what a botch I've made of things."

"You haven't done anything of the sort. Tell me what you're up to these days—now that Teliah's retired from ballet."

"Retired! She may have put the slippers to pasture, but never herself. Committees, fund-raising, benefits, a bit of coaching to keep her hand on the pulse—she'll never retire from the ballet. That keeps me from falling into a state of atrophy as well."

"David," she said, "can you tell me why Gustav was in England just weeks before he died?"

"Was he then? Had no idea." David adjusted his glasses, then squinted at a man who had been standing behind Katherine's chair for the past few minutes. Sounding irritable, David snapped, "Well, what is it, my man?"

Ignoring David completely, the man spoke directly

to Katherine. "*Pardonnez-moi.* I do not like to interrupt your conversation. You are *Mademoiselle* Nikulasson?"

"Yes."

"There is someone who wishes to speak with you." He handed her a small white card. "*C'est tres important.*"

She glanced at the name, then stood. "Where is he?"

"If you go to the garden, I am certain he will find you."

"David, will you excuse me? I have some business to take care of. I won't be long."

"Of course, provided you make that a promise."

As she moved toward the patio doors, she glanced back at the small man who had delivered the message. He was leaning against the wall a few feet behind David, a bent cigarette dangling from his mouth. It seemed odd Kimball would send a messenger—especially one who looked as disreputable as that—instead of approaching her himself. She looked around for Wilde, finding him across the room, too deep in discussion with a group of men to notice her. Good timing. This was strictly between her and Kimball.

Dodging the gestures of two men in animated conversation, she slipped through the doorway to the patio, then walked slowly along the garden path. She'd only progressed a few steps before realizing she'd left her handbag—with the Xeroxes in it—on the table next to David. As she turned to go back for it, someone grasped her elbow from behind.

the **GOLD** *Covenant*

"What are you doing?" she asked, trying to free her arm. "Are you Mr. Kimball?" The man looked more like a wrestler than a business executive. He continued to restrain her arm.

" 'E's in 'is car . . . waitin' for you."

"He was to meet me inside."

" 'E said to tell you it was too late to arrange an invitation."

"And yet, you're here."

"It's not far, Miss. Just outside the gate."

"I don't think so," she said. "Tell Mr. Kimball I'll call him for another appointment."

Before she could move away, she was shunted around the side of the buffet table to a narrow space under an arched trellis. The man was huge. His evening jacket strained at the seams as he crossed his arms over his chest and lodged himself between her and the aisle.

"Do you think we could talk without cramming ourselves into a corner?" She was angry. Said, "I don't know who you are but I'm damned sure Mr. Kimball wouldn't approve of your manners. If you don't move aside—now—there's going to be a scene."

"That would be bloody stupid. You remember the gentleman what delivered my message? Well, take a look at where 'e's standin'. 'E's directly behind your friend there, ain't 'e?" His words were slow and deliberate, hammering at her from inches away. "If there's the least little bit o' disturbance from this 'ere direction, 'e'll sink a lovely, sharp, and very long stiletto between Mr. Forster's shoulder blades. And 'e'll do it with such finesse that no one will even notice until 'e's long since taken 'is leave. Maurice is a nasty little sod. Absolutely no conscience at all."

Stunned, she said, "I don't believe you!" but her conviction faltered noticeably. "No one would be stupid enough to commit murder in front of that many witnesses."

"You willin' to bet your friend's friggin' life on that?"

"Supposing we stay right here?"

"You don' 'alf get it," he snapped, tightening his grip on her arm, pulling her forward. "Look back there."

Across the buffet and bar she could see into the salon. The little Frenchman was leaning against the wall, directly behind David Forster's chair. He glanced up at them impassively as he flicked the butt of his cigarette into a potted plant. There was a glint of steel between his hand and the cuff of his jacket.

"All I 'as to do is give 'im a little signal," the man said. "That what you want?"

"I only met Mr. Forster five minutes ago," she lied. "What makes you think I care what happens to the boring old sot?"

A smile split the man's tomato-red face as he took a backward step and started to unfold his arms. "Then you won't mind watching Maurice do 'im, will you?"

the **GOLD** Covenant

"No! Don't!" Katherine leaned against the trellis, looking at David's nodding head. He'd be there all evening—had probably already fallen asleep. She felt helpless and desperate. "What do you want?"

"Think of it this way, miss, your friend's life for a few minutes a your time."

She cringed, pulling away instinctively as his arm locked tightly around her waist.

"We'll be 'avin' no scenes, now." His breath was close to her ear as he pushed her toward the back of the garden. "An' you won't need t'be sayin' good-by to anyone, neither."

They moved quickly through the yard, the threat to David keeping her quiet in spite of her panic. Kimball had seemed so innocuous on the phone—could he be responsible for this? How else could these men have known about her appointment? When they reached the gate, he shoved her through it then let it slam shut behind them. "You won't be needin' to use that again."

Her inner alarm system had been screaming since she first read the note from Kimball, but she'd stupidly ignored it. Now, they were enveloped by the darkness of the alley. As he guided her along the wall, she stumbled, grabbing a vine to keep from falling. She looked down at what she thought was a tree stump but saw instead a man in guard's uniform propped against the wall. She'd tripped over his legs, yet there'd been no response, no movement,

And no surprise from the hulk who had hauled her out here. She bent down to check the man's pulse.

" 'E's just takin' a wee nap," the hulk said, jerking her upright.

She thought about David, the man waiting with the knife.

Her arms slid around one of the vines that matted the back wall and locked on it tightly.

" 'Ere!" he said, making a half-hearted attempt to tug her free. "What do you think yer doin'?"

"I'm staying right here. Your little creep of a friend can't see us now."

"Look 'ere now. Be a nice lady or I'll hafta haul you off like a sack a rags."

One huge hand closed over hers and began to pry her fingers loose. He was smiling down at her, enjoying the ease of it. She turned her hips slightly. Using her body as a fulcrum, she swung back, smashing her spiked heel into his kneecap. The force of it would have been greater if she hadn't been wearing the long skirt, but it did bite deep into soft pulp, where it apparently hit a nerve. He let go of her, howling with pain as his leg buckled under him.

A sedan was blocking the exit to the right, but if the motor wasn't running, maybe she could make it back to the gate before they reached her. Her legs were restricted by the tightness of her skirt, hampered as well

the **GOLD** Covenant

by her high heeled sandals. In just seconds, she heard pounding steps behind her, close, vibrating the graveled earth beneath them. She hadn't gone more than a few yards before his hand sent her sprawling with a single swipe. He reached down, buried his fingers in her hair and pulled her up. His overripe face was flushed, his small eyes wide with anger.

"I oughta knock you from 'ere t'never, you friggin' bitch."

"What seems to be the trouble, Kenneth? Was the job too difficult for you?"

A man moved up from the shadow of the wall. He was slender, almost delicate, wearing evening clothes, looking as casual as if he had stepped out for a smoke. For an instant, Katherine thought the scuffle had attracted someone from the party, but then, as her head cleared, she realized he had called the other man by name.

"My apologies, Miss Nikulasson." His voice was thick with the raspiness of chronic bronchitis. "Didn't Kenneth tell you I was waiting? I'm Hugh Kimball."

Her head was still ringing from the weight of the blow and the jarring fall but she knew this voice had absolutely no resemblance to the high-pitched voice on the telephone. A cold wouldn't change a quality like that. "Show me some identification," she gasped.

"Identification?" He was incredulous.

With the fog clearing and the hulk's hand wrapped

around the back of her neck, the demand sounded idiotic—even to her.

He broke into a deep rumble of laughter that ended in a paroxysm of coughing. "My dear girl," he said, when he had control again, "one doesn't carry identification around in one's dinner jacket. It just isn't done. But if you'll allow me, I'm sure I can find something in the car to put your mind at ease."

"I'm not going to the car. Why don't you take your baboon and go home. You're a sick man."

"I rather thought you'd be anxious to exchange information."

"Exchange? I don't know what you mean."

"She didn't come along peaceful-like," the other man explained. " 'Ad to give 'er a little encouragement from Maurice, like you said."

The man who called himself Kimball paused to hack into a crumpled red kerchief, his eyes lost in the shadows of his heavy lids. Next to his pale blond beard, his lips looked rouged. He wiped them, tucked the kerchief into his sleeve and smiled at her. "Yes, of course," he said. "I should have expected that. It does put a different light on it."

"Who are you? What's happened to Hugh Kimball?"

"I think we had better find a more convenient place to talk. I have my car waiting at the end of the alley."

"I'm not leaving," she insisted, heart pounding with

fear, certain what she said would have no effect. "David's expecting me back in a few minutes. They'll be looking for me."

"I think not. Didn't Kenneth explain to you what's at stake here?"

She felt a corroborating pressure from Kenneth's fingers clutching her neck.

"Apparently his explanation impressed you enough to bring you this far. I assure you, Miss Nikulasson, it was a very wise choice. If Maurice had witnessed the scene you just made, Mr. Forster would be dead now. You see, Maurice's errors of judgment are never on the side of prudence." He grinned at her, pink lips moist, inches away from hers. She turned her face to avoid the damp heavy breath from his mouth and nostrils.

"What do you want with me?"

"Talk. A friendly, unhurried, private talk. Nothing more. Small price for a life, wouldn't you agree?"

"What're we wastin' time for?" Kenneth said. "I can take 'er along all right."

"There's no need for force. Is there, Miss Nikulasson?"

"Why can't we talk right here?"

"I'm afraid that would be most inconvenient for me."

She stood fast, showing no inclination to move.

"Well, I suppose you do have a choice of sorts," he said, exuding sarcasm. "But remember, some decisions should be predicated on past experience. Evan Babcock failed to understand that. With rather disastrous consequences for his future, I might add. But then, I believe you're already aware of that, aren't you? Yes, I can see you are. I have great hopes that his failure will persuade you to a more astute judgment than he possessed. You see, Mr. Forster's life is as valueless to me as Evan Babcock's was. Now, do you want me to send Kenneth back in there or will you come along like a good little girl?"

CHAPTER 16

Smoke drifted around David Forster's chair, carried by the draft from the open doors behind him. He wasn't bothered by that so much as by the continued presence of the little Frenchman who had delivered the message to Katherine. Something about the man annoyed him, but there was nothing he could say to rid himself of the fellow. After all, it wasn't his party or his home; the little frog hadn't actually done anything to complain about. Except, of course, to deprive him of Katherine's company. That was reason enough to put a man out-of-sorts.

David checked his watch, then once more scanned the crowded room for Katherine. He hoped she hadn't been side-tracked by Sheppard before she got back to him. Not that he'd blame her for wanting to spend the time with someone nearer her own age, or Shep for wanting to keep her to himself. But, drat it, he'd missed the girl. He was sure his own daughter—if he'd had a daughter—would have been like her. It was the conceit of all men, he supposed, to believe they would sire as fine an offspring as she. It was only when he was with her that he ever regretted his and Teliah's decision to remain childless. The years with his wife performing, either here or away on tour, had been more lonely than he'd anticipated in his youth. Gustav Nikulasson's open invitation to join him in the field had taken up some of the slack, along with the time-killing excursions from those sites accompanied by Katherine when she was a child.

She'd never been quite like other children—not those few to whom he'd been subjected by various relatives on various holidays. On the surface she was mature, knowledgeable, and sophisticated, but, as he'd discovered through the years, beneath that surface was a rather large accumulation of adolescent insecurities, all bundled up and labeled *bravado*. He'd never seen her cry. It impressed him to no end when at the age of ten, she'd fallen from a camel, climbed back up while the young Egyptian guides laughed at her clumsiness, continuing the tour without letting on she was hurt. He didn't know she'd fractured the radius of her right arm until she passed out halfway up the side of a pyramid. When he talked to her about it later, she'd said falling off the camel was embarrassing enough without the added humiliation of blubbering in public.

the **GOLD** *Covenant*

It was a tossup whether to pat her on the back for her British-schoolboy-stiff-upper-lip or to give her a good dressing-down. As it was, her father took care of the scolding while he was left with the rather more pleasant role of commiserating ally.

He wished he hadn't gotten off on a left-foot the way he had this time. She wasn't ready to talk about John yet. It must have been hellish for her—watching someone she loved wasting away like that—but wounds heal better when they're opened and cleaned out. Ah, well, she'd get to it in her own time. There were other things to talk about. Unfortunately, he was forbidden to talk about the most important of those. It might have been better if she hadn't come to England, but, even so, he was glad she had. He glanced at his watch again, resolved to leave the comfort of his chair if she didn't return within the next five minutes.

There was the business with Shep, as well. He'd promised to give him an answer tonight, but he was still uncertain about the wisdom of the entire venture. It just didn't set well with him—not since the carrier had been murdered—and now, with Katherine here, it was even more worrisome.

Goddamn, the frog was rude. Bloody damn pest, leaning on a man's chair like that. David's loss of patience may have had more to do with the loss of Katherine and the decision he didn't want to make, but, for the moment, the little Frenchman was the principal irritant. He decided to take the least unpleasant course—to leave the comfort of his chair and to stretch his legs in the bargain. It had been almost five minutes anyway since he promised himself to go in search of Katherine.

Chair's too damned comfortable, he thought, built for snoozing. He gripped the arms and straightened his spine, sitting erect while the circulation brought some life into his quiescent body. He started to rise, felt a cold sting in his back, then a heavy weight within his chest pulled him slowly down into the soft cushions.

David Forster was dead before he knew what had caused the pain. It was sharp and it lasted no more than an instant as the blade cut through the ascending aorta into the right ventricle of his heart. His head drooped to one side. His chin rested on his chest as though he had fallen asleep. He remained in the same position for twelve minutes, attracting only an occasional curious glance.

Having noticed from across the room that Katherine was no longer sitting with David, Wilde had spent that twelve minutes looking for her outside in the garden

the **GOLD** *Covenant*

patios. When he failed to find her outside, he thought she might have been taken in hand by Ian Lewellyn and would probably reappear in David's snug little corner after a tour of the house. He made his way back to the bar, picked up another scotch with ice and one without, then returned to the salon and David.

Shep put the glasses down on the table, and gently prodded his friend's shoulder. David's weight shifted; his body sagged, almost collapsing over the side of the chair. Alarmed, Wilde wrapped his arm around the lifeless form, and, as he did, he bumped the hilt of the stiletto protruding from the back of the soaked dinner jacket. His hand came away sticky with congealing blood. There was no pulse. He eased his friend up and propped a pillow against his side.

The conversation on the facing divan faded to an urgent whisper as interest began to focus on what was happening. Ignoring the stir, Wilde addressed himself in a casual tone to one of the men sitting nearby. "This man is seriously ill," he said. "Would you clear everyone from the room? Move them out to the patio, then tell Colonel Lewellyn he's needed."

A great deal of buzzing accompanied the exodus, but the man delegated—one of Ian's military cronies—seemed to enjoy the temporary command. The room was vacated within minutes.

Wilde sank into a chair, alone with his friend and a

building fury at the senseless murder. What could anyone hope to accomplish by killing David? I never should have brought him into this. The action is too close to home this time; someone's changed the rules. Or someone I hadn't anticipated has entered the game. But why David?

He picked up the scotch, emptied the glass, then started to put it back on the table when he noticed Katherine's first drink, untouched, next to it.

The answer presented itself quickly; she wasn't with Ian. They'd taken her. Furious at his own carelessness, he hurled the glass into the fireplace.

"What's happened?" Lewellyn asked, as he entered the room from the patio. "There's a good bit of excitement building up out there, and now I find you smashing the crystal. What's it all about?"

"David's been stabbed. He's dead."

"Good God, Wilde, you're joking."

"You'd better call the Yard. Get a doctor. Then find Michelle and ask her to take Teliah upstairs. I don't think you should tell her what's happened until the doctor arrives. Her heart's not in the best shape."

"Yes, yes. I know," Lewellyn said, his fingers raking furrows through his rust-colored hair. He stared, unbelieving, at David's body slumped in the chair. "Are you sure he's dead? My God, man, how could it happen here? With all of us—"

"Ian, make the calls."

the **GOLD** Covenant

"Right. Of course." Lewellyn shook himself into action. He darted around the divan, took the steps in one leap and disappeared into the foyer.

When he returned, Wilde was gone.

The driver, Harry Franco, pulled into the alley. He left the motor running while he and Wilde walked down to the Lewellyn property. The back exit had not been in use since the servants' quarters in the mews had been converted to fashionable apartments sometime after the turn of the century. The rear access no longer served a purpose. It was always kept locked. The wild roses growing along the wall had been encouraged to fill in and cover it over. However, when Lewellyn had an illustrious guest in the house, he always hired a guard to watch the alley. A precaution against innovative gate-crashers.

They found the guard slumped against the wall, eyes closed, arms at his sides with his hands open, his head cocked at an angle, legs splayed out in front of him. His clothing was disheveled and dirty, the trousers torn. He hadn't given up without a good scrap.

Wilde knelt at his side, feeling for a pulse. "He's breathing. Tell someone inside the gate to see to him."

"I wouldn't a thought there was a breath left in 'im," Harry said. " 'E's got to have one helluva thick skull."

roberta clark

After he pushed open the gate, he turned back to Wilde. "Look at this. The lock's been sheared off like a piece a cheese." At an impatient nod from Wilde, he trotted off toward the house, returning several moments later with assurance that help was on the way.

"We're leaving before the clean-up committee arrives from the Yard," Wilde said. "Can't waste time answering questions. Those bastards who took Katherine have had a thirty-minute lead."

"Can't believe someone snatched her while we all stood around scratchin' our behinds," Harry mumbled, racing down the alley after Wilde. Breathless, he jumped into the driver's seat and waited for instructions.

At the sound of the electronic bleep, he picked up the phone. "Franco here. Who is it? Hold on, he'll want to talk to you." Harry swiveled around to speak to Wilde. "Mrs. Short's on the line," he said. "Do we stay here or move out?"

"Find a place to hold for a few minutes," Wilde said, "away from here." He took the phone. "When? No message, you say? Did he leave a number? All right, the name will do." He depressed the plunger, dialed, waited for thirty seconds that seemed like thirty minutes. "Hello, Trevor? I need a number and address—and any information you can get on a Hugh Kimball. Can you do it? You'll have to use the name Katherine Nikulasson to verify. That's right. And, Trevor, I need it fast."

the **GOLD** *Covenant*

A few blocks away, Harry pulled into the loading zone in front of the London Hilton. Wilde, still holding the receiver, flipped open his address book, checked a number, then dialed. It rang for a long time before there was a click on the other end, followed by silence. "This is Wilde. If that's you, Taha, tell the man I need a meeting. Tell him I'll be there before morning. I'm in London—on wheels—if you want to verify, but tell him, one way or the other, I'm coming." Another click and the connection was broken.

Wilde sat back, staring out of the window, seeing nothing, swearing under his breath. *I should have sent her home, goddamn it, the day she arrived. I should have been more patient. Another few months—another year—what bloody difference would it have made?*

The buzzing phone put a quick end to the self-recrimination. He snatched up the receiver. "Trevor? Have you got it?" He jotted a number and address on a slip of paper. "Let's go," he said, passing the address to Harry.

The dark brown Rover pulled out of the line of cars and into the stream of traffic along Park Lane. Wilde opened his small notebook, where he recopied the address, along with the extra bit of information Trevor had slipped in before breaking off the call—*Power Line*. So, Mr. Hugh Kimball works for a New York-based television talk show, and Katherine had been in contact with him before she'd been here twenty-four hours. What kind of business was she doing in London?

He couldn't help thinking what a damned foolish conceit it was that he'd believed her coming here had anything to do with her wanting to see *him* again.

CHAPTER 17

"The floor, Miss Nikulasson. It may seem inhospitable, but I'm sure you can understand the necessity."

Katherine didn't answer. She slid to the plush floor of the Rolls Royce, huddling in a corner, her back resting against the front seat. She was shivering. The evening was warm but her body felt as though it had been injected with ice water. She clasped her arms around her knees. When that didn't have the desired effect, she tensed her muscles to stop the shaking.

Her mind was incapable of anything but self-recrimination. There must have been another way to handle this. But what? They would have killed David—she was sure of that, knowing what had happened to Evan Babcock. She supposed there was still the remote chance this madman wanted nothing more than to talk. But about what?

She stared out in silence as the Rolls Royce wound

its way through the city. The rear window was covered with a blind. From where she sat on the floor, the angle of visibility through the side windows made it impossible to recognize the route.

The large man, Kenneth, sat in front with the driver. She could still feel the pressure of his hands on her throat, which caused her thoughts to drift back to the man she tripped over in the alley. There hadn't been time to check for life, but it was obvious he had a run-in with those same beefy hands.

In back, the pale, bearded man seemed indifferent to her silent appraisal, seemed to have dismissed her from his mind altogether. His clothes were expensive, custom-tailored perfection, his grooming impeccable. Too thin for his near six-foot height, he gave the impression of frailty. It was deceptive—she knew from the way he'd gripped her arm as they walked to the car—a trick of coloring. The light hair streaked with white, the fair, almost pink complexion, and the fine blond closely trimmed beard gave the illusion of softness.

"Who are you?" she asked him, her voice barely above a whisper, as if breaking the silence might unleash another attack from the man in the front seat. "How did you know about the meeting with Hugh Kimball?"

"In answer to the first question," he said, without bothering to look at her, "Enrique Quisette. For some people that would be enough to answer the second question as well."

"You're a psychic. Sorry, I didn't catch the vibrations."

"Very amusing, Miss Nikulasson, but I think you'll find me less entertaining than a psychic and far more effective."

"Does Kimball work for you or is he lying in an alley, too?"

"Mr. Kimball's in excellent health. He received your note hours ago and is, at this moment, chasing after his own tail a long way from London. His ego will be painfully ruffled when he discovers he's been played the fool, but I wouldn't be concerned about that. I'm sure his salary more than compensates for such inconveniences."

"Why go to all this trouble—forging notes and threatening people's lives—if all you want to do is talk?"

"My methods," he said, "are dictated by necessity."

"Is that a quotation from Hitler or Stalin?"

"In your position, dear girl, sarcasm is a sorry weapon."

"In my position, there's no other choice."

His laughter deteriorated into a fit of coughing which immediately sobered him. He reached for a prescription bottle in the compact bar opposite his seat, fumbled the cap off, and tossed two capsules into his mouth. When he spoke again, his voice was a raspy whisper. "As for Hitler or Stalin, how are they different from the rest of us? Everyone—including your beloved father—has selfish motivations. Self-interest has always been the prime mover."

roberta clark

Quisette waited, smirking, for an indignant reaction from Katherine. She turned away from him, forcing control of her seething temper.

"You doubt what I say? A little too close to sacred ground, is it? Your beloved father is no more virtuous than Kenneth," he said, taking obvious delight in prodding her anger. "Their goals may vary, and their style, but they're both motivated by money. Everyone is, only some are less willing to admit it."

"How do you make your money, Mr. Quisette?"

"I'm an entrepreneur, an investor, a trader, many things."

"Including kidnapper and murderer?"

"When necessary. However, I've found that sometimes the threat is more effective than the act; more productive and much less final. I hope you'll keep that in mind. If you do, I'm sure you'll find me a reasonable man."

Katherine's hand had been resting on the door handle. When the Rolls slowed to a crawl before turning into an underground garage, she leaned forward to press on it, but there was no response.

"I have the controls," he said, "and you're forgetting we have a deadline to meet regarding your friend, Forster."

"You never mentioned a deadline."

"Oh, didn't I?" his voice disinterested. "How careless of me. Perhaps there'll be no need." He tapped on the glass partition, then turned to her. "You may sit on

the **GOLD** *Covenant*

the seat now, if you wish."

They were inside a huge warehouse. As she pulled herself up, the car rolled onto the flat bed of a freight elevator which was controlled from inside the car. The platform moved down one story, coming to a halt in a spacious garage which housed another Rolls Royce, a Lamborghini, a Ferrari, and black van.

The two men in front got out of the car and opened the back doors. Quisette spoke quietly to the driver, then motioned the other man to follow with Katherine.

The three of them entered a spacious elevator which Quisette activated with a key. The interior of the cage was carpeted with a Persian rug and paneled with peachwood. A Matisse and two Picasso sketches hung on the wall facing the door. They were framed in exquisite hand-carved and gilded wood. They looked like originals. Katherine couldn't take her eyes off of them.

"Yes, my dear Miss Nikulasson, they *are* originals. I see you have an appreciation of art. Perhaps you'll find this experience more stimulating than you anticipate."

The almost-imperceptible motion of the elevator stopped and the doors slid open on a Spartan foyer. They crossed it and entered an equally Spartan room: the rug a closely woven mat of textured gray wool, the walls bare, except for one which housed a built-in bank of electronic equipment behind a glass enclosure. The desk and two chairs were the only furniture. A thick haze seemed to be hanging in the air, but it was only the grayness of the walls combined with the diffused lighting at the perimeter of the ceiling.

Quisette moved directly to the glass and marble desk, where he touched a switch on the recessed control panel on top. Instantly, the drabness was gone. The room was transformed, bathed in a wash of golden light.

"Come sit down, Miss Nikulasson," he said, sinking into the Corbusier chair behind the desk. "Bring me her handbag, Kenneth."

"She didn't 'ave one, Mr. Quisette."

"What!"

"She didn't 'ave one on 'er."

"I heard you the first time, you blithering idiot. Didn't it occur to you to go back for it?"

"Seemed a might too chancy seein' I wasn't sure where she'd put it or if she 'ad one at all."

Quisette was livid. "You'd better hope Maurice is more thorough than you are." He wiped his face with the red silk, then dropped it into a receptacle beside his desk. "Get me a clean handkerchief," he said. The big man rushed out of the room, returning a moment later with an identical red silk cloth. Quisette shook it before tucking it into his cuff. "Now, Miss Nikulasson, what will you have to drink?"

"Nothing."

"Kenneth, bring me a port and Miss Nikulasson a

chilled glass of white wine. Isn't that what you Americans are drinking so much of these days?"

Katherine sat in the chair opposite his. "I thought you wanted to talk," she said. "Can we skip over the phony amenities and just get on with whatever you want to talk about?"

"I'll decide how this business will be conducted," he said, his voice taking on a sharp edge. "I don't think you realize the seriousness of your situation."

Nothing could have been less true. And yet, sitting here, facing this man, listening to his threats, it all seemed unreal to her, as though someone were having a joke at her expense. A very dark joke.

"I don't like doing business with women," he went on. "They're either shrewish, stupid, or hysterical. They have no sense of logic or truth. They're never loyal, and their only consistency is in their weakness. In short, outside of the bedroom I find them completely loathsome."

She was sure *he* would be as loathsome in the bedroom as he was outside of it but refrained from the temptation of telling him. Instead she said, "You *will* let me know when you've decided to get to the point?"

Quisette braced his fingertips against the edge of the desk and shoved his chair back. The instant expression of rage had turned his pale complexion scarlet, his silence more threatening than anything he had said. Before he could act on it, Kenneth entered the room, breaking the silence with a clanking tray. The sound distracted Quisette, gave him a moment to recover control. Indifference now replaced his rage.

After the drinks were served and the big man had returned to his post by the door, Quisette held his glass of port up to the light. He examined it at various angles, then sniffed it before putting it down again without tasting it.

"Liquor has a sensual pleasure to it," he said, "in the color and bouquet and in the texture of it on the tongue as well as in the taste. Enormously stimulating, don't you agree?"

"You said we had a deadline. What is it you want to talk about?"

He stood up, walked around the desk, planting himself in front of her. "Geography, Miss Nikulasson."

"I'll buy you an atlas."

His hand snapped like a spring trigger, striking her across the face, slamming her head against the back of the chair. She pulled herself up slowly, not sure if she was angrier at him or at herself for her inability to control the tears.

"I'm disappointed in your continued lapse of manners. Your behavior has been anything but exemplary." His eyes flashed and then darkened in the shadow of his heavy lids. "Let's see if you can do better now, Miss Nikulasson. What I want from you, quite simply, is the location."

the **GOLD** *Covenant*

"Of what?"

"Let's not play games."

"They're your games. I haven't the slightest idea what they're about."

"I think you have."

"It's a stalemate then," she said. "Where do we go from here? You're making up the rules."

"We're talking about the location of your father's camp."

"My father was killed in a plane crash. Four months ago."

"Oh yes. I'm acutely aware of that news release—a skillful job—the whole scenario neatly arranged by your friend, Sheppard Wilde." He turned, picked up the glass of port, and drained it, holding the liquid in his mouth for a moment before swallowing. "Yes," he went on, "we both know full-well why Gustav Nikulasson had to be put out of the way."

She was shocked. Not certain of what he was saying. The side of her face where he struck her felt hot, the back of her head throbbed from the blow against the chair. He stood before her, grinning, as though pleased with her reaction.

"You're a bright woman," he said. "You don't really believe Mr. Wilde fits the sacred image mold. As I said, we're all the same. When the stakes are high enough, souls are common barter."

Katherine felt cold again. There were doubts before

this, but she'd been afraid to face them. Now Quisette had put the worst of them into words. Her father had been killed by his most trusted friend, Sheppard Wilde. It was the kind of madness that might be true. A tremor shook her body, chilling, leaving her with a sense of complete aloneness.

"You look ill," Quisette said, mocking. "Perhaps you'd like something more potent than the wine?"

"I'd *like* to go back to the reception."

"And I'd be delighted to grant your wish, but first you must accommodate me."

"I have no idea where my father was working."

"I can't accept that."

"You'll have to," she said, desperately. "It's the truth. What possible interest could it be to you anyway?"

"Believe what I tell you. There are people far more influential than I, backed by their governments or by syndicates, all ruthless, all after the same prize, none of whom are going to stand in my way. So you see, my dear woman, you are by comparison the least imposing obstacle. As I told you before, I never waste my time, and I never allow others to waste it either. You are doing just that by pretending to ignorance."

"I'm not pretending to anything. I simply do not know the location of my father's last encampment. Since you seem to be such a gifted clairvoyant, you must know I hadn't seen him for the past two years." She winced

the **GOLD** *Covenant*

defensively as his body stiffened, but he didn't strike her again. Instead, he returned to his chair, leaned forward, pressing his hands down on the cold marble surface.

"We had it from Babcock," he said. "You and Sheppard Wilde are the only ones with the information I want. For obvious reasons, I prefer dealing with you."

"If Babcock told you that, he was lying."

"There are certain conditions under which men do not lie." He spoke with something resembling a smile. "I detest crudeness, however it serves a purpose." His cold eyes signaled Kenneth, who lumbered over to one side of the desk.

Katherine stared at him, fighting the fear that was deteriorating into panic.

"Well?" Quisette said.

"Why should I believe you'd let me go if I did tell you anything?"

"It's a matter of faith."

"Faith in what?"

"In my word, if you will."

She could hardly believe he was serious but there was nothing in his manner to indicate otherwise.

"I'm waiting," he said.

"I want to know what you meant when you said Wilde arranged my father's death."

"What I said was Wilde arranged the scenario. Whether he intended your father's death is another matter. You're digressing, Miss Nikulasson."

"I think you'll kill me—one way or the other—no matter what I tell you."

"On the contrary, that's precisely what I'm trying to avoid. I thought you understood."

"Your method has the opposite effect."

"Then I gave you too much credit for understanding the subtleties. In my business a low profile is essential, and you, Miss Nikulasson, are not a low profile person. I'd prefer to avoid the ruffle that killing you would be certain to cause."

"God! A ruffle. As much as that?"

"Make no mistake," he said, eyes flashing like sun on metal through the hooded lids. "If I don't get my way, you'll leave me no choice."

"What I told you before was the truth. I don't know where my father was working or what he was working on. That's why I'm here. Why I came to England. To find out." Katherine hesitated, fishing for words.

"Do go on."

"What I'm saying is I need time."

"In return for which you'll willingly hand over whatever information you manage to scrape up. That's almost funny." He stood up, stretched, and began to stroll around the room. "Let's say I believe you know nothing," he went on, drawing the words out slowly. "My only viable alternative would be to use you as a hostage

the **GOLD** *Covenant*

to get the information from Sheppard Wilde, assuming he is vulnerable to such a plan—which I do not for a moment believe. But, assuming he were, any such attempt would increase disproportionately the risk on my side, therefore rendering that alternative totally unacceptable. So, Miss Nikulasson, where does that leave us?"

"Nowhere."

"For your sake, I sincerely hope you're mistaken. You see, I've arranged a private showing for you. One that will demonstrate quite clearly what the alternative will be if you don't change your mind."

"You're insane."

"Perhaps."

"I can't tell you what I don't know."

"Kenneth, take our guest to the gallery."

CHAPTER 18

It wasn't a fully enclosed room but instead seemed to be a small section, partitioned off within a larger area. There was no ceiling attached to the partitions. The eerie glow of light shining around the upper perimeter of the nine-foot-high walls was not enough to allow Katherine to see the interior distinctly. Only gradually did she become aware that the light was growing stronger at the top of the wall in front of her. It was minutes before she was sure of what she was seeing. The wall itself was a mural in the style of sixteenth-century Persian art. It was a brilliantly colored, intricate, anatomically detailed, visual compendium of the *Kama Sutra*. The antithesis of everything else she'd seen in Quisette's apartment. No doubt—with his expensive taste—it was authentic, but the aesthetics were on a level with the subject matter—crude.

Bound to a chair by leather straps which restrained

her wrists, ankles, and neck, she had nothing to look at but the wall, which seemed preferable to sitting with eyes closed. The light above fluctuated continuously, almost imperceptibly, giving the painting an illusion of movement, or life. It was strange and disquieting.

She struggled with the straps, trying to slip her hands free of them. In the process, the chair swiveled slightly on its base. With a little added effort, she managed to swing it around a quarter turn until she was facing the adjacent wall. The light followed her, illuminating another mural, this one in a Japanese style. It was every bit as graphic, the acrobatics even more varied than they had been in the other.

The room must be filled with these pornographic pieces, and while there was nothing frightening about them, they were disturbing. Both the brilliant color and the constant motion of the design contributed to a feeling of madness, a feeling that there was no predictability in Quisette's thinking. The sheer insanity in using this room as a method of persuasion was in itself frightening. She had to force her mind onto some other track away from this room.

David Forster was safe now. That was something to think about—to be grateful for. By now, Shep would know she was missing. But would he be concerned about it? Or would he think she'd simply walked out of her own free will? Nothing would indicate she was forced to leave. David would tell him she'd gone off on business of some sort. After the way she'd behaved last night, Shep might believe she'd left without explanation.

No, damn it! Shep isn't an idiot. He'd have to be the worst kind of an idiot to think she'd take off without a word after what happened yesterday.

There was another possibility, one she'd been trying to avoid. Shep might somehow be involved with these people or involved in the same terrible business. Quisette implied—no—he'd accused Shep of arranging her father's death. It was ludicrous, hearing it put into words by a man like that. Yet, hadn't she come to England suspecting Shep of something she'd been too cowardly to put into words herself? Why hadn't she talked to him last night instead of walking out of the room? Perhaps there would have been the answers she needed now, not only for herself, but for the psycho upstairs.

She put the thought out of her mind again. None of her speculations made any difference now. The chance of Shep—or anyone else—finding her here was nil. She was on her own and she'd better start adjusting her thinking to that.

Quisette was not the kind of man who would settle for less than he wanted, substantiation more than adequate. He seemed to have the power to get what he wanted. She'd have to think of a way to convince him of the truth. There was nothing unusual in the fact her father had never mentioned the specific location of his work. In most cases, his campsites had been in remote areas. They were never characterized by quaint little cottages on quaint little streets, let alone even the crudest of tourist accommodations. His letters had been posted from Greece or from England. She wrote to a general delivery address in Athens. If she had wanted to visit his camp, she could have arranged it through Shep or, one other way, through her father's old friend, Sabir Nuri Pasha, one of the few men who could promise safe-conduct in the Zagros mountains. But this was a fact she had to keep to herself. To bring Sabir into this would be to endanger his life as well.

She closed her eyes, saw it again. Vivid blue sky. Babcock's body tumbling, floating.

What was the link? Babcock, Shep, and Quisette....

Again there was a feeling of some other presence—over her right shoulder—in the periphery of her vision. She became aware of a density of darkness inside the shadows, as though someone were standing there. But there was no sound of breathing, no movement.

Shifting the weight of her body from side to side, she managed to swing the chair again, bringing it around another half turn. As she did, the light followed her once more. This time the wall was bare, but in front of her chair, not more than two feet away, was a pedestal with a glass dome on top of it. The dome covered a sculpture which appeared to be the bust of a man . . . she wasn't sure. The piece was no more than a shadowy silhouette against the blank wall.

Gradually, from somewhere inside the pedestal itself, there was a soft glow of light which flickered, then grew brighter until it fully illuminated the enclosed sculpture. Her stomach knotted. She closed her eyes and opened them again, hoping she had only imagined the thing she was looking at inside the glass. It was still there. A man's head—a human head—impaled on a golden shaft. The dark sightless eyes stared at her through a viscous liquid. The skin was almost black with putrefaction, the mouth a taut grimace against the white teeth. The hair and mustache had been neatly slicked with grease as if to hold them in place in the substance which enveloped them.

She couldn't shut it out. The negative image in scorched, flashing light clung to her compressed eyelids. With pulse racing, pounding against her eardrums, threatening to shatter them with the pressure, she fought to keep her stomach from exploding with them. The room was cold—icy—yet her mouth and throat burned with acid bile. Choking it down only made the nausea worse.

In desperation, she flailed at the bindings in an attempt to swivel the chair around as she had before. This time it remained locked in place.

It was the reflection of Quisette's mind—the insane, barbaric depravity of it—but as mad as he must be, he

the GOLD Covenant

could not be mad enough to let her walk out of here after she'd seen it.

Was this a preview of what he planned for her? She had no doubt he meant to kill her even if she did give him what he wanted. But he wanted information she didn't have. That left her without even the hope of an option.

CHAPTER 19

Even with eyes closed, the image was still there, etched on her lids and retina and brain—sightless bloated eyes, the grimace of iridescent teeth, black shreds of skin hanging from the neck, pressing in through silence and darkness, a growing, suffocating essence of madness she would never be rid of.

Her mind grasped at other thoughts trying to lock itself into new channels. Her father's accident. The *scenario*. What had Quisette meant by *scenario*? Shep responsible for the plane crash? It was senseless, but she had almost believed it. Then there was the memory of Shep's voice. His tone was impatient, almost angry. *Gustav may have wanted it that way.* Wanted it. *Sometimes friendship has to be enough . . .*

This was the reason. Clearly, logically, the secrecy, the scenario, all of it had been to protect Gustav's work. Quisette was willing to kill for the exact location of the site. Babcock and this man, whoever he'd been, had probably died because they wouldn't—or couldn't—oblige him.

The plan, to protect Gustav, to protect his work, had somehow gone wrong. Now, Shep was trying to protect her. Or had been until she'd made the task impossible, all the while accusing him of the worst kind of betrayal.

How could she have allowed this lunatic to influence her thinking? He'd killed Babcock—and this—this man . . . No, don't think about it . . . Thinking was a useless exercise anyway. Nothing mattered anymore. There were no options left for her. None she wanted to consider.

Motionless and blind in a self-imposed vacuum, her mind drifted, shedding the stony weight of a body fatigued with the cumulate emotions of the past. Tired. Too tired to care.

There was no awareness of time. She dozed, for how long she didn't know. It might have been one hour or two, or five minutes later when she heard the sharp metallic clack of the bolt. The sound brought fear and, with that, a jolt of adrenaline which snapped her back to reality.

Kenneth's heavy footsteps plodded across the floor and stopped somewhere behind her. Then, the other sound, the viscous breathing. Quisette was there, too. Waiting.

"Look at me!"

She couldn't. It would still be there . . . in front of her.

Quisette leaned closer, his breath moist on her face. "Do you need assistance? Kenneth is infinitely resourceful."

She opened her eyes. He was standing beside the pedestal, his pale face set in a frigid smile. "You're slow to learn, Miss Nikulasson," he said.

Again, acid seeped into the flannel lining of her mouth, an acrid taste that threatened to turn her empty stomach inside-out.

Quisette's hand was fondling the top of the glass dome. "This man was a nothing," he said. "A nothing who thought he could play at Enrique Quisette's game. He now serves as a reminder to people like you who have the same mistaken notion. It's rather a nobler end than the man deserved."

Through shimmering azure, it stared at her—the thing that had been a man—as if its mind still existed.

"I'm going to be sick," she said.

"That would only add to your discomfort."

"I can't talk to you with that thing there."

"Perhaps," he said, "you won't need to talk at all."

After a moment of silence, Quisette left. The door closed behind him. The straps were loosed on her ankles, wrists, and neck, then a large hand gripped her arm, yanking her out of the chair.

the **GOLD** *Covenant*

Quisette's elbows rested on the onyx marble top of his desk, his bearded chin supported by slender interlaced fingers. After she was seated and Kenneth left the room, he reached over to the control panel on his right to press a switch. Katherine heard a whirring sound from behind the glass partition. The frenetic twang of harpsichord music flooded the room. Quisette picked up the file folder in front of him, opened it, and began to read.

It was as if Katherine had ceased to exist.

She pressed her fingers against her temples, massaging her forehead and eyes. She needed rest, could almost fall asleep in the chair.

Quisette's voice revived her. He'd laid aside the file. "I believe this belongs to you," he said, tossing her evening bag onto the desk. "Maurice was good enough to bring it along." His pale fingers drummed on the open file that lay in front of him. "While you were being entertained upstairs, I've done an interesting bit of research. Clever of you to use the Mylar as a wrapping. I almost overlooked it."

"Mylar?" she asked, then remembered the way the Xeroxed photos had been attached to the Picasso print—folded in half, then enclosed in a piece of clear plastic. Plastic . . . Mylar with smudges on it!

With his thumb and forefinger, Quisette traced the

pale growth of his beard around the lips and along the jaw line, lifting his chin, exposing the softness of his neck. He was watching her closely. She began to wonder if her face was as impassive as she wanted it to be.

"I see by your expression you didn't know the significance of what you were carrying. Interesting you should stumble on it so quickly after your arrival. I wonder if your friend, Mr. Wilde, is aware of the acquisition?"

She didn't answer.

"No, I don't suppose he would be," Quisette went on. "It's not the sort of thing he'd allow you to carry around in your evening bag. How fortunate you were planning to enlist help at the party. You were planning to do that, weren't you, my dear Katherine? And how fortunate for me your contact turned out to be Mr. Hugh Kimball."

"Is Kimball another one of your lackeys?"

"I've never met the man." Picking up the evening bag, he fondled it, affectionately, opening and closing the catch several times before finally tossing it to her across the desk. "You know, I had quite accepted the fact that Babcock had nothing to offer in the way of information. The map he tried to sell me was just a copy of the one I'd acquired some time ago. It was quite useless without the addition you so thoughtfully provided. If I were in the habit of making apologies," he went on, "I would have to apologize for not believing you when, apparently, you were telling me the truth. On the other hand, you've not demonstrated the slightest faith in my word, either, have you? I suppose that makes us even."

His voice was drowned in breaking waves, the roaring in her ears. The cold sweat followed, and she knew she was going to pass out if she didn't bend over to get the blood back to her head. Survival had been possible as long as he needed her, now even that slim hope was gone. Behind her, she heard a door open. Quisette was telling Kenneth to bring in something to eat.

"I'm not hungry," she said, when he returned to his desk.

"You have no instinct for survival, Miss Nikulasson." His smile was contemptuous. He leaned back in his chair, studying her for a moment before going on. "I believe," he said, "you are familiar with the name Sabir Nuri Pasha." Although he hadn't stated it as a question, he waited for an answer. Shocked by the surprising change of subject, Katherine was unable to give him one.

"That *is* correct, is it not?" he persisted.

"I've met him."

"Oh, much more than that, my dear Katherine." He went on as if reading a prepared statement to the press. "The illustrious Gustav Nikulasson has involved himself in the intrigues of that quixotic leader for a long time, to the extent that the infamous Nuri Pasha not only nurtures a great friendship for him, but a deep loyalty, a debt of gratitude for past service."

roberta clark

"What an extraordinary idea! Sabir Nuri Pasha, indebted to my father!"

"That is exactly correct." Steel flecks glinted from the shadows under Quisette's brow, the silence deadly. While peering over laced fingers, he weighed his next response. When he finally spoke, his words were deliberate and seething. "You are going to make contact with this man. He is going to lead us to the site of your father's camp."

Katherine was astounded. "You have the map. Why would you need someone to take you there?"

"We both know the answer to that. There are two possible ways of entering that territory: with an invading army or under the protection of a friend. Armies, as we both know, attract unwanted attention. Besides, they are historically ineffectual in that area, therefore leaving but one alternative. Which is why you are still a necessary factor."

Even Quisette couldn't be mad enough to think Nuri Pasha would cooperate in his plan. "Nuri Pasha is a prince," she said, "a leader of his people, a man with great responsibilities. What makes you think he'd respond to a communication from me?"

"Let me put it as simply as possible. If you don't convince him of the urgency to respond, it will be death for you. If that isn't persuasion enough perhaps this will be. Your failure will leave me no other alternative but to supply key Turkish officials with certain evidence which, I guarantee, will instigate military action against Nuri Pasha's people for crimes committed against the government."

"What crimes?"

"You might want to direct that question to Nuri Pasha himself. In the meantime, don't you think it more agreeable to appeal to your friend Sabir on the basis of friendship?"

Katherine was speechless. She stared at him, unbelieving, yet certain he would make good his threat.

"Do you have any idea what a Kurdish village looks like after an aerial attack?" he went on. "Believe me, my contacts are the sort who welcome the kind of information I can give them. It's an opportunity for personal advancement. You, Miss Nikulasson, will be responsible. Responsible for the deaths of thousands of those same people your father has helped and admired for so many years."

Her mind was desperately exhausted, tears beyond control. When she blotted at them, her hand came away muddied with the grime from the struggle behind the Lewellyn's house—so long ago—in another time. She closed her eyes, wanting escape, wanting to remember when life had nothing worse than transient pain.

This was madness.

Quisette's voice was still droning. "This man—this rag-tag Kurdish rebel—knows exactly where your father was working," Quisette rasped, "and he will respond to a debt of honor. It would be well to remind him of that debt in your letter."

"You're the most disgusting excuse for a human being I've ever known."

He smiled before shoving a pad, pen, and typed list across the desk. "These are the details I want conveyed in the letter."

"These people never trust strangers. He won't even acknowledge the message unless he's certain of the source and, maybe, not even then."

"That's why it'll be in your own words and in your own hand, and why it'll be so important for you to be convincing. Think of all those innocent lives."

"I have your promise that no one will be hurt if I can persuade Sabir to cooperate?"

"Of course!"

"And you'll let me go?"

"My dear Katherine, you're my guarantee of safe-passage. I know these people as well as you, and I have no doubt Nuri Pasha would not want the blood of Gustav Nikulasson's daughter on his hands. Therefore it's necessary to keep that option within my control. As I've told you, I have little use for the company of women, but in this case the end makes the means tolerable. You'll be traveling with us as my companion. I'd prefer Nuri Pasha believe it's by your choice."

the **GOLD** Covenant

A faint glow of red lit the control panel, pulling his attention away. He pressed a button and snapped into the speaker, "What is it?"

"Wilde just left the house. Do I stay with him?"

"No. Call the airport. I want the plane ready in one hour with a flight plan for Athens."

He depressed the button and hit another switch. "Kenneth, I want Miss Nikulasson out of here. Now! We'll meet at the plane in one hour. And get her something suitable to wear for the trip. We'll take care of the rest when we get there."

Katherine felt a renewed panic. She'd be on her way to Athens while Shep was looking for her in London—if he was looking for her at all. She wasn't sure of anything anymore, except that she was alone. If she was going to die, she would just as soon put it off as long as possible. This expedition—the wild hope that she could make contact with Sabir Nuri Pasha—would give her more than the zero chance of survival she had at the moment. Somewhere between here and the Zagros Mountains, there might be a chance for escape.

CHAPTER 20

A scruffy-looking Hugh Kimball pulled open the front door before Wilde hit the bell. "Sheppard Wilde? Yes, by God," he said, answering his own question. "You're quite like the photos I have on file. Have an excellent file on you, you know. Not as complete as I'd like, but rather good quality."

The instant aversion Sheppard would have felt at such an admission was assuaged by Kimball's unabashed candor as well as his ingenuous smile. He accepted the extended hand with a nod.

"Come in, come in. Let's go into my study. Won't be disturbed there. Keep it off-limits, is what I say."

Sheppard followed the man into the depths of a long hallway which ended in a large glass-enclosed room. A section of the ceiling and the entire garden wall were constructed of triangular glass panes contained by heavy strips of stainless steel. Nothing inside the room harmonized with the contemporary design. The furniture was old—not antique—just old, an assortment of styles and sizes of things, all of which appeared to have been purchased for some other more suitable place.

Kimball seemed a natural part of the eclectic environment. His accent was mid-Atlantic. He wore a white dress shirt with French cuffs rolled back, a silk scarf tucked into its open neck. His trousers were age-softened corduroy. His sockless feet were shod in Mexican leather *huaraches*. In contrast to his evenly tanned face, the top of his bald pate was sunburned to a bright pink, blotched with patches of peeling skin, which made him appear older than his fifty-two years.

Scattered across the top of his desk were the parts of an over-and-under shotgun and cleaning paraphernalia. "As you can see, I left the house in somewhat of a hurry. Sit down over here," he said, motioning to a comfortable chair away from the cluttered desk. "Can I get you anything?"

"Just tell me about Katherine," Wilde said. "You had an appointment with her?"

"Yes. Look here, you sounded deadly serious over the phone. Miss Nikulasson hasn't had an accident, has she? Rather disturbed when she didn't turn up."

"Where were you to meet her?"

"At the Lewellyn's reception, originally, but earlier today I received a message asking that we change the meeting place." He shuffled back across the room to the desk, where he took an envelope out of a box marked current. "Here, see for yourself. Did have a sense of urgency about it."

Wilde glanced at the elaborate set of instructions. "This must have kept you occupied for hours. Do you have any idea who might want to do that?"

"I don't understand. Are you saying the note didn't come from Miss Nikulasson?"

Wilde shook his head. "I don't believe it did. Who else knew about your appointment with her?"

"Now hold on. I'd like to know what's happened."

"May I smoke?"

Kimball pushed an ashtray across the lamp table between their chairs. He looked tired and impatient, which was understandable after the wild goose chase that had taken up the better part of his evening. "Think I'll join you, if you don't mind," he said. Wilde offered him the pack, then lit both cigarettes. Pulling in shallow puffs, Kimball exhaled thick streams of smoke that swirled in the cone of light above his head. Smoking was obviously not one of his regular vices.

"What did she want to see you about tonight?" Wilde asked.

"No idea. She didn't want to discuss it on the phone. Look here, if what you say is true, I'd better give her a ring at the Lewellyn's. She must be wondering why I haven't turned up."

"Katherine was kidnapped from the Lewellyn home tonight."

"What!" Kimball's high-pitched voice jumped a half-octave. "Kidnapped! Miss Nikulasson? Surely you're joking."

"It's hardly a joke, Mr. Kimball. And it is imperative I know her reasons for coming to England."

"She hadn't discussed the matter with you?"

"No."

"Without going into confidential detail, she was enlisted to approach—to persuade someone to sign on for an interview show in the States. Sorry, but I'm not at liberty to mention names. It's quite innocent, I assure you. Nothing sinister about it. At any rate, how could this have a connection with her being kidnapped?"

"I was hoping you'd tell me."

"Good lord, I've only spoken to the girl once and that was on the phone. I hardly think this has anything to do with me."

"I was under the impression it had. The kidnapper used you—sent you out to beat the bushes, then took your place. He obviously knows who you are, where you live, who you plan to meet, where, and when."

"What in God's name are you suggesting? You couldn't think that I—"

"Mr. Kimball, whether you're aware of it or not, there

is a connection. Perhaps if you gave it some thought."

Kimball slumped deep into his chair, massaging his head and staring at the glass triangles, then pushed himself up. Back at the desk, he picked up the telephone. "You won't mind if I check your story, will you, Mr. Wilde?"

"Not as long as you leave my name out of it."

Kimball nodded, dialed. When he had a connection, he asked to speak with Colonel Lewellyn. "I'd rather surprise him if you don't mind," he said, looking to Wilde for a reaction. "I say, who is this speaking? Scotland Yard, eh? Come off it, I'm not buying tonight." After a moment, his face reddened. "Easy, no need to get ruffled. What's it all about then?" The agitated voice on the other end was clearly audible as Kimball ended the conversation. He lowered himself into the desk chair, nodding at Sheppard.

"Are you convinced?"

"This is dreadful—dreadful. Why would anyone want to kidnap Katherine Nikulasson?"

"More important, who?"

"For God's sake, man, you don't think I would know anyone capable of such a terrible thing."

"We don't always know what people are capable of. Who did you talk to about her? Someone at your office? A secretary?"

"I haven't been to my office since she called." There

was a hesitancy in his voice and then a sudden realization. His tanned face flushed as pink as his scalp. "My God. Gehreich!"

Wilde leaned forward in his chair. "Who's Gehreich?"

"Ernie Gehreich. Former C.I.A. Never actually admitted it, of course, but I knew. Always around when the assignments from Halvern had international implications of some sort or another."

"What does he have to do with Katherine?"

"I don't know."

"Mr. Kimball, there must be something you *do* know."

"I'll try to explain. I work for a U.S. television program called *Power Line*. I'm sure you've heard of it?"

"I'm aware of it. And of Ivar Whalen."

"My office handles leg-work, research, contacts, string-pulling, things like that. Occasionally, we engage in mutual back-scratching with various intelligence organizations. A kind of service-for-service arrangement, if you know what I mean."

"How does Katherine fit into this?"

"All I know is she's working on an assignment for Whalen. His right-hand man, Lawrence Halvern, called me last week. Said to give her anything she needed."

"And Gehreich?"

"Gehreich called me day before yesterday. Said he was working with Halvern on the Nikulasson assignment. Said for her own protection he was to keep tabs on her progress. Not directly, but through me. As a matter of fact, it was he who suggested I meet with her this week-end. She mentioned the reception at the Lewellyn's, so it fell into place rather nicely."

"You didn't question Gehreich's authority?"

"We've always had the tacit understanding that departmental affairs are not questioned, however, I did plan to call Halvern Monday morning. I'm not particularly fond of Ernie Gehreich or his methods. Where he's concerned, I find it wise to—shall we say—cover my ass."

"Where's he staying?"

"I have the number and name of it somewhere about. Didn't strike me as a fashionable place. Not his usual sort. You can call him from here if you like." He rummaged through a pile of papers on the desk and pulled out a folder. "On second thought, I'll dial it for you. He's not at all a cooperative chap."

"It might be better if we don't give Mr. Gehreich advance notice," Wilde said, thinking it might be wise if he covered his own ass, considering he had no idea how reliable Hugh Kimball actually was. "Would you like to come with me?"

"Hoping you'd ask. Couldn't keep an eye half-closed tonight not knowing what's happened to the girl. I feel bloody damned responsible, you know."

"On the way, you can fill me in on the conversation you had with Katherine."

the **GOLD** Covenant

"Better yet, I'll give you a list of the things she wanted done," Kimball said. "Perhaps you'll find something helpful in that."

The shoddy remnants of a once-elegant porte-cochere still clung to the entrance of the Bittner Arms Hotel. The door had been propped open, but the air was static and the lobby stifling with the summer heat. The elderly clerk, immersed in the *Daily Mirror*, gave Wilde and Kimball no more than a cursory glance as they approached the desk.

"The number of Mr. Gehreich's room, please?" Kimball said.

The man grunted, checked the register. "Five-eighteen."

"Do you happen to know if he's in?"

"I'm bloody not 'is mum now, am I?" The old man sniffed and mumbled something else about the bloomin' 'ilton as Kimball turned to follow Wilde into the waiting elevator.

"Didn't imagine anything as bad as this," Kimball said. "Never knew Gehreich to use anything but the best hotels. Not when he was working with Whalen. Always managed to worm the most out of his expense account."

The ancient lift groaned to a stop at the fifth floor.

When they stepped out of the still-shuddering car, they found the hallway poorly lit and oppressively hot. A peeling black arrow pointed left for even numbers, five-hundred-twelve to five-hundred-twenty. A chandelier, stripped of its crystal teardrops, brass fixtures, and all but one of its flame-shaped bulbs, hung from the ceiling at the center of the passage.

Wilde paused outside of five-eighteen to listen, then knocked on the door. Getting no answer, he tried the knob which was draped with a Do Not Disturb sign. The door was locked.

"You don't suppose he's checked out?"

"Let's find out."

Kimball glanced up and down the hall then rubbed a hand over his bald pate. "You mean break in?"

"Mr. Gehreich must be used to that in his business." As Kimball watched nervously, Wilde pulled a set of picks from his pocket. "This hotel," he said, working on the lock to Gehreich's room, "might indicate the man is working more than one street. Tell me, Kimball, does this one have anything to do with *Power Line*?"

"Whatever Gehreich's involved in, I'll wager a month's salary it has nothing to do with Ivar Whalen or the show."

After several tries, one of the picks meshed with the lock. Wilde pulled a pair of plastic gloves from a pocket, handing one to Kimball. He slipped on the other, wiped the knob, turned it, shoved the door open. He entered the room with Kimball reluctantly following. The air was permeated with the odor of stale tobacco and over-ripe garbage.

An overflowing ashtray sat on the bed table next to the phone. The broken pieces of another one lay scattered over the thin carpet along with the ashes, cigar, and cigarette butts. The window had been propped open with a chair, allowing the smell of garbage to drift in from the back alley. Strewn across the mattress and onto the floor were the dingy linens from the unmade bed, a man's slacks and shirt, and several empty beer bottles. A pair of shoes with socks tucked neatly inside sat side-by-side just under the bed. An over-night grip had been tossed into a corner.

"Your Mr. Gehreich is not a tidy man," Wilde said. "Let's have a look around, shall we?"

"I suppose these are both connecting doors?" Kimball said, starting toward one of them. "You don't usually get a private bath in a place like this." He turned the knob, shoved the door, and peered into the small bathroom. "Oh God . . ." he cried out. "Christ . . ." Still clinging to the knob, he swung back against the flaked wood paneling, his hand covering his mouth and nose in a futile attempt to shut out the putrid odor of death.

Wilde crossed quickly to the bathroom. A man's body lay half-submerged in the opaque red water that filled the tub. The head, leaning grotesquely on the porcelain edge, had been nearly decapitated.

Wilde backed out and closed the door. "Is it Gehreich?" he asked.

Kimball was leaning over the window sill between the legs of the chair that had been used to prop it open. When he'd let go of everything in his stomach, he walked stiffly back to the bed, sat down and lowered his head between his knees. After a moment, he straightened up and mopped his face with a wad of tissue from his pants pocket. "Yes, it's him all right," he said, his voice quivering, eyes wide and bewildered. "What's happening? What's bloody happening?"

Wilde didn't answer. He glanced around the small room then focused on Gehreich's luggage. He turned the grip upside down over the bed, shaking out a few items of underwear along with a passport issued in the name of Ernest Gehreich. A dour, nondescript face glared at him from the photograph.

"My God, man, what are you doing? Let's call the police."

"In time." Wilde picked up Gehreich's clothing, examining the pockets, hems, and facings, then went over the belt, gun holster, and strap that were hanging on the bedpost. He checked both shoes—insoles and heels. A stained trench coat lay in a heap behind the door. The lining had been pulled loose, the shoulder tabs ripped off and torn open. He scooped up a second passport and a wad of crumpled paper which had been tossed on top of the torn fabric. The passport had been mutilated, the name and number unreadable, the picture torn out. The wad of paper was an airline ticket to Nassau. He was wrong about his destination, Wilde thought, but he'd bought the right kind of ticket. One-way.

"Let's get out of this room," Kimball pleaded. "I'm not up to waiting in here until the police arrive."

"You can inform the Yard from your home, if you like. After we drive you back."

"We're not waiting downstairs?"

"No. It might be better if the call's anonymous."

Kimball rubbed a hand over his head, thoughtfully. "Yes, see what you mean. God knows what Gehreich was into."

"And, Kimball, try to find out what connection Gehreich's business had with *Power Line*, will you?"

"Right. Anything else I can do?"

"Just be thorough. I'll be in touch."

An hour later, after dropping Kimball off, Wilde's brown Rover was on the M3 heading west toward Andover. As Franco drove, Wilde stared blindly out of the window wondering if the man called Hareb Kassem had already gone to ground.

CHAPTER 21

The gray concrete building that housed Oriental Exports, Ltd. was situated on a large farm west of London, just north of Andover. Sequestered by the surrounding hills in the midst of a thick stand of ancient oak trees, it served as offices for the company as well as private apartments for Hareb Kassem. Its exterior walls were windowless, embellished with an eight-foot wide modern hieroglyphic frieze which banded the circumference between the first and second floors. Electronically controlled access was monitored from several points inside the building, starting with a visual surveillance from the outer gates, over the entire mile-and-a-half drive leading to the main entrance, ending inside the reception area.

The Rover was still rolling along the curb in front of the broad flagstone stairway when Wilde pushed open the car door and leapt out. "Wait here, near the phone," he said to Franco. "This shouldn't take more than thirty minutes."

The entrance doors opened automatically before Wilde reached them, giving him immediate entrée to the building. At the rear of the foyer, two men had taken up guard posts, one of them carrying a Striker revolving shotgun, the other strapping on a shoulder holster fitted with a Beretta .380. Neither of them looked as though he needed the hardware.

Scurrying in from a door on the right, a short-but-husky man with dark frazzled hair, glasses slightly askew, hurriedly pulled a black pin-striped suit jacket over his unbuttoned vest. He skipped over the formalities and spoke to Wilde with snappish ill-humor. "You've taken to strange business hours, Wilde. Is it so important?"

"I'll let Kassem decide that."

"All right. Tell me what it's about and I'll talk to him."

"Where is he, Jamil?"

"You may as well tell me now. It'll end up in my lap anyway."

"When did he start having you run interference for him?"

"I run his business. Running interference is *their* job," he said, nodding toward the men with the hardware.

"Then you can tell him I'm here."

"Tomorrow would have been more convenient."

"*Tomorrow,*" Wilde replied, "*is without substance*, my dear Jamil, *an unobtainable dream, the illusion of an impatient man.*"

"*Patient!*" a voice bawled out from the other room. "*Of a patient man*! For God's sake, get it right. A man's poetry deserves to be correctly quoted. Come in, Wilde. Jamil has the manners of a castrated camel."

Jamil Taha, who had been with Kassem since their college days, rolled his eyes, raised his arms, turned his palms up, and assumed the expression of a martyr.

"A bit harsh," Wilde agreed, shaking his head in sympathy. "Perhaps, not castrated." Leaving Jamil to stew, he crossed the foyer, entered the office from which the voice had originated, and closed the door.

The vaulted room was cavernous, but the cluttered assortment of antiques, lamps, pillows, and prayer rugs, all arranged in small haphazard groupings, gave it an accordant warmth. Except for a large mahogany desk, the room bore no resemblance to an office. It was filled with art objects: tapestries, porcelains, brass and bronze pieces of mid-eastern origin, along with a number of elaborately gilded cabinets and boxes. The furniture—magnificent examples of hand-crafted inlaid woods and tiled mosaics—was of museum quality. A seventeenth-century Caucasian Dragon carpet, its intricately-woven design still vibrant with color, covered the center of the parquet floor.

the **GOLD** Covenant

Hareb Kassem stood in front of a massive fireplace which had been carved out of black marble. He was wearing a blue silk robe over black pajamas, his hands thrust into his pockets, a pleasant smile on his handsome face. The physical antithesis of his name, Kassem was fair-complected with blue eyes and fawn hair—features which were, no doubt, inherited from the Scottish mother he never knew or talked about. His business acumen he magnanimously attributed to the Syrian genes which accounted for half his paternal ancestry, even though the gift had skipped over that closest branch of his family tree. He had been raised in parts of Europe and the middle east by what he referred to as a nomadic father—although others thought the term shiftless more appropriate. He was Oxford educated by his own ingenuity. Wilde was one of the few people who knew his origins, or that the name he used in London society, Arnold Campbell, had any connection with the name Hareb Kassem or with Oriental Imports, Ltd.

He lowered himself into one of the plush chairs in front of the fireplace, propped his legs up on a Louis Quatorze table, and motioned to the chair opposite. Wilde sat down, lighting a cigarette while waiting for the customary silent evaluation to be made over the rim of Kassem's demitasse. Kassem drained the coffee down to the thick dark dregs at the bottom, turned the cup over, and gave it three complete revolutions, then placed the saucer and inverted cup back on the table.

"Would you like a cup?" he asked. "It's an excellent Turkish blend."

"No, thank you," Wilde said. "I see you still look for your fortune in it. Is Jamil coming in for the reading?"

"Later, perhaps. I don't need the cup to tell me when things aren't going well. And, you, Sheppard, you're moving rather slowly. I really expected you a great deal sooner."

"Judging by Jamil's greeting, I rather thought I'd arrived too soon."

"Jamil is over-zealous at times. He likes to feel needed," Kassem said. "Now, about the agreement you were so insistent upon—that we keep a distance?"

"At times like these, distance can breed trouble. It seems we have enough of that already."

"Indeed, yes, some bothersome loose ends, I'd say. The sort of ravelings that have a nasty way of tripping us up."

"Let's talk about them."

"Why not!" Kassem said. "You start, old boy."

"All right. Let's have the unpleasant ones out of the way first, shall we?"

"And those are?"

"The way you handle the loose ends. Since you've come out of retirement, have you changed policy?"

"No change."

Kassem's momentary lift of eyelids indicated he was offended or, maybe, defensive. Either reaction was agreeable to Wilde, who decided a slight push would take it one way or the other. "None in the way of finesse? Inculcation? Discipline?"

Kassem shook his head. "Ah, Sheppard, my old friend, can it be you've lost faith in me?"

"There are times, old friend, when *circumstances alter even the things we hold certain.*"

"You *do* have a way with my words," Kassem laughed. "These circumstances you speak of, am I aware of them?"

"What we both know is that you're aware of most things before they happen." A disarming smile spread over Wilde's face for just a moment, disappearing as he added, bluntly, "David Forster is dead."

Kassem bolted upright in his chair; the uncharacteristic display of emotion seemed the result of genuine shock. Wilde was convinced this was one fact Kassem hadn't been aware of before it happened.

"How?" Kassem demanded.

"Murdered. At Ian Lewellyn's home tonight. Professional, clean, efficient. David never knew what happened."

"Why would anyone want to kill the harmless old boy?"

"Maybe to keep him quiet. Maybe to cover a kidnapping. Katherine Nikulasson was talking to David when I last saw her. I haven't seen her since."

"Katherine Nikulasson? Here? In London?"

"She arrived at Stowesbridge yesterday. We were together at the reception Ian was throwing for an American senator this evening. There were a lot of people. A lot of faces."

"Who's to say she didn't leave the party with someone more interesting?"

"How well do you know her?"

Kassem sat back to flip open an enameled box on the table. He picked out a slender cheroot. Through a cloud of smoke, he said, "I gave her an interview once, did you know that? As Arnold Campbell, of course—the old Scottish heritage and all that. Don't think she believed a word of what I told her. I had to be damned careful; she's quite good at getting what she wants."

"So are you, Kassem."

"I can tell you, I got nothing of what I wanted from her. And I need *not* tell you what that was." He laughed at the memory, then as quickly grew serious again. "My God, Sheppard, I must be getting old. I thought this was going to be a simple affair. No complications, no headaches. Should have known someone would muck things up. It seems we've both waited too long for this meeting. Those damned untidy details!"

"Your gold carrier, for one."

"Ah, there it is then—finesse, inculcation, discipline—I see what you were getting at." Kassem was annoyed.

the **GOLD** Covenant

"You think I'm responsible for that ludicrous killing?"

"Murder isn't your style."

"How very generous of you. I'll return the compliment by telling you I disagreed entirely with Jamil when he credited you with the rather clumsy offing of your Mr. Evan Babcock. It was a logical assumption for him to make, I suppose, given the circumstances and his suspicious nature. However, I can think of no motive whatsoever for either of us having killed Babcock, David, or Barcineh or for having kidnapped Miss Nikulasson. It seems safe to assume, then, if the problem isn't internal, someone is trying to bore in from the outside."

"I want the bloody goddamned bastards before they hurt Katherine."

"Which brings us to the real reason for your visit."

"I need your help, Kassem."

"My help! With your connections?"

"It's your territory. I want shortcuts. I want a mainline to the center of your information circuit."

"That's easy," Kassem said. "What else?"

"Whether you want to believe it or not, I'm convinced there's an internal leak in your organization. If you can find it with your usual efficiency, it might give us a lead to the sods who took Katherine before anything else happens."

"It's not that easy." A long steady stream of smoke drifted from Kassem's mouth before he went on. "You give me too much credit for the quick solution. Remember, I'm a bit rusty after so many years in the pasture. You may be right about the internal problem, though, and, I assure you, it will be my first priority to set things right. You know, Wilde, it was my supposition of the past week that your misanthropic errand boy, Babcock, was the bad connection." Kassem pushed out of his chair to begin pacing in front of the hearth. "I thought he was after the gold, but it just didn't wash."

"Let's talk about the carrier."

"Ahmed Barcineh? The man who lost his head. Very careless of him."

Kassem's ingenuous face displayed the same callous humor that, Wilde knew, had always served him well in school, in business, and in the underworld of gold smuggling he'd occupied until his retirement from it ten years ago.

Drawing in on his cigar and exhaling slowly, Kassem's face sobered in reflection of Wilde's. He said, "You never did appreciate my humor any more than my poetry but, remember, old man, one needed both to have survived in this business."

"The way you survived your business was through an early retirement," Wilde said with a trace of a grin. He used the stub of his cigarette to light another. "At any rate, with airline security what it is now, I didn't think you'd be using the old carrier system for this deal."

"There are ways to make it work, even now. Sometimes the very fact that a system is out-moded can make it useful again."

"About the carrier, Kassem. Who killed him?"

"At this point, I'm not sure. Barcineh was an old hand—experienced, reliable—but on this last trip he made a mistake. His delivery was at least five kilos short. We would like to have discussed it with him, in a civilized way, you understand," the smile flashed briefly again, "but he was dead when we made the pick-up. Interesting question, Wilde. If he was killed for the gold, why did they take only five kilos? Why not the whole lot?"

"His weight was checked when he left?"

"Always! He was carrying forty at the start."

"Only five kilos short . . ." Wilde mused. "Hardly worth killing for."

"Exactly." Kassem leaned through the cloud of white smoke circling his head. "And why would anyone leave thirty-five kilos behind? Do you know what that's worth on today's market?"

"In the neighborhood of three-quarters of a million dollars?"

"Close enough. What kind of self-respecting murderer helps himself to ten percent of the profits, leaving the corpse with ninety?"

"Supposing," Wilde said, "Barcineh *had* raked off the five kilos. Supposing the thirty-five was all he was carrying at the time . . ."

"You're suggesting he was killed for some other reason than the gold? Perhaps you're right, but we didn't turn up the missing kilos and we, my friend, are very thorough."

"Maybe a bit rusty though? As you pointed out, you've been in retirement a long time, Kassem. What about the pay-scale? Does it still buy loyalty?"

"Of course. Whatever that fool was involved in, it couldn't have been worth risking his scrawny neck over. He should have been satisfied with what he had—a chance to crawl out of that dunghill he came from—a chance to make a fortune by his standards. There's no accounting for human greed, is there?"

"You have no complaint on that score," Wilde said. "Greed is what kept you in business all those years."

Kassem laughed, dropping back into his chair. "So. Where does this lead us?"

"Have you checked your security system on the other side? Someone inside fingered Barcineh."

Kassem waved a hand, dismissing the possibility. "He must have given *himself* away. He could have become over-confident—tried to make another connection for a bigger percentage. And that might lead us back to your own doorstep, my friend. Directly to the late Mr. Evan Babcock."

"Babcock the connection?" Wilde grew thoughtful. "He would have to have been familiar with your operation—point of origin, point of entry. It's possible. Still, Evan wasn't a killer, nor was he fool enough to siphon off small portions of shipments. He would have known there wasn't sufficient profit in that to compensate for all the trouble he'd be buying."

"There aren't many men who have the resources to take on Hareb Kassem. Not now, and not when I was running the syndicate," Kassem said with pride. "It would be foolish to the point of stupidity."

"*Complacency gives birth to ruin.*"

"Again, you remind me of my own wisdom which I too often forget."

"Have you also forgotten that sometimes the unexpected can make a success of a foolish act?"

"Go on, Sheppard."

"Suppose someone thought he had the perfect way to revive your gold syndicate. Suppose he could unlock a new source. With the right key, he just might be able to do that. Wouldn't it be worth the gamble then?"

"Katherine Nikulasson!" Kassem exploded. "This *someone* thinks she's the right key. But she knows nothing!"

"Let's hope he doesn't find that out. This is the same someone who's using people like disposable toothpicks. I want his bloody goddamned hide. If he's hurt her I'll skin him alive and fly his carcass from a flagpole."

"You, my friend, are supposed to be the civilized one."

"It's been a nasty evening all around."

roberta clark

Kassem rose to fetch a decanter of brandy, looking to see if Wilde would join him. Wilde shook his head. After pouring himself a glass, he returned to his desk. From the intercom, he summoned Jamil. "Get in here on the double." Then he picked up the phone and asked the voice on the other end for an update on smugglers. Still holding the receiver, he nodded at Wilde. "All right, Sheppard, give me a few hours on this, will you?"

The door flew open and Jamil rushed into the room, his hair now neatly brushed, vest buttoned, face—as always—a visual display of abdominal distress. He took the phone from Kassem, pulled up the desk chair, flipped open a pad, and pulled a pen from his pocket with a self-satisfied glance at Wilde.

After briefly filling in Jamil, Kassem returned to his chair in front of the fireplace. He picked up the demitasse, turned it over, then studied the configurations in the fine grounds of coffee clinging to the side of the cup. "She something special to you?" he asked. The ensuing silence made him glance up at Wilde. "Yes! I can see she is."

"While the wheels are spinning, Kassem," Wilde said, "see what you can get on a man named Ernest Gehreich: American, likely a moonlighting operative, some connection with a TV show called *Power Line*. He turned up dead at the Bittner Arms Hotel. Same style as Barcineh."

the **GOLD** *Covenant*

"Another disposable," Kassem said in disgust. "Let's hope Katherine Nikulasson can keep herself alive until you find her. I like the girl, too. She's the only female who ever gave me a twinge of sentimentality."

CHAPTER 22

Katherine sat up on the bunk, wakened by the noisy snap of a lock, followed by the thud of a foot against the door. They were the sounds which announced the arrival of every meal, but this time the swarthy man who entered the room was not one of the stewards she'd grown accustomed to seeing. He was older, near forty, much bulkier, his biceps putting a maximum strain on the rolled-up sleeves of his white sweat-stained shirt. The grip of a revolver protruded from his leather belt.

One thing she was sure he would have in common with the other stewards was a severe case of aphonia. No one had spoken to her since she'd been locked in the stateroom. No one had even acknowledged her existence when she spoke to them. It wasn't the silence of a language barrier; it was a well-trained, disciplined silence, no doubt based on fear of Quisette.

the **GOLD** *Covenant*

She propped the pillows against the cabin wall and sank back into them, watching as the man crossed the room, deftly balancing a loaded tray on one huge hand. "Another goon," she said. "They must have run out of waiters. You and Kenneth look well-matched. The two of you ought to think about going on the road—a kind of Two Stooges act." Talking was therapeutic even when it was lost on deaf ears. She continued with her monologue. "Subject's too personal, I guess. Bet you'd rather talk about something innocuous. The weather, maybe? Must be a lovely evening. Outside, I mean."

With practiced indifference, the big man flipped the folding mahogany table out of its wall bracket, locked the support in place, and deposited the tray on top of it.

"Actually," she went on, "it's a miserable, sweltering, goddamned rotten evening, and I don't really give a pig's ass what you think about it."

The man turned to stare at her for a moment, then smiled, baring a mouthful of perfectly-aligned but darkly-stained teeth. It was the first reaction she'd provoked during the entire week she'd been confined to the stuffy cabin.

"Amazing!" she said. "The light of understanding still shines in Attica."

He replied in English with a trace of a Greek accent. "You will join Mr. Quisette on the afterdeck when you have finished."

"The man talks! How extraordinary. Do you have a name?"

"Pavlos Xenides."

"Did Mr. Quisette come back alone, Pavlos?"

He shrugged in answer to the question. Still smiling, he left the cabin, closing and locking the door behind him.

My God, she thought, after all the time in this sweat box, I'm almost looking forward to seeing that bastard Quisette again. She padded over to the recessed porthole that was her only link with the outside world. The tiny radius offered a view of a section of the active harbor at Piraeus—passing cruise ships, ferry boats, all sorts of pleasure craft, and a number of luxurious yachts similar to the one that had been her prison for almost a week.

Any doubts Katherine held about Quisette's influence were dispelled when they arrived in Athens. There had been no customs check, no show of passports or visas, no opportunity to talk to an official of any kind. The moment his Gulfstream II put down at the airport, they were shunted to a waiting helicopter that flew them directly to Piraeus. The landing pad was the upper deck of a private yacht which was, at the least, three-fifty to four-hundred feet in length. Her tour of the ship had consisted of a direct route to the cabin she now occupied.

The compact accommodations, she judged, were a part of the crew's quarters. In spite of the air conditioning, the room seemed stuffy and claustrophobic. Only the porthole—the umbilical to the outside world—kept her from going completely crazy. Since that first night, her sleep had been fitful, half-conscious dreams continually distorting the time and waking her sporadically with feelings of desperation instead of allowing the restorative strength sleep should have brought.

It had been days since she'd seen Quisette. The last time was on the night after they'd arrived, when she had been wakened and brought into the grand salon. Quisette had redrafted the first copy of her letter to Sabir Nuri Pasha—the contents of which he found suspect. She was to paraphrase the new version more convincingly. The result had been acceptable but, in her own mind, would not achieve the desired result.

My dear and honored friend, Sabir Nuri Pasha,

As you know, the loss of my father, Gustav Nikulasson, has been a great sorrow to me. It is in the name of his memory and your friendship for him that I make a humble request of you. The details of this request will be conveyed to you by the bearer of this letter, Mr. Enrique Quisette.

In introduction, Mr. Quisette has requested that I assure you of the purity of our motivations. In brief explanation, we wish to undertake an expedition to the place where my father was working at the time of his death.

roberta clark

We respectfully ask if you will provide us an escort, as he always assured me you would do in his absence. The purpose of this journey is twofold: [1] to search for remnants of his unfinished work, and [2] to publicize his sympathy for the plight of your people and his dedication to helping them in their struggle for independence. This, I believe, would be an appropriate memorial to his life and to those principles to which he devoted it.

It is most important you receive Mr. Quisette as soon as possible. The reasons are urgent and cannot be conveyed in a letter, but will make themselves clear when you have spoken to him. Mr. Quisette, who is close at hand to await your reply, will make any arrangements which you specify and pay any costs which might be incurred on this expedition.

I remain hopeful for your assistance in this matter and beg to hear from you at your earliest convenience, as we wish to accomplish our work before the coming winter season.

With best wishes to you and to your family, I am your devoted friend,

Katherine Nikulasson

Katherine had no doubt the letter would reach Sabir. It was his custom to spend the summers in Beirut with his family. At any other time of year there would've been little chance of finding him. He might be anywhere: in the Zagros Mountains, in Paris, or England, in Cairo, or even in the United States. Sabir's major occupation was

the **GOLD** Covenant

the raising of funds for hospitals and medical supplies, for schools, and for the army fighting the continuous, endless battle for Kurdish independence.

But, however meticulous Quisette's attention to detail might be, he couldn't predict Sabir's response to the letter. She was almost certain Sabir would find her request whimsical at best, an imposition if not an impertinence at the worst. If he refused to see Quisette the first time, it would be that much more difficult to make contact again. They would have lost any chance to go into that volatile area peacefully.

Still, Sabir was unpredictable. There was always the remote chance he would be moved by his friendship for her father. The question in her mind was whether it was right to be hopeful, or whether the hope itself was a betrayal of an old friend. What little of her confidence that remained had slowly deteriorated as each silent, muggy day blended into the next with no word.

Now, with Quisette's return, she was certain the plan had failed. The time had seemed long while she was waiting, yet, it was much too short to indicate success. Sabir would not have been so quick to make a positive decision. There were too many contingencies, too many necessary precautions that would entail long-range planning.

She wandered over to the tray of food. It was enough to feed four or five people—baked lobster, filo pastries with cheese filling, moussaka, yogurt with cucumber, baklava, a plate of assorted fruit, and a small carafe of thick sweet Greek coffee. It looked as good as she knew it would taste but the heat and confinement of the small cabin left her with no appetite.

Picking up a stem of plump grapes, she entered the bathroom, which was, like everything else in her quarters, compact but elegant: the walls, sink, and shower all of black marble, the fixtures polished brass. She shed her wilted clothes, turned on the cold tap, then stepped into the shower stall, eating the grapes while standing under the cool spray. Slowly, she began to feel a rejuvenation, inside as well as out.

When the door of the cabin was unlocked, precisely an hour later, Katherine was waiting, dressed in a fresh pair of Bermudas and a clean white shirt. The large man, Pavlos, led her down a narrow passage toward the stern of the ship. The revolver still protruded from the back of his belt—within reach—like a dare to anyone foolish enough to try to take it. He stopped at the companionway connecting the galley with the afterdeck lounge, motioning for her to go up alone.

When she reached the deck, a soft breeze from the sea touched her skin with the tantalizing promise of freedom. The sun, though low in the sky and casting a long red glow across the water, was still hot and brilliant. Quisette was waiting for her at a linen-covered table beneath a blue-and-white striped awning near the stern rail.

the **GOLD** *Covenant*

Kenneth, who seemed never to be farther than twenty-five paces away and who apparently was never caught in a sitting position, stood near the bulkhead where the sun hit him full-face. His complexion had the angry flush of blood pressure about to peak. His stance went on immediate alert as she moved past him.

"Ah, Katherine. I see the clothes are an agreeable fit." Quisette's apparent good humor sounded forced. "Now, if you'll pour me a cup of coffee," he went on, "cream, sugar, brandy, we'll get started." He laid down the newspaper he was reading and indicated the silver service on the table.

After pouring a cup, she stirred in the requested additions and set it in front of him.

"Help yourself as well," he said. "It's Brazilian, brewed American style. You should find it a touch of home."

"It's too hot for coffee."

"Suit yourself. Sit down, my dear Katherine. We can't have you acting the too-servile female, even in this part of the world. Sabir Nuri Pasha wouldn't find it characteristic of the free-spirited American woman, now would he?"

Katherine's heart began to race. "Does that mean you've made the contact? Sabir's given his consent?"

"It means, dear girl, your letter—our letter—had the predicted effect." He picked up the cup, raised a toast to her, then took a sip. "We can expect an emissary from your friend, Sabir, at any moment. Unannounced. It seems he dislikes predetermined appointments so we must be ready at all times to put on the proper show. I don't think it necessary that we make gauche romantic pretenses, but as we speak, your things are being moved to the stateroom adjoining mine. I'm sure you'll find it much more spacious and comfortable than your former quarters. Enjoy it while you can. You'll find very little luxury once we're under way."

"*You* may find that more of a problem than I will."

"I see the heat has done little to wilt your acerbic tongue." He unfolded the newspaper at his side and tossed it across the table. "Perhaps this will help to convince you that any deviation from the plan will be dealt with harshly and swiftly. Those same consequences will touch many more lives than your own."

She picked up the paper—a day-old copy of the *London Times*—and stared at the two photographs, one of David Forster and, next to it, one of herself. The headline read Murder-Kidnapping Baffles Yard. She scanned the copy, not wanting to believe it, every word a needle piercing deeper. David dead! They'd killed him. In spite of everything. For nothing. For the hell of it . . .

Her eyes filled with tears, her mind with agonized frustration. She bolted to her feet with a visceral howl that paralyzed Quisette and yanked the edge of the linen cloth, dumping the coffee service into his lap.

the **GOLD** Covenant

He reacted too late. The sudden frantic movement of his chair tipped it off-balance and slammed him to the deck on his back. His shocked yelp of pain was drowned out by Katherine's furious voice. "You goddamned slimy bastard—"

Kenneth reacted too late as well, but it took only seconds for him to recover. Oblivious to the human tank charging across the deck, Katherine continued to shout until the words were choked off by the huge hand which clamped around her neck like a vise. He dragged her around the table, reached down and offered his other hand to Quisette.

Quisette angrily waved him away. "I'm all right!" he said, spitting the words out like venom sucked from a wound, fixing the two of them with a murderous glare.

The intense hatred was directed at both Katherine and Kenneth. She had caused his humiliation; Kenneth had allowed it to happen. Both of them had witnessed it. That, Katherine thought, must have angered him more than anything else. He looked ridiculous, sitting on the deck next to his overturned chair in the midst of spilled coffee, cream, sugar, serving pieces, and linens. His anger, which should have been intimidating, instead had a calming effect on her but she watched with a good deal less than satisfaction as he pulled himself up and dabbed at the stains on his white slacks. A loss of dignity wasn't enough.

As if sensing her contempt, he slapped the napkin down on the table. "Let her go," he said to Kenneth. "I don't want her marked. And get someone up here to clear away this mess."

Kenneth's hand dropped to his side. He stood glaring at Katherine, red-faced, eyes spilling fury, then turned and went to the intercom built into the varnished mahogany of the after bulkhead.

Almost immediately, two stewards scurried up from the galley and cleared away the debris, scouring the deck and replacing the soiled linen. As they worked, Quisette pulled aside one of the chairs and sat a few feet from the table.

"Sit down!" he commanded. His brows lifted for an instant, revealing the glacial core behind the pale blue irises. Katherine felt an involuntary shiver as she moved to the chair opposite. He went on speaking, softly emphasizing each word. "I keep score, Miss Nikulasson. And I always come out ahead. I assure you of that fact. Like death, I win."

"*Like death, I win*," she mimicked, her voice shaking, barely in control. "I'll see that engraved on your tombstone." She could feel Kenneth close the gap between the bulkhead and her chair but it didn't bother her. The quiet rage was still there and it gave her a total disregard for the consequences.

David's murder had left her angrier than anything

she'd ever experienced. Everyone dies, goddamn it—no one knew that better than she did—but that had to do with luck, or the way the cards are dealt, or God's will, or whatever the hell you wanted to call it. This was different. This was someone reaching out and switching the cards. Playing God. Somehow or other, she had to even things out for David before it was too late for her as well. The fact she was still sitting here in one piece could only mean Quisette needed her—intact—and she had every intention of using that to her advantage.

Quisette's temper flared for a moment before it simmered into an acid smile. He signaled the big man to back off. "You really shouldn't tempt Kenneth," he said. "It shows lack of discipline and lack of control over the tongue, even to the imperilment of the body. But then, that's just another manifestation of female weakness, isn't it?"

Ignoring the question, she said, "Have you ever thought someone might be keeping score on you, as well? It'll take a damn sight more than a lapful of hot coffee to pay for David Forster's life."

"By *someone*, I take it, you mean a vengeful God?" He made a rasping sound of amusement in his throat. "If, indeed, there is a God, my dear, ask yourself who he's favored up to now."

There was a compulsive snort from Kenneth, who remained at the rail within a few feet of her chair, doggedly determined not to repeat his previous error. The stewards retreated from the afterdeck, as Pavlos arrived with cups and fresh coffee. He deposited the tray on the table before joining Kenneth to wait for further instructions.

Quisette's voice was all condescension when he spoke again. "I must admit to the momentary weakness of thinking you different than the ordinary female," he said. "In fact, I was rather enjoying your display of courage. It's a quality I find totally lacking in women of beauty. Unfortunately, what I mistook for courage was, in reality, emotionalism. Like all the rest, you are a great disappointment."

Katherine looked beyond him, at the mountains above the harbor, a superimposed series of gray, rugged silhouettes in the fading light. A serenity beyond reach. Tantalizing. Intangible. Here, all around them, was activity, the beginning of the night's celebration. The sound of parties and laughter carried across the water like currents of electricity. Emotions. How wonderful it would be to use them again for enjoyment—for love— instead of grief, anger, and hatred.

"The purpose of this discussion," Quisette went on, "was to be the *modus operandi* of the next few weeks. It seemed wise to have the David Forster matter in the open. As it turned out, I was quite correct. Better these fiascoes are done with before your friend, Sabir Pasha, makes his appearance."

the **GOLD** *Covenant*

At a motion, Pavlos stepped forward to pour a cup of coffee, stir in cream, sugar, and brandy, then place it in front of Quisette. He moved back to the rail without offering Katherine the same amenity. After tasting the coffee, Quisette placed the cup on the table and dabbed his lips. "Now," he said, "back to business."

Katherine's focus returned to Quisette's face. The adrenaline-fed bravado had deserted her, leaving a leaden sadness in its place. "Why did you kill him?" she asked.

"*I* did not kill him, dear girl. Simply think of it as the uncontrollable forces of nature meant to teach us the realities of life."

"What realities? Spell it out for me."

"If you cooperate, Sabir may survive."

"*May*! As with David Forster? You promised if Sabir cooperated—peacefully—there would be no one else hurt."

"I am a master of human nature, my dear. With people like you, the words *may survive* have an enticing persuasiveness whether you believe them or not."

Her energy, like the bravado, was consumed by the heat of the afternoon, the aftermath of emotion, and the growing horrible conviction that David would not be the last one hurt. She stared at Quisette but she was seeing David Forster, Evan Babcock, and that pathetic creature who'd been mutilated. Her thoughts were filled with the words she'd written in the letter to Sabir. Would it have been better if she hadn't written it? Would Quisette have carried out his threat against Sabir's people? It was possible, if he had influence in the right places, and she had no reason to believe he hadn't.

The sound of an approaching launch brought Quisette to his feet and a hustling of activity at the port side. With Katherine following, he moved to the rail, where he watched the shore boat cast its lines to the boarding platform.

There were two passengers in the launch, both men of medium height and build, both in dark business suits oddly out-of-place in the present setting.

"It looks like your friend, Sabir Pasha, is a man of action," Quisette said. He signaled the waiting crew, who immediately lowered the boarding ladder, then he turned to Pavlos. "Take them into the salon," he ordered. To Kenneth he said, "Keep the girl up here until I've had time to change. We'll make our entrance together."

CHAPTER 23

Wearing white linen slacks, ice-blue silk shirt, and pale gray paisley scarf, Quisette seemed to blend into the decor of the salon. Everything in the salon was soft—soft peach walls, soft gray-blue divans bordering both sides, their long lines broken here and there with soft cushions, and low white tables with floral arrangements in the same soft colors. It seemed to Katherine a deliberate attempt to anesthetize his adversaries.

She was still wearing her casual uniform of khaki shorts and white shirt when she followed Quisette into the salon. As they entered, the two waiting visitors immediately rose to their feet. Both were lean and muscular under their dark suits, both of medium stature, but there the similarity ended. One was, at the most, in his early twenties, olive-skinned with piercing, brown, deep-set eyes and a thin, dark mustache. The other was fairer—

his eyes a metal-gray, his hair and mustache a reddish brown—in the neighborhood of sixty. He looked as though he had spent a lifetime out-of-doors.

"Gentlemen, it's a pleasure to see you again so soon," Quisette said. "I don't think you know Katherine Nikulasson."

She extended a hand to the younger man first.

"*Mademoiselle*," he said, with a slight bow, "I am Lieutenant Mohsen Raza."

She nodded, smiled in acknowledgment, and turned to the older man, hands at her sides. He studied her with cool, intense eyes, then, bursting into a pleased smile, clasped her shoulders with outstretched arms. "Katherine Nikulasson!" he said. "You are well. I was most concerned."

"I didn't think you would come yourself."

"Katherine," Quisette interrupted, "perhaps it would be more enlightening if *you* made the introductions."

"I thought you'd met in Beirut," she said. "Sabir Nuri Pasha."

"You will forgive us if we failed to introduce ourselves properly at that time," Sabir said. "Names are a luxury we cannot always afford."

"I quite understand," Quisette said, his annoyance obvious to Katherine. "Please, be seated. May I offer you some refreshment? Something cool to drink?"

"Thank you, no. Time is also a luxury, *monsieur*. Our business will be brief and to the point."

the GOLD Covenant

The two men seated themselves opposite Katherine and Quisette. They sat stiffly on the edge of the cushions, backs straight, as if to counteract the passivity of the room. Sabir spoke first, going directly to the point.

"If, as you suggest," he said, "this expedition is academic in nature, then you must have a plan indicating a specific goal."

Quisette reached for a folder on the coffee table. "I believe this will answer all questions in regard to that." He handed the older man a sheaf of documents. "Our plans for the expedition must seem rushed or haphazard to you, but, I assure you, they're not. As you know, Katherine is familiar with the area. Neither she nor I suffer from false illusions nor unrealistic expectations. Her major concern is to lay to rest that debt to her father, to his work and to his memory."

Sabir gave the documents a cursory reading before handing them to Lieutenant Raza. "This so-called attention to the plight of our people that you propose to air to the world," he said, with sardonic humor. "In what manner would you undertake to accomplish such a monumental feat?"

Quisette mumbled, paused, reached for his handkerchief and pressed it against his mouth. The preventative action did nothing to stifle the coughing spell which erupted in spasms, shaking his entire body. When he recovered, his voice had regained its confidence. "There is interest in many areas, several magazines of international stature as well as a prestigious television show—a program produced in the United States. Perhaps you're acquainted with *Power Line?*"

Katherine was stunned. *Power Line.* Why had he picked that show? It couldn't be coincidence. They'd sent her to London on the simple matter of recruiting Sheppard Wilde, paying her far more than the job was worth; yet, the thought was ludicrous—that *Power Line* could have any connection with a man like Quisette. Lawrence Halvern had seemed straight. He'd also been the one to put her in contact with Hugh Kimball, and it was her appointment with Kimball that had led her to Quisette.

"You have influence with these people?" Sabir was saying.

"I've talked to them. They'll buy it, if the material is accurate, exciting, and timely."

"And commercial," Sabir added with an ironic smile. He sat back on the divan, his posture relaxed as he continued. "They will use such phrases as *unwavering dedication to freedom, heroic men and women in an heroic struggle,* and *the brave symbol of all oppressed people throughout history.*" Sabir made a dramatic mockery of his words. "Then, one week later they will be speaking of our enemies in the same terms. I am familiar with such programs and such expediencies."

the **GOLD** Covenant

"It may seem ignoble to you," Quisette replied, "but, you must admit, such commercialism does serve a purpose. Without it there would be no supplies, no arms, no guns, no ammunition, no support of any kind with which to fight your war."

"Hah!" the younger man, Lieutenant Raza, exploded. "I shall tell you something, my friend, the Kurd has learned to live without. We fight now as we have always fought—without supplies, without arms, without guns, without ammunition," he paused for emphasis, "without support. The Kurd has no friends."

"In spite of that," Katherine said, "*the tree will last forever.*"

Sabir looked hard at her, then suddenly laughed. "You are right," he said, "but *only if the worm cometh not from within.*" He turned to Quisette and asked, "You are familiar with the proverbs of my people?"

"No. My background is not as rounded as Katherine's, regrettably," he said, his manner suddenly petulant as he turned to Raza. "If you'll forgive my contradiction, Lieutenant, I would remind you that Katherine's father has been a friend of the Kurds as well as of Sabir Nuri Pasha for a longer time than you can remember."

Sabir raised a hand, silencing Raza before another outburst. "This journey. Is it so important?" he asked Katherine. "Is it not a need that can be satisfied in some other way?"

"It is important," she said. "Please, believe me."

He studied her, intently. "Very well. The difficulty is unimportant so long as it is the right way."

"I can't promise you that it is," she said. "I just don't know any other way."

"I think our business here is at an end."

Quisette's face mirrored his disappointment. "Does this mean you refuse our request? You refuse to honor your friendship for Gustav Nikulasson, a man who has always remained loyal to the Kurdish people?"

"Sabir Nuri Pasha does not need a lesson in honor," Raza said, angrily. His steel-gray eyes narrowed when he spoke. "Nor does he fail to understand the truth when he hears it."

"Of course not," Quisette said, flustered. "Then you do intend to help—"

Interrupting with a wave of his hand, Sabir said, "Let's dispense with the lies, *monsieur*. I do not exist in a vacuum. The circumstances of David Forster's murder and Katherine's simultaneous departure from London are not coincidence. I do not believe Katherine left London of her own accord. I know her well enough to be certain you could not use her in this scheme of yours unless you held a substantial threat over her and, quite possibly, over me and my people. Now, it is time you clarified the details."

"Very well." Quisette seemed relieved to drop the

the **GOLD** *Covenant*

pretense. "It's quite simple really. You're protecting something of great value, something in which I have a particular interest. There is good reason why you would prefer to keep this something from becoming public knowledge. Now, let's say, as a matter of conjecture, the Turkish authorities should be apprised of this thing of value and your reluctance to share it with them. What do you think their reaction would be?"

"Go on." Sabir's voice was seething.

"We both know the answer, so let's look at it from another viewpoint, a more practical one, based on a sharing of assets. You have something I want. I have the power to prevent something you do *not* want. A fair trade, don't you think?"

"What exactly do you want?"

"A look at the assets—not only without interference but with your blessing. I want a free choice of whatever I can transport in one load of the Gulfstream's cargo compartment."

"After which—?"

"After which, we dissolve our partnership as though it never existed, leaving you free to carry on as before—in perfect security."

"Why should I believe you have the power to cause this thing that I do not want?"

"Whether you believe or not is immaterial. The fact is I do." Quisette reached for the file again. He extracted an envelope which he offered to Sabir. "This is a copy of an identical document which is in the possession of a most reliable colleague. He is not now, nor has he ever been, connected with my business so, you see, it would be fruitless to try to find him. I think you're familiar with the name on the envelope, the man to whom it's addressed."

Sabir glanced at the name of the Turkish official. Without comment, he pulled out the letter. When he finished reading, he tossed the letter on the table as though it were a piece of contaminated waste. "So, you have the location," he said, stiffening. "If you are denied your wishes, the Kurdish people lose what is rightfully theirs. In the process of losing what is rightfully theirs, they lose their lives as well."

"What I am offering, Sabir Pasha, is a peaceful alternative."

Sabir rose from the divan. "You will be ready to leave at a moment's notice," he said, "your plane fueled, your pilot standing by. You will tell no one where you are going. You will bring only the barest essentials—bedroll, soap, toothbrush, comb, razor, one change of clothing—all rolled into packs which you will each carry for yourselves. You will have no more than two companions, beside yourself and Katherine, and one pilot. I will supply the other. The flight plan and destination will be provided after take-off." He did not wait for a response. With, Lieutenant Raza following on his heels,

the GOLD Covenant

Sabir was gone.

Quisette settled back, visibly elated by the outcome. With a motion, he dismissed Katherine who walked back to her new quarters filled with apprehension. What seemed at the moment to be a reprieve for all of them could change at Quisette's slightest whim. He was not a man to abide by his word. He'd given her proof enough of that. She had to talk to Sabir. He needed to know more about Quisette—needed to have a better chance than David Forster.

CHAPTER 24

Besieged with the endless set-backs of the past five days, Wilde was in a vile humor. The dark mood persisted in spite of his attempt to sweat out his frustration in the fields at Stowesbridge. Patience was a requisite of his work, but this was different. It was inactivity that magnified his helplessness and the realization that this time, unlike other times, he would not be able to bear the failure. This time, it was Katherine's life at stake.

Blaming himself was easy—he'd let the affair get out of hand—but there was nothing useful in dwelling on the fact. It had all been so simple in the beginning, just a promise to a friend, made in good faith, a promise Wilde now regretted more than anything he'd ever done. At the time it was made, the promise had seemed inconsequential. It was highly improbable the circumstance which would necessitate its fulfillment would

the **GOLD** *Covenant*

ever occur. Unfortunately, it did occur—with Gustav's death. Under the terms of their agreement, the details of his death had to be kept secret even from his own daughter. Wilde hadn't liked doing that, both for the pain it had caused Katherine as well as for the mistrust that caused the gulf between them.

There seemed always to be something between them—age, pride, distance, another man—yet she'd continued to occupy his thoughts over all those years. It was something he'd never understood, but then what man ever understands the chemical element that draws him to one woman and repels him from another. His misfortune was in timing. It had never been right. Even in Gstaad—when he'd thought everything was as perfect as it ever could be—when she was too young and yet, in some ways, so much older than he.

Her first time on skis and she was terrible at it. No coordination, she'd said. They'd found other things to do—indoors—where her coordination had been spectacular.

But it was more. It was knowing he'd never be satisfied with anyone else. Never be whole.

Then she'd left. God! He'd never been so angry with anyone for being so bloody stupid. She hadn't trusted herself. Hadn't trusted him. He'd never have her until she did—with no help from him. That's why he'd let her go.

Now he'd lost her again. Before he'd had a chance

to tell her that nothing had changed, she'd been caught up in the terrible machinery of his own making. Now, here he was, incapable of finding her, let alone pulling her out. Every informational resource at his disposal had been exhausted.

After the initial investigation of David's death and Kat's disappearance, Superintendent Hopkins had been assigned both cases on the assumption those crimes were connected with the murder of Evan Babcock at Stowesbridge. His progress had been no better than Wilde's. The descriptions of the murderer-kidnapper, made by guests at the Lewellyn reception, had varied to an extent that made anyone from Wilde to Katherine, herself, a suspect. That fact, as well as Wilde's disappearance before the arrival of the police, had done little to ingratiate him with the superintendent or the Yard.

The murder of Ernest Gehreich—thanks to Kimball's anonymous report—had been tied to another case with a more closely related M.O., the recent unsolved murder of a gold smuggler, an unidentified corpse minus head. If not for Kimball's precautionary measure, Wilde may not have been temporarily cleared in the Forster-Babcock investigation. He would certainly have been more than just one of the suspects near the top of Hopkin's list.

Both Hugh Kimball and Hareb Kassem had come up with zeros in the inquiries on Gehreich. He was what he appeared to be: a disenchanted, self-serving operative

the **GOLD** *Covenant*

who had been trying to turn a greased palm into a fistful of gold, and who had been permanently burned in the process. His association with *Power Line* had been legitimate; what he did with it had not. For some unclear reason, Kat had become entangled in the mess Gehreich had created.

Wilde's first break came on the fifth day, from an unexpected source. It was late afternoon when he returned from the fields, grimy and in need of a cold shower. He entered the back door, detoured through the kitchen for a drink of water, and then went out to the front hall to pick up his mail. Mrs. Short had just hung up the phone when she saw him.

"If I'd only known you were 'ere," she said, looking extremely distressed.

Wilde's pulse quickened with the prospect of news. He took the message from her and read it as she continued.

" 'E said it was urgent—about Miss Katherine. Said you was to call 'im the moment you came in."

"Sabir Nuri Pasha," he said, looking at the name on the paper while trying to check his optimism. He'd already spoken to Sabir, the day after Kat disappeared. As with every other inquiry, he'd learned nothing. He didn't want his hopes to get out of hand when it was more than likely Sabir was calling for a progress report rather than with any new bit of information.

"You're certain he said *urgent*, Mrs. Short?" Wilde

asked as he dialed the number.

"Indeed, 'e did, sir. 'E said it plain and clear." She stood by, anxiously fussing with her apron and using it to dust off the spotless banister. "Do you suppose 'e's found Miss Katherine? I wisht I'd 'ave known you were in the 'ouse, I'd never 'ave—"

He nodded at Mrs. Short who looked relieved, straightened her apron and scurried back to the kitchen. "Hello. . . . Sabir Pasha? Is he there? This is Wilde, Sheppard Wilde. . . ."

After a moment he heard the booming voice of Sabir. "Wilde . . ." a voice boomed from the receiver, ". . . How soon can you get to Athens?"

"Four, maybe five hours—depends on the weather. What's happened, Sabir?"

"I have seen her—Katherine—talked to her. She is held by a man named Enrique Quisette—on his yacht, *Zereda*, in Piraeus."

"Make it three-and-a-half, and damn the weather."

"Listen to me, Sheppard. You cannot go after her until we talk. She is hostage. You must know the terms. This Enrique Quisette—do you know his reputation?"

"I've heard the name. He used to be one of the most successful art smugglers in the business, but he was taken out of circulation about two or three years ago."

"Yes, he spent a year in prison. He used the time well. He is not only—as you say—back in circulation,

the **GOLD** Covenant

my friend, but with a great many more greased palms at his disposal. That is why it is vital you stay away from the *Zereda* until we've talked. You must promise me, Sheppard. There is more than Katherine's life at risk."

"How did she look? Are they treating her all right?"

"Her eyes have some fear, but, as I could not speak with her in private, it is difficult to say for what exact reason the fear exists. I think, if we do not do anything stupid, she is safe for the present."

"Where do I find you?"

"Attica Palace Hotel. Sheppard, there's something else, before you leave England . . ."

Harry Franco skidded through the round-about, then floored the accelerator as he hit the final turn onto the M3 motorway. Oblivious of the speed, Wilde sat in the front passenger seat trying to get through to Hareb Kassem before they reached the airport. He'd been trying from the time he'd hung up the phone with Sabir until now.

Jamil Taha answered again with the same information. Kassem was unavailable at the moment, would call as soon as was possible. Jamil would be most happy to convey any messages.

Wilde's answer remained the same. "I'll convey the message myself. Tell Kassem to keep his phone in

roberta clark

reach. I'll get back to him in three hours." With that, he dropped the receiver, sat back, and closed his eyes. In three hours he'd be fifteen-hundred miles closer to Katherine . . .

CHAPTER 25

Katherine spent the next day in relative freedom. She was allowed on deck but only in the aft lounge area, with Kenneth never more than a few paces away. The only place she could escape the omnipresent shadow was in her stateroom, but after the long days of enforced confinement she had no desire to lock herself away willingly.

Quisette had not made an appearance on deck since the previous afternoon. It would have been the preferred *status in quo* if there hadn't been a noticeable increase of activity aboard the *Zereda* throughout the day. Meetings had been taking place in one of the salons. She didn't have to be there to know what was primary on the agenda; however, she would have leaped at the chance to hear the details.

The pilot, who'd flown them from England to Athens, arrived early, had a brief meeting with Quisette, then left in the helicopter. A short time later, he returned with a passenger-load of five men. From her vantage point on the afterdeck, Katherine watched them move from the landing pad, down the ladder, and along the passageway to the forward salon. The two men who brought up the rear—both conspicuously armed—had a military bearing but wore civilian clothing. The men who preceded them were dressed similarly in stiff dark suits, but carried briefcases instead of arms. Leading the contingent with long purposeful strides was a fifth man whose presence was riveting. He stood a head taller than the others, even without the addition of his black-tasseled maroon fez. Between his dark glasses and his salted-black beard, his nose was like a blade making a diagonal slash across the center of his face.

All five men remained closeted with Quisette for several hours. In the early afternoon they emerged from the salon and climbed up to the helicopter pad from which they were ferried back to Piraeus or points beyond. She knew with absolute conviction she would see them again.

Just after dark, she retired to her room but was unable to sleep. She had lain in bed reading for about an hour when she heard the launch pull alongside. It was im-

the **GOLD** *Covenant*

possible to see through the open porthole, but she could hear the boarding ladder being lowered, followed by the unmistakable sound of Sabir's voice. They were leaving tonight—she was sure of it. She was dressed and ready when Pavlos knocked on her stateroom door.

Sabir Nuri Pasha was waiting in the aft salon with Lieutenant Raza. The lieutenant was outfitted like a Hollywood extra, straight out of a flick on WWI fliers. His leather jacket was cracked and soft with age, a white silk scarf was tucked neatly inside of his open shirt collar, and a pair of goggle-like glasses hung from a black cord around his neck. The only thing missing was the leather helmet. Both men stood when Katherine entered, followed by Kenneth and Pavlos. Ignoring the bodyguards, Sabir greeted Katherine warmly, relieving her of her pack before grasping her hand in his.

"There is much risk in this," he said. "Can we not dissuade *Monsieur* Quisette from taking you with us?"

"I don't think it's possible," Katherine replied. "Even if it were, I couldn't be the cause of bringing you into this, then leave you to face it alone."

Just outside, Quisette issued last minute orders to the ship's captain. When they'd finished, he strode into the salon, clearly pleased with himself.

"I'm impressed with how quickly you act, Sabir Pasha," he said. "It's my hope you might reflect on the advantage of extending our partnership beyond the present contract."

"Rest assured, my reflections encompass all possibilities."

"I'm happy to hear it. I believe you met Mr. Farr and Mr. Xenides last night. They'll be traveling with us."

"Your preparations are in order then?" Sabir asked, without a glance at the men. "In my country, a man who needs more than a moment to pick up his feet will reach eternity in less."

"In that case," Quisette replied, "we shall try not to lag."

"I did not mention yesterday that Lieutenant Raza must pilot the plane after a certain point of departure."

"But I have my own pilot, Douglas Sanger. Mr. Xenides acts as co-pilot. They're both well-qualified and experienced."

"No question," Sabir said. "But, in what capacity?"

"It's a short hop," Quisette insisted, "a matter of three or four hours, at most. I see no need for another pilot."

"I'm sure your men are expert, having been trained in the rigorous field of smuggling; however, this area is not a common route of smugglers. It requires a knowledge beyond the ordinary if we are to go unnoticed. As you know, we must fly beneath the radar fields. For that, we must have someone at the controls who knows the topography as well as he knows his own face. Not only is Lieutenant Raza an excellent pilot—trained by courtesy

the **GOLD** *Covenant*

of the Iranian Air force—but he is also familiar with the height of every chimney, of every tree, every rock, every mountain. Our safety, my friend, depends on those irreplaceable talents—"

Sabir was cut off by the noisy roar of an engine as the salon door opened and Quisette's pilot entered the room.

"Are we ready?" Quisette asked. The pilot, Douglas Sanger, nodded to Quisette who turned to Sabir. "Raza can act as co-pilot and navigator. Is that satisfactory?"

Sabir raised both hands in a gesture of acquiescence. "The question will settle itself when Mr. Sanger is faced with the realities of the flight," he said.

"They're ready on the other end as well, sir," Sanger said. "I've just spoken to control."

"We'll be right along."

Sanger seemed fit in body but his face was gaunt to the point of dehydration which made him appear even smaller than his average height. He glared at Lieutenant Raza, raking him over with overt distaste. Raza touched his forehead in a casual salute as Sanger brushed by him.

Quisette motioned for his men to follow. Pavlos reached for Katherine's pack but she shook her head. "Carry our own," she said. "Requirement of the trip, wasn't it?" Slinging the pack over her shoulder, she followed the others.

roberta clark

The vintage-aged Gulfstream II was in mint-condition, custom-tailored for Quisette's business: long range capability at moderate speeds, drab matte-gray exterior for low visibility from land or air, and—as Sabir was assured earlier—modified for short distance landing and take-off, a vital requirement for their destination.

Immediately after transferring from the helicopter, they were given clearance by the control tower. Twenty minutes from the time they left the ship in Piraeus, they were airborne over the Aegean Sea with Sanger at the controls. Thirty minutes later they would put down at a small landing field on the island of Kasos. That was as far as the approved flight plan would take them. Officially, they would be vacationing on Kasos for an indefinite time. In actuality, they were off again within the hour—without a registered flight plan, Mohsen Raza at the controls, heading east toward the southern border of Turkey.

Katherine flicked off her overhead light and stared out into the darkness below. The water was rough, the wind splintering the seas and scattering them in patches of fluorescent spume. Sabir hadn't exaggerated when he said they'd be cruising at extremely low altitudes the rest of the way. She hoped he also hadn't exaggerated Mohsen Raza's talents.

the **GOLD** *Covenant*

In contrast to the drab exterior of the plane, the interior was bright and luxurious. The forward lounge they occupied was fitted with club chairs, tables, and a bar; the aft lounge with another grouping of club chairs and a desk-office. The rear of the plane was furnished with a galley, lavatory, and sleeping berth. The entire cabin was aromatized with the herb tea Kenneth had brewed in the galley. After delivering a steaming mug to Quisette, he moved back to his seat across from the big Greek.

Quisette bent over the aromatic steam. "You should have some," he said to Katherine while inhaling the vapors. "It would relax you."

"I'm not sure I want to relax."

Sabir's gray eyes showed concern. "You look tired. You will need rest before we reach our destination."

"If you want to use the berth," Quisette said, "you'll find it quite comfortable. No one will disturb you until we land."

"Maybe later. I'm much too wide awake right now." She picked up a magazine and turned on her overhead light.

"Women are stubborn creatures," Quisette said. "I've yet to meet one who knows what's good for her. They have no natural instinct for survival."

"You haven't met *our* women, *monsieur*. They not only know how to survive, but they are instrumental in the survival of our men. I think you will find Katherine no different. Now, let me ask why you insist on bringing her with us? I can see no reason for it in the terms of our contract."

"My dear Pasha, if given the choice, she would insist on being with us, isn't that right, Katherine?"

She looked up without answering. There was nothing to be gained by allowing him to drag her into the pointless discussion.

"Is that your reason for bringing her?" Sabir persisted. "Because she would insist? It is said that a man who is ruled by a woman is but a flavorless mouse in the jaws of an unsatisfied cat."

Katherine couldn't contain her laughter, although she tried to bury it behind the magazine.

"The reason she is here," Quisette snapped, giving her an infuriated glance, "is that I see fit to bring her."

Sabir smiled and shrugged his shoulders. "Are you acquainted with our country, *monsieur*?"

"As much as anyone."

"Ah, then, not at all!"

Quisette laughed himself at the less personal jibe. "I expect to become well-acquainted with it on this trip," he said.

"In only one trip? After many years, my own children and grandchildren have yet to learn its essence."

"How many children do you have?"

"I have three sons and a daughter. Not many, but

enough to fill the house with grandchildren," Sabir said with pride. "The son of my daughter, Zarif, will follow in my steps someday. He has that rare quality of leadership that comes to only a few."

"I find children to be a nuisance. Except in rare cases, they are microcosms of every weakness of the human race."

"Were you one of those rare exceptions?" Katherine asked.

"Of course," he said, without hesitation. "One cannot possess uniqueness without recognizing it—*and* the lack of it in others. I had no more toleration of children as a child than I do now as an adult."

"It is my experience," Sabir said, "that, like adults, children who set themselves apart are often unhappy in their own company."

Quisette made a sound somewhere between a cough and a snort. "You make elementary Freudian assumptions, my dear Pasha. All I've done is to state a fact. Children prattle of nothing, laugh at anything. They cry as a matter of coercion. In my opinion, the creatures have no more place in a house than livestock. They should be quarantined until they reach maturity."

"You're certainly eloquent on the subject," Katherine said. "Tell us, as a rare specimen, did you find yourself isolated or were you first choice on everyone's team."

"Judging by the sharpness of your tongue, you were

probably, as a child, a prime example of what I'm talking about. In actual fact, one needn't *like* children to raise them properly. It's a simple matter of discipline, and making the proper distribution of assets at the proper time. I suspect most parents abhor their children. I, for one, don't find that fact particularly shocking." Quisette waved off the subject with a flip of his hand. "For myself, I prefer to leave their breeding to those who lack the imagination for more stimulating occupations."

"A strange attitude," Sabir said. "I would find it unnatural *not* to feel affection for the children who are, after all, the future—the reason we work, fight, and care whether our enemies prevail."

"The future? Nonsense!" Quisette said. "There is no future beyond ourselves. Everything ends with me, just as it does with you, my friend. The concept of a future beyond ourselves is self-deception, designed to enslave and empower one over another. It causes men to grub for pennies, for vague promise of rewards they never see, all for the benefit of offspring who will someday regard them as nothing more than compost."

"You have the wisdom of a sophist. You forget, the compost of which you speak—that which is of blood and bones—is both necessary and beneficial. From it everything else grows. Freedom, for example. If I do not live to see the freedom of my own people, then I pray my children do, and that they remember those who nour-

the **GOLD** *Covenant*

ished it with their bodies and made it possible."

"I'm certain they'll remember you, Sabir Pasha," Quisette said, a tone of condescension creeping into his voice. "You're already a legend. People need heroes and heroic philosophies to keep them functioning."

"Your words have the sound of cynicism."

"I find nothing wrong with being honest—or cynical, for that matter—on a subject about which most people are hypocritical."

"It would be better to be neither honest nor cynical." Sabir smiled at Quisette, the picture of affability. "You see, *monsieur*, I have the advantage of years, and the years have taught me that cynicism is nothing more than a loss of faith caused by one's own inadequacies. Honesty of opinion is often confused with the ignorance and cruelty of prejudice."

"I find your viewpoint quaint, unrelated to the times. Both cynicism and prejudice are the outgrowth of truth—of reality, my dear Pasha. Contrary to what you say, idealism creates inadequacy, which ultimately leads to failure."

The conversation was doing little to strengthen Katherine's hope either she or Sabir had any future beyond the next few days. She laid the magazine aside, unbuckled her seatbelt and stood. "It's a woman's philosophy of expediency to avoid the controversies of men," she said. "I think I'll have a look at where we're going."

"A nap would be more sensible," Quisette snapped, making it sound like an order.

"I'll sleep better when I know Mohsen Raza is as good a flyer as Sabir Pasha says he is."

CHAPTER 26

Douglas Sanger slid from his seat in the cockpit. "Be my guest," he told Katherine.

She slipped in beside Lieutenant Raza, who had been at the controls since they took off from the Island of Kasos. Sanger slumped into the jump-seat directly behind them, pulled a thermos from underneath, and poured himself a drink which smelled like whiskey lightly laced with coffee. Although he seemed content—relieved of duty and the immediate company of Raza—he showed no inclination to move out of earshot.

Katherine relaxed, allowing her gaze to scan the hundred-and-eighty degree expanse of window in front of her. Her intake of breath was a clearly audible reflex. Beneath them, hurtling past at a dizzying speed, were brilliant streaks of light, diamond-like facets of moonlight shooting at them from the surface of the sea. She felt as if she could reach down and shear off the crests of the waves with her hand. It was like nothing she'd ever experienced before, nothing like the view from those little portholes in the passenger compartment. There was no motion. Only frightening proximity, speed, and exhilarating vulnerability.

"Do you ever get used to it?" she asked.

"Not so complicated." The lieutenant swept an eye over the array of instruments. "These babies pretty near do everything for you."

"I meant the view."

"Oh, that. Never," he laughed. Then, glancing at her out of the corner of his eye, he added, "Well, maybe enough so breathing stays more steady."

"Will it distract you if I talk to you, Lieutenant Raza?"

"Name's Mohsen! And I like company. Your kind! Makes me sharp, you know?" His grin revealed a row of teeth that looked like they were auditioning for a commercial. "I'm a naturally-born show-off. Prettier the lady, better I perform."

Katherine laughed. "It's beautiful," she said. "Nothing like the view from back there."

"You like it? Me, too." His phrases were short and punctuated with pauses that invited interruption. "It's the moonlight. Never fly without it. We're off the record, you know? Invisible. Like that guy in the book, only, in our case, it's a plane. Bigger worry, don't you think?"

"Do you ever get lost?"

He laughed and waved a hand at the elaborate instrument panel. "Difficult to get lost. Look at the radar there. See that spot? Cyprus. And that one? Headland at Anamur. It's like road map. Easier every time. We come off Kasos, head northeast for Rhodes. Then it's due east, past Antalya Korfezi—Gulf of Adalia to you—and, in about ten minutes, we pick up headland at Anamur—right there." He pointed to one of the shapes on the radar screen. "That's when we look for Musa Dagh—dead ahead. Very famous mountain, Musa Dagh. You know it?"

"I've read the book."

"Hey! Pretty good. Me, too." He flashed his spectacular smile. "You're going to see plenty mountains this trip. Best way to be invisible. I fly them like roller coaster."

Behind them Sanger grunted, "And probably get us all killed." Then, not quite under his breath, he added, "Fuckin' towel-head, A-rab hot-dogger."

Katherine looked at Mohsen, wondering if he would react to the slur. His pleasant face remained impassive but his hands tightened on the controls. His eyes were glued to the attitude indicator. Suddenly, and very smoothly, he pulled back on the control yoke and snapped a hard left. The plane nosed up twenty degrees, then rolled over like a puppy. Sky, water, moon, stars, everything before them spun three-hundred-sixty degrees.

Behind them, Sanger was caught off-guard. He

grabbed for support, letting go his cup which hit the floor of the cabin in a spray of liquid and fumes. The thermos rolled into the cockpit, where Mohsen retrieved it and tucked it into a corner. There were no audible comments from the area of the jump-seat. Katherine thought it best not to inquire about Sanger's loss. It had—she was sure—been a loss of more than a cup of whiskey-laced coffee.

Mohsen was not so politic. "Amazing affect the alcohol has on the coordination," he said, winking at Katherine, "and the mouth. Some men have no idea how to talk when lady is present."

With the altitude indicator riding the horizon again, Mohsen's hands relaxed a little on the control yoke. Katherine reached down for her seatbelt, just realizing it hadn't been fastened. "Amazing!" she said. "I would have thought we'd all be on the ceiling."

"Centrifugal force. Pretty good, huh? Any time you like to go 'round again, you let me know, okay?"

"Thanks," she said, fastening the belt. "That'll do for awhile."

"You got to fly these planes, you know?" Mohsen said, his voice becoming intense. "I mean, really fly them. You got to feel them in your hands. You can't flip auto pilot switch and sit like fat sultan. If you don't want trouble, you got to read this baby. Like a woman, she doesn't always say what she means. If you want to stay

the **GOLD** *Covenant*

out of trouble, you got to know what she means. You got to know what she feels, what she thinks, and how you gonna do that, huh? Only one way. You got to hold her, that's how. You got to have your hands on her. You know what I mean?"

"I know."

It works the other way, too, Katherine thought. John never talked about his pain, but she could feel it through his hands, his touch, until the time he stopped holding her because the pain was all that was left.

Why think about that now? Why remember the pain? Why not the way he'd been before? Before they'd stopped seeing people, stopped walking on beaches, stopped all the for-granted things? Why not remember the strength in his hands, not just the affection or the love, but the way they could make you feel, the way they could tell you how he felt?

And Shep, all those years before. Why hadn't she believed what she felt then? Why hadn't she trusted? Why had she stopped the holding? So easy to grow apart when the touching stops. It isn't something planned, it just happens.

"You know Sabir Pasha a long time?" Mohsen asked.

"Since I was a child."

"Me also. I am Persian, but I am raised as Kurd. In my heart I am Kurd. Very difficult to change the heart. Look," he pointed to the radar screen, "ten minutes, then you see it down there. Euphrates. Very big river. Like Mississippi, huh?"

She glanced at the screen, then looked up again. Suddenly, the moonlight vanished. She saw a huge mass rushing toward them, filling the entire window frame with darkness.

"Musa Dagh," he said.

"Musa Dagh," she whispered, not even realizing she'd spoken. The sea fell away beneath them and they were climbing. Her scalp was taut, hands gripping the edge of the seat trying unconsciously to lift the plane over the crest. Then, in a burst of stars and sky, they broke clear. Her heart and stomach were all mixed up somewhere in the vicinity of her throat, but she began to breathe again, unaware she'd ever stopped. "My God," she said. "I've never been so thrilled or scared in my entire life."

"You like it, huh? Maybe I teach you how to fly before we get there."

"Why not?" Katherine said, smiling at the wry look on his face.

He continued to chuckle at the idea while he scanned the instrument panel. Minutes later, they had leveled off, returned to an altitude where shadows whipped by like pieces of exploding shard.

She could almost feel the brush of the great peaks as the plane slid into the protective folds of the mountains.

the **GOLD** Covenant

The forward lounge was dark. Enrique and Sabir lay in a disharmonious chorus of soft snores, propped by banks of pillows in their reclining club chairs. Two overhead lights flickered in the aft compartment, guiding Katherine from the cockpit where she'd spent the last hour and a half. It was the most exhilarating time she'd had in years, doing more to revive her than any amount of restless sleep could have done.

Pavlos sat beneath one of the lights, reading the latest edition of *La Monde*, Kenneth under the other, asleep with one hand supported in the sling of his shoulder holster. She settled in a chair across the aisle from Pavlos.

"We're gone two, maybe two and a half hours," he said, looking up from his magazine. "We should be coming in soon, eh?"

"That's why I came back. According to Lieutenant Raza, we should sight the field within ten minutes."

"Hah! I like to know where that is," he laughed. "These fellows do not bother much with details."

"He seems to know what he's doing."

"You betcha. He's got good team. Some peasants burning cow dung next to dirt strip on top of plateau which is somewhere in Zagros Mountains and which they give us fifteen, maybe twenty minutes to find. Pretty good arrangement for landing fancy jet planes, eh?"

"And if we don't find them?"

Pavlos shrugged his massive shoulders and made a diving motion with one flat hand into the other. "Your friend Sabir makes no room for—how you say it?—fuck up!" When Katherine reached down to fasten her seatbelt, the big man laughed, nodding his approval. "Even the fatalist is cautious," he said, then fastened his own belt. "That Raza fellow—Mohsen—he flies like a jack rabbit with wings. I think maybe is no reason to worry so much. Maybe we come down like so, eh?" He made a smooth palm-down landing on top of *La Monde*.

"Why do you work for Quisette?"

The big man's expression went, in seconds, from surprise to amusement, to reflection to resignation. "Why does any man work? To have money in his pocket, to keep peace in his house, to feed his children, to drink, to entertain women. Who knows? You think I am different than these?" He nodded at Kenneth.

"Just a stray hope . . ."

"You think blood money, eh? Maybe so." He shrugged with a broad grin. "Or maybe, if you are born where I am born, you will not be so—how do you say it?—squeamish. In my village, you work twenty years, you save enough to buy a television. For Quisette, you work ten years, you save enough to buy the village."

"Is that what you plan to do?"

"Is not such a bad plan, eh?"

"Either way, you'll end up watching television," Katherine said. "I wonder if you'll enjoy it more than the man who waited twenty years."

"You think I am bad fellow, eh? Maybe so." He shrugged again, turned off the two overhead lights, then raised the shade on his window. Outside was nothing but darkness.

When Katherine settled back in her seat, she picked up the discarded magazine and tried to convince herself Pavlos had been exaggerating the slim margin for error. When the big Greek's breathing fell into the same rhythmic pattern as the other's, she flicked off her own light, raised the shade, and peered out into the night. Almost as if on cue, she was aware of a change in speed. Seconds later, she felt a jolt of land under the wheels.

The others, jarred awake at the first touch, were at the windows of the forward lounge, watching the eerie flicker of lights rush past as the plane bounced to a stop. Outside, along the edge of the field, vague shadows of figures were visible in the glow of flames shooting skyward from a row of oil drums. One by one, the fires were being extinguished.

Sabir was the first to release his safety belt. He moved to the aft cabin where Katherine was sitting. "The journey will be good." He clasped her hand. "God is with us."

"I hope you're right," she said. "We can use the help."

Sabir replied in Kurdish and gave her a reassuring smile which she found anything but reassuring. Not only was she unable to understand his words, she was also frustrated there was never a chance to speak with him alone. Quisette had made it clear she would lose her relative freedom if she didn't behave. Kenneth and Pavlos were there as constant reminders.

"Come. It's more comfortable up there," Sabir said. "We must wait until they cover the landing strip before we leave."

They both moved to the forward lounge, where Mohsen had just emerged from the cockpit. He nodded to both of them, flashing Katherine a *thumbs up* before heading aft to the luggage compartment. He was followed immediately by Pavlos. Quisette, who'd been talking to Douglas Sanger, dismissed him and turned his attention back to them.

He seemed elated, his pale skin flushed, his voice excited as he said, "I congratulate you, Sabir Pasha. You are a man of your word. Your efficiency is most impressive."

"It is one's choice of allies that makes it seem so. Do you understand Kurdish, *monsieur*?"

"I'm afraid not," Quisette said. "It's not what I consider a useful language."

"We have a saying, *Bezin be pieh kho, Me shin be pieh kho*."

"And the translation?"

the **GOLD** Covenant

"The idiom does not do well in the English," Sabir explained. "It is merely a tradition when one enters the land."

Katherine had recognized one word, *goat*. Whatever Sabir had said had nothing to do with tradition, of that she was certain.

CHAPTER 27

What they called a landing strip consisted of three-quarters of a mile of unpaved rock and shale situated on a high plateau in the Zagros Mountains. The sharp snow-topped ranges of the Zagros sprawled across southeastern Turkey, northeastern Iraq, and the western rim of Iran with no respect for the sanctity of borders. Pale pre-dawn light had just begun to tinge the sky, turning it translucent, making the barren terrain appear even more forbidding than it had been in the darkness.

After five minutes of waiting, a shrill whistle from outside, signaled all clear. They moved out of the plane, Katherine following Sabir Pasha with Quisette close behind her. The air still reeked of smoke from the beacon fires though all of them had been extinguished after they'd touched down. Ashes, carried by the gusty winds like gray snowflakes, settled on their clothing and in their hair, filling their mouths with the taste of carbon. Mohsen and Pavlos kicked up even more dust at the rear of the plane as they unloaded the baggage compartment, tossing the gear onto the barren ground.

With work on the air strip completed, the band of ten or so rebels congregated near the plane. Most of them were no more than dimly-defined figures in the darkness. The few nearest the bottom of the ladder were touched by the light of hand-held torches. Their features were cut from the darkness in harsh lines and angles; their faces burnt-umber, the ingrained hue of men who live and work without shelter. Their draped turbans, shirts, and jackets, slept-in, hand-wrung, were lined with creases. Some of the woolen jackets and double-breasted tunics were belted with ammunition clips, others tied with bright sashes. Here and there, the hilt of a dagger was visible in the folds of cloth. Their trousers were rough woven, striped, full at the waist, pegged inside heavy woolen socks and boots. Each had a rifle slung over his shoulder.

In the eerie shadows, the men seemed fierce and threatening but the greeting they gave Sabir was warm and filled with exuberance, showing great affection as well as respect. They provided him with a rifle, an ammo belt, and a strip of cloth—his turban—which he draped around his head with practiced expertise.

Turning to Quisette, he said, "The camp is not far but

it would be well for us to leave at once. Light is our enemy and it grows quickly. My men will see that the plane is properly serviced and housed before they follow us."

"Sanger will go with them," Quisette said.

"As you wish."

At that, several of the men carrying torches led the way for the two pilots toward a nearby escarpment that seemed to thrust from the mountainside. Stopping at the center of the mound, two of the men shoved aside branches and logs. Another operated a pulley device that opened two huge doors which broke cleanly from the surrounding sod. As the men moved inside, the light of the torches revealed the interior of an enormous barn, its sides and roof supported by rough timbers. On the outside it was camouflaged with earth to look like an extension of the natural geological formation.

"It is not necessary we wait for them," Sabir said. "The fewer we are on the trail at the same time, the less noticeable we will be."

"Surely, you intend to leave someone here to guard the plane," Quisette said.

Sabir seemed amused at the thought. "If the plane is found, a guard could do little to protect it. In the words of my ancestors, 'We rely on the preserving hand of Allah'."

the **GOLD** *Covenant*

Sanger stayed at the plane with two others as a concession to Quisette's lack of faith in the *preserving hand*. The rest of them followed the rebels. The trail consisted of a series of steep and narrow hairpin cuts carved into the side of the mountain, starting with an abrupt drop at the end of the landing strip. Katherine's respect for the flying jack rabbit, Mohsen, increased even more when she realized how easily they might have overshot the field.

In the short time since they'd started, the threatening dawn hadn't materialized. The sky remained dark. Sunrise, which had just tipped the peak of the mountains, was now hidden behind a swath of roiling gray clouds. The storm moved over them quickly, without warning, bringing first a bitter wind followed by cold, biting rain. They were drenched to the skin within minutes of the deluge.

What started as trickling rivulets, twisting and winding back and forth across their path, soon became full racing streams, spilling from their natural course before tumbling down the mountainside. Already slippery with rocks and loose shale, the scrubby ground was made treacherous by the torrents of water. Katherine tested her foothold with each step before trusting her weight to it. Collar raised, hunched down into her jacket, she tried to protect her wet body from the stinging wind. Her backpack was heavy with soaked clothing and gear.

roberta clark

It grated against the unhealed scratches on her neck and shoulders, a reminder of what a short space of time there was between a world of comparative sanity and this endless nightmare.

It seemed years since she'd left David Forster sitting in the safety of the Lewellyn's home. The memory of it was tainted, haunted by the man stationed behind David's chair, leaning casually on the French door, playing with the cuff of his sleeve, playing steel against light as though he held a harmless prism against his wrist. Why hadn't she yelled, caused a commotion, anything that might have stopped him? Why hadn't she even tried? Looking back on it, she'd made all the wrong choices. Looking back was always so clear.

Now Sabir and his men were being swept along, as she was, with a momentum that seemed ungovernable. Though they were armed and deep in their own territory, she couldn't believe they weren't in more danger than Sabir anticipated. The images of the men she'd seen on the *Zereda* yesterday were with her as vividly as if they stood before her now. All had the mark of professional soldier. Mercenaries. Or hired killers. Quisette's apparent vulnerability in this setting was only an illusion, like all the other illusions he'd created to mask the ferment of his sick mind.

She had to arrange, somehow, to talk to Sabir alone. He knew about David Forster's murder but not about the

the **GOLD** *Covenant*

gallery in Quisette's apartment—the decapitated head—the aberrations of insanity. Once and for all, she had to know the truth about her father's death—about Sheppard's involvement. Sabir was her only hope of that.

At the moment, she could hardly see Sabir through the sheet of rain. They were separated by Mohsen and, directly in front of her, Quisette. Quisette was struggling as hard as she was to keep his footing. Branches snapped at her from the edge of the trail as he brushed past them. She had to pace herself to avoid being hit. Her leg muscles were beginning to ache from the constant effort to keep from slipping.

After a precipitous half-mile, the trail leveled off. The slope became gentler, easier to manipulate, but narrower. She moved slowly, sliding one hand along the wall of rock on her left, the other gripping her pack to steady it, the straps adding irritating friction to the discomfort in her legs. She was trying to adjust the straps when a chunk of earth gave way under her feet. Her immediate instinct was to pull back but the ground continued to crumble in a chain reaction precipitated by the weight of Kenneth and Pavlos behind her. In a blur of motion, the three of them fell. She somersaulted, hit the ground on her back, then began to tumble, bumping over rocks, grabbing for scrub, only to have it wrenched from her hands as the weight of her body propelled her downward.

Seconds later, she slid to a stop at what seemed to be

the bottom of the mountain but was, in reality, a clump of shrub and rock on the edge of a narrow shelf. Disoriented, half-conscious, she drifted.

They ... John, Shep, and her father ... and David ... dragging her from the ruins of a plane ... have to tell them something ... tell them to run ... to leave her ... they can't hear ... won't listen ...

The insistent voice was asking, "Are you all right?" She opened her eyes to see Mohsen beside her on his knees, his face near and very serious. "Anything broken?"

Immediately, she took silent stock of herself. There were bruises but no extreme pain—nothing that would indicate a broken bone or a torn ligament. Apparently the mud had cushioned and greased the fall. She stared up at the dark eyes and tried to smile. "It's still raining," she said, thinking, *that isn't the right answer.*

"Yes." His laughter had a degree of relief in it.

"Where are the others?"

"Down there."

She followed the movement of his eyes. Twenty feet below, Kenneth was dragging himself up the slope. A few feet below him, Pavlos lay sprawled on a small ledge, conscious and groaning loudly, his head propped against the boulder that had stopped his fall.

"Looks like we need litter for that one," Mohsen said. "From size of him, team of mules would be very good idea, too, eh?" He put an arm around Katherine to

the GOLD Covenant

help her up. "Can you walk?"

Instead of using the support to pull herself up, she gripped his arm and held onto it. "I have to talk to Sabir Pasha. Can you tell him? He doesn't know how dangerous . . . He doesn't realize—"

"He knows."

"You don't understand," she said, more desperately. "He doesn't . . . he can't know. Quisette won't keep his word. Sabir shouldn't have come. You have to get him away from here."

"But you sent for him."

"I was wrong to do that. If anything happens to him—"

"If you did not write letter, do you think this Quisette would not find another way?"

"I had no right—"

"Bloody 'ell!" Kenneth bellowed at them. "What you standin' round talkin' for? Get yourself up there and get us some 'elp. Can't you see the man's busted both 'is goddamn legs?"

Before Mohsen could answer, Sabir Pasha shouted from above. "Stay where you are, we are coming down. The trail switches back below the ledge."

Mohsen helped Katherine to her feet and said, "Wait here. I find your pack, then we go down together. Okay?" As an afterthought, he turned to Kenneth and added, "Better start to look for other two packs, Mr.

Farr. Not such good idea to lose gear in place like this."

"I don't bloody take my orders from you, you little sod." Kenneth waited until Mohsen had started up the slope. Glaring with disgust at the steep mud-soaked mountainside, he moved off to the left, following the path of their fall.

After watching for a moment, Katherine decided it was foolish to stay where she was when she might be of some help below. She slid the rest of the way down, reaching Pavlos at the same time as the four men who ran the trail ahead of the others. They had pulled themselves up to the ledge and were starting to probe the damage to Pavlos' legs, when he stopped them with a howl of pained protest. They shrugged, gave up the examination, and began work on a litter. She knelt beside the big Greek, wiping away a clot of mud that had lodged on his eyelid.

He looked up at her and said, "Pretty damn fast way to travel, eh?"

"How bad is it?" she asked.

He shrugged, tried to shift himself to a more comfortable position, but the effort brought visible pain. "Maybe you think is good lesson for Pavlos, eh?"

She put her hand on his forehead. He didn't appear to be in shock although his skin was clammy.

"Let me take a look at your legs," she said.

"Not now. Too much hurt."

the **GOLD** *Covenant*

"If your legs are broken, they'll need splinting. You'll never be able to stand the ride otherwise."

"Hey! In my pack is whiskey. You find, okay? Then you send Kenneth to put on splints."

When she scrambled off to help search for the packs, Kenneth slipped back down to the ledge and worked on the big Greek to the music of his howling. The alcohol anesthesia would have to act as an after-the-fact consolation, she thought. She found both packs lodged in a cluster of scrub and boulders about half-way up the slope. There was a canteen inside one of them wrapped in a black wool sweater. A quick whiff told her the contents were whiskey. After replacing the top, she tucked it back with the sweater and hoisted the pack over one shoulder. By the time she reached Pavlos again, the others had climbed up to the ledge.

"I'll take care of that," Quisette said. He tossed the canteen to one of the men and turned back to her. "When Kenneth's finished, we're going on ahead. There'll be six men carrying the litter. They'll be moving too slowly for us."

"He needs a doctor," she said, turning to Sabir.

"We do what we can," he said. "You know doctors are a scarcity here. We live and die without them. And," he added, searching the sky, "if we do not start moving very soon, we may be close to achieving the latter."

CHAPTER 28

The sound of water was everywhere, although the rain had stopped shortly before they made the three-thousand-foot descent to the base of the plateau. Here, the valley was a comparatively lush narrow strip of land cradled in a canyon six thousand feet above sea level. The trail followed the course of a stream through the canyon and along the sheer face of rock towering above them on either side. Scattered oak thrust their limbs through the groves of walnut and fig trees, some knotted with the vines of wild grapes, all carpeted under with grass and patches of blooming scrub. The natural camouflage of branches and leaves shielded them from the stray reconnaissance flights that covered the area with unnerving irregularity.

Katherine was tired. Like a massive shadow, Kenneth Farr followed her, pushing her along with the mere proximity of his bulk. As the path meandered closer to the rocks, she stopped, suddenly, forcing him to an abrupt stop behind her.

" 'Ere. What're you doin'?" he said. "Let's move on."

When she pointed to one of the springs gushing from the wall of the mountain, he gave her a grudging nod. Silently grateful, she leaned over to take a long drink. The water tasted of the earth but it was fresh and cool as she let it trickle over her face and neck. When she looked back, it was clear why Kenneth had allowed her to stop—he needed the break himself. Far more meticulous than she was, he pulled out his crumpled handkerchief, wet it in the spring, then used it to dab at his forehead and cheeks. His fastidious motions were a clumsy imitation of Quisette's with the red silk, but the wet compress did nothing to improve the flushed puffy face or the disposition behind it. It would be easy to believe the altitude had weakened him, or that he'd suffered an injury from the fall, but Katherine knew—even if either possibility were true—it would have no effect on his adherence to duty. His thought processes were permanently programmed to accommodate Enrique Quisette's orders on demand.

Readjusting her pack, she began walking, almost closing the gap between her and the others before Kenneth's plodding footsteps caught up with her again. The group had shrunk considerably since they'd started. Six men had been left behind: four to carry Pavlos on the litter, two to test the condition of the trail or to spell the others if necessary. That left them with an escort of only two partisans. One of them led the single-filed column, followed by Sabir, Quisette, Katherine, then Kenneth, with Mohsen and the other partisan forming the rear guard.

A half mile upstream, the trail veered off into a deep gorge, protected by an overhanging limestone escarpment. The sharp-angled twists and turns made it impossible to estimate how far they'd traveled but Katherine was feeling the pace, as well as the new bruises she'd added to the fading collection of older ones. The path had not been worn by recent travel. It was paved with a slippery scree and strewn with huge boulders which years of erosion had crumbled and dislodged from the mountainside. The rock barriers were not impassable but getting over them required the full concentration of the hikers, without which an untested or unstable footing might cause a fall resulting in serious injury.

When the column finally came to a halt, Katherine sank to the ground in quiet relief. She rested her head and arms on her knees as Sabir held a hand up for silence. He cupped both hands around his mouth and shouted something in a Kurdish dialect. The stone walls acted as sounding boards for his voice, carrying it high into the canyon. Before the echo had died away, two men materialized from the rocks above them, rifles held at their hips, faces rigid, menacing.

While one trained his weapon on the group below,

the **GOLD** *Covenant*

the other started a sure-footed descent down the slope. When he reached the trail, Sabir moved toward him speaking calmly in short phrases. The conversation was animated and brief. When it was over, the man began to laugh. He clapped Sabir on the shoulder, then raised his rifle over his head as a signal to the man above. Still laughing, his weapon now slung harmlessly over his shoulder, he climbed back to his post.

Sabir turned to Quisette and said, "They were expecting more of us. It was necessary to explain."

"How many men do you have in these mountains?"

"We have no census takers here, *Monsieur* Quisette. The count would change too rapidly to be of any use. I'm going to send one of the men ahead to tell them to prepare food and beds."

Quisette pulled out the red silk and wiped it over his damp forehead. "How much farther to the site?"

"Our destination, for now, is a cave we call Rashe—a quarter of a mile from here. For centuries it has been a refuge for the people of my tribe."

"Why not go on? I want to reach the site as soon as possible."

"If you wish to reach it at all, you will let wisdom override your impatience. The jet reconnaissance of our enemies has destroyed our two natural defenses: remoteness and isolation. At Rashe there will be food and a place to rest for the day. At nightfall we can move again."

The cave appeared deserted. The entrance, a huge proscenium arch of stone, was over fifty feet high and about the same distance across. Beyond the arch, the cave was sparsely furnished with pieces of wood and stone, straw, blankets, boxes, and a few cooking and eating utensils. The fire pit at its center contained a bed of hot embers, the only sign of recent occupancy. The man Sabir had sent ahead was nowhere in sight.

"There should be a guard on duty," Sabir said, addressing the comment more to himself than to anyone else. "These men! Sometimes they have too much a mind of their own."

"Maybe they've gone for supplies," Mohsen said, without conviction. "Wait here. I'll look around inside." He moved past Sabir, picked up a torch at the side of the pit, and lit it from the embers before he entered one of the dark apertures at the back of the cave.

"Go with him!" Quisette snapped at Kenneth. Listening to their footsteps echoing through the passage and into the chamber beyond, Quisette turned to Sabir and asked, "How deep is it?"

Sabir shrugged his shoulders. "No one knows. Some of the passages are very small, like honeycombs, unusable. Come, I'll show you." He lit another torch

the **GOLD** Covenant

and started into the cave. Quisette followed, taking Katherine's arm, pushing her ahead of him. "We'll stay together," he said.

Katherine wanted to hold back, to stay near the entrance where she could feel the air and see the sky, but Quisette's grip was painfully resolute. The absolute isolation of being underground drove her to panic. Imagination, vivid and uncontrollable, possessed her— buried her alive in suffocating darkness. Her father had worked in places like these without the slightest misgiving, while she had always made excuses to stay outside. If he sensed her fear, he'd never spoken of it, nor had she confided it to him. Confession would have given the fear substance. So long as no one forced her to deal with it, it could be kept in the abstract—in the privacy of her own mind.

Mohsen and Kenneth were just returning to the first chamber as they entered it. "Empty!" Mohsen said, eyes fixed on Sabir.

"No matter!" Sabir's words were like a reprimand. "Come with us. We can use more light."

When they reached the center of the second chamber, Mohsen raised the torch to full height, casting its light on the upper walls. Slowly, recognizable forms distinguished themselves from the natural irregularities on the surface of the stone. As the light moved, the forms took the shapes of men and animals.

"I am not a scholar," Sabir said, "but I would guess some of these drawings to be as old as time. No one knows their exact origin and date. In our time, they've been viewed only by those in my tribe. So, you see, you have been given a singular privilege."

Quisette was fascinated. "Are there others? Have you taken photographs, kept records of locations? And artifacts, have you found any?"

Sabir launched into the history of Rashe, but his voice was little more than a droning in Katherine's ears. The stagnant air, combined with the smell of burning tar and the mustiness of the earth, was becoming more dense and less breathable. She desperately hoped they would go out; instead, they moved on to the third chamber.

"I have to get out of here!" she said. Wrenching her arm from Quisette's grip, she pressed her back against the wall, visibly trembling. To go deeper into the cave would shatter the last remaining layer of control. She felt paralyzed. Her pulse raced, the erratic rhythm of her breathing was audible. The men stared, amazed. In their preoccupation with the cave art, none of them had noticed how the confined atmosphere was affecting her. Sabir realized first what was wrong.

"The caves can be oppressive," he said. "It's not unusual. You'll be all right, Katherine, when you can see the sky and breathe freely. We'll take you back."

"No, please. I don't need help." She began to

stumble along the wall toward the opening. When she reached the outer cavity with its huge archway framing the mountains and the sky, it was like having a weight lifted from her chest. She sank onto one of the straw mats, resting against the smooth wall of stone, her body absorbing the restorative coolness of it.

Everywhere around her was the imprisoning immensity of the Zagros Mountains. There was no place of escape; even if there had been, she was too tired to go on. Fatigue was destroying her resiliency and her strength. If she didn't reverse the process soon, it would also destroy her will to survive. How had she ever allowed herself to become so weak?—allowed the mental fatigue to leech away her physical strength? It had started so long ago—before England and Quisette and the madness—when she'd let go of hope. When? At what point did hope become resignation?

Strange. She would have thought resignation would bring peace but it hadn't, it had brought debilitation instead. Now it was robbing her of whatever was left of her inner resources. Soon, she'd be altogether incapable of thinking. Unless she could rest. Sleep without dreaming...

...and turn off the endless questions...

Why was Sabir so acquiescent, so docile? Not like him. Why? Why bring Quisette here—with hardly any resistance—to a place sacred to his people? What did he know of Quisette? Where were Sabir's own men? His troops? The women who cooked for them? Cared for them? Sabir hadn't expected Rashe to be deserted—she had read it on Mohsen's face as if it had been written in ink.

And Sheppard.

If only she could relive that evening in the library. If she hadn't been so hostile, Shep might have relented, might have answered her questions. Things might have been different.

Her thoughts vaporized into wisps of smoke, shapeless tendrils grasping at form and dissolving into nothing. She tried to focus on a single thought—one truth filtered from the rest, one truth that would make sense of what was happening—but she was conscious only of the sun, the warmth of it on her face, and the coolness of the rock against her back. What good were answers now? What did it matter? Would anything be changed for the knowing why?

She was asleep for only minutes when the first explosion reverberated from the stone, through her body, registering harmlessly in her brain. Thunder! She opened her eyes and was looking out from the cave's entrance into the clear blue unclouded ceiling of sky when the second round of sharp explosive rifle fire crackled through the gorge and echoed from every direction. A moment later Sabir and the others raced from the interior of the cave.

She pulled herself up, moving farther out onto the rocky ledge which sloped to the floor of the canyon. They all stood there, as if transfixed, listening to the echoes fade and die. When they were silent, Sabir abandoned the protective proximity of the cave to find a better position to scan the mountainside. Slowly, he searched the ragged outcroppings of stone. Nothing moved. He motioned for Mohsen and the other partisans to follow. They scrambled down the rocks to the dusty canyon below and, again, studied the terrain above and surrounding the cave.

As Katherine started down the incline after them, a shower of small pebbles rained from the slope above. She spun around and looked up, shielding her eyes from the sun. Directly over the archway of the cave's entrance, a man in olive-drab uniform rose to full height, towering over those below. Pavlos stood next to him. Each of them held a submachine gun gripped in his hands.

Sabir pivoted around slowly, careful to keep his arms extended away from his body. The cliffs above them were dotted with olive uniforms and the glitter of sun on metal. The man standing next to Pavlos shouted orders as the rest of the unit began to move in from either end of the gorge.

Sabir turned to Mohsen and the others. His voice

was low and firm as he told them to drop their weapons, raise their hands over their heads, and remain passive. Quisette stood at the entrance, hands crossed over his chest as Kenneth, using his .44 magnum as a pointer, ordered Katherine to climb the rest of the way down to join her friends.

"Your man has made a miraculous recovery," Sabir said to Quisette. He watched Pavlos slide and skid down the slope at a half-run, following the other man.

"He has, indeed," Quisette said. "The Greeks have always been remarkable actors, haven't they?"

"You promised," Katherine said. "No killing—"

"Promised?" Quisette said. "Did I? Well then, think of this as my guarantee. There are only two worthwhile principles in life, my dear Katherine, self-interest and self-preservation. And I'm fanatically devoted to both."

As the man with Pavlos reached the floor of the canyon, Quisette started down to meet him. The man was tall, his black beard salted with white, his nose a misaligned slash across his face. The fez had been replaced with a white turban, but the features were unmistakable. He was the man she'd seen on the yacht in Piraeus—the man who'd been closeted in the meeting with Quisette for over two hours.

The sun burned down, leeching strength, leeching consciousness. As if removed from her body, she could see the ground spinning out from under her feet . . .

CHAPTER 29

Sheppard Wilde looked at his watch; he was fifteen minutes late. This tie-up was even more hopeless than the others they encountered on the ride from Piraeus. The street was alive with chickens. A collision between a bus and a poultry truck had catapulted the terrified birds from their broken crates into the stream of cars. The resulting chaos had paralyzed traffic in all directions. Wilde paid his driver and climbed out of the taxi. Several cars behind him, another man climbed out of a cab. He was lean, wiry, and dark complected. His eyes were deep-set and glossy, darting like a ferret's. He moved off in the same direction as Wilde.

With the noise of horns and angry voices fading in his wake, Wilde covered the last four blocks at a fast clip. At Pandrossou Street, he turned into the hustle of the Flea Market where his pace was hampered slightly by the crowded stalls. In spite of the heat, the street was filled with bargain hunters shuffling through copper, brass, jewelry, and clothing heaped together in unsorted piles of treasure and junk.

At Eolou, he veered off to the right, then strolled in the direction of the Acropolis, keeping ten paces ahead of the bulky shadow he'd picked up somewhere in the market. A half-block past the Library of Hadrian, the man fell into step beside him. His bald head was the same dark-roasted tan as his face; his belly looked the size and weight of a beer keg.

With the panache of a magician, he flipped a card from his palm to his fingers and held it up for Wilde to see. It was a creased, discolored, over-used business card announcing the name Stavros Sikelianos.

"Sorry I'm late," Wilde said.

"Is expected. Come, you follow me, eh? I know *ouzeri* not far. Good sausage—the best!"

There was no further conversation until they arrived at their destination. The *ouzeri*, Xenia, was a seedy but active bar permeated with a mixture of aromas promising the best of Greek cooking. Its only decoration was a WWII-vintage jukebox with lights flashing behind blue, green, yellow, and red glass.

As they entered, Stavros Sikelianos's voice boomed over the din of conversation in the room. His barrage of Greek, directed at the kitchen, received a disembodied answer which was loud, crude, and friendly, reducing

Wilde's companion, Stavros, as well as the other customers, to raucous laughter. With a greeting here and there, Stavros steered Wilde to a paper-covered oak table toward the back of the room. The spot was well-chosen, situated in the draft between the doorway and a large window.

Unnoticed, the ferret-faced man slipped in after them, moving to a corner of the bar, out of sight of their table.

Wilde took out a pack of Camels and offered one to Stavros. The Greek accepted with a smile, said, "I have matches," and patted the two pockets of his white shirt. Finding them empty, he reached into his black trousers. In the back pocket, he found a box of safety matches. After he lit both cigarettes, he sat back and inhaled deeply.

"I like these American brands," he said, "but you are English, no?"

"Yes."

Wilde showed no sign of elaborating further so the Greek went on talking. "I do much business with your friend, Kassem," he said. His eyes darted around the room then lit up expectantly as they focused somewhere over Wilde's shoulder. "Now, you see I am right. Best sausage in all of Athens." He flipped the ember of his cigarette into a copper plate on the edge of the table and tucked the stub over his ear.

A moment later, the heavyweight owner of the disembodied voice arrived at their table wearing an apron splattered with unrecognizable food stains and carrying a large plate of sausage, a loaf of dark bread, two glasses of ouzo, and a couple of worn checkered napkins on a tin tray. He set the tray down at the center of the table, gave Stavros a good-natured slap on the back and returned to his kitchen.

"You like?" Stavros asked, handing a glass to Wilde.

"I like." After a sip, Wilde put the glass down. "You said you might have something for me."

The Greek broke off a hunk of bread, stabbed a sausage and placed it on top, then held it out to Wilde.

"I've eaten."

"A pity." Stavros hesitated only slightly before biting off an enormous hunk of the dripping mass. With his mouth stuffed, he nodded.

"Does that mean the sausage is still the best in Athens or you have information for me?"

Stavros shook out a napkin to wipe the drippings off his chin. "Both," he said, before taking another bite.

Wilde pushed the remainder of the sausages and bread to the end of the table. "Maybe you could hold off on the snack until we've talked."

Stavros grinned, finished off what he already had in hand. Wiping his chin of grease and his forehead of perspiration, he tossed the napkin on the table. "You pay in dollars?"

Wilde laid an envelope on the table between them.

"What do you have?"

"I have check on certain hotels. Places where is very relaxed about papers. You understand?"

"Go on."

"There is a Turk. He is—how you say?—a mercenary. Anything for money, eh?" He paused for a moment as music blared from the front of the room where someone had dropped a coin in the jukebox. Wilde flicked an ash into the copper dish and waited for him to continue. "This mercenary, he has business in Piraeus, at a certain yacht. It is very-fast-in, very-fast-out kind of business."

"The name of the yacht?"

"*Zereda.* Is very beautiful ship. Owner is man called Enrique Quisette."

"And the name of the mercenary?"

"Abdul Hareem Bey. You know him?"

"Only the name."

"I have photograph." He began to pat down his pockets again, ending with the top left shirt. "Is not new. One, maybe two years."

Wilde took the picture from Stavros. It was a telephoto shot of two men standing in front of the Benaki Museum. For the first time in days, he felt a surge of hope—not because of the tall, blade-nosed Turk, but because of the man who was standing next to him. Although the picture was on the fuzzy side, it was clear enough to see the second man bore a remarkable resemblance to the man he'd seen in a shoddy room at the Bittner Arms Hotel. It was the same dour face that decorated the passport belonging to the late Ernest Gehreich.

"This man with Hareem Bey, do you know him?" Wilde asked.

Glancing at the envelope, Stavros massaged his rotund belly and made a gesture to the effect it was unlikely there was anyone he *didn't* know.

"You can count it, if you like," Wilde said, nodding at the envelope lying between them on the table. "There's more than enough to cover the fee."

"Is okay. Stavros Sikelianos does business only from the best reference, and Hareb Kassem is best, eh? Whatever he say is okay with me and he say you are reliable customer." Stavros glanced at the cooling sausages and back at the picture again. "The man is called Jongen... Hans Jongen."

"Are you sure?"

"Is absolute for sure."

Wilde's disappointment was momentary. Gehreich had to be using an alias. That would explain the second, mutilated passport they'd found in his room. "What else do you know about this Hans Jongen?" he asked.

"Is long time, hard to remember. I am thinking you have interest only in other man, Hareem Bey. This one . . . nothing much to know. Business man, small-time smuggler."

the **GOLD** Covenant

"I'd like to keep the photo."

Stavros picked up the envelope, flipped through the contents and beamed. "Hey, I get you whole damn family album for this." He stuffed it into his hip pocket and reached for the plate of sausage. Before he dove into it, he looked up at Wilde. "Maybe you change your mind, eh?"

"Do you have more photos of this Hans Jongen—with any of his other contacts?"

"Not here."

"Where? There's a bonus in it for you."

"My place." The Greek gave the plate a longing look. "Wait here. In five minutes, go to kitchen. My brother-in-law, Timotheos, will tell you where to go."

Stavros crossed the room, slid behind the bar, and disappeared into the kitchen. Wilde glanced at his watch, then picked up the glass of ouzo.

In the active crowded room, he didn't see the small ferret-like man slip into the hallway leading to the back exit.

The kitchen was hot and steaming with spicy odors. A wooden counter took up one entire side; a large, deep porcelain sink on pipe fittings occupied the space between two chopping blocks at the center of the back wall. Opposite the counter, Timotheos stood in front of the huge black stove covered with pots in varying sizes. He nodded at Wilde and held out a folded piece of paper.

"You go out this way," he said, indicating another door. "There."

The door led to a storeroom lined with jars, cans, kegs, and sacks smelling heavily of cumin and garlic. Through it was an access to a hallway, at the end of which was a dingy door, the crude hand-lettered word for exit painted on it.

Wilde turned the knob and pushed. The latch clicked back, but the door seemed to be jammed. He pushed again, this time with more weight behind it. As it gave, slightly, a man's arm dropped across the small opening at ground level. The unlit butt of a Camel cigarette was clenched in the fingers. There was no sound. Wilde placed his left hand and right shoulder against the door, forced it open as gently as possible, and stepped through to the alley.

Stavros Sikelianos's body, which had been seated against the door, was slumped face forward on the dirt, a dark stain growing around the head. Wilde turned him over and placed a hand at his wrist but the gesture was futile. The man's neck was slit from ear to ear, halfway through to his spinal column. Like Gehreich's . . .

Wilde grew alert at a sound behind him—a movement . . .

He dove forward, instinctively, getting his own neck out of range within milliseconds of the whip lash that bit

the **GOLD** Covenant

into his left leg. The sting was sharp but he didn't pause. He rolled, whirled around and came up in a crouch next to the row of garbage cans at the back of the building. A kick sent one of them hurtling toward his attacker. The wiry little man dodged it easily then made a quick jabbing movement with the stainless steel noose.

Wilde's mind was racing. The Lewellyn's. He'd seen this man before. The night David Forster was killed. The night Katherine was kidnapped.

"You goddamned son of a bitch."

The man grinned, baring a perfect row of pearl-white teeth. His right hand continued to jab, demonstrating its speed, daring Wilde to choose a direction as his left hand slowly edged toward Wilde's back.

Wilde knew the right hand was just a distraction. He'd never get close enough to use the lethal piece of wire. He made a sudden movement to his right, causing the weasel to bring his left hand up defensively. Then, as he watched, the man's left hand began to move toward his back again. If there was a knife buried in his belt, there'd be no warning. He'd pull it out and throw it in one motion.

Wilde's peripheral vision had spotted the garbage can lid propped against Stavros's feet. It would have to do. There was no time for anything else. All in the same motion, he thrust himself forward, grasped the lid, then launched himself into the smaller man like a run-away truck. With the lid acting as Wilde's shield, they fell together, landing with Wilde's more substantial weight on top. Wilde lifted the lid and smashed it down, again and again, until limp fingers released the steel noose and the groans faded to silence.

Only then did he become aware of Timotheos standing in the doorway. Soberly, the man removed his apron to lay over Stavros's face. He straightened from his task to stare at Wilde. "You are hurt," he said, "your leg. Is much blood. Come in. I get doctor."

"I haven't time," Wilde said. "You understand? No time for police. Tell them this man is wanted in England. I'm sorry. About Stavros . . ."

The man shrugged. "All time I say, 'You're in bad business, Stavros.' He says, 'You make best sausage, Timotheos, but you don't know how to have fun.' Stavros knows, eh? He knows how to have fun."

Timotheos turned and went back into the bar.

There was no identification in the dead man's pockets. He was a professional and he worked for Enrique Quisette, of that Wilde was certain. He was also certain the man had murdered David Forster as well as Ernest Gehreich and Kassem's gold carrier, Ahmed Barcineh. With Interpol, it wouldn't be long before the Yard was fitting

the **GOLD** *Covenant*

the pieces together.

Wilde ripped off the bottom of his shirt, wrapped it around the slash on the back of his left leg. The wound was deep but the metal hadn't hit an artery. He tucked in the torn shirt tail, dusted himself off, and walked several blocks before hailing a taxi.

The lower half of his trouser leg, his sock, and his shoe were soaked with blood, his light-blue shirt stained with the blood-dampened grime of the alley. It was not an unobtrusive appearance to present in public, but a change of clothing would have to wait. If he was going to find anything worthwhile in Stavros Sikelianos's room, he would have to get there before the police arrived.

CHAPTER 30

The address Stavros had written on the scrap of paper was in the Plaka—less than a mile from the *ouzeri*. Wilde asked the driver to wait. The exterior of the small residential hotel appeared neglected; by contrast, the interior had a warm respectability about it. The immaculate walls of the lobby smelled of fresh paint. The varnished surface of the registration desk reflected the glitter of an amber glass chandelier suspended from the center of the high ceiling. With a nod to the clerk and a familiar Greek pleasantry about the weather, Wilde moved past the desk to the stairway.

Stavros's room was on the second floor facing the rear of the building. The lock was easily negotiable with the picks he carried as standard equipment. Once inside, he slipped on a pair of thin plastic gloves—also standard.

The room had all the characteristics of a disorganized office that was being used, incidentally, as a bedroom.

the **GOLD** Covenant

Occupying one small corner were a sink, a sideboard holding a hot plate along with basic cooking utensils, a table, chair, and an oak chiffonier with an array of toiletry articles on top of it. One black sock hung from a bottom drawer. The rest of the room was filled with an untidy desk, a vintage file cabinet, bookshelves stuffed with everything but books and, on the floor, stacks of cardboard cartons that seemed to be holding the overflow of Stavros's *business* records.

More of the make-shift file boxes were strewn over the unmade bed along with folders, manila envelopes, and photographs. Judging by their content, these were the files Stavros had hurriedly searched through before their meeting. All of them contained material relating to Abdul Hareem Bey. It seemed to be an on-going record, started years ago. Wilde recognized Stavros himself standing next to Abdul in several of the earlier photographs. Their uniforms were identical. From mercenary to informer—Stavros's career choices weren't related to an interest in longevity.

Another familiar face was that of Ernest Gehreich—a.k.a. Hans Jongen—which appeared in more than a few of the photographs with the Turk. None was dated later than two years back. He wondered if the association had started then or whether Stavros had not bothered to pull out earlier records.

What had he said? *Is long time. Hard to remember.*

roberta clark

The dates on the boxes indicated Stavros was not a man who ever got around to up-dating his files. If that were true, the older files, would be in the metal cabinet.

The drawers of the file cabinet were jammed full. He flipped through them, more concerned for time than neatness. The pile on the bed had grown considerably before he found a manila envelope with the name Jongen scribbled over the top of an old address. He carried it to the table, shoved aside the dried remains of a meal, and dumped out the contents of the envelope. There wasn't much in it—photographs, mostly, with a few pages of Greek script—but to Wilde it was much more. It was the price of a ticket to the Zagros Mountains.

By the time he reached his room, the wound on his calf was bleeding again. He sent out for bandages, tape, and a bottle of Scotch—the latter to serve two purposes. His next call, to Hugh Kimball, would be delayed—he was assured by the operator—by no more than thirty minutes. While he waited, a quick shower washed off the dried blood and grime from the alley. When the scotch arrived with the bandages, he poured a shot over the wound, then covered it with a pressure pad and tape.

When the call from Kimball finally came through an hour later, Wilde was dressed and working his way through a second Scotch while he waited for room service to deliver his dinner. The day before he'd subsisted on coffee alone. Tonight, his appetite was healthy for the first time since Katherine had been kidnapped.

Kimball, Katherine's British liaison with *Power Line*, had managed, so far, to keep the Yard at bay in the Gehreich matter. Beset with a strong sense of guilt over his inadvertent involvement in Katherine's kidnapping, Kimball had also been extremely accommodating with both his information sources and his expertise. At Wilde's request, had done so without informing *Power Line's* head office in New York.

Taking the cue from Wilde, Kimball restrained his natural inclination to chat. He jotted down the lengthy set of instructions, promising the fastest possible action. "Stay put," his cheerful voice shouted into the phone. "I'll get back to you within twenty-four hours."

"I'll be an arm's reach," Wilde said. "And, Kimball, be sure the Campbell matter is first priority."

"Done!"

He wasn't any closer to Katherine, but, thanks to Stavros Sikelianos and the thoroughness of his records, he had a chance of getting there now. A good one. Waiting in Athens after Kat and Sabir had gone was one of the most difficult things he'd ever been forced to do. The most difficult was letting *her* go—knowing she was on the *Zereda*, knowing he couldn't even make an attempt at taking her off the ship before they left.

His promise to Sabir had been necessary; too many other lives were at stake. Neither Wilde nor Sabir could make a move until Quisette's connection was broken. Permanently! It had been agreed Wilde was in the best position to break it. In return, Sabir would do everything possible to assure Katherine's safety. They both knew the tenuousness of that promise, but neither had the heart to mention it.

Early the next afternoon, Wilde had the first report from Kimball. It verified Stavros Sikelianos's information about Abdul Hareem Bey, filling in some of the details as well. Hareem Bey was a Turkish mercenary but not in the usual sense. He came complete with his own army—experienced troops, ordnance, and loyalty to the highest bidder. He was expensive. That he'd been on the *Zereda* in Piraeus the day Quisette left was not a coincidence. It meant Quisette had hired a private army, an army that was going to rendezvous with him somewhere between Athens and the Zagros Mountains.

The prognosis was not encouraging—except for one small possibility. Quisette's threat to Sabir Pasha might be a bluff so far as the immediacy of execution was concerned. Since outlaws like Abdul Hareem Bey were not

the **GOLD** Covenant

persona grata with legitimate agencies, Quisette was more than likely acting without the knowledge or sanction of anyone he might know in the Turkish government. In that case, he'd be as anxious as Wilde to keep this affair quiet. His investment was heavy. To make it pay off, he would have to avoid expensive bribes. His official connections would have to be used as a last resort, and only after he removed himself from the scene. Quisette, better than anyone, would know how quickly a so-called ally could turn and sink its fangs in your throat.

It was speculation, an exercise to consume minutes, to build hope, to try to convince himself the loss of time was not as crucial as he knew it was. He'd always been patient—had to be in his business—but this was different—this was Katherine's life. The only way to keep her alive was to sever Quisette's connection. That had to be done before any part of this affair was made public. If it wasn't, not only Katherine's life and Sabir's would be forfeit, Kurdistan itself would be steaming with the blood of its people.

Wilde poured the last drop of coffee into the cup on his lunch tray, on the point of dialing room service to ask for another carafe, when the phone rang. He was relieved to hear the familiar voice of Hareb Kassem on the other end.

"Wilde? That you?"

"Where the hell have you been, Kassem?"

"Campbell, old chap. I believe your message was for Arnold Campbell."

"Kassem! Campbell! Whatever the bloody hell you choose to call yourself today, I'd still like to know where you've bloody been! I've been trying to reach you for twenty-four hours."

"Awfully oblique way you went about it. You could have called me at O.I., directly, instead of having your Mr. Kimball leaving messages all over Scotland for Arnold Campbell. You know my office always knows where I am."

"Does Taha know you're talking to me now?"

"Look here, Wilde, what's it all about? What difference does it make whether Taha knows or not?"

"Does he?"

"No! As a matter of fact, I'm calling from the club. My caretaker caught the message from Hugh Kimball. He relayed it directly from Scotland. I'm meeting Kimball at his house in a half hour. *Now* will you tell me what this is about?"

"We got lucky with Stavros Sikelianos. Unfortunately, it didn't turn out as well for him. He ran into our friend with the portable guillotine."

"Bad luck. It's not easy to find reliable informers."

"You're all heart, Kassem. Look, we haven't time enough to go over everything twice so I'll let Kimball fill you in on the details. He'll also give you a packet I sent

the **GOLD** *Covenant*

over. I think you'll find it interesting—especially the photographs. Our friend Taha is extraordinarily photogenic."

"Jamil Taha?"

"The same. The photos will explain why I've been kept on the oblique by your O.I. office. Look them over and let me know if I have a go."

There was a long pause on the other end before Kassem spoke again, his voice stripped of any trace of pleasantness. "He's skipped!"

"Taha? Are you sure?"

"I *wasn't* until now. He asked for a few days off."

"How soon can you catch up to him?"

"Depends on how far he's run."

"Call me." Wilde dropped the receiver. "Bloody hell!" he said aloud. "The timing. The goddamned rotten timing!"

He poured a Scotch, carried it to the bathroom, flipped on the cold tap in the shower, and had just begun to strip when the sound of the phone brought him back across the room in two strides. It was Hugh Kimball, confirming he'd reached Kassem.

"Just finished talking to him. What about Gehreich? Have you turned up anything on his alias?"

"Have I!" Kimball's high-pitched voice shouted into the phone. "You're not going to believe it. I thought it was a long shot. Didn't think it would pay off. They don't usually. Long shots, I mean—"

"Kimball . . . slow down. What have you got?"

"You were right. Absolutely right. Gehreich wasn't staying in that broken down room at the Bittner Arms. It was just what you said it was—a meeting place."

It had been Kimball's own words—the comments he'd made when they arrived at the Bittner Arms just before discovering Gehreich's body—that Wilde had remembered on the way back to his hotel room yesterday afternoon. *Never knew Gehreich to use anything but the best hotels. Always managed to worm the most out of his expense account. . . .*

"You still there, Wilde?"

"I'm still here. Did you find out where he was staying?"

"He was registered at the Gatwick Hilton, under the name you gave me, Hans Jongen. They had his stuff in storage."

"Did you get a look at it?"

"Got it right here in my study. Never guess how—"

"Never mind the details," Wilde said, impatiently. "Tell me what you found."

"Went through every damn thing in it, right down to his socks and skivvies. Used gloves, as you so wisely—"

"Kimball!"

"Right! Sorry. Not used to this kind of excitement. There was a letter . . . addressed to Angela Gehreich, his wife. Not much in it. Financial statement, power of attorney, full title to all of their joint properties, a short, rather nasty note telling her he was leaving her. Must have been stashing away money for himself in a secret account over the years, judging by the tone—"

"Skip the personal details and get on with it, will you?"

"Sorry again. Seemed like a good indication of his intent. The important thing, actually, is the small leather address book I found stuffed into a box of souvenir coasters. It lists names and phone numbers."

"Run down the list for me, will you?"

Kimball read off the names, pausing expectantly after each one, but Wilde waited until he'd finished before asking, "Is there a name next to Oriental Imports?"

"No. Just a number. Do you know the company?"

"I've heard of it," Wilde said. "Give the address book to Campbell along with the packet. And, Kimball, it's important you tell him where you found it."

CHAPTER 31

Katherine woke with the amicable aroma of tea bringing a momentary feeling of security. The feeling was short-lived. Above her, spidery shadows played across the cathedral rock ceiling, crawling down the smooth gray walls and over the stone floor where they attached themselves to the dark figures moving about in the light of the fire. Slowly the figures themselves came into focus: Quisette with the man she'd seen on the yacht in Piraeus, and a number of white-turbanned men in dark olive uniforms. They were sitting around the fire pit, some talking, some eating, some cleaning rifles. Near the foot of her mat, Kenneth slouched on a bench, eating out of the stainless steel pan from his camper's kit. There was no sign of Sabir, Mohsen, or the other partisans.

She sat up on the hard mat, leaning against the stone, exhausted from the small effort required. One

the **GOLD** Covenant

of the men glanced over at her and said something to his companions that made them laugh. She didn't need to understand Turkish to recognize the sentiments expressed—the contempt for a sub-species. It was an attitude she'd encountered often enough in some of the countries she visited with her father. She'd learned to deal with it by keeping a distance—restraining her tongue and her temper. It was apparent these men would enjoy an angry reaction from her. To oblige them would be to guarantee defeat in a fixed game. A game these men relished playing.

Turning her back to them, she began a slow process of stretching. The aches were too numerous to count, but the tenderness of skin was most uncomfortable. The coarse, irritating surface of the woolen blanket had acted like a dermabrasion on her arms and legs.

Someone nudged her and said, "*Ya sou.*" It was the basso voice of Pavlos. She turned and looked at the towering figure grinning down at her, his teeth almost as dark as his sun-baked complexion. "I bring you something to eat in few minutes," he went on. "You like to wash first?"

"Well . . ." she said, ". . . if it isn't the star of the Greek chorus miraculously restored to health, courtesy *Deus ex machina*. Where can I get one for our side?"

"Sorry, I have only tea, bread, and goat cheese this morning. You don't like my offer?"

"Where do I wash?"

"I show you facilities." He laughed at the word. "They're not so fancy, but view is very beautiful."

She tried to stand but the effort hit her inner ear like barrel-riding on a rough sea. Forced to stop midway on her knees, she asked, "Who slipped me the mickey?"

"Very funny." He laughed at the thought. "You sure don't need mickey! You sleep pretty damn good with no help. More than twenty-four hours. Sleep is good for the fever."

"Fever! Twenty-four hours!" She looked at the sky, astonished. The light had faded just a little. She didn't remember lying down on the mat, closing her eyes, falling asleep. It seemed only moments since they'd been standing in the canyon, surrounded by the small army of mercenaries. "It couldn't have been that long," she said.

"More than a day. Your fever was high but sometimes that is good thing. Makes body fight harder. Is good body take control of mind when mind cannot take care for body."

"Conditions haven't been conducive," she groaned, tried to get up again but her body wasn't cooperating yet. "Given the opportunity, I'll take better care of both in the future."

"It is good you keep sense of humor."

Katherine looked over at the men around the fire pit. "Where are the others, Sabir Pasha, Lieutenant Raza?"

Anticipating her question, he motioned toward the inner caves. "They are restrained but unharmed. *Monsieur* Quisette is not patient man though. For short time he was persuaded fever made travel impossible for you. Now he threatens to leave you in this place. That is not good prospect."

"I'm not so sure the other alternative is any better. Who is the man with Quisette?"

"Abdul Hareem Bey. These mercenaries are his men. Next to him I am—how you say? Little Bo Peep." He roared at that. "I rather do business with devil. Devil is more pleasant fellow."

Suddenly, Kenneth, who'd done nothing but grunt until now, slung his leftovers on the ground. "Enough a that," he snapped. To underline the point, he banged the pan on a rock, whipped out his handkerchief, and began to burnish the metal with a fury. "I thought you come over 'ere t'give the woman somethin' to eat."

"Is so. But first . . ." Pavlos extended a hand to Katherine.

She rejected the offer, pulled herself up the rest of the way on rubbery legs, then followed his directions to the primitive toilet facility. It was a hundred or so yards from the cave: a burlap-sided pit with a rusty shovel for sanitary purposes and—as also promised—a spectacular view over the top of the cloth walls.

When she returned to the cave, Pavlos poured a

basin of water from one of the suspended rawhide jugs, set it down on a flat ledge, and motioned that it was for her use.

Her body felt dehydrated after the fever and the twenty-four-hour hibernation. She picked up the tin cup next to the basin, scooped it full, drank, and filled it again. The pure icy spring water was like a hone, putting a sharp edge to all of her senses. Her thirst quenched, she splashed her face and neck, then sponged off her arms and legs with what was left of the water. As she washed, she was again conscious of the men watching her, their silence even more unnerving than their laughter.

Pavlos stood close by which gave her a sense of security, a feeling she wasn't certain she could trust. She picked up the basin, carried it out, and dumped the dirty water over the rocks. When she returned, Pavlos exchanged a plate of food for her basin. With the fading sunlight, a chill had crept into the shade of the cavern. She chose a spot under the outer arch where she could sit in what was left of the sun's warmth while she picked at the dry bread and pungent cheese. Before she was finished, Pavlos returned with a large, chipped enamel cup. It was steaming, filled with strong syrupy tea. The first sip was shockingly sweet, but she found it energizing and polished off every drop.

"Good for waking up the head," Pavlos said, relieving her of the plate and empty cup. "You feeling better now?"

She nodded. "How far do we go tonight?"

"In miles, not far. In time, long way. Eight hours, maybe more."

"Will we reach—?"

"Well, now," Quisette's voice cut off her question, "do you think, my dear Katherine, you're well enough recovered for us to carry on with this little expedition? I assume Pavlos has made it clear to you I don't intend to lose another day on your account."

Quisette looked as meticulously groomed as he had on the yacht, and much healthier. It seemed odd he should appear stronger under conditions that should have been debilitating to a man with his apparent ailment. It wouldn't have surprised her if the impression he gave of consumptive weakness was deliberately cultivated. The coughing spells, raspy throat, the bloodless look of a vampire victim were beginning to look like a pose.

She said, "I'm ready when you are."

"Well then," he said, his voice reeking of sarcasm, "let's make it now, shall we?"

She glanced over at Hareem Bey. "This friend of yours," she said. "Aren't you afraid of bedding down with another viper?"

"I'm like the Kurds," Quisette said, relishing the comparison. "I have no friends. Friends are the least reliable of Homo sapiens. Friends would worry me, vipers never. You're a hopeless idealist, my poor pathetic girl. I *buy* what I need—whether man or material. It's the only way to assure loyalty. Even from vipers like Hareem Bey."

Katherine stifled the impulse to reply. "If you'll excuse me," she said, "I have to check my backpack."

The trail began with an almost vertical climb upward to the top of Rashe and then along a narrow ridge of mountain. In front of them, the sharp splintered peaks of the Zagros were growing more forbidding. The moonlight cast sprawling shadows across rocks and gullies plunging their depths into abysmal darkness. Katherine desperately wanted to hug the mountainside, but to do so made it impossible to keep up with the others. The pace was set by Hareem Bey, and though it was grueling for her it was even more difficult for Sabir Pasha, Lieutenant Raza, and the partisans who were tethered to each other by a long length of rope.

The weather, at least, was friendlier. The air was crisp, the sky clear. The ground underfoot was dry and firm. During the first two hours of the relentlessly steep uphill grade, Katherine's legs rebelled. It was sheer will that forced them to keep moving. She ignored the complaints of her body, concentrating all her effort on maintaining the distance between herself and the man

the GOLD Covenant

in front of her. Finally, putting one foot in front of the other became as automatic as taking the next breath.

Turning off the contradictory workings of her mind was not so easy, and she actually found herself growing eager to reach the site. To see the place where her father had last worked. To see for herself what these men considered more important than human life.

No, she thought, that isn't the real reason. It's the hope of finding Gustav there. Alive. God, I've got to stop reaching for what's gone. Wanting the truth is not the same as wanting the truth to be what you want it to be. Gustav is dead. Like John. No amount of wanting can change that. As for our destination, reaching it is analogous to reaching the end of my own life. Hardly a thing to be eager for.

She'd flown to England for the truth, but had turned away from it. She'd treated Sheppard as an enemy right from the start. Might he have told her more if she hadn't done that? Why hadn't she asked more questions of Sabir? If she really wanted answers, he would have given them to her. The truth is she hadn't wanted answers. She was relieved with Shep's reticence. It had given her an excuse to go on hoping. And she *had* hoped Gustav was still alive—that the news of his death was a mistake, a hoax, a cover, something that could be explained away. There'd been no evidence of his crash, no body, no proof. Death was something you had to witness—as she had witnessed John's. It was that incontrovertible firsthand knowledge that made it true.

The terrain was changing, gradually, becoming less punishing. Katherine had so inured her brain to the tortured nerve-ends in her muscles she didn't know exactly when the grade had begun to reverse itself. The leveling-off brought about a palliative recovery, physical first then mental, but nonetheless welcome. They continued moving on a slow decline for another hour before the trail sloped upward again, this time on a more gentle rise.

Several hours before dawn, they reached a plateau which looked out over the chasm of the valley below to the panorama of sharply-cut angular peaks surrounding it. On the rim of the plateau, Hareem Bey halted the straggling group to give his men a curt list of orders. It seemed they were to stop here briefly, before starting down the last hazardous section of trail.

Katherine sat near the edge of the cliff, separated from Sabir and the others by the guards, kept at a distance which made it impossible to converse. The altitude here was greater than at the airfield. How much greater she didn't know, but the landscape was more barren, the breathing more difficult. The thin clear atmosphere was luminescent, the full moon an enormous beacon balanced on the peak of a mountain. She shivered and clutched the collar of her shirt around her neck.

Looking directly down the slope of rock below, she

the **GOLD** *Covenant*

was surprised to see a system of pipes—an ancient aqueduct. It appeared to have been carved from the stone itself. She knew there were similar aqueduct systems in this area. Gustav had taken her to see the most famous—the Shamiram Su—which had been built by the Vannic monarch Menuas early in the eighth century B.C., long before the rise of the Persian Empire.

She turned to look up at a parallel course to the mountain behind her where, fifteen or twenty feet above the plateau, a flood gate was still recognizable. When she turned back, she saw Quisette with Hareem Bey and Kenneth strolling along the edge of the plateau. They seemed to be following a set course.

Looking closer at the ground under the loose covering of dirt and pebbles, she saw a rail line with close-set tracks running along the slightly curving terrace, ending at a dark depression in the side of the mountain—another cave. A second later, the three men disappeared into the opening.

"Interesting, eh?" Pavlos had moved up beside her, watching the place where the others had vanished. "You like to go in and look around? Is maybe last chance you get."

His words sounded like a death sentence and yet he'd spoken them with the geniality of a tour guide. The incongruities of the man amazed her. She stared at him for a moment, then shook her head.

That seemed to amuse him. "Afraid, yes?" he

asked. "But you have no fear to go in tall buildings. Is very funny, you know? These caves are more safe than anything. These caves are here for couple thousand centuries. Still be here couple thousand centuries after your buildings fall down."

His laughter began with a slow rumble and grew to a great basso roar. She couldn't help smiling but was annoyed with her own reaction. It was too easy to forget where Pavlos' loyalties lay. Next she'd be trusting him as a friend and friendship is a slim value to a man whose prime motivation is hard cash. She stood up and walked along the edge of the cliff with the big Greek following.

"Twenty-five-thousand-foot drop," he said. "I think is village down there. Is called Luisse. Name means light."

She started to ask about the village, but her attention was distracted when Kenneth's hulking form emerged in the stone archway. She watched him approach Sabir Pasha, remove the tether line, then lead the older man back into the cave. Curious, Katherine followed them along the tracks as far as the opening. While she stood listening, Kenneth came out again, stooping to avoid hitting his head. He was in short sleeves, his shoulder holster stuffed with a .44 Magnum, his face florid. His intake of breath was audibly intermixed with grunts.

"They want you inside," he said. When she drew back, he took a lumbering step toward her, his twisted mouth mimicking a smile. "Maybe you'd like a bit a 'elp?"

the **GOLD** Covenant

Pavlos moved up beside her. "Is okay," he said to Kenneth. "You let me bring her in. Okay? No trouble."

Kenneth looked as though he might like a bit of trouble. His wheels visibly spinning with indecision, he glared for a full thirty seconds at the casually disarming and slightly shorter Greek before he finally shrugged his massive shoulders in agreement.

Turning to Katherine, Pavlos said, "Is not so bad, you know. Just think it is house—only more safe than house."

"I don't have trouble with logic, only with the panic."

"I stay with you. You feel sick, I take you outside. Okay?"

She looked at Kenneth's determined expression. "I guess there won't be a better offer," she said.

They'd hardly gone past the opening when the loud bang of an engine shattered the stillness. The rhythmic pounding was more than just sound; it reverberated from the stone into the core of her body. She froze.

"It's just the bloody ore crusher," Kenneth shouted over the noise. "Get a move on!"

Pavlos' huge hand came down on her shoulder. "Is okay. You take a look, eh? You don't like . . . offer still goes."

Her inclination was to bolt for the outside, but behind Pavlos was the solid barrier of Kenneth. There was nothing incongruous about *his* character—it was pure malevolence. She thought about what Pavlos had said about the caves. They would be there beyond time. Her hands tightened into fists and her nails dug into her palms. She turned and slowly followed the beam of the flashlight Pavlos directed along the tracks.

Just a few yards ahead, the narrow passage spilled into a cavern, a huge vaulted area with the dark mouths of tunnels radiating from its walls. The cavernous room was lit with oil lamps and filled with mining equipment. Picks, sledge hammers, drills, and buckets were stacked on shelves against one of the walls. An ore car, empty and coated with dirt, sat on the rails at one of the tunnel openings.

Quisette and Hareem stood beside one of the machines, watching as Sabir operated the controls. It was an ore stamp—crudely made but effective and not uncommon in primitive places like this. Each stamp was enclosed in a heavily-framed cylinder, each attached by pulleys and belts to an engine which powered the vertical hammer blows, driving them down with tremendous force to crush the ore.

The smell of diesel fuel nauseated Katherine. Added to the inner tension already restricting her lungs, it became a suffocating weight. She leaned against the wall, closed her eyes, and began a conscious effort to draw in each breath slowly and deeply.

"You should not have come into this place."

the **GOLD** Covenant

She opened her eyes to see Sabir approaching. Her face was perspiring; she could feel the beads of moisture on her upper lip and forehead. "No choice," she said, glancing at Kenneth.

"Hold on then, we leave soon." He bent closer. "It is almost dawn and we are still alive."

She nodded, trying not to show a weakened confidence in the continuation of that state of being. Think about something else, she told herself—anything to keep the panic in check. "This place. What is it?" Her question echoed loudly throughout the cave as the ore stamp suddenly fell silent.

"Gold, my dear Katherine," Quisette said, answering for Sabir. "*This* is a gold mine. Rich and operational." With Hareem at his side, he walked over to join them. "Imagine that—gold—great veins of it. And your friend Sabir Nuri Pasha has been using the proceeds to illegally finance his humanitarian activities. Interesting, isn't it, the rationalizations that so-called honest men make for breaking the law they pretend to respect?"

"The laws of which you speak are not ours," Sabir said. "They are merely an attempt to supersede our own ancient and sacred statutes. It is a question of where one's allegiance lies."

Quisette's hoarse deprecating laughter was magnified in the vaulted room. "Call it what you will," he said. Treating Katherine to the same air of condescension, he added, "Did you know your father was involved in this highly questionable and very lucrative enterprise?"

"I'd rather hear it from a more reliable source," she said.

"You do enjoy being difficult. Perhaps what we both need is a closer look at the *real* motivation. I think that may convince even you."

"Gold would not motivate my father to anything illegal."

"Nor me!" Quisette added emphatically, his arms spread in a gesture of innocence, eyebrows lifted over frozen blue irises. "Not in the form in which we find it here. One may as well be sentenced to a life of hard labor. Not my cup! Crude ore is much too primitive. Too far removed from its more refined, more desirable, and much more highly motivating end product."

"Which is?"

"Unfortunately, you missed Sabir Pasha's magnificent description of what awaits us in Luisse. Since you were instrumental in bringing us here, I'm going to allow you the pleasure of seeing it with us before you and the others join David Forster and your—"

"It would be advisable for you to keep your bargain, *monsieur*," Sabir interrupted, angrily. "My people do not treat kindly the breaking of a promise."

"Indeed. Are you speaking of the people you've sworn to preserve? I think, old man, your days of advis-

the **GOLD** *Covenant*

ing are over."

"If you harm Sabir," Katherine said, "you'll never leave here alive."

The muscles of Quisette's jaw snapped like wire under his transparent skin as his hand slashed across her face, reeling her backward against Sabir. The older man steadied her, his eyes molten with rage. When she recovered her balance, he lunged at Quisette, hitting him squarely in the mid-section. Almost simultaneously, the butt of Hareem's rifle slammed into the side of Sabir's head. The two men fell to the ground, Sabir unconscious, bleeding from the wound on his head, Quisette pinned beneath his body.

"Get him off of me," Quisette roared at Kenneth who was already dragging the older man to one side. Glowering at the crumpled body, Quisette stood, impatiently brushing himself off. "I'll not have him die yet," he barked at Hareem Bey.

"You son of a bitch," Katherine said. "You stinking piece of garbage."

She knelt down to press her kerchief against the deep gash above Sabir's ear. Shaky from his fall and his rage, Quisette gripped Kenneth's arm to steady himself, then lashed out with his booted foot. The kick slammed into her ribs with an audible crack, sending her sprawling onto the hard stone.

Quisette's voice, trembling with anger, seemed to

come from a long way off. "Get them out of here and ready to go. I'm through with civilities."

CHAPTER 32

It was an hour before dawn. Two miles east of the ancient city of Luisse, a plane skimmed over a spiny ridge of mountains, gliding into an approach from the south. The landing strip was lit by a row of oil lanterns in perforated metal drums which marked both ends and the length of the runway along the left border. Kicking up the fine pebbles from the dirt-and-gravel surface, the plane rolled to a stop. As it turned and taxied back to the camouflaged shed which served as a hangar, three men stepped out of the darkness. They were dressed as Sabir's men had been, in khaki shirts, their wool trousers stuffed into heavy socks and boots, ammunition belts slung across their chests, turbans tied with ends flapping.

They had been waiting through most of the night and, now, working swiftly, they began to dismantle the primitive equipment, first extinguishing lanterns. They nested the drums, rolled them back to the shed for storage, then moved out again to erase the wheel tracks from the field. When they were finished, they returned to the hangar, where Sheppard Wilde was unloading his gear from the plane.

Wilde moved forward to grasp the hand of the taller, square-shouldered man standing in front of the others. "Nahil!" he said. "Good to see you again."

"And you, Sheppard Wilde," the younger man answered warmly. "It's good to see you, as well. And on time."

Nahil was Sabir Nuri Pasha's grandson—in his early twenties, educated in France and England, the only male heir who hadn't been lured away from his country by the cushier temptations of Western Europe. Even in the dim light of the shed, his ruddy complexion, brows, and mustache had a tinge of fire about them. The strength in his lean body could be felt in the gentle firmness of his grip. He'd inherited his grandfather's passion for the independence of Kurdistan as well as the older man's coloring and—in Nahil—both still had their unfaded fiery brilliance.

Nahil motioned the other two men forward. "Massud Suwar and Vahad Agha—my best men. Two, as you requested. And you? Alone?"

"Fastest way to move. How do things stand, Nahil? Are we on schedule?"

the **GOLD** Covenant

"All workers were evacuated from the mine and the city the same day of your message. As my grandfather boasts, our people are stones of the mountain that move on the wind." Nahil said it with an obvious pride of his own. "They wait in the rocks above the reservoir on the north. The signal is three rifle shots in quick succession. When they hear that, the plan is in motion."

"Katherine, Sabir Pasha, and the others?"

"We've had them under surveillance since they landed three days ago. I sent in ten men to give them escort to Rashe but because of some pretext of injury they separated into two groups. Abdul Hareem Bey took one before they reached the caves and the other after. Truthfully, Sheppard, I didn't expect this mercenary, Hareem, to take them before they reached Luisse. It worries me."

"The man to worry about is Enrique Quisette. Hareem Bey is only a tool, fueled by one thing. Money. When the fuel line is plugged he'll fold his tent and move on. If we can check Quisette, we'll have a better than even chance of defusing Hareem."

"I can think of several interesting ways to defuse this bloodless viper. What have we been waiting for?"

"Up to now, we've been waiting for confirmation."

"The matter my grandfather mentioned," Nahil broke in. "And you have it? The confirmation?"

"It hasn't been notarized, but the odds are at least

even. How will your men feel about that?"

"For myself, I can tell you it's better than the odds we're accustomed to, but I'll ask them."

Nahil turned to Vahad and Massud, giving them a translation of the conversation. The two men looked at each other in silent agreement, then Massud shrugged and responded for both.

"He says, *A weak heart attains no satisfaction*," Nahil explained. "Is that answer enough?"

Wilde nodded. "When do you figure our friends will arrive in Luisse?"

"By dawn, I think. The mules should arrive at the same time," Nahil said. "If this man with the pale hair is as greedy a mongrel as I think, they will have loaded everything by sundown. I tell you, this order of my grandfather's—to have my men submit without resistance—goes against my blood. Especially when I must stand by and watch how those dogs mistreat him."

"You won't have to stand by any longer. Everything's squared away here. It's time we were moving."

Nahil didn't respond. His dark eyes stared at Wilde, fired by the lanterns. He seemed suddenly indecisive.

"What is it, Nahil?" Wilde asked. "You've something more on your mind."

"They were hurt, Sheppard. Sabir Pasha's head was bloodied. I don't know what happened to the girl, Katherine, but she was in pain, too. I'm sure of it."

the **GOLD** *Covenant*

Wilde was silent, his face rigid. He knew his anger would have to be controlled if they were going to get Katherine, Sabir, and the others out alive. The matter of Quisette would have to wait.

"Perhaps I should not have told you," Nahil said.

"It's better you did."

"Sheppard, when you spoke to my grandfather in Athens, did he tell you everything—all of his plan?"

"He had no plan when I spoke to him, other than my contacting you for all arrangements. Is there something else I should know?"

Abruptly changing the subject, Nahil said, "I think we should start before the light."

Wilde nodded. He knew by experience that what was on Nahil's mind could not be extracted by persuasion—not before he was ready.

Minutes later, with their packs of equipment and supplies strapped to their backs, the four men climbed the narrow ridge from which the roof of the hangar was cantilevered. At the crest, they lay flat on their stomachs, waiting for their eyes to adjust to the more intense darkness below. The city was a network of squares and rectangles vaguely delineated within the deep shroud of shadows cast over it by the mountains.

The ridge on which they were lying formed the eastern rim of the valley. From it they had a panoramic view of the basin and surrounding mountainsides. Directly below them, the slope angled down for three-hundred feet, ending at the ruins of a fortress built over the upper gate of the city wall. Out of the crumbling bricks of the fortress, the twenty-foot-wide stone wall curved around the sides of the basin, dipping another hundred feet on the north side and two-hundred on the south before it dissolved into the mountain. Facing them, the western wall—a towering mass of granite—rose twenty-five hundred feet above the valley floor. Within this lopsided bowl, the city of Luisse filled the basin like age-old sediment.

It had been almost a half-year since Sheppard Wilde had last seen it. Five months ago, he'd flown to Luisse with two friends. Before he left, he'd had to bury both of them: Gustav Nikulasson, a man he'd respected—loved—better than his own father, and Kevin Arman, a colleague who'd become an irreplaceable friend. It was a time he didn't like to remember. Too easy to blame oneself. Too easy to feel responsible for the decisions that had brought them here. Decisions, he knew—without hindsight and given a second chance—would have been made in exactly the same way by him, Gustav, or Kevin.

Wilde shook off the maudlin feelings, looked at his watch, and pulled a pair of binoculars from the case slung over his shoulder. "I count six guards on duty—two at the reservoir, two on the west wall, two patrolling. Any more, Nahil?"

"One—in front of the fortress—but he's not likely to wander inside. Fortunately for us, it's infested with bats. I don't think Hareem's men are fond of the ugly little demons."

"Is anyone?"

"We have thirty minutes until they change guards," Nahil said. "If we start now we'll be in before that."

Wilde raised himself to a crouch, slid over the edge of rock, and started down the slope toward the fifty-foot-high slab of clay brick that was the outward wall of the fortress. The others were close behind him. They moved fast, keeping low, using outcroppings of boulders as shields until they reached a point below the line of vision of the guards inside the city walls.

At the base of the fortress, Wilde slipped a coiled line from his belt, shot the grappling hook over the top of the wall, yanked it tight.

"Remember," Nahil said, "when you reach the top, don't be in a hurry to go anywhere. There's no roof and it's a long way down on the other side. Do you remember the layout?"

"Like a picture." The drop from the inner wall was sixty-five feet, fifteen feet longer than the outer wall. The building was stepped into the side of the hill, with little remaining of the original floors. "I'll wait at the top," Wilde said.

"Good. We'll enter the city wall from the opening,

three-quarters of the way down the south side of the fortress. You'll remember that a large section of the floor beam protrudes enough to give us a platform—just big enough for one person. We'll drop a second line directly in front of the opening. Then we lower ourselves to the beam, one at a time, as quickly and quietly as possible. Once we're inside the wall, we have a clear route to the prison."

"Have you figured the distance?"

"Exactly one and seven-eighths of a mile," Nahil said. "I have the place marked where we've loosened the stones. Inside the wall, watch for obstructions. Stones. Bricks. There is much debris left where partitions have been ripped out in the past."

"Otherwise, it's downhill all the way?"

"Exactly. If we can keep from disturbing the bats. Keep a hand on your jugular, Sheppard."

"Maybe I won't have to. I'm taking the outside route—nothing to do with my lack of love for the wee creatures—but it'll be the fastest way to make contact with Sabir. He could be needing immediate help. You, Massud, and Vahad can manage without me."

"It's too much of a chance. You'll be spotted."

"Not if I get in before light." Wilde gripped the line and started the hand over hand ascent to the top of the wall.

CHAPTER 33

The city of Luisse lay twenty-five hundred feet below the cliffs but the distance was more than tripled by the switchbacks that cross-hatched the surface of the mountain like sutures. The narrow trail was terrifying in the darkness. One misstep meant a non-stop, half-mile drop. Katherine hugged closely to the jagged rocks, brushing them with her left arm as they plodded down the mountain in single file.

Clouds drifted overhead, shrouding the sky with slate-gray patches thinly rimmed with moonlight. The air had grown increasingly colder with the approaching dawn. Her layered clothing did little to keep out the chill and she thought of the extra sweater in her backpack wishing she'd put it on earlier. Neither she nor Sabir had been allowed to recover their belongings after being dragged out of the mine. Her right side throbbed painfully where Quisette's foot had slammed into her ribs. By keeping her arm pressed against the rib cage, she could relieve the pain a little, but doing so also made it more difficult to keep her balance on the steep grade.

The darkness and the dry slippery condition of the trail made it necessary for all of them to move at a slower pace than had been set by Hareem Bey on the first leg of the trip. Feeling awkward and vulnerable, Katherine was grateful for that but at the same time wished she were able to work up some warmth in her stiffening joints.

In front of her, Quisette and Hareem had been talking sporadically since they'd left the plateau. Their voices, hardly more than a dull droning at first, were gradually increasing in volume.

". . . already lost a day," Quisette was saying, the unmistakable sound of irritation in his tone. "We'll make up for that by starting the loading before dawn this morning."

"It takes time for the men to bring the mules," Hareem said. "I waited for the landing of your plane before I radioed . . ."

"That was bloody stupid," Quisette barked.

Hareem stopped, turned to face him, the substance of anger surrounding him like a dark vapor. His voice was a venomous whisper when he finally spoke. "Your tongue offends me, Quisette. I have cut them out for less."

Quisette stared back at him, coldly. "Don't play the prima donna with me, Hareem. I pay your salary, plus a

the **GOLD** *Covenant*

healthy percentage. You can't do one tenth as well without my connections. We went over the plans together. You agreed on the schedule."

"Schedules can hang you. To survive is to move with caution. I told you last night, something is not right in this place. You would be wise to trust my judgment."

"I trust performance and that's what I'm paying for. Don't disappoint me. If the mules aren't in Luisse by morning, your men can carry the packs on their own backs."

"We shall see," Hareem said, moving, on in silence.

Exhausted by the cold and the persistent throbbing in her side, Katherine's mind wandered, through vague memories of warm baths, sunshine, and sleep—undisturbed sleep—far away from this place. Gradually she became aware of pale-orange light filtering into the darkness, the promise of morning, of warmth, possibly even survival. She watched with anticipation, amazed she was still capable of such an emotion.

Below, she could barely distinguish the pattern of the city, which seemed to be a part of the cliff, spilling out of the stone itself and lying cupped in the bowl of the valley. Like a monochrome diorama, its streets, rows of uneven roofs, and encompassing walls appeared serenely quiet within the natural boundaries of hills and mountains. Only a few distant figures, moving along the walls like sedulous insects, gave it life.

This is where her father had worked—where he had been alive and happy. The importance of it, his mood, his optimism, were all so apparent in his last letter to her. She had to remember that. To remember he would never have turned away from what he'd found here, even knowing the dangers and the risk. It would have been turning away from life—the way she had—something Gustav would never do. Had never done. He may have been killed in a plane crash in the Mediterranean, but he had never left this place. The irony was that she might not leave it either. If only she had come here when Gustav was alive. If only she'd listened to him.

With the growing light and the closer vantage point, the detail in the layout of the city became clearer. The aqueduct system she'd seen from the plateau fed into an open reservoir adjacent to the elevated north wall. It was impossible to determine whether the water that supplied it came through the pipes from the floodgate above or was an accumulation of rainfall. Whatever the source, the reservoir was full—a serene oval reflection of its mountain setting.

The final approach into the city stretched out in a smooth ribbon of earth that spanned the great wall, carrying them directly into the heart of Luisse. The city did, in fact, emerge from the side of the mountain as if caught in mid-evolution, half-in and half-out of the earthen face. At some point in its history a slide must have buried part of it beneath the dirt and rock.

It was a depressing realization, strongly suggesting something Katherine hadn't wanted even to consider: Gustav had been working underground. If that were true, she would never see what he'd found. The caves had been difficult enough to enter, even though they were natural cavities, carved in stone and preserved for centuries. That she could contain her fear in an area like this—an area buried under a slide, under thousands of tons of loose earth—was inconceivable.

The keenness of her own disappointment surprised her. How could she be resigned to death while at the same time be concerned about the things of life that no longer mattered? Maybe the resignation was premature, the product of the fever. Certainly, her thinking had changed since she'd been ill. She'd given up hope. Sabir Pasha hadn't. He'd been trying to instill that same optimism in her but she'd passed it off as a paternal attempt to placate, to protect her from the reality of what was inevitable.

No. She was wrong to believe he would do that. Sublimation was an extravagance. There could be no divorce from the harshness of life in this place where harshness was an everyday reality. Sabir would not have tried to give her hope if there were none. Nor would his men have surrendered so easily if they hadn't been ordered to do so. It was not consistent with their character, their reputation as fighters. For that matter, why had there been so few partisans? Where were the others? These mountains should have been filled with Kurdish rebels. What about the city? Except for Hareem's men, the city seemed to be completely deserted as well.

A few white-turbanned mercenaries moved about in the growing light, standing guard at the top of the towering south wall, positioned at regular intervals around its perimeter. Other than the one patrol they'd passed in the narrow street, there had been no sign of life within the walls, no remnant of the people who belonged here, no smells of cooking, no tools of work or play. The lop-sided clay-brick houses were hollow shells, open to the wind that funneled through them, leaving layers of sand.

Maybe they were already buried—the people who had lived here—like John and Gustav and David.

She was almost asleep on her feet—her mind drifting, forgetting the purpose of her thoughts—when Hareem stopped abruptly. Katherine sensed a commotion behind her. Turning, she could just distinguish Sabir's figure in the line of men. He seemed to be in pain. Silently, in slow-motion, he dropped to his knees, sagging against an empty door frame. She started toward him but Hareem grasped her arm and held her back. He barked an order to his men who, in turn, prodded the partisans on with their rifles. Satisfied, Hareem released his grip on her and strode on after Quisette, who hadn't bothered to stop.

She waited until one of Sabir's men managed to help him to his feet again. As she watched, another man seemed to materialize from the shadows inside the house. The light was still dim. The man had appeared so quickly, Katherine wasn't sure of what she'd seen. Her mind had played tricks on her since the fever. Now it was conjuring phantoms. Yet, there was something . . .

There had been one man helping Sabir, now there were two. The one supporting Sabir's weight—what was it about him? His height? He was stooped with the burden of the older man, but still he was taller. None of the partisans with them were as tall as Sabir.

She stood aside to wait for this new helper, but one of Hareem's men pressed his rifle against her shoulder, and shoved her forward. Stumbling, she grabbed at the rough bricks protruding from the wall. The move saved her from falling but twisted her torso. This had the same effect as piercing her ribs with a hot knife. Every breath magnified the pain. She swore at the mercinary through gritted teeth. As if he could read her mind, he laughed and made threatening motions with his rifle, holding the others back until she started to move again.

With both hands clasping her right side, she walked

roberta clark

slowly, making no effort to close the distance between Hareem and herself. They continued in single file, finally veering off to the south after reaching a central plaza. Directly ahead of them was a large building which seemed to be a structural part of the city wall. It was their destination.

As they entered the courtyard minutes later, it came alive with mercenaries. They scrambled from inside the building in a disarray of clothing and equipment. A man in dark-brown uniform strutted out of the door behind them. There were sergeant's stripes on his sleeves, and a large revolver protruded from a holster at his hip. His body had the shape and density of a truncated bull, with a massive black-turbanned head directly and rigidly attached to the shoulders. The man's face was embellished with an over-sized mustache. His bulky chest bore a shoulder-to-shoulder display of ribbons and medals.

Hareem Bey spoke to him in low guttural phrases, motioning toward the prisoners, then, leaving the sergeant to carry out his orders, entered the building with Quisette, Kenneth, and Pavlos. The sergeant waited until the door closed behind them before relaying Hareem's orders to his men.

Immediately, Katherine and the others were prodded on to the back of the courtyard where they were herded through a heavy planked door into a windowless room.

CHAPTER 34

The roof was constructed of split-beams covered over with rough boards and earth. Its condition attested to long years of neglect, but the resultant gaps in the dry earth allowed a frail dawn light to filter through it. But for that, they would have been enveloped in total darkness. The cell—a forty-by-forty-foot space—lacked even the usual rudimentary furnishings. The floor was hard-packed clay, the walls the same adobe brick used throughout the city.

While the others filed into the cell, Katherine moved to one side of the doorway to wait for Sabir. He entered, still leaning on the shoulders of two men, one of whom was Mohsen Raza.

"How is he?" she asked the lieutenant.

Sabir answered for himself. "A headache only. Nothing to be concerned about."

"Back there, in the street," she said, "I was afraid you

weren't going to make it."

"Ah, then you were watching? You saw . . .?"

Sabir looked at the tall man on his right. Although the light, above and behind him, cast deep shadows over his features, she could feel the intensity of his eyes when he looked at her. He was the man who'd seemed to materialize from the shadows when Sabir fell, she was sure of it. But there was something else . . .

"Kat!"

The word, affectionate, warm, only one small word, but the voice . . .

She stared, her mind rejecting. It was impossible for him to be here. It was the fever again, fatigue playing tricks with her mind . . .

He placed a hand against her cheek, brushed the matted hair away from her face, looked at her for a long moment before slipping his arms around her shoulders, pulling her close.

"Shep," she whispered, afraid he would vanish.

"I'm here, Kat." His arms tightened and pain stabbed through every nerve of her body. She stiffened and clasped a protective hand against her side but didn't try to disentangle herself from his arms. The strength and the security were too wonderful to let go of for any reason at all.

Her mind struggled for words, but all she could say was, "Shep . . ." Tears started down her cheeks leaving grimy tracks. They had nothing to do with the pain.

"What is it, Kat?"

"How . . .?" still tentative, still afraid it was a dream.

"First, you," he said. "You're hurt."

"No. Yes."

"Let's have a look."

She shook her head, feeling alive again for the first time in days. "Where did you come from, Shep? How did you get here?"

"*First* we take care of you."

"It's my ribs. Just bruised, I think. Sabir Pasha's in worse shape. They hit him with a rifle butt. He might have a concussion."

Sabir waved off the concern. "As I said, it's no more than a headache. I need only to rest a little." He motioned toward a corner of the room where Lieutenant Raza was scraping together a pallet out of scattered clumps of straw. "Come, we will talk there."

"Good strategy. Rest while the enemy dances." The words came from Raza who immediately took his own advice, lay down, propped his head with his flight jacket, and closed his eyes.

After Wilde helped Sabir get settled, he caught Katherine's elbow. "Let's get that shirt loose before you sit down. Martyrs don't travel well."

It was a no-argument order, the kind that normally made her bristle, but this time she had no desire to bump wills. She pulled the shirt-tail out of her pants, rolled it up with the sweater, then hiked it over her rib cage. The incredulous whistle that followed was not inspired by her feminine assets, of that she was certain.

"My God, girl, you're a pretty sight! A bloomin' rainbow. That's more than a bruise. Cracked a few, I'll wager. It's a wonder you didn't go through the roof when I hugged you." He began to unwind his turban. "Clamp your hands on top of your head for a minute. Can you manage that?"

She nodded, raising her arms while he anchored the long piece of cloth at her waist, then wrapped it snugly around her diaphragm.

"Feels better," she said when he was finished.

"Good. We have to have you in shape to move quickly."

"Move where? When?"

"Out of here—and soon. Since we'll be moving fast, the most productive thing you can do until we get the signal is to rest." He put his hands around her face again, smiled, and shook his head. "You really are a pretty sight to see, Kat. Dirt, tears, and all—or did I tell you that already?"

"It's for damn sure you haven't told me anything else. When do I find out what in hell is going on? Where you came from? Where and how we're going? Just for starters."

"To think," he said, "that for a slim moment there, I thought you might have mellowed." The broad grin on

the **GOLD** *Covenant*

his face was one of relief as well as amusement. "Try sitting down. I hate to talk on my feet."

The simple act of lowering herself to the floor was a painfully difficult process. She held her breath with the effort, releasing it slowly as she leaned back against the rough brick.

Wilde settled down beside her. "Who did that to you?"

"Enrique Quisette. Lovely man. Ever meet him?"

"I'm looking forward to the pleasure."

"It's one I could have done without," she said. "It seems miraculous we're still alive. The man has a gourmand appetite for killing."

"Imagine we have Abdul Hareem Bey to thank for keeping the reins on him."

"Hareem! How did you know about him? Were you ever involved with these people, Shep?"

He was silent for what seemed like a long time. Finally, sounding more sympathetic than hurt, he said, "I asked you to trust me but it seems I gave you little or no reason to do so. Isn't that right, Kat?"

Her first impulse was to blurt out *Damn right!* but the concern in his eyes kept her from saying it. There was a deep, very real sorrow there; it had been present the night he caught her snooping in his study. The night she'd been so angry with him—so quick to condemn him.

"Damn it, Shep!" she said, her instincts getting the best of her. "It hurts too much to cry."

He smiled. "Can I take that as a vote of confidence?"

"Only if I start getting some answers." She accepted the handkerchief he offered, wiped her eyes and face, then handed it back to him.

"Keep it," he said. "You might not be finished with it yet."

"What did you mean about Hareem keeping the reins on Quisette? He isn't exactly a paragon of virtue himself."

"No, he isn't, but he *is* a survivor. And he survives because he's prudent. Expediency comes first. He knows Sabir's popularity with the Kurds. To kill him on his own soil would be not only inexpedient, it would be stupid—an avoidable risk. Vengeance is a matter of honor here. Hareem's method is to carry out his mission, stirring up as little animosity as possible. He'll only do that so long as the silver keeps pouring into his palm. We're planning to turn off that supply line."

"That's another question. Why was Quisette so disinterested in the gold mine?"

"The mine would be useless to him. In this area, it's strictly hit fast and get out faster."

"Then there really is something here that's materially more valuable?"

"Far more!"

"That's why my father was killed?"

"Gustav was killed in a strafing attack, he and Kevin

Arman. You remember Kevin—he flew with me for years. We were moving supplies when the plane dove on us. It was a reconnaissance flight—Turkish, Irani, Iraqi—we were never sure which. No reason to attack. Just a mindless spraying of bullets into whatever was moving on the ground. It's one of the ways they entertain themselves."

"What about the newspaper account of the plane crash in the Mediterranean?"

"A cover. It was part of the agreement your father made with Sabir. We never dreamed—no one dreamed—it would ever be necessary. That it would ever come to reality."

"But why was it necessary to lie about the way he died?"

"To preserve a heritage," Sabir answered. "A heritage buried almost three-thousand years ago in the rubble that covered half of this ancient city."

"This isn't an ordinary village," Wilde added. "It was a center of artisanship for the Vannic Empire. Dates back to somewhere around 840 B.C. Amazingly, the Chaldians—or Alarodians, as your father called them—kept the city a secret from their enemies for a great many years. Luisse survived every invasion of the Assyrian army up to the time of Sargon. Then, it appears, under threat of discovery, it was destroyed from within to keep its treasure from its most hated enemy."

"That period was Gustav's great passion," she said.

"He always said there were gaping holes in it. He wanted to be the one to fill in the missing pieces."

"He would have if he'd lived," Wilde said.

"But I still don't understand why it was necessary to lie about his death."

"Let me explain," Sabir said. "As Sheppard told you before, it was part of the agreement. If we had not lied, it would have brought attention to this place. The archaeological treasures, the heritage of the past, are not the only things that would have been lost forever. The more immediate and, by practical standards, the greater loss would have been the heritage of Kurdistan's future. A heritage yet to be established."

Katherine remained silent, still doubting the need for lies and deceit.

"Think of it, Katherine," Sabir continued, his voice growing more fervent. "Think what the gold, the treasure, could buy. Not just arms and ammunition, but hospitals, medical supplies, the means to educate our children, science, technology, a pathway into the twenty-first century alongside the modern world. I had to choose between the past and the future. Can you understand that? If I had allowed your father to publish his work at this time, others would have come—not just scholars, but government representatives and the military. We would have lost control. We would have lost the small amount of freedom we have in this area. We would have

the **GOLD** *Covenant*

lost the mines, their profits, *and* the opportunity for advancement they represent. Your father understood this. He was willing to withhold the publishing of his work."

"Are you saying Gustav began his work here knowing it would never be published?"

"It was nothing as final as that," Wilde said. "It was a temporary agreement. He was willing to wait. He used to say 'Thousands of years have passed already, history has all the time in the world'."

"How did he come to be involved in the first place?"

"Sheppard arranged it," Sabir said. "He knew the importance of preserving the archaeological find. He also knew the importance of secrecy. Your father was the only qualified man we could trust. We made a pact—a covenant—the three of us. In exchange for Sheppard's help, I would allow Gustav and Sheppard freedom to work here undisturbed. In return, they agreed to withhold publishing, to keep the location secret, to remove nothing from the excavation site."

"Were you collecting a percentage on the gold, Shep?" Again she saw the look of disappointment in his eyes and again she regretted her too-hasty assumption.

"Without Sheppard there would have been no gold," Sabir said, answering for him. "He came at my request. He confirmed the value of the mine, then he made it workable. He arranged the contacts for transporting and converting the gold to goods. His connections and his knowledge brought this about for the welfare of my people in the only way possible. With," he emphasized, "no profit to himself."

She looked at Wilde. "Is that true? You had nothing to gain by this covenant?"

"That, Katherine," he said, "depends on what you consider a gain to be."

"What's the value of a man's work?" Sabir asked. "Of friendship? Of loyalty? Of regard for another man's desire for freedom and for knowledge? You should have seen your father when he first arrived in Luisse. It was, for him, like setting foot in heaven."

It had to be true. Gustav would have come here even if, by some miracle, he'd known what the outcome would be.

"His notes, his manuscripts? Are they still here?" she asked.

"I have them," Wilde said. "Gustav left them with me to hold in trust for you. They're in that strong room you almost managed to break into."

"It should not have ended this way," Sabir said, "but man cannot always direct his paths. It is for him merely to serve his purpose while he is here, no matter the obstacles life presents to him. The Kurds have a saying: *The horse and mule fight but the donkey is knocked down*."

"That, Sabir Pasha," she said, "is the sum total of all history."

the **GOLD** *Covenant*

"So it is." His laughter filled the room.

"There've been so many excavations in these areas," she said. "How did Luisse escape discovery for so long?"

"There are a number of reasons," Wilde explained. "The slide covered everything of value. Then the terrifying devastation of it frightened people away for generations. Even if it hadn't, there was no reason to return—nothing survived but the homes of servants and the slave quarters. The ruins were of little interest to anyone except the occasional wandering sheep herder."

"Also," Sabir added, "it is an area traveled by no one outside of my people, and they, for as long as I can remember, have always regarded it as a place of evil." He ran a grimy hand over his beard, massaging his chin thoughtfully. "Of course, it was a superstition which was most likely invented to protect the wealth buried here, but, however it began, it has persisted with the desired result. Superstitions only grow stronger with age; nothing is more pervasive or enduring among the unenlightened. This city has been under that curse of ignorance—or the devil, according to how one chooses to believe—since the day of its destruction. But, to my way of thinking, that very superstitious fear has preserved it for my people."

"Who discovered it? You? Sheppard?"

"It was during one of my periods of—shall we say—retreat, when I came to spend a lengthy time in Luisse. Because of the superstition, it has always been an ideal sanctuary. After a particularly heavy rainfall, I became aware of something odd. The springs from the mountain had partially washed away the earth from one of the buried houses. It was of a completely different character than the others. Its walls were of hand-cut stone, layered in patterns—light and dark—its floors tiled in elaborate mosaics.

"In my excitement, I began to explore the periphery of the city. This led to the discovery of the remains of a conduit system—also uncovered by the rains. I followed it to the cliffs above and, ultimately, to the gold mine. My grandson, Nahil, realized the significance of, and the connection between, the mine and the city. Further exploration of the ruins revealed an access through the south wall which led to enormous pockets beneath the earth."

Sabir's words brought a painful disappointment. What she'd feared was a reality.

"Gustav was working underground."

"It is much like the remains of Pompeii, buried in an instant of life after the eruption of Vesuvius in 79 A.D. Much of Luisse was left intact under the rubble."

"How in God's name did Quisette find out about it?"

"We had a breach in the system," Wilde said.

Sabir sighed and looked at him. "What Sheppard does not say is that it was one of my own men who betrayed us—who fell into that breach. The temptations

the **GOLD** *Covenant*

were too much for him."

"Not surprising," Wilde said. "They would have been too much for most men."

"Why didn't Hareem load up everything and take off before we got here?" Katherine asked.

"To steal is one thing," Sabir said. "To profit by it is quite another."

"He's right, Kat. It takes very special contacts to make a big profit from the illegal sale of antiquities. Quisette's a master of the art. Hareem could never hope to do as well on his own and he knows it. Also, in this way, he quite wisely leaves the door open to further dealings with Quisette."

"What about the others? You'd think some of Hareem's men would be tempted."

"I suppose that's possible, but a man like Hareem Bey has effective ways of discouraging betrayal. It's probably the first lesson he teaches in basic training."

"Usually, it is taught by example," Sabir added. "Dismemberment, disemboweling, removal of the skin. Such methods do wonders to inspire loyalty in the most treacherous of men."

Katherine shuddered. She knew he wasn't exaggerating. The thought that Quisette could turn them over to Hareem's mercenaries was terrifying. "How are we getting out of here, Shep? Shouldn't we be doing something?"

He laughed. "We are!" At that, he stood and approached the back wall. "Can you hear them yet?" he asked one of the partisans.

The man nodded. Shep ran a hand along the edges of stone protruding from the wall. Behind them, the scraping sound was growing louder. "It's here," he said, indicating one of the larger stones. "When you feel it move, give it a hand. We don't want to disturb the guard with unexplainable noises." He turned and had started toward Katherine when another sound made him freeze—wood grating heavily against wood on the outer side of the door. Immediately, he stepped back with the other men to form a shield in front of the wall.

The bolt lifted, the door swung open, and the thickset figure of the sergeant stood spraddle-legged under the lintel, outlined by the morning sunlight. Moving his bulky upper torso as if it were on a swivel, he scanned the room. When his eyes lit on Katherine, he slapped a hand at the weapon on his hip and lifted his chin in a movement indicating the open door. Her failure to respond immediately brought on a louder invective which seemed directed as much toward the courtyard as toward her.

Mohsen lifted his head and said, "What's all the noise?"

"I think he wants me to come out," Katherine said.

"I wouldn't go near him. The man has the breath of a camel and a brain of the same source."

Two of the sergeant's reinforcements entered the room, advancing on Katherine. One of them nudged her

the **GOLD** *Covenant*

shoulder with the barrel of his rifle. She turned—could see Wilde begin to move and Sabir tense as he made a subtle restraining motion with his hand. She knew then if she didn't comply quickly, their whole plan would be jeopardized.

"Okay! Okay!" Her voice was loud and frightened as she pulled herself to her feet. Looking at Wilde, she pleaded, "Stay cool, chum. No wild cards. Remember the odds."

A guttural outburst from the sergeant cut her off. She turned and walked out of the room. The door slammed behind her, and the bolt fell into place again.

CHAPTER 35

With help from both sides of the wall, the huge stone slid forward, grating against the abutting stones, grinding the remaining mortar into powder. As it was lowered to the hard clay floor, Nahil climbed through the opening to a restrained cheer from the men inside. Brushing aside the rush of questions, he hurried to Sabir and knelt beside him. His hand touched the blood-soaked turban.

Angrily, he turned to Wilde. "I'll kill the man who did this."

"No! You will not!" The stern command came from Sabir Pasha. "You forget, Nahil. Personal matters are secondary. There will be no change in plans. *Monsieur* Quisette will find his recompense, as will the others, in the prescribed order. Now, help me to my feet." Sabir stood, steadied himself against Nahil's arm for a moment, then said to Wilde, "You and I can wait here. Perhaps, in time, they will bring her back."

"Katherine?" Nahil asked, looking around the cell. "Where is she? She was to be with you. This is not good."

"They took her out a few minutes ago," Wilde said. "I rather doubt they'll oblige us by returning her on our schedule."

"We're ready to move now," Nahil said. "The mules have arrived. They've been taken into the excavation. The loading won't take long, so we must be out of here before they've finished."

"We cannot leave the girl behind," Sabir argued.

"Nahil's right," Wilde said to the older man. "As you just reminded him, we can't let personal matters endanger the plan. Too many lives are involved. You go on with Nahil and the others. I'm going after Katherine."

"The odds are not good enough," Nahil said. "I'll go with you."

"Easier to move if I'm alone. There'll be plenty of distraction when the rest of your men get here."

Nahil hesitated. "There's something you should know, under the circumstances." He stopped to glance at his grandfather as if for permission to go on. The older man's eyebrows lifted in a barely perceptible expression of approval. For a moment, Nahil watched Sabir quietly begin the evacuation of his men from the cell, then he turned back to Wilde. "My men aren't going into Luisse," he said. "We've planted explosives along the entire length of the aqueduct system and at strategic places throughout the city. We're going to level it. Bury it!"

"When?" Wilde asked, his expression masking the sudden feeling of apprehension.

Nahil looked at his watch. "Starting at 7:00 a.m., it'll go up in five minute increments."

"Can you delay it?"

"We have no communication from here."

"Goddamn it, Nahil, why the change?"

"Your plan will still be in effect. We've given the vermin time to get out before the city goes under."

"That's hardly an explanation." Wilde was angry. Katherine was out there, somewhere, and there might not be enough time to find her. No matter how well they planned, there were always the unpredictable things that could go wrong, that could bring failure at any time. He glanced at his watch. Becoming emotional now would only be a waste of valuable time. "How many increments?" he asked.

"Four within the city. That should allow time for everyone to get out—even with complications—before the side of the mountain blows. The detonations should be in five minute intervals; however, the timing may not be accurate. One more thing, Sheppard, when you find Katherine, avoid the streets. I'm not sure which or how many buildings are wired to go up. Kurds are independent; it's never a surprise when they take it on themselves

the **GOLD** Covenant

to embellish the plans. The only thing certain is that the reservoir will be the final blast at this level. When that happens, you'll have five minutes to get out of the city before the mountain goes."

Wilde nodded toward the opening where Sabir waited. Nahil gripped his arm, said, "Good luck, my friend," then turned and entered the passageway.

Wilde kicked the door with a heavy-booted foot, and slipped a thousand-lira banknote between the warped wooden planks. On the other side, a voice muttered, "*Bu nedir?*" Wilde was silent, waiting for the first touch. When it came, he snatched back on the note, leaving a torn scrap in the hand of the guard. Cursing came first, followed by the sound of the bolt scraping in its ancient metal fittings.

A narrow stream of light crawled into the dimly lit room. The guard's eyes widened. Not only was the room empty, but the trail to the displaced stone in front of the escape hole was paved with thousand-lira banknotes. There was caution at first as, rifle poised, he entered, then squinted into the shadowed corners. After a surreptitious glance out at the courtyard, his interest turned back to the banknotes. His mental processes—almost audible—were what Wilde had counted on. Why sound the alarm before collecting the money? Who would be the wiser?

The guard lowered the rifle to reach for the first note, but his fingers never touched it. Wilde swung from the beam, his boots hitting the turbanned head with the solidity of spilled concrete.

The guard's filthy clothes served as binding and gag. Wilde wrapped the equally unsavory turban around his own head—ignoring the probability of its being home to any number of microscopic creatures. From a distance, the white cloth would be enough to identify him as one of Hareem's men. He dragged the unconscious man into the opening in the wall, sliding the huge stone back into place. With the man's rifle slung over his shoulder, Wilde moved outside, closing and bolting the door behind him.

As nearly as he could tell, most of the mercenaries had been commandeered from their guard duties, or their leisure, to expedite the loading. Quisette's impatience was beginning to show in lack of caution. Wilde spotted two men on the wall next to the reservoir, another two at the fortress. None of them seemed aware of any unusual activity in the courtyard.

Wilde paced in front of the prison while he studied the layout of the central building in the complex. On the third lap, he cut across the walkway at an angle between the two buildings. An unshuttered window at the rear opened into an unoccupied barracks room cluttered with clothes and gear. He climbed in over the splintered window frame and crossed the clay-dirt floor to the door opposite, which led to a long hallway.

The only sound in the building was the crackle of dice, the slap of wood against wood, and a sporadic murmur of voices. There were six rooms opening into the hallway, all with only the warped doorjambs framing the entrances; all of them unused except the barracks room from which he'd entered and the one at the end of the corridor from which the voices emanated. There was no sign of Katherine.

Wilde paused outside the last room, listening. The conversation had become more animated. Although his knowledge of Turkish was basic, he understood enough to know the backgammon game in progress was coming to a close finish. Only two voices were distinguishable, but that was no guarantee Katherine wasn't in the room—along with any number of silent onlookers. Only one way to find out.

Rifle raised, he stepped inside. His khaki jacket and the borrowed white turban gave him the second's advantage he needed. In the center of the small room, two men sat at a table with a game board between them, one man facing Wilde, one with his back to him. Before either of them had a chance to react, he snapped the barrel of his rifle catching the closer man just below the padding of his turban. The dice shot from the out-flung hand as the man crumpled to the floor. Across the table, the sergeant's quizzical expression froze into disbelief as the muzzle of the rifle came to rest on the back of the chair, pointing directly at his own face.

Wilde's Turkish was rusty but adequate. *"The girl, where?"*

There was a recognizable smirk behind the sergeant's enormous mustache. His confidence restored, the man lifted his massive shoulders in a shrug of incomprehension. The muzzle shot forward, hard, connecting with his sternum just above the xiphoid cartilage. The force of it sent the man backward off his chair, doubled over with pain.

Wilde stepped around the table, now pointing the rifle at the man's groin. *"Listen, you ugly head of a jackass. The girl! Or you become a woman. Understand? Yes?"*

"The mountain," the sergeant spat out, "inside the mountain with Hareem Bey and the others."

"Stand up."

Wilde relieved him of the automatic tucked in his belt and patted him down for other loose hardware. He turned up three knives: one from the back of the belt, another in an underarm holster, a third stashed in a boot top. He tossed the lot out the window, shouldered the rifle, and shoved the automatic into the man's barrel-stave ribs. "Let's go," he said.

The sergeant pivoted, arm raised, stiff, hand slashing. Wilde side-stepped. The sudden move threw the heavy man off-balance. The butt of the automatic caught him just above the eyebrows. He folded face-first onto the dirt floor.

Wilde checked his watch. Five minutes before the first blast. Barely enough time to get to the site and get Katherine out. There was no telling what condition she'd be in considering the depth of the excavation. When Gustav had begun work here, he'd talked about her fear of caves—of any underground enclosure. It was one of the reasons he hadn't pushed her to visit the site. Never seemed important enough to bother about, he'd said. Supposed she'd get over it sooner or later. Wasn't anything she couldn't do if she set her mind to it.

Wilde moved quickly across the courtyard and into the street where he could see the two sentries above the level of the houses, following his movements. He raised an arm, made an ambiguous motion at them before he turned and doubled back around the outside of the courtyard until he reached the southern perimeter of the city. From here it was only a few minutes to the point where the wall disappeared into the rubble of the slide area at the base of the mountain.

The wall itself was hollow. Shored up by massive timbers, a cross-section of the structure had been laid bare at the entrance to the site. The six-foot-thick stone walls, varying in height from thirty to fifty feet, sheltered the twenty-foot-wide interior passageway. The honeycomb of niches, rooms, and lofts, used for storage of food and weapons in ancient times, had been entombed fully stocked. Dust permeated the air, as did the smell of mold and decay—and a more recent smell of animals. A maze of dirt-laden cobwebs hung from the ceiling shimmering like soft stalactites in the beam of his flashlight.

Wilde was as familiar with the passage as he was with his own home. In front of him was a hundred yards of stone wall on either side, a sharp right turn, and then, dead-ahead, the first of the two ground-floor workrooms. Interconnected by a ten-foot-high stone archway, they were all that remained intact of the Vannic temple to the God Khaldi that had been the dominant center of Luisse. The temple had been built in the form of a ziggurat, the fourth side being the mountain itself from which it was partially carved. With the stone rising and blending into the towering cliffs, the structure would have had a monumental grandeur unique in its time.

The workrooms were dedicated to the glorification of Khaldi. All the resources of the kingdom—silver, bronze, precious and semiprecious stones, along with the gold of Luisse—were used to produce the treasures commissioned by King Rusas of Van. All of these had been buried when the Assyrian king, Sargon, invaded Van in 714 B.C. According to the records Gustav had deciphered, Rusas had ordered the sacred city destroyed in preference to surren-

the **GOLD** Covenant

dering its treasures to the hated Assyrians.

The corridor was lit by oil lanterns hanging from hooks embedded in the stone. As Wilde approached the abrupt turn that would bring him directly in front of the first excavation, he slowed his pace to a brisk walk, banking on the probability everyone would be occupied with the loading—too occupied to take notice of a stray mercenary.

As he rounded the corner, he found the pack mules nearly blocking the entrance—a bit of luck he hadn't anticipated. It gave him time to check location of men and activity before entering the room. Slipping by the mules, he noticed three of them had already been loaded with crates.

The first room appeared to have been swept clean of everything Quisette considered valuable. The rest—pieces which were either too large to take or those on which he'd placed a lesser value—lay scattered about like rubbish. Among the discarded treasures were a large statue of the God Khaldi and Bagmastu, his wife, lying on a silver-and-ivory bed, chariots still in the working, forging implements, hand tools, work benches, scraps of metal, unfinished lances, swords, shields, scattered chips of gemstones, casting molds of all sorts. And, piled in one corner, the shards that Gustav had so carefully numbered and catalogued.

As Wilde had hoped, everyone in the adjoining room was engrossed with the packing still in progress under Quisette's direction. A workbench running the length of the facing wall bulged with the larger pieces that appeared slated for the crates. The smaller pieces lay on the shelf above it. All were priceless: gold and silver candelabra, the great bowls used by the kings of Van for libations in honor of Khaldi, stone carvings of Vannic kings and goddesses all embellished with gold and gems, silver shields decorated with images of lions and wild oxen, all sorts of vessels and cups, silver censers, gold swords, daggers of ivory and hardwood in gold or silver settings, golden keys in the likeness of protecting goddesses, gold seal rings, and bows, arrows, and lances of silver inlaid with gold.

Katherine stood in the midst of the commotion, arms protectively hugging her body. She was watching calmly—too calmly—as the pieces were wrapped and crated on the work tables. Her eyes were glassy, staring, but not at the unbelievable treasures in front of her. They seemed to be fixed on a point in space. She was on the edge. An explosion, now, could send her over it, irretrievably.

Wilde hefted an unfinished casting of a bronze shield, hoisted it in front of his face, and entered the second room. A quick glance gave him the complete layout and disposition of men. They were all packing, with the exception of Quisette, who stood near Katherine supervising the work. There was no way to reach her without

the **GOLD** *Covenant*

a distraction of some sort. He needed a moment to get his bearings. As he started toward a corner where some of the empty crates had been stacked, Quisette's voice snapped at his back.

"What are you doing, you idiot? I said to leave the unfinished work."

As Wilde lowered the shield, Quisette was diverted from his tirade by a sudden movement from Katherine.

"He knows the value of what you're destroying," she said, her voice a detached monotone.

Quisette turned on her. "As you find the leavings so much to your taste, you can stay here to enjoy them after we've finished." Satisfied with the effectiveness of his threat, he turned his attention back to business.

At first Wilde thought Katherine had spoken out to keep Quisette from discovering him, but now—looking at her—he realized she hadn't even seen him. Her submissive silence seemed to be caused by something more than the claustrophobia. She looked physically ill. In the elation of seeing her again, he hadn't noticed it in the prison. Her face was pale; there were dark depressions under both eyes. She held her hands clenched into fists as she leaned on the workbench for support.

Wilde picked up one of the empty crates and carried it over to the bench Katherine rested against. He slid it onto the cluttered surface and turned to face her, but, before he had a chance to speak, he was startled by the sound of his own name shouted out from across the bench.

"Wilde! Sheppard Wilde! Bloody hell!"

He looked up to see the equally startled face of Jamil Taha, Hareb Kassem's trusted executive secretary—the same familiar face he'd found over and over again in Stavros Sikelianos's collection of photographs.

"Well, well," Wilde said, "if it isn't the indispensable, trustworthy, man-of-two-faces Jamil Taha."

Aware Quisette and the others had stopped to watch the exchange, Wilde put his hand around Katherine's arm and pulled her close to him.

"Taha!" Quisette spoke the name like a threat. "What is this? What's going on?"

Still incredulous, Taha glanced from Wilde to Quisette and back again. "You don't know him? Sheppard Wilde? You didn't know he was here?"

"Of course not, you imbecile." Quisette turned to regard Wilde, looking pleased to find the unexpected intruder.

Wilde tightened his grip on Katherine, moving her slowly toward the exit. The automatic in his hand pointed at the center of Quisette's chest.

"You have less than a minute to get out, Quisette," Wilde said. "This whole place is coming down."

"Did you suppose I'd be as gullible as that? You know, Mr. Wilde, I imagined you might be a problem to deal with in future, but now, thanks to your thoughtfulness, we can deal with you—"

The explosion cut him off. Muted by the mountain, the sound of it was like distant rumbling thunder, but the vibration shook the dry earthen walls of the basement room like the aftershock of an earthquake. The air filled with a dense powdery dust. Breathing was difficult and visibility reduced by the loss of several lanterns as well as from the thickened atmosphere. Metal clattered against metal; crates thudded to the floor, spilling their priceless contents.

Panic radiated in an immense shock wave.

The mules, left untethered, stampeded into the passageway, trailing rope and packing, jamming the interior of the wall with their braying clamor. Behind them, men shoved and cursed, trying to fight their way past the terrified animals. At the first explosive shock wave, Katherine had wrenched free of Wilde's grip. He searched for her in the tangle of human shapes still struggling to get out of the room but she seemed to have vanished into the dust. If he hadn't heard the quiet sobbing, he might have passed over the figure huddled among the fallen crates and packing materials under the bench. She was curled up in the cluttered debris, head buried in her hands, not moving.

He knelt down and wrapped his arms around her. "You're all right, Kat. We'll get out of here now."

As he started to pull her to her feet, a hoarse voice

shouted at him from across the room. "You! Get over here and help with this box!" In the settling dust, Quisette had mistaken him for one of the mercenaries. Behind him, Taha grappled with one end of a crate. It seemed to weigh as much as he did. The other end was supported by a grunting six-foot-five hunk of red-faced beef which, as nearly as Wilde could tell, was human.

"Did you hear me?" Quisette was shouting now, on the verge of hysteria. "Goddamned Turks can't understand a word of English. I said—"

"Carry it yourself," Wilde said. "You've got two minutes before the next blast."

Quisette peered through the murkiness that separated them. This time there was fury in his eyes when he recognized Wilde. He stared at the automatic still gripped in Wilde's hand. "Do you realize what you've done? You ignorant fool . . . you peasant . . . Get him, Kenneth. Kill him!"

Wilde said, "You're down thirty seconds . . ."

"Kenneth . . . move!"

The big man began to lower the crate, his eyes never leaving the automatic. Wilde was wondering how many bullets it would take to stop him when the second explosive blast hit. The crate fell. Quisette, arms stretched out in front of him, lurched and stumbled toward the exit. Kenneth stood in the dirt cloud like a pillar, fists clenched at his sides, still staring at the weapon. Wilde

the **GOLD** *Covenant*

steadied the gun in both hands, leveling it at the massive chest.

Kenneth blinked the dust from his lids. "Bloody 'ell. I ain't stayin' 'ere to get buried for nobody." With a dismissive scowl at Wilde, he lumbered off after Quisette.

Wilde dropped to his knees again and gripped Katherine's shoulders. "Listen to me, girl. Do you want to get out of this hole or not?"

She lifted her head and looked at him, eyes staring wildly out of a mud-tracked face. It took several seconds before she accepted what she was seeing. Finally, through the labored breathing, she said, "Did you say something about leaving? Can't be too soon for me."

She tried to tack on a smile and even though it was hard to recognize on the grime-covered face, he thought he'd never seen anything more beautiful. "The side?" he asked. "How're the ribs holding up?"

"They hurt like hell but that's the least of our worries, isn't it?"

He grinned. "Let's go then," he said.

The third explosion came as they reached the turn at the southwest corner of the wall. Katherine froze. Wilde tightened his hold on her hand and started to break into a run when he saw something else that instantly rooted him to the ground. Just ahead, between them and the sunlight streaming through the entrance, a familiar, cone-like cylinder dropped and rolled to a standstill in the rubble. A grenade.

Without a word, he yanked her back around the corner, pulled her down and dropped, covering her body with his. The sound was deafening. Stone chips and debris showered the passageway and the crash of collapsing timbers left them with only the dim light of one kerosene lantern that hadn't been extinguished in the blast.

"Wait here," he said. "There might be another."

He disappeared around the corner. When he returned, it was obvious from his expression another grenade would have been overkill. The entrance had been sealed effectively and permanently by the first.

"They've buried us," Katherine said, quietly. "Buried us alive."

"You're not going to get hysterical on me, are you?"

"I'm not sure. Somehow, it's not so bad with you here. Stupid, isn't it? Feeling more secure because someone else is going to die with you? I'm sorry, Shep."

"You'll have me completely disillusioned if you start indulging in that sort of slop now. Let's start digging, shall we?"

"What else have we got to do?"

Another explosion. More distant. Then a low rumbling.

Somewhere under the mountain the rumble was growing louder, coming from the direction of the excavation.

"Come on!" He pulled her toward the remnant of

crumbling stone that had once been an access to one of the upper storerooms. "The steps, let's go!"

They were halfway up when the water roared through the archway, sweeping crates, packing, timbers, and abandoned pieces of treasure with it. The rush of water smashed into the barricade at the end of the passage, then sloshed back from the uphill stretch in a subsiding wave, leveling off beneath them at a depth of four or five feet.

"The reservoir," Wilde said. "It looks like the charge they planted must have blown away another section of the wall." He stood up, suddenly excited. "That means there's another way out. If the water got in—"

"Oh, God! I can't go back there."

"It's no worse than staying here. There's a chance—at the very least—a chance of getting out."

"Tell me the truth, Shep. Will there be more explosions? Are they going to bury the city?"

"If we talk," he said, "we waste time."

CHAPTER 36

The water was receding, slowly, but the dampness in its wake intensified the odors and thickened the air. The increasing stuffiness together with the aggravated pain in Katherine's side made each breath she took a conscious, labored effort. In spite of the humid warmth inside the walls and the warm drops of perspiration dampening her forehead and upper lip, she felt cold. She could no longer tell whether her body was reacting to the injury or to the thought of returning to the excavation, but it was clear she would pass out if she didn't keep her head lowered.

"Listen to me, Kat " Wilde's voice grew urgent. "We have one chance of getting out of here. It's not guaranteed, but it is a chance."

She made an unintelligible sound from under the mat of hair that had flopped over her inverted face, then, suddenly, sat up, clasping the hair to the top of her head.

the **GOLD** *Covenant*

Something had touched her, chilling the perspiration on her neck. Cool. Refreshing—like a whisper of air conditioning. When she turned around it was still there, on her cheeks and eyes and forehead. It wasn't imagined.

"A draft," she said, "there's a draft."

"Kat! There's no time to waste."

"There is. Shep, I can feel it. What's up there?"

"Storeroom. Armory." He stopped talking and looked up. The stairway above them was a stubble of broken beams and jutting pieces of mortar that had, at one time, supported the stone steps. At the top, there was a metal door askew on rusted hinges. There was a draft coming from somewhere behind it.

"You're right," he said. He leapt down the steps, into the water, sloshing along the corridor toward the rubble that had once been an exit. Seconds later, he was back lugging a length of the shoring timber. The remnant structure of the stairway reached to within four feet of the door. Balancing precariously on two of the stones, braced against a beam for leverage, he rammed the timber into the door. After several attempts, the metal slab swung free of its upper hinge, where it dangled for an instant until its own weight snapped the lower hinge and sent it plunging down into the water. At once, they were both struck by an overpoweringly fetid odor.

Wilde played the beam of his flashlight into the storage space above them. They saw fluttery movement and then, suddenly, the air became dark. They were enveloped in moving, live, pulsing creatures. Hundreds, thousands of them—slapping their faces, arms, hair, displacing the air with a black, nightmarish, living kaleidoscope of frenzied wings. The vibration was deafening, paralyzing. Katherine slid to her knees, swatting wildly, trying to shield herself from the onslaught of thick small bodies but there were too many of them. Wilde grabbed her as she teetered near the edge of the steps. He knelt beside her and held on, steadying them both against the wall until the commotion subsided as abruptly as it had started.

She lowered her arms, peering up into the eerie gloom of the storeroom where nothing was left but the silent swirling of dust. "What was it?" she asked.

"Bats. Disturbed them with the light, I'm afraid. They live in the walls—a nuisance but harmless. The odor's a dead give-away." He checked the time and winced. "I'll go across first, Kat. Do you think you can manage as far as the top beam?"

She looked up at the timber and then at the four- or five-foot gap from there to the opening. Her ribs were on fire; even normal movement was painful. "I can get to the beam but I don't think I can make that jump across."

"You won't have to. I'm going to use the wood to bridge it. I'll be close enough to give you a hand over." She nodded an uneasy assent. "One more thing, stay in my footsteps up there. Guano's heavy. It can turn dry-rotted floors into a booby trap."

The storeroom was an armory, running along a hundred-yard length of wall under a battlement with access to the top of the wall through several trap doors in the low ceiling. The draft had come through one of these, apparently reopened by the blast of the grenade that had turned the wall into a tomb. Wilde boosted Katherine through the opening, then pulled himself up after her.

"Like emerging from a grave," she said.

From the top of the battlement, forty or fifty feet above the streets, they had a panoramic view of the entire area. The first two explosions had been in the sections farthest from the mountain, apparently with the intention of collapsing the outer rim inward to fill the natural bowl that contained the city. The fortress at the east gate had been leveled, its remains forming a rock-stubbled ramp from the top of the wall to the hill behind it. Below them, the streets had been muddied and, in the lower areas, flooded by the destruction of the reservoir.

Beyond the walls, an unmistakable trail of white turbans was highlighted by the sun. They were moving into the mountains to the north—a company of men and two pack mules. Quisette had apparently managed to salvage a part of the treasure as well as his life. He'd not only survived, he was going to profit.

"They're getting away," Katherine said, her disappointment, anger, and frustration overwhelming.

"Let's move, Kat, we're not out of trouble yet."

Ten minutes had elapsed since the reservoir had gone up. That meant Nahil had reached the airfield in time to radio for a delay, but there was no telling how long the delay would be.

As Wilde and Katherine raced their way along the top of the wall toward the high ground east of the city, the base of the mountain blew in a shower of earth and rock.

"Hit ground!" he shouted and dropped beside her, arms and shoulders over hers.

They were scarcely up and running again before the next explosion came, seconds after the first, sending them sprawling into the ruins of the fortress. When the hail of dirt, pebbles, and rock subsided, they scrambled to their feet, clambered over the heap of stone and mortar, and sprinted up the hill toward the airfield.

When they felt safely out of range of the avalanche, they turned to watch as one by one the blasts sent rock and earth thundering down on Luisse, filling streets, shattering houses, burying everything. The sky was a haze of silt suspended in thick gray layers. The city was enveloped in a halo of dust which rose from the ground and shimmered like grains of gold in the filtered sunlight. It was fascinating and terrible.

the **GOLD** *Covenant*

Wilde's hand tightened around Katherine's and she could feel his disappointment and sadness as keenly as she felt her own—as keenly as if he'd reached inside of her and touched the essence of her being. For the first time, she felt comfortable with that—wanted him to be that close. Like coming home to something familiar, like re-discovering a stored-away treasure. It had been there from the beginning—in spite of the confusion, in spite of the inexorable contradiction of emotions he always stirred in her—it had been there. Waiting.

Tears muddied her face again. Lately, there seemed to be enough of them to make up for all the past years of arid stoicism. Maybe it was just exhaustion, physical and mental, or maybe it was the rekindling of memories that should have been laid to rest. Whatever the reason, she let herself cry—without restraint and without guilt—enjoying the quiet, patient, security of Shep's arms.

When she finally stopped, Wilde rummaged through his pockets for a handkerchief.

"I still have the one you gave me," she said. "Looks like you were right. I wasn't finished with it." Her attempt at wiping up was a failure. The moisture combined with several layers of dirt turned her face into something resembling a topographical map.

Wilde took the cloth to add a finishing touch, then smiled at the result. "Seems as though every time I find you, you're in desperate need of a bath. I think it's time we did something about that, don't you?"

"I think it's time we did something about the two of us."

"I couldn't be as dirty as you are."

"Are you evading the issue, Sheppard, or are you just slow?"

"Slow. Very, very slow," he said, "but it hasn't been entirely my fault, you know?"

"I know."

"Do you really? No more doubts?"

"None."

"We're going home, Kat."

"You're the boss."

"Healthy instinct," he said, making her laugh.

When she started to speak, he blocked the words with a touch of his fingers, and when he bent down to kiss her, she wondered if the taste of Luisse was on his lips or hers.

CHAPTER 37

Mrs. Short stopped midway on the stairs and waited for Sheppard to re-emerge from the library. The set of her shoulders expressed a silent admonition as she stared at the dry leaves and grass clippings that had blown through the front door with him when he entered a moment before.

Striding out to the hall again, he looked up at the housekeeper. "Is she upstairs?" he asked.

"Outside gettin' some exercise an' it's about time, I can tell you. It be the same every day—workin' right the way through lunch and tea, then takin' dinner on a tray in the library."

"Have you packed her things yet? We're leaving for New York tonight. Twelve-forty flight."

"Packed herself before breakfast. Started workin' in the library directly after, and didn't come out from under them papers until Mr. Kimball popped in 'bout an hour ago."

"Where are they now?"

"Went for a walk down by the brook. Said they wouldn't be long so I put the tea tray on the table out by the pool." Turning her eyes from the leaf-cluttered floor of the otherwise- immaculate entryway, she added, "Guess you'll be wantin' a bag packed for yourself then," and started up the steps without waiting for an answer. "It's not so often I count the leavin' of a guest as a loss." The addendum seemed to be addressed to the paintings on the wall of the stairwell rather than to Wilde.

"Why, Mrs. Short, I had no idea you'd grown so fond of Mr. Kimball."

"You know *exactly* who I'm speakin' of, I'm sure."

He knew. His own feelings had taken the same direction. Not surprising, he supposed, since, for him, Katherine had always possessed some special quality beyond that of other women. Even in those years when he'd considered her a child, it had been difficult to dismiss her as such.

He tossed his coat and tie onto the banister, loosening his collar and rolling up the sleeves of his white shirt on the way out to the patio. After pouring an ample Scotch he sank into the deep cushions of a lounge chair and took his first swallow with a renewed admiration for Mrs. Short's talent with a tea tray. The woman had a clairvoyant insight. The fact that, before five o'clock,

the **GOLD** *Covenant*

she insisted on the propriety of supplying the Scotch via a teapot was small price to pay.

It was good to be back at Stowesbridge, to have all the details settled. The first few sessions in London with Superintendent Hopkins, then the later ones with Hareb Kassem and Hugh Kimball had taken up a good bit of time. They'd been an annoyance to him, knowing Katherine was here working. He wanted to be with her, wanted to look up and see her there—wherever he was. Wanted the talk, the comfortable silences, the spark of humor—and sometimes temper—and the holding her. Most of all, he wanted the holding her, loving her, knowing she would be there tomorrow. And the next day and the next . . .

After she'd left him the first time, he had made Stowesbridge a place apart, a place of solitude and privacy. He'd locked out the social world of London. And the women. Kept them on neutral ground where there could be no complications, no mistaken intent.

The idea of a woman filling a void or providing the answer to loneliness was, to his mind, the kind of absurd nonsense that doomed marriage or any other relationship to total disaster. Knowing Katherine taught him there was only one reason for wanting to be with a woman rather than without her. The reason was, simply, that being with her was better than being without her.

No one would ever take Katherine's place. She'd

brought to Stowesbridge a dimension he hadn't known it lacked. No one would ever have that unique quality of belonging without loss of essence or independence. He'd waited a long time for her to feel the security of it—that quality she'd always possessed—had waited a long time while she learned it wasn't a strength she'd borrowed from Gustav or John. Or from him.

Since they'd come home to England, she'd needed time to heal physically and emotionally. But, surprisingly, with the challenge of organizing Gustav's papers—the hours and days buried in work—her emotional state had grown sounder than his. He felt like an idiot schoolboy. Quite simply, he'd not yet become secure in the reality of her being here. He wouldn't be secure until she was in his bed, in his arms, in his life. Permanently. Nor would he be secure until every last piece of the past had fallen into its proper resting place.

Mikhail Czerny at Rhodes-Corinthian Publishing was anxious to discuss the possibility of her editing Gustav's manuscripts herself—the prime reason for her submersion in work. Every moment of her recuperation time had been spent organizing the material for their meeting. That time had slipped by all too quickly. Now, he couldn't rid himself of the feeling that *she* might slip away from him as well.

In the distance, he could see Katherine and Hugh Kimball walking slowly toward the house along the stand of trees at the edge of the lower field. The sunlight was brilliant, a visible radiation rising from the cropped golden fields behind them, catching fire in Katherine's hair. Odd the way her hair changed color with the light.

"I think he's fallen asleep," Katherine said. She and Hugh Kimball sank into neighboring chairs both facing the dozing figure.

"Must be the sun," Kimball's clipped staccato noted with amusement. "Hasn't had time to drink himself into a stupor quite yet."

Wilde raised one eyelid and peered at their grinning faces. "What are you two babbling about? Sounds like typical media drivel—rumor by innuendo."

"Truth, my dear Wilde. The plucked-arse, unadorned, naked truth." Hugh wiped a hand over his sun-burned head and chuckled. "I've told Katherine about your arrangement with Ivar Whalen to do the *Power Line* show. Hope you don't mind. There was no other way of explaining the check."

"Or explaining your flying to New York," Katherine added.

Wilde smiled. "There might be other reasons for that."

"Why are you doing it?" she insisted. "The man's a barracuda."

"It seemed a good idea. One should always try to fulfill one's agreements. Don't you think?"

"That's rot and you know it. I made no promises to Ivar Whalen. And things have changed considerably since I left the States."

"Do you think the effects have been felt as far away as New York?" He smiled placidly, took out a cigarette and lit it before going on. "No matter. It's still a brilliant solution, all around." His tone changed to a humorous irony. "And think how it might enhance your professional standing."

"Quite right," Kimball put in, "accomplishing the impossible. Snagging the great recluse, Sheppard Wilde—"

"Bullshit!" she snapped. "That's nothing but a goddamned evasion."

"Are you shocked, my dear Kimball? The girl is not only profane, she is sneering at twenty-five thousand dollars. Is that a sum to be passed over lightly? By the way, Kimball, is that the only reason you're here? To make delivery?"

"It's the more pleasurable reason."

"I'm impressed with Whalen's promptness. And the *less* pleasurable reason?"

Rocking back in his chair, Kimball raised his arms and cradled his sunburned pate against his folded hands. " 'Tis done, lad. And most efficiently, if I do say so myself. Wrapped, shipped, and not a thing left to chance."

Katherine looked from one grinning face to the other. "Will you two spit the feathers out and tell me what you're talking about?"

"What do you think?" Wilde said, turning to Hugh. "Can we trust her?"

"Goddamn it, Shep!" she exploded. "What's going on? Haven't you two finished with this business yet?"

"Just a few loose ends that needed tidying up."

"It seems to me you've tied up the ends very neatly," she said, "thanks to the expert doctoring of fuel tanks and gauges on Quisette's plane."

"Nahil and his efficient band of rebels get the credit for that."

"T'was your idea, though," Kimball laughed, "and a lovely one at that. Can you picture the look on Quisette's face when he realized they were out of petrol over Turkish territory? God! Imagine it! You believe you've gotten away with a mammoth chunk of a priceless treasure, and, suddenly, you're faced with two choices—both unthinkable! Either you land in Syria with your illegal cargo or you land in Turkey with your illegal cargo. Not an easy choice."

"Do you know for sure he's in Turkey?" Katherine asked.

"Checked on it myself," Kimball said. "Quisette & Company, and that includes Jamil Taha, are sitting in a Turkish prison—charged with the crime of stealing national treasures from the people and state of Turkey—waiting for a trial that has a guaranteed outcome. If he ever manages to bribe himself out of that situation, he'll have Scotland Yard standing by with a few dozen questions of their own, and, very likely, a delegation of Kurds, as well."

"I think the rebels have finished with the man," Katherine said. "Luisse is gone. Sabir Pasha will stay in hiding the rest of his life to insure that. He'll never give up his dream that the next time Luisse surfaces it'll be in a free state of Kurdistan. What other loose ends are there?"

"Just one. Ivar Whalen."

"My *former* employer," Kimball added. "Tendered my resignation. As of yesterday."

"But why?" She looked at their faces, obviously both in wonder at her ignorance. Had she been so deeply buried in Gustav's papers over the last few weeks that everything had slipped by her? "I seem to have missed something," she said.

"Right from the beginning—"

"It was Ivar Whalen who set you up," Kimball interrupted. "Before you left New York. In exchange for all sorts of goodies from a man named Ernest Gehreich."

"Do you mean Whalen knew Quisette was going to kidnap me?"

"With Gehreich dead we'll never be certain about

that," Wilde said. "The rest isn't difficult to figure, though. Gehreich was working for Jamil Taha—the manager of a gold smuggling syndicate who wanted to relieve his boss, Hareb Kassem, of control. Taha needed cash but he couldn't get caught with his hand in the gold till. The only other source was the treasure."

"But how did he know about that?" Katherine asked.

"Let's just say, simply, that his boss, Kassem, as a favor to an old friend, had been applying his expertise to Sabir Pasha's problem. Sabir didn't have the luxury of ordinary channels for converting his gold into usable commodities."

"Hareb Kassem, " Katherine said. "That has a familiar ring to it. Slightly Scottish, if I'm not mistaken."

"And retired," Wilde added, smiling.

"About Taha," Katherine said, "what connection did he have with Quisette?"

"Taha needed someone to convert the treasure pieces to cash. He knew that would require an experienced dealer, a man with the best contacts. Gehreich provided the man—Enrique Quisette—and Quisette double-crossed them both. Gehreich went first, after you'd been delivered to England. Taha was handled more subtly because Quisette wanted to use his syndicate connections in Turkey to threaten Sabir Pasha. After killing Taha's courier, Quisette kept Taha in line with blackmail—exposure as a traitor in the smuggling world was the same as a death sentence. Unfortunately for their plan, Taha panicked and ran when he realized he was about to be offered up to Hareb Kassem as the Judas. Quisette lost his ace trump and Taha went down with him."

"But how does Whalen fit in?"

"Gehreich had been doing legitimate agency business with Whalen for years. It was a perfect connection. He knew Whalen's weaknesses, knew how to manipulate him. He didn't even have to tell Whalen why he wanted you in England. All he had to do was offer the right motivation—a small slice of the treasure and enough information to give his show a massive shot in the arm."

"And I thought Whalen was just a pea-size bastard," she said.

"If he'd been any bigger, he wouldn't have underestimated Gehreich," Wilde said. "He'd have known Gehreich would try to cover every inch of his backside, including leaving tapes of their conversations."

"And you have the tapes? Is that how you're going to tie up the loose ends with Whalen?"

"We have something a bit more poetic in mind."

"Which is?"

Kimball jumped in, unable to contain his pleasure. "We're sending him a few little mementos from Luisse—courtesy of Ernest Gehreich. It seemed he ought to have something for his trouble."

"You're joking!" She stared at the two of them. Saw

they were both suddenly serious. She shook her head in disgust. "I don't believe this. You're *not* joking!"

"Dead serious!" Wilde's tone confirmed the statement.

Katherine picked up the teapot, poured a cup, dropped a spoonful of sugar into it, and took a sip. "My God!" she spluttered. "Scotch!"

Kimball picked up her cup and took a whiff as Wilde roared with laughter.

"Try the other pot," Shep said. "I forgot to warn you about Mrs. Short's little eccentricity."

"Magnificent woman!" Kimball said. He poured himself a shot from the same pot, gave it his approval, then went on. "One thing good out of all this mess. Whalen came through with the twenty-five thousand dollar bonus. Made certain of that before I mailed him my resignation."

"I'm not sure I want it anymore." Katherine pulled the bank draft out of her shirt pocket. She frowned at it before dropping it onto the tray. "I'd rather see Shep cancel."

"That would spoil everything," Kimball said. "Talked to Lawrence Halvern this morning. He said Ivar's not thrilled with the terms, but he recognizes the barrel."

"What other terms beside the immediate payoff?" she asked Wilde

"Nothing out of the ordinary."

"I beg to differ," Hugh said. "The terms are completely out of the ordinary for *Power Line*. The show will be telecast live, no editing—subject doesn't approve of the editing process—and the audience will be a limited few, personally invited by Mr. Wilde. Strictly from a professional viewpoint, Sheppard, my lad—and not to be taken as a derogatory remark—I don't think you're worth the risk Whalen's taking. But then, I've never been much of a risk-taker myself."

"Even with all the concessions," Katherine said, "it isn't worth having you go through with it. I don't need the money. I told you that."

"You've bloody-well earned it," Wilde said, "even without the interview."

"But you're *doing* it!"

"Yes."

She stared at him for a moment in frustration. Finally, she said, "It has nothing to do with the money. There's another reason, isn't there? And it's something to do with those little mementos. And you're damn well not going to tell me what it is!"

Sheppard turned to Hugh with a helpless grin. "Stay to dinner, will you, old boy? I think I'm going to need an ally."

CHAPTER 38

The taxi cut across the path of a delivery truck before screeching to a halt in front of Rockefeller Center. Katherine, already running thirty minutes late, climbed out, handed the cabby a bill, then rushed into the NBC building. She draped her jacket over her light-weight silk dress as she rang for the elevator, shivering from the coldness of the lobby. Lawrence Halvern wanted to see her before the show began and she'd been curious enough to agree to a meeting. Now, she doubted there would be time to discuss anything more complicated than the weather.

The filming of *Power Line* was scheduled to begin in less than a quarter of an hour. She still felt uneasy about Shep's appearance on the show—responsible as well—but he couldn't be dissuaded from doing it, and he wouldn't discuss his reasons. Since they'd arrived from England, he'd been using Gustav's rooms in the Park Avenue apartment but she'd seen little of him during the past two days. Her time had been spent with Gustav's editor at Rhodes-Corinthian while Shep was occupied with his own business, which, it seemed to her, entailed more than the preliminaries for a television interview.

On the twenty-first floor, she entered the circular reception area, hesitating before a glimmering expanse of gray marble. The high-pitched thrum of an industrial waxer was the only sound in the after-hours emptiness of the foyer. The maintenance man guiding the waxer was the only sign of life. He glanced at her before he continued with the business of polishing the last quadrant of marble flooring which already bore the hazardous look of a sheet of ice. Before she started across it, Lawrence Halvern appeared in the doorway directly opposite the bank of elevators. He motioned for her to wait, closed and locked his door, then strode over to meet her.

"It's late. We can talk downstairs." He shook his head at the noise generated by the waxer, waited until the elevator doors closed before taking up the conversation. "Thank you for coming," he said. "I thought you might've changed your mind."

"My last appointment dragged on. I tried to reach you—"

"The switchboard is down, and, earlier, I was out of the office. We still have a few minutes before filming begins."

the **GOLD** *Covenant*

The studio was small, intimately arranged in a semicircle starting at a level below the thrust stage, rising to a few feet above it. A central aisle parted five tiers of plush seats, none of which were occupied. The set had been converted from Whalen's usual chrome, glass, and leather to one meant to compliment his guest. The corner of a traditional English country room had been reproduced on the stage. A book-cluttered antique table separated two over-stuffed chairs placed in front of an oak-paneled wall hung with two landscapes by Turner. The chairs were already occupied by Ivar Whalen and Sheppard Wilde who were in a huddle with a technical advisor.

Halvern led her directly to the control booth, where they sat slightly apart from the technicians, facing a clear view of the panel of monitors inside the booth as well as of the stage and the large screen above it. "I thought this might be more interesting for you," Halvern said. "The auditorium looked rather lonely. Would you like a cup of coffee? Or a drink?"

"No thank you."

"I'm ready for the latter myself, but I think I'll settle for the coffee right now. Will you excuse me for a moment?"

She nodded and watched him as he walked over and spoke to one of the gofers. In the booth, as everywhere else, Halvern seemed a man set apart by his air of meticulous impeccability. He was the personification of a retouched photograph: immaculate suit, flawless complexion, cobalt-blue irises created by tinted contacts, every hair in its prescribed place.

"Sure you won't change your mind?" he asked when he returned to his chair.

"I'm sure." Her voice was deliberately cool. As before—when he'd come to her with the Wilde contract offer—she found him pleasant and easy to like. She had to keep reminding herself he worked for Ivar Whalen. He belonged to Ivar Whalen. "What did you want to talk about, Mr. Halvern?"

He smiled with the practiced patience that absorbs abuse without taking offense. "It may seem to be a limp bid for absolution," he said, "still, I wanted to say I was sorry for all the trouble"

"Apologies aren't necessary . . ."

"Nevertheless . . ."

". . . and they aren't the reason you wanted to see me before the show, are they?"

"Only in part."

"Tell me, Mr. Halvern, how much did you know when you came to me with that first offer?"

"Very little. Next to nothing, actually. I wouldn't blame you if you didn't believe that, however, it's true."

"Would you have acted differently if you *had* known more?" She didn't need an answer—his hesitation was a moment too long. "What about Whalen? I suppose it would be legally inadvisable to tell me how deeply he was involved?"

"Between the two of us—and off the record—I think you're entitled to an explanation. Ivar isn't dedicated to what he calls *the unveiling of souls* for public edification, although that is one of the side effects of his business. He has no burning drive to crusade for the betterment of mankind, nor does he make any pretense of purity or messianic purpose. At worst, he can be verbally brutal, sometimes slanted, coldly clinical, and always relentless. At best, he's pure, enlightened entertainment." Without seeming to notice the intruding elderly gofer, Halvern reached for the mug of coffee and shoved it onto the shelf behind him. "What I'm leading to," he went on, "is that Ivar is never dishonest."

"Never?" Katherine couldn't help smiling, her amusement tacitly implying Halvern was a victim of his own sales technique.

"Never intentionally!"

Her reaction was an extended silence that left him to decide the next tack. He reached up with a manicured hand, smoothed his well-trained eyebrows, and at the same time shaded his eyes from the overhead lights. "I seem to get off on the wrong foot with you very easily," he said. "Quite simply, Ivar wanted you to know he appreciates the job you did for *Power Line*."

"I already have the bonus. What else did you want to talk about?"

roberta clark

He looked out at the stage where Whalen was beginning his introductory speech. Sheppard's face filled the large screen above, registering no emotion or reaction to what was being said. "Would you like to hear it?" Halvern asked. He handed her a set of earphones and slipped a set over his own head.

The customary flattery in Whalen's opening was already dissolving into a mire of innuendo: *"There has always been speculation about the origin of Mr. Wilde's wealth. Some of the speculation is based in small part on rumor and envy, in large part on political differences. We're aware that there are adequate reasons for speculation and for the subsequent criticisms given voice by the media on both sides of the Atlantic. It has been said that Mr. Wilde's clients do not always—how shall I put it—operate within the letter of the law."* He paused for dramatic emphasis. *"Nor is it generally thought his clients are in any way dedicated to the common good . . ."*

Katherine pulled off the headset and stood up. "If you don't mind, I'd like to watch the show from the auditorium."

Quickly removing his own set, Halvern said, "Please stay. I haven't had a chance to say what I wanted to say." Losing the battle with her own curiosity, she sat again without replying and waited for him to go on. "What I was trying to tell you before was that Ivar is looking forward to a continued association." He stopped when

the **GOLD** *Covenant*

she made a move to get up again. "You're right," he said. "It's even sounding like bullshit to me. I need to get off on another foot."

Her eyes were on the bank of monitors—at the line of close-ups of Shep's impassive face—knowing how he must be hating every minute, wondering why he'd ever broken his policy of absolute personal privacy. She would have liked nothing better than to be out of the studio, to be home, to be anywhere else. It was Shep's insistence that brought her here and her promise to him that kept her from leaving. She could hardly have refused the one thing he'd ever asked of her, even though it would have been more bearable to watch the show in private.

Forcing her eyes from the screen, she turned her attention back to Halvern. "I'm sorry," she said. "You were saying?"

"You're looking remarkably well." His attempt to start again soured immediately with what was obvious to both of them: that she was alive at all was not by courtesy of either him or Ivar Whalen.

Resisting the impulse for sarcasm, she simply said, "Thank you."

"What I was trying to explain was that Ivar's only involvement was in trying to sign Sheppard Wilde for the interview. He could in no way have known or be held accountable for what happened after you arrived in England."

"He wasn't paying me twenty-five thousand dollars for anything as simple as a name on a contract."

"Fifty!"

"Only with the signature. Do you really believe he expected me to get it?"

"Of course. He's wanted Wilde for years. He would have paid even more if it were necessary. You're reading too much into his motives. What happened later was unfortunate but it had nothing to do with *Power Line*." Their conversation was interrupted by one of the men at the control panel who turned and tapped Halvern on the shoulder. "What?" Halvern asked, impatiently. "What is it?"

The technician pointed to a young couple entering the studio. The man could have passed for a teen-ager if it weren't for a prematurely-receding hairline; the woman was an attractive blonde, her trim athletic body neatly enveloped in a soft pastel suit. They both seemed confident about where they were and, without hesitation, moved down to take the aisle seats in the second row.

"Who the hell let them in?" Halvern asked, his voice rising.

"Beats me," the technician said. "They must be looking for the *Newlywed Game*."

"No one's supposed to be in the studio audience. Send someone down there to get them out. And do it quietly!"

There was a brief flurry before a page was sent off

the **GOLD** *Covenant*

to do the ejecting. Halvern turned back to Katherine. "Where was I?" he mumbled, irritably. "Oh, yes, the contract. That's all there was to it. Ivar thought you were a guaranteed entree to Wilde. If anyone could snag him for an interview, it was you."

Katherine held his eyes for a moment, then without a trace of doubt, said, "Sending me to England was part of Whalen's bargain with Ernest Gehreich."

Halvern seemed shocked at the mention of Gehreich's name. She could see the wheels spinning behind the blue irises. He had two choices: play dumb assuming she was bluffing, or assume she knew everything and treat it casually. "Gehreich?" he said. "What would Gehreich have to do with the matter?"

"Ask Whalen yourself," she said. "Ask him what Gehreich promised him—to make it worth the price. *Then*, ask yourself if I'm reading too much into his motives."

"What are you talking about?" Halvern seemed genuinely disturbed. "I knew Ivar had an arrangement with Gehreich and others like him," he went on, "but they were usually concerned with information gathering of one sort or another. There was nothing criminal involved. And, certainly, nothing that would've affected his contract with you."

"One more question you might ask Ivar," she said. "Ask him if he knew Gehreich was an errand boy for Enrique Quisette."

roberta clark

"We're running a little off the track here, Katherine. This isn't at all where I intended to go with our little talk."

She was silent for a moment, wondering where he *had* intended to go with their little talk. Suddenly it was obvious. "You're afraid of a goddamned lawsuit! That's what this meeting is really about, isn't it?"

He gave her a weak, acquiescing smile. "It's routine."

"Let's drop the dance and hustle," she said. "Ivar probably thrives on lawsuits. It would be stupid for me to fight on his home ground. Besides, I'm not the least bit interested in supporting a lawyer for the next two years just for the doubtful satisfaction of a judgment against *Power Line*."

"There's also the matter of articles," Halvern said, visibly gaining confidence. "You are a journalist, Katherine, and you know the ramifications of libel."

"Is that some kind of a threat?"

"It's nothing you haven't heard before in your business."

"Loyalty's a rare quality," she said. "It's a goddamned shame you've wasted yours on Ivar Whalen. He doesn't deserve to come up clean."

"He's not a bad man. I've known him—worked with him—for years. You're mistaken about him and so is Wilde. I know Wilde's up to something. He wouldn't be here otherwise."

"If it worried you, why didn't you cancel the show?"

"I would have liked nothing better, but Ivar was set on . . ." Suddenly distracted, he leaned forward on his chair. "What in hell is going on down there?"

In the studio, the gate-crashing couple had spoken briefly with the page but they remained in their seats after he started back to the exit. Passing the booth, the page glanced up at Halvern, his face a maze of furrows. Halvern didn't notice. His attention had shifted to what was happening on the stage and on the enlarged screen above it. There was a glint of panic in the cobalt eyes. His hands fumbled with the headset, disheveling his hair as he hurriedly pulled it on.

Katherine was watching too, fascinated and incredulous. She pulled on her own headset and stared at the photographs Sheppard was holding up for the cameras.

"*These*," Wilde was saying, "*were taken shortly before Gustav Nikulasson's death. He's standing at the entry to the site where he was last working. The pieces he's holding are part of the Luisse treasure. The dagger sheath is solid gold, encrusted with rubies, diamonds, and emeralds. The necklace is a collar, wrought-gold, intricate as lace and studded with diamonds and sapphires . . .*"

In the studio, the couple became quietly animated. The woman reached for her briefcase-styled bag, pulled out a manila file, and opened it. The man leaned over to examine the contents with her, both of them glancing back and forth from their papers to the photos Wilde was displaying on the large screen.

"Get a camera on them," Halvern yelled. "I want to see what they're looking at."

Some of the cameras zeroed in and a moment later close-ups registered on several of the small screens in front of Halvern and Katherine. Slowly, the couple below shuffled through a set of glossy eight-by-ten photographs. They were of the same artifacts Wilde was describing, only these were in various stages of uncrating by customs officials.

On stage, Whalen was asking, "*Where are the pieces now?*"

"*Stolen,*" Wilde said. "*Smuggled out of the territory, I suppose. Doubtful we'll ever see them again.*"

"*Pity,*" Whalen said, seeming distracted as he glanced up at the booth. "*What a waste!*"

"*Not altogether. We still have what's most important. Gustav Nikulasson's nearly completed studies.*"

Removing the headset, Katharine said good-by to Halvern, who followed her out of the booth. In the hallway, he grasped her arm. "You knew, didn't you?"

For a moment, she stared at him silently, amazed at the intense, barely-controlled anger in his usually placid face, then she said, "Knew *what*, Mr. Halvern?"

"About the artifacts!"

"Do you mean the photographs? Why should they be so upsetting to you?"

the **GOLD** Covenant

He started to answer but was interrupted when a technician poked his head out of the booth. "There's a foul-up, Larry," he said. "Ivar's on the boil. Better get in there."

Halvern looked at Katherine, his anger turned to resignation. "The crate was delivered a week ago," he said. "Labeled PROPS. It was the way Ivar planned it with Gehreich. I couldn't convince him there was anything wrong. I knew we had trouble the moment I laid eyes on it, but Ivar couldn't' see it. Didn't want to see it! He couldn't give up the stuff, not when he had it in his own hands. He wanted it too much."

Clinging to an outward stoicism, Katherine found the tumble of words slowly evolving into a revelation. It explained why Shep had insisted on doing the show. It also explained Hugh Kimball's sudden resignation from Ivar's staff. The two of them had been busily orchestrating this whole thing.

"It wasn't Gehreich, was it?" Halvern was saying. "You and Wilde sent the crate. And made sure customs knew it was coming."

Another shout from the booth: "Larry! Do something!"

Halvern pushed the studio door open. From behind him, Katherine could see the commotion on stage. The filming had stopped. Ivar, in a fury, was talking to the young couple from the audience. Wilde was walking toward the exit where they were standing. Halvern looked back at her. "Tell me," he said. "Just for my own satisfaction."

"You won't believe this," she said, "but I didn't have a clue."

"She didn't, you know." They both turned to see Sheppard standing in the open doorway. "Ready to go, Katherine?" he said. "The interview ran a bit shorter than expected."

They came out on Fifth Avenue into a piercing autumn breeze that promised an end of one season and a short path into another. The touch of night air was exhilarating—the coolness of it pressing through hair and clothing—the clean sharp sting of blood to the face.

"Walk or ride?" Wilde asked.

"Why didn't you tell me?"

"I liked the surprise on your face. Reminded me of the night I found you standing on a ladder in your Yugoslavian resort wear. I rather enjoyed that as well."

"Did he have a chance?"

"Who? Our Mr. Ivar Whalen? You're worried about fair play for that bastard?" He shook his head and smiled at her but there was a hint of self-satisfaction in it. "He had more of a chance than he deserved. One whole week to be exact. If he'd reported the items to the Treasury Department, they'd've gone much easier on him.

the **GOLD** *Covenant*

They knew the crate was sent by Gehreich—the detour Kimball and I gave it is unimportant—and they knew Gehreich's connection with Quisette."

"Then the young couple in the studio . . ."

"Treasury agents. They had no proof of Whalen's involvement. Not until he accepted the shipment with the false customs declaration. He convicted himself."

"What'll happen to the two treasure pieces now?"

"I suppose they'll end up in some dusty little museum after a long legal battle over who rightfully owns them," he said. "Have you settled on the terms for your father's manuscripts yet?"

"This afternoon. I'm going to work on the first draft myself. Mikhail Czerny will do the second, then we'll do the final draft together."

"Here? In New York?"

"I'd rather work some place quieter."

"I know a nice quiet place in the country," he said. "Long term lease, though. No escape clauses."

"Any fine print?"

"None. On the contrary, there is something in the way of an enticement." He reached into his pocket, pulled out a key, and handed it to her.

"A key to the library?"

"Strongroom!" he said.

"That *is* strong enticement," she said. "It'll take serious consideration. Let's walk."

TOLTECA
K. MICHAEL WRIGHT

His name is Topiltzin. He is the son of the Dragon, a blue-eyed Mesoamerican hero. He is also a godless ballplayer, a wanderer, a rogue warrior. He will become known as the Plumed Serpent, the man who became a god, who transcended death to become the Morning Star.

In the world of the Fourth Sun, Topiltzin is the unconquered hero of the rubberball game. When he comes with his companions to a city to play, children flock to meet him, maidens cover the roadway with flowers for him to tread on, and people gather to watch the mighty Turquoise Lords of Tollan. They are the undefeated champions of the ancient game of ritual, a game so fanatically revered that spectators would often wager their own children on its outcome. To lose meant decapitation. The Turquoise Lords of Tollan never lost. At least until now.

The Smoking Lord, descended from Highland Mountain kings, has come with vast armies. He has learned of the splendid Tolteca from a priest who tried to teach him the true way of the one god. After offering the old man up as a sacrifice to the midnight sun, Smoking Mirror has now come north to see if the legends are true.

An army has come, and a new age. Topiltzin witnesses its horrors. He finds cities destroyed, villagers raped and ritualistically slaughtered by sorcerer priests sent as heralds to offer up human sacrifice. Unable to stop the blood slaughter of innocents, realizing the vast armies of the Shadow Lords will annihilate even the mighty Tolteca, Topiltzin becomes obsessed with one final objective, one last move in the rubberball game: the death of the Smoking Mirror.

ISBN#1932815465 / ISBN#9781932815467
Platinum Imprint — US $26.95 / CDN $35.95

scott kauffman
IN DEEPEST CONSEQUENCES

Calvin Samuels is a public defender with a passion for sticking by the underdog. His clients are desperate men and women with desperate cases. Like John Rogers. Although Samuels saved him from a life behind bars, he couldn't save his life. Within months of his acquittal, Rogers' body is fished from the Ohio River, two bullet holes in the back of his head. Police speculate his death was the result of a drug deal gone bad.

Believing he failed a friend who depended on him, Samuels seeks redemption in the representation of Mark Alexander, accused of the brutal murder of two drug dealers. Needing to believe in his client's innocence, however, Samuels is blind to clues that Alexander is not what, or who, he seems. Until he meets Allison Morris, Alexander's former lover and the prosecution's most damning witness. Could Alexander actually be Rogers' murderer? But when the trial finally reaches its stunning conclusion, Samuels' descent into the maelstrom has only just begun.

ISBN#1932815627
ISBN#9781932815627
Gold Imprint
US $7.99 / CDN $10.99
Available Now

THE WITCH
mary ann mitchell

Deep in the basement a wooden box sits on a table. Demons that were called into the world are etched on the box. With tiny claws they writhe, push, and scratch at the wood, attempting to gain freedom. The forked tongues flick the air, bulbous noses scent, swollen cheeks pulse. Their icy determined voices vibrate the atmosphere with inaudible high-pitched screeches calling for revenge.

Five-year old Stephen's mother, Cathy, is dead. Her body was cremated, her ashes cast into the ocean. Yet her spirit hovers over Stephen. It urges him to go down to the basement. For Stephen is meant to be the demons' instrument. His innocence will be their mask, his love their weapon.

Because Stephen's father ended his affair with the babysitter too late. And Stephen's oppressive, demanding grandmother must pay for the pain she selfishly forced on her daughter.

With blue eyes and cherub smile, Stephen will set out to punish Mommy's persecutors.

ISBN#1932815813
ISBN#9781932815818
Gold Imprint
US $6.99 / CDN $8.99
Available Now
www.maryann-mitchell.com

RICHARD SATTERLIE

SOMETHING BAD

Gabe Petersen can't cross the borders of his rural Tri-county area—even the thought triggers the erratic cardiac rhythm and breathing difficulty of a panic attack. And he doesn't know why. His memories stop at twelve years of age, his early years nonexistent.

But when a strange little man arrives in town, Gabe feels an unsettling sense of familiarity. Then families begin to die, all because of bizarre natural disasters, and the events trigger glimmers of memory for Gabe. Memories pointing to Thibideaux, the strange little man.

Returning memories open a door on rusty hinges in Gabe's mind. Behind the door is a catatonic Catholic priest who fled the area years ago after he was found sitting on the church altar surrounded by the slaughtered remains of several animals. And Gabe now remembers . . . he was there. Along with Thibideaux.

The past explodes, revealing Gabe's deepest fears. This time, his family is Thibideaux's prize. And Gabe's only weapon to defend them is his mind . . .

ISBN#193383613X
ISBN#9781933836133
Gold Imprint
US $6.99 / CDN $8.99
July, 2007

First, there is a River
Kathy Steffen

A family conceals a cruel secret.

Emma Perkins' life appears idyllic. Her husband, Jared, is a hardworking farmer and a dependable neighbor. But Emma knows intimately the brutality prowling beneath her husband's façade. When he sends their children away, Emma's life unravels.

A woman seeks her spirit.

Deep in despair, Emma seeks refuge aboard her uncle's riverboat, the Spirit of the River. She travels through a new world filled with colorful characters: captains, mates, the rich, the working class, moonshiners, prostitutes, and Gage-the Spirit's reclusive engineer. Scarred for life from a riverboat explosion, Gage's insight into heartache draws him to Emma, and as they heal together, they form a deep and unbreakable bond. Emma learns to trust that anything is possible, including reclaiming her children and facing her husband.

A man seeks revenge.

Jared Perkins makes a journey of his own. Determined to bring his wife home and teach her the lesson of her life, Jared secretly follows the Spirit. His rage burns cold as he plans his revenge for everyone on board.

Against the immense power of the river, the journey of the Spirit will change the course of their lives forever.

ISBN#1932815937
ISBN#9781932815931
Gold Imprint
US $6.99 / CDN $8.99
www.kathysteffen.com
August, 2007

"Fast, engaging – a fine debut." —Lee Child
NY Times bestselling author of *One Shot*

GUNS
PHIL BOWIE

Sam Bass is tall and lanky, loves old western movies, wears cowboy boots and drives a beat-up Jeep Wrangler. He has a gorgeous girlfriend, Valerie, a Cherokee widow with a young son, and he's a hot shot pilot. A hot shot pilot with a past. And when Sam makes a daring and dangerous rescue of a couple lost at sea in a storm, he gets publicity he definitely doesn't need.

The Cowboy, as he's known in certain circles, has finally been located and a hit team is dispatched to take care of unfinished business. A bomb is planted in the beat-up Jeep. But it isn't Sam who drives it that day.

Grief stricken, Sam visits Valerie's grandfather in the North Carolina mountains to tell him he plans to avenge Valerie in the ancient Native American way of members of a wronged family seeking justice — with no help from the law. With only the old man's help, Sam trains his mind and body for the task ahead. And then the bloody hunt is on . . .

ISBN#1932815597
ISBN#9781932815597
Gold Imprint
US $6.99 / CDN $8.99
Available Now
www.philbowie.com

MEN OF BRONZE

scott oden

"Sing, O Goddess, of the ruin of Egypt..."

It is 526 B.C. and the empire of the Pharaohs is dying, crushed by the weight of its own antiquity. Decay riddles its cities, infects its aristocracy, and weakens its armies. While across the expanse of Sinai, like jackals drawn to carrion, the forces of the King of Persia watch... and wait.

Leading the fight to preserve the soul of Egypt is Hasdrabal Barca, Pharaoh's deadliest killer. Possessed of a rage few men can fathom and fewer can withstand, Barca struggles each day to preserve the last sliver of his humanity. But, when one of Egypt's most celebrated generals, a Greek mercenary called Phanes, defects to the Persians, it triggers a savage war that will tax Barca's skills, and his humanity, to the limit. From the political wasteland of Palestine, to the searing deserts east of the Nile, to the streets of ancient Memphis, Barca and Phanes play a desperate game of cat-and-mouse — a game culminating in the bloodiest battle of Egypt's history.

Caught in the midst of this violence is Jauharah, a slave in the House of Life. She is Arabian, dark-haired and proud — a healer with gifts her blood, her station, and her gender overshadow. Though her hands tend to Barca's countless wounds, it is her spirit that heals and changes him. Once a fearsome demigod of war, Hasdrabal Barca becomes human again. A man now motivated as much by love as anger.

Nevertheless honor and duty have bound Barca to the fate of Egypt. A final conflict remains, a reckoning set to unfold in the dusty hills east of Pelusium. There, over the dead of two nations, Hasdrabal Barca will face the same choice as the heroes of old: Death and eternal fame...

Or obscurity and long life...

ISBN#1932815856 / ISBN#9781932815856
Gold Imprint — Mass Market Paperback
US $6.99 / CDN $9.99
Available Now

LINDA JACOBS
RAIN OF FIRE

The world's largest volcano does not reside beneath Hawaii's mountains, or in Washington state, but Yellowstone National Park. Past eruptions have darkened our continent and covered it with a blanket of ash that smothered both plant and animal life. Now the supervolcano, with its earthquakes and geysers, is monitored on a daily basis for signs of the beast reawakening.

As a terrified child, geologist Kyle Stone watched her family die in the 1959 Hebgen Lake Earthquake near Yellowstone. Fighting a lifetime of fears, she is one of the scientists with a finger on Yellowstone's pulse. When a new hot spring appears overnight in the park and a noted naturalist is scalded to death, Kyle mounts an expedition into the Yellowstone backcountry to unravel the mystery. Accompanying her are Ranger Wyatt Ellison, former student and friend, and Dr. Nicholas Darden, volcanologist and former lover. More than just a volcano is heating up.

Amid personal conflict, earthquakes uprooting the land, and poison gases killing wildlife, Kyle finds herself in the unenviable position of convincing park officials to evacuate Yellowstone before tens of thousands of people die. As the earth shudders, Kyle must also choose between past and present, and defeat her darkest terror simply to survive.

ISBN#1932815279 / ISBN#9781932815276
Gold Imprint
US $6.99 / CDN $9.99
www.readlindajacobs.com